WRONG
LIGHT

Also by Matt Coyle

WRONG LIGHT

A RICK CAHILL NOVEL

MATT COYLE

OCEANVIEW (PUBLISHING
SARASOTA, FLORIDA

ACKNOWLEDGMENTS

ALL NOVELS ARE a team effort and this book was no exception.

My sincerest thanks to:

Kimberley Cameron for her continued support and friendship.

The crew at Oceanview Publishing, Bob and Pat Gussin, Lee Randall, David Abolifia, and Autumn Beckett for behind-the-scenes heavy lifting. Special shout-out to Emily Baar for dealing with my never-ending editing process.

David Ivester and Ken Wilson for overtime marketing efforts.

Carolyn Wheat, Cathy Worthington, Grant Goad, and Penne Horn from the Saturday group for their thoughtful critiques.

My family, Jan and Gene Wolfchief, Tim and Sue Coyle, Pam and Jorge Helmer, and Jennifer and Tom Cunningham for support and mouth-to-ear marketing.

Nancy Denton for a key early read.

Gordon Hunt, Lisa Gussin, Ana Rabelo Wallrapp, and David Truett for info on 1969 Camaros.

Kathleen Dengerink for her expert knowledge of autism.

George Fong for info on the FBI.

David Putnam for advice on firearms.

A biotech insider who wishes to remain anonymous for his knowledge of the science and business of stem cell research.

And last, but not least, Jeff Dotseth for his encyclopedic insight into the world of talk radio.

Any errors regarding Camaros, autism, the FBI, firearms, stem cells, or talk radio are solely the author's.

WRONG
LIGHT

CHAPTER ONE

HER VOICE, A low purr ripe with memories of long-ago crushes, vibrated along the night's spine. It pulled you close and whispered in your ear. *You're not alone. We'll get through this. I won't abandon you.*

I'd listened to it on the radio during nighttime stakeouts. Nine 'til midnight. Five nights a week. 1350 Heart of San Diego on your AM dial.

Naomi at Night.

No last name. None needed. Her voice was all that mattered. And your imagination.

Counter programming. A palate cleanse to the syndicated political braying, sports shouting, and conspiracist ranting that bloated talk radio. A throwback to an earlier decade. When talk radio meant just that—talk. And listen. A disembodied voice in the night meant to soothe, not agitate.

People eager for something else, someone else, someone who seemed to care, started listening. So much so that listeners began calling in from as far away as San Francisco. The station's long-held, but underutilized blowtorch 50,000-watt signal was finally paying dividends. Syndication had to be the next step. An entire nation waiting to hear the "Voice." To be soothed. To be heard. To be validated.

That is, if Naomi could stay alive that long.

* * *

I pulled into the 1350 radio station's parking lot at nine p.m. The station sat a couple streets west of Interstate 15, just north of where the Traitors—I mean, Chargers—used to play before they took their lone championship from the old AFL in fifty-seven years of existence up to Los Angeles to play second fiddle to the Rams while LA yawned. Not that I carried a grudge.

The parking lot had no gate, no guard, no lights, no security camera that I could see. Anyone could drive in. There were six other cars in the lot besides mine. No one inside any of them.

I turned off the ignition just as the moody bumper music for *Naomi at Night* came on. No need to let my imagination wander when I was about to meet Naomi. In the flesh. 1350 The Heart of San Diego was painted in red and blue lettering on the glass doors leading into the lobby. The "o" in San Diego was heart-shaped.

The doors were locked. A relief, but that still didn't solve the problem of the unguarded parking lot. Any five-night-a-week lonely listener who was convinced that he and Naomi were destined to spend eternity together had only to wait outside until his afterlife wife finished her show and walked out to her car. Even if somebody escorted Naomi through the parking lot, they'd be no match for a crazy with a gun in his hand and twisted love in his heart.

I pushed the button on the intercom next to the door.

"Yes?" Male voice.

"Rick Cahill to see Chip Evigan."

"I'll let you in."

Evigan was the Program Director who contacted me about threats to Naomi. He'd sounded as if he was in his late forties or early fifties. A little old to still go by "Chip." One man's opinion. Then the name came back to me. He'd had a show on the radio years ago that I'd listen to on my morning drive to Muldoon's Steak House when I ran the joint. *Morning Joe with the Chipster.* It was pretty awful, but his frenetic energy was a good wake-up call for opening the restaurant at 7:30 a.m. after closing it the night before at 1:00 a.m.

Either time or his new position had sapped the frenetic from him. The man who opened the door to the radio station was slump-shouldered with a mouth to match. Purple circles were engraved under his drooping brown eyes. He stuck out a hand and tried to lift the corners of his mouth in a smile. Failed.

"Chip Evigan, Mr. Cahill. Thanks for coming."

I shook his hand, then followed him through a door down a narrow hallway.

Naomi's sultry voice wafted out of the speakers in the hallway. "Welcome, fellow wanderers of the night. What secrets shall we whisper tonight? What lies can we tell that reveal the truth? Find shelter here from the dark night, the cold world. Bring your lives with you. You're safe here."

Her standard opening. A siren call to every socially awkward shut-in from San Diego to San Francisco. My only surprise about the threats to Naomi was that they hadn't come earlier. Like her first week on air two years ago.

I stayed abreast of Evigan and walked by an open area dotted with a few desks. A woman sat at one looking at a computer monitor.

"That's the News Nest. Rachel is scanning the wires for stories for the bottom of the hour news break." He nodded at the woman. She looked up and smiled. Red hair, freckles across her nose like a teenager, even though she was in her forties. Rachel Riley. She'd worked at the station for years. I'd heard her read the news at various times of the day for over a decade. Even had her own show for a while. Seemed like everybody who worked at the station did at one time or another and then either got promoted or demoted. The common factor being they couldn't hold onto their own shows' audiences.

A business that lived and died by ratings made for shaky employment. Naomi was the station's brightest star. A lot of resentment could grow in the shade deflected from all that sunlight.

On the right just past the News Nest was the studio. A big picture-frame window looked in at the talent. A sign next to the window said "On Air" in lighted red letters.

"Naomi," Evigan said and walked past.

I slowed a tick. Involuntarily. I'd worked security at a radio-sponsored country music festival a while back during a lean month. The lone country radio station in town had a booth featuring their on-air personalities at the event. That day, I'd learned the true meaning of the saying, "A face for radio."

Naomi had a face for billboards. Dark eyes, hair to match that peaked to a point on her forehead and outlined a heart around her face. Cheekbones that could cut and blossomed lips that couldn't help but make every word she spoke seem sensual.

I didn't know exactly what I expected, just not the woman I saw. I wondered if her harasser had ever seen her. If so, more fuel for the demented fire. She wore a '60s hippie-brimmed hat that hid her eyes and most of her face in the picture on the station's website. Shadows and mystery. Her show. Her persona.

She caught me looking at her and stared back. Piercing, unblinking eyes. No smile. Heat flushed my cheeks. I felt like a schoolkid caught ogling the substitute teacher. I sped up to catch Evigan as he opened a door into a small office.

He sat down behind a utilitarian desk. I took a seat opposite him in a wooden chair that was probably older than me. A whiteboard with the station's program lineup hung on the wall behind him. The lineup was written in erasable black ink for easy replacement in the volatile world of talk radio.

Signed photos of Evigan with local celebrities back in his radio hosting days covered one of the other walls in the small office. Or at least, his younger days. The man sitting across from me looked to be twenty years older than the one in the photos, most of which were probably less than ten years old. I guess time flies faster behind a desk than a microphone in a radio station.

"Everything I show you and that we discuss has to be kept in the strictest confidence, Mr. Cahill." The purple circles under Evigan's eyes seemed to have embedded deeper in the sixty seconds since he let me into the radio station. "Do you understand?"

"All my clients' cases are confidential, Chip. That's why they hire me." I needed the work, but if I was going to be scolded like a child, I'd prefer it came from the woman behind the microphone and not a man named Chip.

"Well, alright, as long as I have your word."

"You not only have my word, Chip, you have it in writing on the contract I sent you and that you signed." Middle management. "Why don't we move onto the reason you hired me?"

Evigan frowned, deeper than his default expression. He took out a letter envelope from his desk drawer and set it down in front of me. "This arrived a week ago."

I looked at the envelope without picking it up. It was addressed to Naomi at Night with the station's call letters and address. The return address was also the station's. The postmark was from San Diego. That narrowed things down a bit. The writer probably stuck the letter in a post office drop box somewhere in the city. Untraceable. The handwriting on the envelope was in block print. Each letter leaving a deep indentation into the envelope. Anger bordering on fury or someone who didn't know their own strength? Neither option was on my best-case-scenario list.

"And you contacted the police, but they declined to investigate?" Reiterating what he'd told me on the phone.

"Yes."

"Why not?"

"I read them the letter, and they didn't think it sounded threatening enough to investigate."

I pulled out a pair of nitrile gloves from my jacket pocket and put them on. I opened the envelope and removed the letter, careful to hold it by the edges of the paper, in case there came a time when there'd be a reason to fingerprint it. There were six pages of hand-printed stationery in the same block lettering as the envelope. Same deep indentations, too.

"How many people have handled this?" I asked Evigan.

"The daytime receptionist, Naomi's producer, and me. I think that's it." Evigan's face slipped back into a deep frown. "Why?"

"Wait a second." I put the letter down. "Naomi hasn't read this?"

"She gets so much mail that she doesn't have time to read it all, so we have her producer, Carl, read some of it and pass along any letters to her that need a reply. Naomi likes to personally answer letters from her fans. After Carl read the letter, he brought it straight to me."

"And you didn't tell Naomi about it?"

"No."

"And you told Carl not to tell her about it, too?"

"Yes."

"Don't you think you should alert her to this situation if you think it's dangerous?"

"I'm not sure it is dangerous." His eyebrows rose.

"You called the police and then me when they wouldn't help you. I think you're sure."

"Just read the letter and tell me what you think."

I started reading the letter, again holding each page on the edges. The first five pages were fairly innocuous. The writer praised Naomi and recounted some of the things he claimed she said during her shows, putting quotation marks around them.

"Don't fight the lonely night. Let it in to comfort you until your Other presents herself." "Don't pollute the freedom of your mind with the restrictions of your body." "Peer into the darkness. Only then can you find your true light."

There were another twenty or so quotes. It sounded like New Age mysticism. Naomi had ventured into that area when I'd listened to her, but not too often. Mostly, she just listened and found the perfect question to ask at the perfect time to unlock the caller's true angst. She was remarkable. She should have been a psychiatrist. Or a homicide cop.

The author turned one of Naomi's quotes back at her on the last page of the letter. *"I was lost in the darkness until I peered into it and found my true light, you. Cora, you have given me a purpose in this darkness underneath."*

The letter ended: *"Until that night, that sweet night when our prophesy is fulfilled, I ask that you just acknowledge that you've listened to my words on paper as you have on the air. Just say my name once during the show by the end of next week and I'll know our hearts are twinned forevermore. Don't disappoint me and awaken my rage.*

"*Until, sweet Cora,*

"*Yours, Pluto.*"

Evigan was pacing behind his desk by the time I finished the letter. He stopped when I set it down. "Well?"

I reread the last paragraph out loud and looked at Evigan when I finished. "Is Naomi a stage name? Is her real name Cora?"

"No. Her real name is Naomi."

"What about her middle name?"

"Ursula. But I Googled Cora." Evigan looked like he was waiting for a pat on the head.

"And?" No pat.

"It was made famous by James Fenimore Cooper in *The Last of the Mohicans*. She was the dark-haired heroine in the book."

"The dark hair fits Naomi." I wondered if there was some connection with the novel. I also knew Cora was a shortened version of the Spanish name for heart, *Corazon*. I had to dig deeper. "What about Pluto?"

"It's a planet. Or used to be. I can't keep track." He sat back down.

"I know that." He still wasn't getting a pat on the head. "Odd choice for a name for a potential stalker."

"Why do you say that?" Evigan's eyebrows and voice rose in unison.

"If I was an insecure creep who fixated on a woman I could never have, I'd pick a bigger planet to enhance the size of my penis, like Jupiter. Not some dot in the sky you could never see that lost its planet cred. Pluto is also a Roman god. Did you try to find a connection between it and Cora?"

"No."

"That's okay. I'll do it. Has there been any other communication from him?"

"Maybe."

"What do you mean?"

"Naomi received an angry voicemail asking her why she didn't acknowledge a letter she received." Evigan walked around his chair like he was about to sit down, then went back behind it and put his hands on the headrest. "The voicemail date was 12:01 a.m. last Saturday morning. Right after the last show of last week."

"Can I hear the message?"

"No. Naomi deleted it."

"Then how do you even know about it?"

"She asked Carl why he hadn't told her about a letter asking her to acknowledge its author over the air and told him about the voice-mail." Evigan scratched at the side of his face with four fingers. "As I said, she likes to respond to her listeners."

"But you didn't give her the chance to on this one." I held up the letter, then carefully put it back into the envelope. "Don't you think she deserves to know that some creep listening in the night wants his and her hearts to be twinned forevermore or feel his rage?"

"I don't know what twinned forevermore even means."

"Neither do I, but the kook who wrote that letter knows exactly what it means. He's got it all laid out in his twisted mind waiting for the right instant to put his plan into action. And now, by not saying his name on the radio, she's awakened his rage." I stood up and pointed in the direction of the studio outside his office. "And that woman has no idea. Does someone walk her to her car? Does she have an alarm system at her home? Does she have a dog?"

"Settle down, Mr. Cahill." Evigan furrowed his forehead and patted the air with his hands. "The police didn't see the letter as a threat."

"Was that their finding after they performed a threat assessment?"

"I don't think they performed a threat assessment."

"Have you talked to any psychologists?"

"No. That's why we hired—"

A knock on the office door interrupted Evigan. He looked at the clock on the wall. It read 9:15 p.m. Rachel Riley read the traffic report through the speakers hanging in the office.

"Shit." He bobbed his head once and opened the door.

"You're here awfully late, Chip." Naomi stood in the doorway. Curve-hugging jeans, beige tank top that highlighted her bust and athletic shoulders. She was only five-six or so, but her presence seemed to fill up the whole room. The cool roundness of her radio voice had sharpened into an edge. "Are you going to try to micromanage my show again?"

"No." Evigan swallowed and turned red. "You're doing great. This is Mr. Cahill. He's consulting on the station's security. Nothing to worry about."

"Hello, Mr. Cahill." She put some of the purr back in her voice. Melodious and sensual at once. The kind of voice that inspires fantasies in lonely men trying to hold back reality and the night. "Everything secure tonight?"

"So far." I wanted to tell her why I was really there, but she wasn't my client. The radio station was. Still, if Evigan didn't tell her soon why he'd hired me, I would. Five grand check or not.

Naomi looked at Evigan. "I hope you're not getting paranoid again, Chip. You know what happened the last time."

She threw me an over-the-shoulder look that a bent letter writer could twist into an invitation, and left the office.

CHAPTER TWO

EVIGAN LOOKED LIKE Naomi had just kicked him in the balls. He sank down into his chair and avoided my eyes.

"What last time was she talking about?" I asked.

"It was nothing." Still no eye contact.

"I don't get you, Chip." I hit the "P" in his name hard and leaned toward him. "You hire me because you think your on-air talent is being threatened, you show me a spooky letter, and Naomi references an earlier incident, and now you're downplaying it all. I already cashed the check for five grand. I'm keeping the money, but tell me now if you don't really want me to investigate."

"No. I want you to investigate." Evigan's shoulders slumped. "This is a delicate situation, Mr. Cahill. Naomi is important to this station. Important to the ownership. But I have to tread lightly."

"What do you mean?"

Evigan wrung his hands in front of himself and avoided my eyes again. I noticed that he wore a wedding band. "I don't want to do anything to upset Naomi. She and ownership are in the process of negotiating her next contract. She means a lot to this station and she has other offers from all over the country."

"Are you keeping the letter from Naomi so she doesn't take a job somewhere else?" I stood up and grabbed the letter off the desk.

Evigan spasmed in his chair. "I don't want the job, Chip. I'll send you a check. I'm going to wait until Naomi's next break and then I'm going to tell her that you're keeping information from her about a potential stalker. Good luck in the negotiations."

I walked toward the door. Evigan bolted from his chair and jumped in front of me. "Wait! That's not it. I want to tell her, but I can't."

"I can."

I shot my hand behind Evigan and grabbed the doorknob. He leaned against the door, his hands open at chest level, eyes wide. "Let me explain. Please."

I released the doorknob. "Talk."

"Can we sit down?"

"No." I took a step back from his coffee-and-desperation breath.

"Naomi mentioned another time." He scratched his cheek again. "We had a board op when Naomi first started who had a crush on her."

"Board op?"

"Board operator. He controls the audio, runs commercials, and used to screen calls. Now we have a separate screener for Naomi because of the volume of calls she gets. Sometimes, the board op helps with the overflow." Evigan pushed an open hand toward my chair. I sat down, and he continued. "Anyway, we had this young board op who wrote Naomi poems and asked her out a couple times. She turned him down, and he started calling her at home. So, I had to fire him."

"I don't see the problem. Sounds like you did what anyone in management would do."

"I did, but Alex, the board op, sued for wrongful termination and harassment."

"Harassment?"

Evigan stared at his desk. There was more to the story.

"I called the police because I thought Alex was a danger to Naomi. I read one of the poems and it sounded threatening." Evigan blew out a long breath. "I was wrong. The poem was a joke in response to something Naomi had said to him. It was a big misunderstanding. Anyway, he won the lawsuit against us and the station had to pay him two hundred fifty thousand dollars."

"So, Naomi didn't feel threatened by Alex?"

"No. His lawyer called her to testify on his behalf."

"Did she back his version of the story?"

"Yes."

Thus, Naomi's jab at Evigan about being paranoid.

"I'm still going to need Alex's full name and whatever information you have on him."

"I can't give you that. He has a restraining order on the station and on me."

"What?"

More staring at the desk. Finally. "I went to his house after I read the poem and told him to leave Naomi alone."

"That doesn't sound like enough for a restraining order."

"I said some other things and that I'd make sure he'd never work in radio in San Diego again."

"And you physically threatened him." Had to for a restraining order.

Another deep exhale. "I got carried away and told him if he didn't leave Naomi alone, he'd spend the rest of his life in a wheelchair."

That's not a station manager protecting an employee. That's a man protecting a woman he has deep affection for. How deep? Was it reciprocated? Judging by Naomi's demeanor tonight, I doubted it. Did Chipster have a wedding band on his finger during that time? This *was* a delicate situation.

"So, Naomi wasn't happy about Alex getting fired, and you're worried if you show her the letter, she may think you're overreacting again and that might give her a reason to go elsewhere?"

"More or less. It's the owners' call, not mine."

"Well, it's my call whether or not to tell her that she could be in danger, and I am going to. Job or no job."

"The contract we both signed had a confidentiality clause in it, Mr. Cahill. The owners will sue you."

"They won't have much standing if I quit."

"They have better lawyers than you'd ever be able to afford." Matter of fact, not spiteful. "They'd find a loophole that said the confidentiality still stood. I know you just want to make sure nothing happens to Naomi. So do I. The fact that you want to tell her makes me certain that you're the right man for this job. Investigate for a week, and if you don't have this figured out, we'll tell Naomi about the letter."

"I'm not sure how much standing the station would have before a judge when he found out that they were trying to hide a potential threat from her." I stood up. "But, I'm staying on the job. Let me handle it my way. Naomi needs to know about the letter, but if she decides to work somewhere else, it doesn't mean the threat is over. If the letter writer is really a sicko, he'll follow her anywhere to act out his fantasy."

"Can you at least wait until tomorrow?" Evigan wrung his hands some more. "I don't want her to worry about it while she's on the air. I'll call her tomorrow and set up a conference call where we can all get together and talk about it. Will that work?"

"I can wait until tomorrow, but I want to talk to her alone and I want to do it face-to-face."

"I don't think the owners will go for that." Deeper circles under the eyes.

"I don't care. That's the only way I'm doing it. I know they wrote me the check, but someone else's safety is at stake. That takes precedence. Bean counters or not. They can fire me, if they want. Either way, I'm telling Naomi about the letter."

Evigan already had his phone to his mouth by the time I left his office.

CHAPTER THREE

I WENT OUT to my car and scanned the parking lot. Six cars plus mine. Good. The same number as when I arrived a half hour ago. Still, I walked over to each car and peeked through the windows. No crazy with ink-stained hands hiding in any of the back seats. I got in my car and drove around the nearby business parks looking for anything out of place. Nothing. I drove over to a FedEx store on Areo Drive and made a copy of the letter and put the original and the envelope in a plastic freezer storage bag as possible evidence if needed later.

Naomi's smoky voice oozed from the speakers and filled my car as I drove back to the radio station. "Step back from that ledge. There's a window right behind you. All you have to do is go through it. It may be dark on the other side, but only in darkness can you find true light."

Sobbing sounds from the caller on the phone.

"Let the tears fall, Cindy. Only tears can cleanse the past."

The words coming from someone else would have sounded like New Age mumbo jumbo. But spoken in Naomi's soothing, unrushed cadence they sounded like the truth. Even to me. And I saw the truth as my life's calling, outlined in black and white. But you could get lost in that honey-brandy voice and want to believe that everything was going to be okay. And maybe it was, at least for three hours, five nights a week.

I wondered what happened to her listeners with thinner tethers to reality than I when the dream burst and the disappointments and desperation of life grabbed hold and pulled them under. Did they spin one-eighty on their savior? Write letters and leave angry voice-mails? How far would they go to inflict retribution for a lifetime of trespasses?

Nothing out of the ordinary in the business park. I circled back to the 1350 parking lot and parked ten spots away from the nearest car and fifty yards away from the lone streetlight that gave the lot its only illumination. My black Honda Accord blended into the night. Good for surveillance and perfect for testing 1350's buddy system at the end of Naomi's show. Plus, tonight I could take the place of the nonexistent security guard and watch for letter writers or the next desperate loon.

Chip Evigan exited the radio station ten minutes into my vigil. He walked over to a white BMW 328i twenty yards from my car. He started to open the door, then stopped. He appeared to be looking at my car. I doubted he could make me out through the darkness or even if my car was occupied. He pulled a cell phone from his pocket and touched the screen. My phone vibrated in my jeans. I pulled it from my pocket, pressed its face against my chest, and turned away from the window to block the illumination.

"Hello." I dimmed the screen and looked back at Chip.

"Mr. Cahill?" He held the phone to his ear and stared at my car. "This is Chip Evigan. There's a car I've never seen before in the parking lot. It's parked in a dark area like whoever parked it there doesn't want it to be seen."

"Hmm. You need to go check it out. Make sure no one's hiding in it, waiting for Naomi to go to her car at the end of the night."

"I'm not sure that's safe."

"You're the last line of defense right now, Chip. You have to man up."

"Maybe I should go get Carl and Kevin to come with me."

"And leave Naomi alone in the studio?"

"The call screener and Rachel will still be in there."

First test of the 1350 buddy system. Chip Evigan wasn't a hero. Which was fine. He was management, practical. Weigh the pros and cons and make an informed decision.

I ended the call and got out of my car and walked toward Chip. He ducked below the roof of his Beemer.

"It's me. Rick."

Chip's head slowly emerged from behind his car. Hard to tell in the limited light, but his face looked flushed like he had a fever. Or was embarrassed.

"Why didn't you tell me that was you?" A mixture of anger and shame.

"I was just testing the station's defenses." I stopped in front of the passenger side of Evigan's car. "It needs work."

"I would have checked the car." He looked down at the roof of the Beemer.

"I'm not worried about that. You did fine." I turned and extended my arm. "It's the parking lot itself. There's no fence or gated entry to keep people out. No security guard. Anyone can park here and wait to catch Naomi or anyone else alone at the end or beginning of a shift. You should tell the owners to invest in fencing and a security guard. Or at least one of the two."

"I have, Mr. Cahill." He opened the car and tossed his briefcase inside. "Even before the situation with Naomi."

"They don't listen?"

"They listen." A pinch of pink back in his cheeks. "They listen to me when it comes to everything inside those walls. When I took over as program director, we averaged a 1.7 overall share. The last book we were a 3.2."

I pretended like I knew what all that meant. "When did you take over?"

"Two and a half years ago."

"Isn't that when Naomi started?"

"Two months later. I hired her. That's why the owners listen to me."

"Except when it comes to the station's security."

"Yes." He hissed the "s," got into his car, and peeled out of the parking lot.

I didn't know what the numbers or the book that Evigan mentioned meant, but I had a greater understanding of how important Naomi was to him. I'd have bet that he made a few passes at her in the early days and probably still carried a crush. But Naomi's true importance to Evigan was what she'd done for his career. He was the guy who signed the golden goose. Discovered the sultry nighttime star whom radio stations all over the country coveted. If she left 1350, the program director with the Midas touch would have to prove that his keen eye for talent wasn't just a case of a gift falling into his lap.

* * *

Naomi and a large round man exited the radio station at 12:17 a.m. The man's dark skin blended into the night. I hadn't seen him during my brief tour of the station. He may have been Naomi's producer or board operator. I was just happy Naomi didn't have to walk to her car alone. Her hair was now in a ponytail pulled through the back of a ball cap. She wore a waist-long leather jacket that fit as well as her Levi's.

The two walked up to a mint-condition metallic blue 1969 Camaro with dual white hood stripes. It was parked closest to the streetlight just outside the parking lot. I'd noticed the car when I'd arrived three hours earlier. A buddy in high school had owned a similar Camaro without the stripes. We'd loved the car and marveled how something built ten years before we were born could be as cool as we were. I haven't been cool for twenty years, but the '69 Camaro still is.

Naomi and the man hugged, then she got into the Camaro. It fit. Classic. Hip. Not of this millennium, but still relevant. The V-8 engine rumbled and the headlights went on. She backed out of the parking space and headed toward the exit. I was parked just beyond the exit. The headlights caught me broadside. I held my pose. No need to duck down. I wasn't on surveillance. Only playing guard dog and my shift just ended.

The Camaro pulled up alongside me. Naomi leaned across the passenger bucket seat and hand-cranked the window down. A task most people my age had never attempted. I rolled down my window. Her face shadowed in the dark.

"Working late, Mr. Cahill?"

"Not anymore. Heading home."

"Are you going to tell me the real reason you met with Chip tonight or will I have to wring it out of him? I'd prefer not to have to go in early tomorrow and catch him before he scurries home."

"I'll tell you tomorrow over lunch." I handed her one of my business cards through the open window. "Call me in the morning and pick a restaurant."

"No cliffhangers, Mr. Cahill. Follow me."

CHAPTER FOUR

NAOMI PULLED THE Camaro into the parking lot of a squat square building fifteen minutes later. The Night Owl, a longtime dive bar in Pacific Beach that's never tried to be anything but. You have to respect that. Knowing who you are and being comfortable with it. I'd never started a bender at the Night Owl, but in my earlier years, I'd ended a few there.

I followed Naomi inside the dark windowless bar to a wooden benchlike table in the back. The swivel of her hips would have been a put-on from another woman. On Naomi, the movement was natural. And hard to ignore. The bartender, gray but fit in his sixties, noticed and nodded at Naomi when we walked by. We sat on square barstools opposite each other against the wall. A jukebox behind us played "Born To Be Wild." A couple of sixty-something lifers shot pool on the lone table in the back. Five or six men and a woman of the same vintage sat at the bar muttering at each other. The woman let out a loud cackle. Nobody seemed to take notice of us except the bartender who now leaned over the nearside of the bar and asked us what we wanted to drink. Naomi ordered a Dewar's White Label rocks. I did the same.

"Sports bar more your flavor, Mr. Cahill?" The tilt of Naomi's head kept her eyes hidden under the bill of her ball cap. Her voice, less smoke and purr than on the radio, but still smooth and beguiling.

"Call me Rick." I took a sip of the scotch the bartender just delivered. "I don't go to bars much anymore. If I do, it's not for the ambience. This is fine."

"Sounds like there's a story in there that I could probe on the show sometime." Naomi gave me the first smile of the night between full lips. Definitely not a face for radio. "But tonight, I want to hear about Chip's latest ill-conceived scheme and how he's pulled you into it."

"He told you the truth. He hired me to tighten security at the station." I needed to tell Naomi about the letter, but I suddenly felt an allegiance to Chip. Her disdain made me feel a little sorry for him. He was in a tough spot for a number of reasons and ill-equipped to do battle with Naomi. And probably the station's owners.

"'Tighten security' covers a lot of ground, Rick. Let's narrow it down in regard to me." She took a sip of her drink. "Does this have anything to do with Alex?"

"The board op who was fired?"

"Yes."

"Probably not, but it's possible." Naomi's testimony on his behalf or not, I needed to investigate Alex before I could eliminate him as the letter writer.

"That's a little cryptic. Please explain."

"The station received a letter last week that seems a bit menacing. Chip thinks the angry voicemail you received last Friday about not acknowledging a fan on air may have come from the letter writer."

"I don't know why Chip keeps things from me." She shook her head. "It just makes everything worse. He treats me like I'm a porcelain doll. I'm his one-figurine glass menagerie. Do you have the letter?"

"A copy."

"I need to read it." She held out her hand across the table. "This is about my life, not the station's Nielsen numbers."

I pulled the photocopied letter out of my inside coat pocket and handed it to Naomi.

She read it. Her lips held a soft line. No facial tics that I could see. After a few minutes, she pushed the letter across the table at me.

"Does any of the language sound familiar to you?" I picked up the letter, but didn't put it back in my pocket. "Similar to something one of your callers may have said?"

"This is just Chip overreacting again." She lifted her head. Her eyes, dark half-moons. "When I started at 1350, Chip told me not to think about the thousands of people I was talking to each night. He said to concentrate on talking to one single person. Just like we're talking now. After I became skilled at it, he told me that there are a lot of lonely people listening who consider me a friend even though I don't know them. That it was a privilege and I needed to respect it. I took him at his word, and now he flies off the handle when one of those lonely people wants to take that friendship to the next level. The letter is harmless."

"You may be right, but you still need to take precautions. I'm going to try to force 1350's owners to get some security at the station. You should do the same at home. Do you have an alarm system?"

"No."

"A dog?"

"I used to. They give you all their love and then leave this world too soon. I can't take that heartache anymore. Men come and go. Dogs mean something."

I understood her feelings about dogs, but that didn't solve her protection problem.

"Whether or not this Pluto is a nut, you should still get a house alarm. You can hide under a hat, but you're a public figure and need to take precautions. Not every lonely person listening to the radio has good intentions."

"I take precautions, Rick." A smile with a little nasty in it. "I can take care of myself. I don't need a hired hand to look after me because the station wants to protect what they think is their property. Or Chip wants to protect the myth that he's the next John Mainelli."

"Who's John Mainelli?"

"He was the Program Director at WABC in New York who hired a little-known conservative blowhard who'd been on the radio in Sacramento and gave him a megaphone."

"Rush Limbaugh," I said. "That's a little different style of radio than yours."

"Right." She nodded. "But it's all about audience size and Chip thinks mine can be huge if I go into syndication, which would make him the man behind the new voice."

"And you think Chip is more concerned about maintaining his own legacy than protecting you?"

"Yes."

"Don't you want to go into syndication? The money would be a lot better than what 1350 can give you, right?"

"We'll see." She dipped her head a fraction, the bill of her hat hiding her eyes.

"What about Alex? Was that another instance of Chip protecting his legacy or something else?"

"You're an independent thinker, aren't you, Rick? The owners had Chip hire you to investigate the person who wrote this letter without me knowing. They don't want me to get spooked while we're in negotiations over my next contract. But you're not an automaton who stays in between the lines." She tilted her head and gave me a look that would have quickened the pace of faceless letter writers had they been in my seat. My pulse rippled. "You see life in full color, don't you?"

"I watch and ask questions."

"And your question is does Chip see me as more than his goddess of fortune? The answer is yes. More like Aphrodite."

"Has he ever acted on those feelings?"

"Sort of." She curled her lips and blew air through her nostrils. "He wined and dined me after he hired me. He was my new boss, and I couldn't risk pissing him off. He made a couple passes, but I shut him down before it got too icky."

Naomi was different from the character she played on the radio. That didn't shock me. Everyone has a different persona for each audience they encounter. Almost everyone. I'd known a couple people in my life who never wore masks. They were pure of soul. Life was crueler to them than the rest of us.

Yet, I couldn't deny Naomi's pull on me. The flesh and blood behind the voice.

"What happened with Alex?" I still had a case to figure out.

"Alex was a sweet boy who fell in love with a voice on the radio and the face behind the glass." Her mouth fell and her eyes drifted over my shoulder. "He didn't realize they were two different people."

"What about the poems?"

"The poems were professions of love from a young man out of the hood who'd never felt real love in his entire life."

"Do you still have any of them?"

"I'm not sentimental, Rick. Life's too hard for that."

"Except when it comes to dogs?" I asked.

"Dogs don't try to trade career advancement for sex or try to make you their girlfriend after one drunken mistake."

"Did the station know you had sex with Alex?"

"Chip did. Ownership didn't until the wrongful termination hearing. The shocked looks on their faces almost made all the hassle worthwhile."

"How did Chip know about it before the hearing? Did you tell him?" I wondered about the boundaries of her torment of Evigan.

"No. He followed me home after the station Christmas party. The freak."

"And he fired Alex after that?" Chip told me he'd read something threatening in one of the poems.

"A week later."

"Did you know that Chip threatened Alex?"

"Alex told me."

"Was that before or after the Christmas party?"

"That was after he'd already fired Alex."

"Why then?" Was Chip still carrying a crush at that time? What about now?

"I don't know. Ask him."

"I will. After I talk to Alex. What's his last name?"

"Evans." She gave me his phone number and home address.

We each finished off our second round of Dewar's. Naomi slipped the tip of her tongue between her lips and stared into my eyes. Bold. The words would come next, but she'd already made her intentions clear.

"Follow me home, Rick. You can look for weaknesses in my security."

I had a rule about getting involved with clients. I'd broken it once before. No one had gotten hurt. Except me.

"Not tonight, but I'll walk you to your car." I stood up and dropped a twenty on the table for the bartender. "Wouldn't want either one of us to make a drunken mistake."

CHAPTER FIVE

My black Lab, Midnight, met me at the front door. The one constant in my life. I cooed at him and scratched him behind the ear. I grabbed a Ballast Point Scottish Ale out of the refrigerator and led Midnight into the backyard. He half-trotted with his nose to the ground looking for just the right spot to empty his bladder one last time before bed. I sat down on a patio chair on my deck and started to fill my bladder one last time before bed.

The malty ale sitting on top of the Dewar's could make for a sluggish morning. It was already close to two a.m. Despite the two shots of scotch and half a beer, I wasn't tired. My mind was running too hard to let sleep creep in.

1350 Heart of San Diego might as well have been the set of General Hospital. Drama, internal politics, and sex. All revolving around Naomi. Add on the creepy letter and the back of my neck started itching. Something was off with the whole scenario. Naomi didn't seem worried about the letter or the angry voice message. She'd been around. She was tough. Still, her lack of concern surprised me. She'd lived long enough to know there was pure evil in the world. She had to know her late-night purr out into the shadows could stir a demented soul. One hibernating, waiting for the right trigger to wake the evil within.

I took another sip of beer and stared out beyond the lights of Mission Bay at an ocean I couldn't see. A sliver of a view during the day, a black expanse at night. Midnight finished peeing on a favorite bush and sat on his haunches next to me. I scratched his head, and he leaned against my leg.

This wasn't life's promise I'd envisioned as a kid growing up. I was thirty-eight. I didn't have a steady woman in my life or children to chase Midnight around in the backyard. Life doesn't keep promises on its own. You have to work to make them come true. And sometimes get lucky. I could live with that. This was the life I'd made. I owned it. And it could continue on in its presently unruffled state if I put the hours in on the Naomi at Night case and left the subtext and the attraction alone. Investigate the specifics, write a report, and move on to the next case. But the back of my neck itched. And underneath that irritation was truth waiting to be scratched.

I headed into the kitchen for beer number two and probably a morning headache. My cell phone rang before I made it to the refrigerator. I didn't recognize the number on the screen and froze. I'd spent the last year dreading a call I hoped would never come, but had to answer. Every unknown number a stab in the gut.

I held my breath and answered the phone.

"Rick? It's Naomi." The sultry thrum in her voice replaced by a fast-twitch quaver. "Someone stole my gun."

"What gun?" Naomi hadn't been flippant at the Night Owl when she said she could take care of herself. But, maybe not as well as she thought she could.

"I keep a Glock in the glove compartment of my car. I bring it into the house when I'm home for the night. It's gone."

"And you remember putting the gun in the glove compartment this morning?"

"Not this morning. When I left my house to go to work at seven o'clock tonight."

That meant someone had stolen the gun while Naomi was at the radio station or when we were together inside the Night Owl. A random robbery or the person who wrote the letter? The timing of the theft pointed to the latter. A letter, angry voicemail, a breach of the target's property.

Escalation.

"Call the police and report the gun stolen. Then you need to stay at a friend's house for the rest of the night." I couldn't take a chance with Naomi's safety if the letter writer was responsible.

"I can't report the gun stolen."

"You don't have a license for it?" Not a big deal. Many people had hand-me-down guns from family members. "Considering the circumstances, I think the police will cut you a break."

"I can't get a license for a gun, Rick." The edge I'd heard in her voice when she talked to Evigan in his office.

I'd just uncovered one reason for the itch on the back of my neck. Naomi couldn't get a license for a gun because she couldn't own one. She was a felon.

"Okay. We'll deal with that later. In the meantime, it would be best if you stay with a friend tonight. Do you have someone you can call?"

"No."

"Give me your address."

"Why?"

"I'm coming over."

CHAPTER SIX

NAOMI LIVED IN Del Mar, an upscale bedroom community true to its name, by the sea. It was twenty miles north of downtown San Diego and had some of the priciest real estate in the county. Her house was a modest single-story sitting up on a hill, a mile or so back from the ocean. No Camaro in the driveway, but the porchlight was on. She'd probably parked in the two-car garage.

I parked in the driveway and phoned Naomi.

"Rick?"

"I'll be at the front door in thirty seconds." I didn't want to knock on her door unannounced and frighten her.

I scanned the street and surrounding houses. Empty street and no lights on in windows at 2:25 a.m. I popped the trunk of my car and pulled out a Mossberg 590A1 Pump-Action Tactical shotgun. The Smith & Wesson .357 Magnum holstered under my left arm was fine for a shootout during the day. I wanted something with wider dispersal and a bigger kick if someone invaded the house in the dark.

Unlike Naomi, I not only had licenses for the weapons, I had a conceal/carry for the Magnum, as well.

I double-knocked the front door. Naomi opened it, looked at the shotgun, then me.

"Come on in, but do you really think that's necessary?" She nodded at the shotgun.

"Probably not." I stepped into a small foyer that opened into the living room. "But I like to prepare for all contingencies."

"Apparently." She closed the door and walked into the living room. The house had an open floor plan below a maple wood-slat ceiling with a large skylight over the center of the living room. The furniture was leather. Expensive and masculine. The whole house had a masculine feel.

Naomi still had on the blue jeans and tee shirt she wore at the station, but had removed her leather jacket, ball cap, and shoes. Her brown hair danced on her shoulders as she sat down on a leather sofa that had a Native American blanket draped over the back. It didn't fit with the decor of the rest of the house. Maybe the one accent piece Naomi owned. It worked. She looked comfortable and sexy in a home that didn't suit her. But then, it did.

A driftwood coffee table loaded with a bottle of Dewar's White Label, two rocks glasses, and a marijuana joint sat in front of the sofa.

"Have a seat." She pointed at a matching stuffed leather chair perpendicular to the sofa, then lit the joint with a steel Zippo lighter.

"Not yet." I went down the short hall and checked all three bedrooms and bathrooms, then circled back. Clear.

"I could have told you no one else was here."

"Was anything else missing from your car?"

"No."

"How about the house? Does anything seem out of place here?"

"No."

I walked to a sliding glass door that led out to a wooden deck. Sliding glass doors are easy to breach even when locked. Moving them up and down can pop open the spring-loaded lock.

"You either need to get a lock installed at the top of the door that screws into the frame of the house or a broom handle or long, thick dowel to put on the door track. Anyone could break in through this door in ten seconds."

"Yes, sir." She put a hand to her forehead and saluted me.

"It's not a joke."

"I know." She put her hands in her lap. "I'm trying to lighten things up."

I opened the sliding glass door and walked out onto the deck, which wrapped around the side of the house. The landscape dropped away from the house into vast darkness. Some headlights and taillights shone from Interstate 5 to the east and flowing north and south. A few lights twinkled from the west, probably the racetrack and fairgrounds. The black empty of the ocean was a mile or so to the west.

Million-dollar views during the day. Optimal opportunity for a concealed breach at night.

I went back inside and locked the slider. Naomi lifted the joint toward me.

"No thanks." I sat down in the chair opposite Naomi and laid the shotgun across my lap. "I'll take it from here if you want to get some sleep."

"I'm a little wired." Naomi replaced the joint in her hand with half a rocks glass of scotch.

"That's understandable. It's been an eventful night."

"That's not it." She took a sip of scotch. "I'm always wired after a show. Tired, but my brain won't slow down enough to sleep."

I had the same sleep patterns when I managed a restaurant years ago. Dealing with the public was exhausting but exhilarating at the same time. It must have been exponential when you had a listening audience in the tens of thousands.

I looked at the furniture in the living room and my eyes rested on the out-of-place blanket.

"How long have you lived here?"

"I don't really live here." Naomi took a hit of the joint and held it in. She finally exhaled. "I'm house-sitting for a friend who's out of the country for a year."

"How long have you been here?"

"Nine months."

"How many people know you're staying here?"

"Just a couple of the neighbors." She pulled the blanket off the back of the sofa, tucked her bare feet under her, and spread it across her lap.

"No one at 1350 knows you're staying here?"

"No."

"What about Alex?" The ex-employee with the crush.

"No. I haven't talked to him since the lawsuit last year."

"Is your mail forwarded here?"

"No. I use a PO box for all my mail. Always have."

The photo of Naomi with her face hidden by the hippie hat on the 1350 website wasn't just to maintain the mystery of her radio personality. She was a private person. Maybe that was because of her past life.

"How long ago did you do time?"

"Small talk over? Now it's time to get down to the facts, just the facts, ma'am?" Naomi set her drink down on the coffee table.

"We don't have to talk." I stared at the front door. "I'll keep watch until the sun comes up. After that, you should convince 1350's management to hire a bodyguard until we deal with your stalker."

"I'm not convinced I have a stalker."

"Yes, you are. You wouldn't have called me tonight about the stolen gun. You would have waited until tomorrow, if you told me about it at all."

"Maybe I just wanted to get you up here so I could make another drunken mistake."

"Maybe." I shifted my eyes from the door to Naomi. Her red-tinged brown eyes at half-mast, ripe lips parted. I'd made worse mistakes. I think. "But you were shaken when you called me a half hour ago."

"And here you are, armor shining. Is the hero complex a shield you use to block out a time when you were unheroic?"

"Could be, but I was hired to find out if someone was stalking you. It looks like someone probably is, so I'm just doing my job."

"I'm sure holding my hand isn't in the contract." Another sip of scotch.

"I took the job. You're my responsibility now."

"I like the sound of that." She shimmied deeper into the couch. "But I'm not the one paying you. The station is."

"My job is to find out who's stalking you, stop them, and keep you safe." I shifted my gaze from Naomi's enticing eyes to the sliding glass door facing the deck. "It doesn't matter who's paying me."

"Does that mean you'll keep a secret?"

"As long as you're not planning on committing a felony, yes."

"I've already committed one of those."

"Is that what you want to tell me about?"

"No." Naomi held in a hit of the joint and finally exhaled musky-scented smoke. "If I tell you something in confidence, that means you won't tell anyone, right? Not even the station."

"Right. It's between you and me. Nobody else." The contract I signed put a lie to my statement. I'd keep my end of the bargain with 1350, but I'd keep Naomi's confidence, too.

"Please don't tell Chip about the gun."

"He doesn't know you have a gun? I mean *had* a gun?"

"No."

"I guess it's none of his business, but he and the station need to know about the potential escalation." I peered through the sliding glass door and caught the red eyes of a lone pair of taillights going up I-5 a mile away. "They need to get serious about protecting you."

"How can you tell them you think this creep has escalated if you don't tell them about the gun?" Naomi hugged her knees over the blanket. "Are you going to make something up? That someone broke into my car? What if they report the break-in to the police? They'll question you. Are you going to lie to the police, too?"

I didn't tell her that I'd lied to the police before. More than once. But usually to protect my own ass, not someone else's. At least not someone I'd met five hours earlier.

"The police need to get involved, Naomi. The gun possession can be worked out. Dealing with an armed stalker can't. The cops can arrest this guy. I can't. Either contact the station's lawyer tomorrow or hire one of your own. A lawyer can get an agreement from the police before you admit to anything. They'd much rather throw a stalker with a gun in jail than you."

"You can't tell the police or 1350 about the gun." Naomi shot a hand through her hair. "You promised me."

"1350 doesn't know you did time?"

"No."

"Okay. I'll figure something else out." I set the shotgun down against my chair and leaned over and rested my hand on Naomi's knee. I felt her warmth, even through the blanket. "But you have to come clean with me. I need to know about your past. What were you convicted of? Where'd you do your stretch? Whoever's stalking you may be someone from your other life."

"I don't have another life." Naomi brushed my hand away and stood up. "It was a mistake to call you."

She hurried down the hall and slammed the door to the master bedroom.

But she didn't ask me to leave.

CHAPTER SEVEN

I HEARD WATER running in the house at eight fifteen. Longer than a toilet flush or a face scrub in the bathroom sink. Naomi was in the shower and up for the day. Only a few more minutes of playing bodyguard. Unfortunately, my never-ending day would continue.

I walked out onto the deck for the third time since the sun came up. I scanned the sagebrush hillside below. No one creeping up it toward the house. No one anywhere in sight. The morning sun sparkled across the San Elijo Lagoon. The northern end of paradise. But paradise was just a pretty bow around the eighth largest city in the country that had its fair share of kooks and psychopaths. They just had golden suntans and blond hair.

I went back inside and found Naomi in a terrycloth robe with her hair twisted up in a towel. She wore glasses that couldn't conceal the blue glow of her eyes. She must wear brown contact lenses. Why? The natural color of her eyes was spectacular. Cobalt blue that damn near vibrated. How much of her true self did she hide every day? A radio persona at night. Did she play another role during the day?

Naomi had made it clear last night that her past was off limits. I'd give her the space. For now.

She stood in the kitchen next to a coffeepot. Last night hadn't ended pleasantly. I didn't want to stick around long enough to find out how the morning would start. I went to the front window in the living room and peeked outside for the twentieth or so time since I arrived at the house at 2:25 that morning. Clear for the twentieth time.

"You should be safe at home during the day." I walked into the kitchen. "I'll see you at the station tonight."

"You look like you stayed up all night," she said and took a sip of coffee.

"I did. Uneventful. Whoever stole the gun from your car may have just been an opportunist and has nothing to do with the letter writer."

"Maybe." She took another sip of coffee. "Some coffee before you go?"

"No thanks."

I walked to the front door with the Mossberg at my side. Naomi followed and stopped me with a hand on my back. I turned to face her.

"There are some things I just can't talk about, Rick." Her piercing blue eyes locked onto mine. Her voice empty of the ingrained seduction. Direct. Warm. Guileless. "Not to anyone. Even someone I . . ."

She went onto her tiptoes and kissed me on the lips. Tender. Warm. Lingering.

My lips kissed her back before my brain could calculate the error of their actions. Rule one, don't get romantically involved with a client. The rest of my body ignored my brain and rules. It drank in the warmth and rode out the buzz.

"I . . . I . . ." My brain hadn't reengaged yet.

"Shhh." Naomi put her fingers on my lips. "I'll see you tonight at the station."

Words finally formed in my head, but I left without saying anything. I finally uttered the word stuck in my head when I got behind the wheel of my car. "Wrong."

I pushed the last minute I'd spent with Naomi into a compartment in my brain. I had a few that were still empty. There were other things to think about. The case. I had to keep Naomi and my job separate. The long night pulled at me as I hit the tail end of the morning rush hour on the drive home. I'd been up for over twenty-four hours and just wanted to go to sleep. But I couldn't. I got home and fed Midnight then let him outside. I got back on the road by nine fifteen.

More traffic down to the radio station. But I didn't park in its parking lot. I drove across the street and parked at the business park. I got out of my car and walked the circumference of the four identical three-story glass buildings that formed a cube.

I spotted a security camera on the outside of the building making up the west side of the cube. It was pointed at the back parking lot, which was in line of sight of 1350's. Bingo. Now I just needed to see the footage of last night from the time Naomi arrived at the station until I staked out the parking lot.

Easier said than done. I didn't have a badge and I couldn't report a crime to the police so they could investigate. Maybe I didn't need a badge. I did have a paper license from the California Bureau of Security and Investigative Services. That might impress someone.

A large sign in front of the building said Lansing Business Park. I went inside. The building was inhabited by ten or twelve businesses. This could take a while. I searched the roster next to the elevator and lucked out. Suite 1-D read *Lansing Security*. I found the suite in the right corner of the ground floor.

The suite was small with a slider window like a drive-thru fast-food restaurant just inside the door. A dark-haired man with mutton-chop sideburns wearing a gray Lansing Security work shirt sat on the other side of the window. His name patch read "Quint." Could have been a first name, could have been a last name. Or, it could have been both like Cher. He opened the slider after I walked in.

"Can I help you?" He didn't sound like he really wanted to.

"Yes." I smiled like I meant it. "Does the security camera facing the back parking lot belong to Lansing Security?"

"Yes." His face scrunched up. "Why?"

"I'm a private investigator working for the radio station across the street and there may have been a crime committed in their parking lot last night." When you don't have a good lie, go with the truth.

I pulled out my wallet and showed Quint my paper badge. He looked even less impressed than his default expression.

"Don't they have their own security cameras at the radio station?"

"They should." I raised my eyebrows like I shared his disdain. "But they don't."

"And you want to look at last night's recording."

"Yes." Couldn't be that easy.

"Well, that's against company policy, so I can't help you."

"Maybe I could talk to your boss. Is he in?"

"You're talking to the boss." He folded his arms across his chest.

"Since you're the boss, maybe you could make an exception to the policy." Probably too late to appeal to his ego. "I'm just trying to do my job and make sure people are safe over at 1350. It's probably less than two hours of footage. We can fast-forward through it in ten minutes."

"Come back with the police, and I'll show them whatever they like." He smiled. Not in a friendly way. "Because your little piece of paper doesn't give you the right to act like a cop."

Zero for one.

"Okay." One final question. "Is the daily footage archived or do you tape over it each day?"

"Proprietary information." He slid the drive-thru window shut and looked back at his computer. Discussion over. Quint and I had failed to bond.

I traced the route I took last night when I followed Naomi to the Night Owl. I parked in the same parking lot on the east side of the building where I had last night. The bar had a wraparound lot. A self-storage business sat behind the bar on the other side of a chain-link fence in the back. I walked a three-sixty around the Night Owl. No security camera. There was one on the storage facility, but it was pointed in the wrong direction.

An Enterprise car rental agency was next door on the east side of the bar and a Sonic drive-in restaurant on the west. There was a Citibank across the street. At least two out of the three businesses would have security cameras. That left just two questions. What were the cameras pointed at and how would I get a look at last night's footage?

I left my car in the bar parking lot and did a walkabout. Bingo. All three had multiple security cameras. Each with at least one pointing in the direction of the Night Owl. Sonic had two cameras facing the bar, but at the opposite side of the lot where Naomi and I had parked last night.

I did my paper badge routine with each of the businesses and got the same result as I had with Quint at Lansing Security. Just more politely. Contacting the police wasn't an option. I'd given my word to Naomi, which now looked like a bad idea. But it was my word.

I sat in my car in the Night Owl parking lot. Last night tugged on me. My head felt like an overstuffed sofa cushion. I hadn't slept in thirty hours. My senses were going into hibernation. If I went home now, I could get five or six hours of sleep before I went back to the radio station. Sleep. A siren call that I was ready to crash my ship on the rocks to heed. But, I couldn't.

Citibank was the only one of the three businesses that archived the daily footage from its security camera. Sonic and Enterprise automatically deleted the previous day's footage every day at midnight. If Naomi's gun had been stolen while we were in the Night Owl last night, the only shot I might have at getting a glimpse of the thief was to somehow look at the security camera footage from Sonic and Enterprise.

I pulled out my cell phone and punched a number I never expected to call again.

"Special Agent Mallon."

"John, it's Rick Cahill."

Silence. Which was better than the reaction I got from most other members of law enforcement in San Diego County.

Mallon was a Special Agent at the FBI. I'd made enemies of his boss, the Special Agent in Charge of the San Diego field office when I'd encountered him and Mallon a couple years ago.

Finally, "How can I help you, Rick?" He sounded about as eager to help as Quint at Lansing Security.

"I need your help."

"I already assumed that's why you called me. Unless you have information regarding an ongoing federal investigation, there's not much I can do for you."

"I don't know what it could lead to. Possibly something federal." Maybe the stalker was a felon himself and had crossed state lines with a gun of his own. Maybe not, but I needed law enforcement help, and Mallon was my only shot.

"Please explain, Rick. I'm kind of busy right now."

"I need help with viewing footage from security cameras owned by private businesses."

"Have you contacted the police department in the jurisdiction where the businesses reside?" Mallon asked.

"Unfortunately, I can't do that. And even if I could, you know there's not a police department in the county that would agree to help me."

"I'm afraid that's not my problem, Rick."

"You owe me, John."

When I'd first met Mallon two years ago, he'd risked his job to help me off the books. He'd done it because it was the right thing to do and because someone else's actions broke the FBI's sacred trust with the Constitution of the United States. By the time the case concluded, I'd killed a murderer who had John as next on his list. But that's not why I told him he owed me.

He'd hired me about a year ago to tail his wife. He thought she'd been fooling around on him. She had, just not in the way he feared. She'd been stepping out on him onto a dance floor. He didn't like to dance and she did. The Salsa. She took lessons and snuck out to dance with a partner whenever she got the chance. The dancing with the partner never went horizontal. She just loved to dance and didn't want the man she loved to feel badly that he wouldn't provide her that enjoyment. By far, the most saccharine reason for deceit I'd ever investigated. Actually, the only saccharine deceit case I'd ever investigated.

However, being the upstanding guy he was, Mallon felt awful about distrusting his wife and worse about hiring me to uncover the truth. I didn't charge him anything. He sent me a check anyway. I ripped it up.

Though not as upstanding as John, I did feel a bit sleazy telling him he owed me. But not enough to keep me from trying to use him to find the truth. The truth was my life's mission.

"I sent you a check, Rick. You never cashed it. That's not my fault." A piff exhale. "Oh, I get it now. That's why you didn't cash the check. Or are you threatening to tell my wife I had her followed? You've been waiting for a time when you needed something and you could hold it over my head. I didn't think you were that kind of man."

I didn't know what kind of a man I was, but I knew what kind of a man I wasn't. I'd ripped up the check because Mallon had risked a lot to help me find the truth once, not because I wanted to leverage him later. But that's exactly what I was doing.

"You're right. You don't owe me anything. Hang up right now and we're at least even." I let go a deep breath. "But a woman's life may be in danger. I can't go to the police. She needs our help."

"Who is *she*?"

"I can't tell you that. I'm sorry. She's a public figure who's being harassed and probably stalked. I'm sworn to secrecy. I wish I wasn't."

Silence, then a long exhale. "Tell me what you can."

I told him about the letter, the voicemail, and the theft of something from Naomi's car. I left out the gun and enough information that he wouldn't figure out who I was protecting. Hell, he probably didn't even listen to talk radio. It didn't matter. I'd given Naomi my word.

"I'm not a threat assessment expert, but if the stalker broke into her car, that is rapid escalation."

"We're on the same page."

Mallon was a good man who'd spent his life doing the right thing. He'd been an accountant when his brother was killed overseas fighting for our country. John then joined the FBI to try to cut off the money trail that funded terrorists like those who killed his brother. He cared about people. So did I. He just helped them without screwing up their lives. Or his own.

"Give me an address."

CHAPTER EIGHT

MALLON WAS DUE to meet me in the Night Owl parking lot in an hour. My brain and stomach battled each other to fill their immediate needs. As usual, my stomach won. The nap I desperately needed lost out to the rumbling in my belly.

Sonic was a thirty-second walk next door. In-N-Out was five minutes in the other direction. Not even close.

I conked out in my car after I finished a Double-Double with Animal Fries. And a chocolate shake. A tapping in my brain woke me. I opened my eyes and saw Special Agent John Mallon rapping his knuckles against my window and staring at me. Even with his eyes hidden behind his aviator sunglasses, I could tell he wasn't happy. I rolled down the window.

"Are you drunk?" He glanced at the In-N-Out detritus strewn on the floor of the passenger seat, then back at me.

"No. I was up all night guarding the woman's house. Thanks for coming." I opened the door and Mallon stepped back to let me exit.

"This bar first?" Mallon pointed at the Night Owl. He wore his standard issue blue suit with a neutral tie, short brown hair perfectly coiffed. We were about the same height, but I had a few years and a few pounds on him. Most of the pounds were muscle. Except for the pound of fast food I'd just shoved down my gullet.

"It doesn't have a security camera. Enterprise next door does."

We walked to the car rental agency and talked to Kelsea, the manager I'd talked to earlier that day. Late thirties, blond and pretty, she wore a gray business suit with a white shirt. Special Agent Mallon flashed his shield and Kelsea was happy to help. She led us into her office, sat down in front of a computer, and hit a couple keys.

"There. You've got the two outside views and the one in the showroom."

"Can you pull up the outside feeds and see if they cover the area of the Night Owl's parking lot we need to see?" I walked around the desk and looked over her shoulder.

The computer monitor was split into the three different camera feeds. The video was in color, but grainy and washed out. A rental agent walked a customer around a car, inspecting it before handing the key fob over. The movements juddered a bit due to the frame-rate conversion from camera to computer screen. The bottom right of the screen showed the right side of the Enterprise parking lot and a few feet of the Night Owl's. The hoods of both my and Special Agent Mallon's cars were visible. I didn't think that would be enough to show anyone entering Naomi's car last night, but it was worth a look.

"The camera in the lower right of the screen is the one we need. Thanks."

The manager tapped a few keys on the keyboard. The screen changed to a single image of the Enterprise parking lot and the thin slice of the Night Owl's.

"What time do you want to look at?" she asked.

"From about 12:30 a.m. to 1:30 a.m. If you'll just show us how to run the footage, we'll let you get back to work."

Mallon came around the desk and stood next to me. Kelsea showed us a toggle switch on the screen we could use to forward and reverse the recording. She also showed us how to zoom the image. Pretty simple.

"Thank you, ma'am," Mallon said. "We'll alert you when we're done."

I took Kelsea's seat. Mallon grabbed a chair from the table in the corner of the office and planted it next to me.

The image on the monitor was frozen on 12:30 a.m. The right side of the screen showed the three-foot sliver of the Night Owl parking lot. The three feet were larger on the full screen, but the image still only revealed hoods of cars. The hoods were at the top of the camera feed meaning they were parked near the entrance to the parking lot. About a third of the right-hand lane of Balboa Avenue was visible across the top of the screen.

I hit the play button. No movement on the screen. I fast-forwarded on the slowest speed.

"What are we looking for?" Mallon asked.

"The woman's car and mine should enter the parking lot in the next minute or two. I want to see if someone breaks into her car while we're in the bar."

"But you can't tell me who the woman is or what was stolen from the car, correct?" Mallon gave me the Special Agent eyes again.

"Right." I nodded my head. "But now, I owe you."

"I can't imagine a scenario where I'd need your help."

No hurt feelings. I couldn't imagine a scenario, either. I almost felt guilty.

A few seconds later, a hood became visible pulling into a parking space in the middle of the frame. The first three feet of dual racing stripes were visible on the far right of the screen. Three seconds later, a black hood appeared below Naomi's Camaro. My Honda Accord.

"That's us."

"Back it up." Mallon pointed at the screen. "I want to watch the cars come down Balboa again."

Mallon was ahead of me. I'd been concentrating on the parking spaces where I expected our cars to show up, and he'd been watching the full screen. I reversed the video and watched slices of our cars disappear backwards. I watched the far left top of the screen. The passenger side of Naomi's Camaro came on the screen, easily recognizable because of the one racing stripe visible in the image. I followed the Camaro as it neared the Night Owl parking lot entrance. It passed through the top right of the screen, slowing slightly before it disappeared. Then headlights shone through the wrought-iron fence separating the Night Owl parking lot and that of Enterprise Rent-A-Car. The hood of the Camaro appeared. My car followed a few seconds later. I paused the tape.

"We can't see cars turn into the parking lot. Hard to tell if someone was following you." Mallon's eyes stayed on the screen.

"There weren't that many cars on the road after midnight on a Monday."

"Did you know where the woman was leading you to?"

"No."

"So, you were concentrating on following her rather than on anyone who might have followed you."

"I would have remembered someone pulling in behind me." He had a point. That didn't mean I had to acknowledge it.

"There is another parking lot that's on the west side of the bar."

"You get all of that while I was asleep in my car?"

"I pay attention." Mallon may as well have been wearing his sunglasses for all the emotion I could read in his eyes. "Let the tape run."

"Roger." The Feds didn't miss anything. At least Special Agent Mallon didn't.

We both watched the top of the screen. Sure enough, headlights and then the right side of a black sedan drove down Balboa. The car didn't appear to slow like mine and Naomi's had near the entrance of the Night Owl. A white SUV passed by a few seconds later.

"It looks like neither car parked in the Night Owl parking lot. At least not the one you parked in." Mallon seemed to enjoy the chase. Looking at videotape of a bar parking lot must have been more exciting than scouring bank accounts.

"Shall we continue?"

"I'm noting the time so we can compare them to the Sonic tape. 12:32 a.m."

I reversed the tape, then let it run on normal speed and watched the hoods of Naomi's car and mine. And watched. Nothing happened. The camera angle couldn't see our car doors opening and the two of us walking into the bar. I watched the top of the screen for someone walking by on the sidewalk. Nothing. I sped the tape up on the slowest fast-forwarding speed. No action on Naomi's car or on the sidewalk beyond. An occasional car would pass by on the top of the screen and I'd rewind and we'd watch in regular speed. None of the cars appeared to slow to turn into the parking lot.

Finally, at time stamp 1:17 a.m., the Camaro and my Honda Accord hoods pulled back out of the screen and disappeared for good. Mallon and I had been in the cramped office for about the same time Naomi and I had been in the Night Owl and we came up with nothing.

Next stop, Sonic.

CHAPTER NINE

THE SONIC MANAGER, Rudy, was a clean-cut kid who looked eighteen, but had to be older. His eyes went big and his face turned red when Special Agent Mallon showed him his badge. He led us through the kitchen, which was surprisingly clean, into a small office in the back. Rudy sat down in front of a computer and pulled up the security camera feeds. There was one overhead in the office with a live view of the three of us. No thinning hair spots on my head yet. There were two cameras in the dining area and two on both sides of the restaurant that covered the drive-in stalls where people were served by carhop girls on roller skates.

"Rudy." Mallon took control. No question, he liked being out in the field. Even if it was my field and he could get into a jackpot with his boss by playing on it. He pointed at the computer monitor. "We'd like to see the footage from this camera from 12:30 to 1:30 a.m. last night."

Mallon pointed at an image that had the entry into the drive-in from Balboa as well as three stalls. The camera faced the Night Owl, but a five-foot-high cinder block privacy wall blocked any view of the west-facing parking lot. It did have a view of the right lane of Balboa and the entry into the Night Owl's parking lot.

"Okay." Rudy tapped the keyboard a couple times and a black-and-white still shot from the one camera filled up the screen. The time stamp read 12:30 a.m.

"Thanks, Rudy." Mallon put his hand on the back of the kid's chair. "We can take it from here."

"Um." Rudy tugged at his shirt. "I'm not allowed to let anyone use the computer. I can run the video for you."

"Do you remember the badge Special Agent Mallon showed you, Rudy?" I couldn't keep a smile from lifting my lips. "He's here from the FBI."

"I know, but the owner is very specific about the computer." He turned in his chair and looked at Mallon with a sad smile. "I can show you what you want to see, but nobody can touch the computer. We were robbed once and the police used the computer to look at the security footage on their own and somehow lost some sales data."

Mallon put his hands on his hips. His authority had been challenged by some kid a couple years out of high school. Not that it was the kid's fault. He was in a tough position. If Mallon wanted to go to the wall, he could find a way, worst case involving a judge and a warrant, to get custody of the computer. Of course, he wouldn't. That would shine light on what we were up to and could get him fired.

The facts of the situation rolled over his normally impassive face.

"That's fine, Rudy," I said, but looked at Mallon. "We're not looking for anything involving national security."

I grabbed the only other chair in the room on the opposite side of the desk and set it down next to Rudy. I nodded at it to Mallon, but he stayed standing with his hands on his hips.

"Can I ask what you're looking for?" Rudy asked me.

"We're looking for any cars turning into the Night Owl's parking lot or anyone entering the lot on foot." Mallon joined back in on the hunt and leaned over Rudy's shoulder. "Go ahead and start in real time."

The kid clicked the mouse and the image on the screen moved. It was a bit clearer than the feed from Enterprise, but still juddered a bit. Two minutes in, we saw half of Naomi's Camaro and my Accord turn into the Night Owl parking lot. A few seconds later, the black sedan and white van that we'd seen in the Enterprise video showed on the computer screen. At least the right side of the vehicles did. The sedan pulled into the Sonic drive-in and passed through the radius of the security camera's view. The van continued west on Balboa out of sight.

"Pause," I said to Rudy. "Can you pull up the other camera views so we can see if that black sedan stops for food or exits the other side of the parking lot?"

"Sure." He clicked the mouse a couple times and the screen now had all four outside camera feeds up. He fast-forwarded the video on the second outside camera next to the one we'd focused on. He paused at 12:33 a.m., which was the time the car passed out of our camera's view. Sure enough, the nose of the sedan appeared on the far-right corner of the camera feed.

"Perfect." I winked at Rudy. "Now start that video up at regular speed."

The sedan, which looked like it might be a Toyota Corolla, pulled into the stall at the far end of the drive-in.

"So much for that lead," I said. "Just some guy getting a late dinner or an early breakfast. Let's go back to focusing on the camera with the eastern view of Balboa."

Rudy clicked the mouse and the screen filled up with the single camera view. We watched for the next half hour at the slowest fast-forward speed until Naomi's Camaro and my Accord exited the Night Owl parking lot. No cars followed us. Another forty-five minutes of futility.

Or maybe not. Two different camera angles from two different businesses and neither showed anyone entering the parking lot on foot or by vehicle. It could have been someone from inside the Night Owl who went into the lot and broke into Naomi's car. The view we had of the car was only its hood. Except, I'd been facing the door that night at the bar and didn't remember anyone exiting before we did. Or entering. The regulars who were there when we walked in were still there when we walked out. Probably just another Monday night at the Night Owl.

Zero for two. If the camera at the bank across the street from the Night Owl had similar results, that left the parking lot of 1350 AM. I hoped I didn't have to take Mallon to Lansing Business Park to meet my pal Quint from Lansing Security.

I gave Rudy my business card, thanked him, and we left the restaurant.

"One thing seems certain—no one entered the parking lot from Balboa Avenue while you and the woman were in the Night Owl." Mallon asked me as we walked up Balboa to the crosswalk, "You sure no one came in or out of the bar while you were there?"

"Ninety-five percent."

"Maybe the bank camera has an angle the others missed."

We crossed the street and went into Citibank. Mallon flashed his badge to the bank manager I'd talked to before I called for the FBI's help. Lisa Beathard was in her late thirties with a clipped efficient manner that matched her clipped brown hair. She led us back to her desk and showed us how to use security camera footage, then stepped back and watched over our shoulders.

The bank had four cameras. One in the vault, two on the floor, and one on the outside of the building facing the street. The one facing the street picked up both sides of Balboa Avenue and the entry into the Night Owl parking lot. Its view didn't go all the way to where Naomi and I had parked our cars, five spaces deep, but it did catch the door to the bar. We fast-forwarded to 12:32 a.m. and watched Naomi's and my car enter the parking lot and disappear out of the camera's view. Ten seconds later, two figures were visible walking from offscreen into the Night Owl.

The video was grainy and juddered as badly as the images from the Enterprise camera. All you could barely make out was that a man and a woman entered the bar. No defining features were visible. Not great, but the key was we could see if anyone else entered or left the bar while Naomi and I were in there. We watched at regular speed so as not to miss the second or so air time when the bar door could open and emit light, designating someone coming or going.

Forty-five minutes later, we were zero for three. No one entered or exited the parking lot or the Night Owl itself. We thanked the bank manager and left.

Mallon stopped outside the bank and faced me. "Your secret client must have been mistaken about the time of the break-in of her car. It must have happened earlier in the day, or a scary thought, while she was at home."

"She seemed pretty adamant. She puts the item in her glove compartment every time she leaves her house in the afternoon and takes it inside when she's home for the night. Every day. No variations. She had the item yesterday when she left her home at 7:00 p.m. It was gone when she got home around 1:45 a.m."

"Does she have a conceal carry license for the gun?"

Shit.

"I didn't say anything about a gun." Mallon had figured it out. He was smart and in law enforcement. He had to figure it out.

"Nobody's going to put a diamond necklace in their glove compartment when they leave the house each day and bring it back inside when they return home. Or a sex tape for that matter. Does she have a conceal carry?"

"I doubt it."

"Is this woman in some sort of legal trouble, beyond committing a misdemeanor every day she leaves her house?" Mallon threw up his hands. "On second thought, I don't want to know. Plausible deniability."

"She's not in any legal trouble." At least not at present. As far as I knew. "The gun's for protection and you can see why. She's in the public domain and that attracts crazies. You and I would do the same thing in her situation."

"Like I said. I don't want to know. I did what you asked and that's the end of it."

"There's one more camera at her only other stop last night."

"What? Why didn't you tell me that earlier?" Mallon's face pinched up.

I'd been hoping we'd get lucky. Whether Mallon listened to 1350 AM or not, he'd be able to do some simple research to easily discover that Naomi was my client. What he'd decide to do with that information was up to him. I had to risk it to get a glimpse of the man who was stalking Naomi.

"I didn't think we'd have to look at it. I figured the break-in had to have occurred at the Night Owl."

"Doesn't matter." Mallon wiped one palm over the other. "I've done all I can. Good luck."

"John, this woman is in danger. She just needs another forty-five minutes of your time."

"And what if we see someone stealing the gun on the security video? I'll have to follow up on it and report it to the police. I have no other choice. Then what are you going to do?"

"That's fine." I'd cross that bridge when I saw it burning in front of me. "Her safety takes precedence."

"Where's the other camera?"

"Off Aero Drive."

"Damn." Mallon looked at the smartwatch on his wrist. "We have to make this quick."

"Roger."

I gave Mallon the address of Lansing Business Park, and we walked back to our cars and headed out. We were just ahead of the meat of the rush hour and got to the business park by 3:35 p.m. The drive home would be a bitch though.

Quint sat behind the drive-in window staring at his computer screen at Lansing Security. Looked like he hadn't moved since I left him five hours earlier. He turned his head toward us. Same disinterested, aloof look on his face as this morning.

"I'm Special Agent Mallon with the FBI." Mallon flipped open his leather badge holder and held it in front of the window. "We need to take a look at your security camera footage from last night."

Quint's eyes rounded big and his face flushed like we'd just caught him looking at porn on the Internet. Maybe we had. He tapped a key on his keyboard without looking.

"Okay." His eyes shrunk back to disinterest. "Come through that door on your right and make the first left."

We did as instructed and ended up in his tiny office, maybe twice the size of a toll booth.

"If you'll show us how to run the footage from last night, we'll let you attend to your other duties," Mallon said to Quint.

I had the feeling Quint didn't have any other duties. He seemed to just sit in front of his computer all day.

"I'm sorry, sir." He looked up at Mallon. "But I'll have to operate the computer."

Another stickler for the rules.

Mallon let go a breath, then looked at me. "Give this gentleman the time parameters we need to look at."

"Let's go from 7:30 p.m. last night until 10:00 p.m." I smiled at Quint and tried to keep a smirk out of it. I'm sure he thought he'd never see me again after he brushed me off this morning. I had friends in high places. At least for another half hour or so. "You can fast-forward until you see a 1969 Camaro enter the 1350 parking lot across the street. Then go real time."

Quint tapped some keys and the feed from the security camera from last night came onto the screen. The view caught a couple of the outer rings of the business park's parking lot, the street, and the middle section of 1350's back parking lot across the street. He started fast-forwarding and stopped as soon as a car with two stripes on the hood parked in the 1350 parking lot.

Quint had caught the car quicker than I did, but he did spend his days staring at a computer screen. Probably spent his nights home alone the same way playing *Call of Duty*.

A woman got out of the car at 8:03 p.m. Like the other videos we'd watched today, the feed was grainy and the night washed out the color, but the car was obviously Naomi's and she was the woman. She walked inside the building. We watched in the slowest fast-forward mode until my Honda Accord pulled into the parking lot at 9:00 p.m. Two men exited the station at 9:10 p.m. Again, the images were fuzzy, but the two were probably Jeff Palet, the political talk show host before Naomi, and his producer. They got into separate cars and exited the parking lot without approaching Naomi's car.

No one else came into the parking lot until I exited the station to do my ride-about around the business park. No one came in or out of the parking lot while I was gone. My car returned ten minutes later. I didn't need to see any more. I'd guarded the parking lot for the next two-plus hours until Naomi came out and I followed her offscreen to the Night Owl.

"You can shut it off," I said to Quint.

"There's still a couple hours until Naomi finished her show," Mallon said.

"Who?" Mallon had figured out who my client was, as I expected him to. That didn't mean I had to confirm it.

Quint stared straight ahead at his computer screen

"It's pretty obvious, Rick. We drove right in front of the radio station with its big 1350 sign out front to get here. I've heard Naomi's show." Mallon put his hand on Quint's shoulder. "Let it run."

"No, we're good." I nodded at Quint. "I stayed in my car in the parking lot until the subject left a little after midnight. Nobody broke into her car while I was there."

Quint's eyebrows went up and he looked at me. His job as computer jockey just got interesting. But it really hadn't. What had gotten interesting was why Naomi lied to me about having her gun stolen. If she ever really owned one. To be generous, maybe she'd gotten confused about when she last brought the handgun into the house or how many stops she made before or after work last night.

"What would you like me to do?" Quint looked at Mallon for instruction. The one with a badge.

"Keep rolling," Mallon said to him, then turned to me. "We need to see if someone followed her from the radio station."

"I followed her and no one broke into her car. Not here, not at the bar."

I felt like a jerk for pressuring Special Agent Mallon to help me and risk disciplinary action or worse on a wild goose chase. The goose and I were going to have to have a talk.

"We can't be a hundred percent sure about the bar. We didn't see every angle. We're here. Let's finish it. Then we'll be all done."

Quint may have thought that Mallon meant that we'd be done watching video feeds. I knew he meant something else. Scratch the FBI off my "I Need a Favor" list. Quint started the video again.

"Fast-forward until the Camaro leaves the parking lot," I said. "That should be around 12:15 a.m."

He had the image of Naomi leaving the parking lot with me in tow in less than twenty seconds. We exited stage left and Quint stopped the video.

"Let it run for another thirty seconds," Mallon said.

Quint did as instructed. No other cars appeared on the screen.

"That's good," I said. "We'll let you get back to your job. Thank you."

Mallon frowned and left the tiny office. I followed him out to the parking lot. My lack of sleep over the past thirty-six hours hit me like an anvil. The adrenaline of the chase had kept me going, running on fumes. The revelation that Naomi had lied to me evaporated what little fuel I had left. I felt like a mastodon in the La Brea Tar Pits. Mallon turned to me when we reached our cars.

"I don't know what's going on here, Rick, and I don't think you do, either." He opened his car door. "But I suggest you figure it out before you get yourself in too deep."

Special Agent Mallon exited the parking lot leaving his words spinning in my head. Right next to my own.

CHAPTER TEN

I WOKE UP on the couch to Midnight staring me in the face. From two inches. I checked my phone—7:28 p.m. Over an hour past his dinnertime. I got off the couch, went into the pantry in the kitchen, and shoveled dog food into Midnight's bowl from the forty-quart container where I stowed it. He did his dinner dance, and I put the bowl down onto the floor. He didn't wait to see what I was having.

The sleep deprivation anvil still sat on my head. I'd gotten about two hours on the couch. Enough some nights, but not right after going sleepless thirty-six hours straight, sans a ten-minute car nap. I called Naomi. Voicemail.

"It's Rick. Call me."

I hadn't talked to her since I left her house this morning. I'd been too busy trying to find ghosts. Besides, after the kiss, I wouldn't know what to say. "Wrong" popped into my head again. But that was my issue, not hers.

She needed a welfare check. Not the kind that comes in an envelope from the government. The kind police perform when someone may be in danger or physical distress. Whether she lied about her gun being stolen or not, the letter and the angry voicemail were real. Some creep hiding behind a fake name had an unhealthy interest in her.

Naomi was probably on her way to the radio station. I let Midnight out into the backyard to take care of business, then back inside.

I needed dinner, a shower, and another four hours of sleep. I grabbed my keys and went out to my car.

Chip Evigan answered his cell phone on the first ring. "Mr. Cahill?"

"Have you talked to Naomi today?" I turned right on Balboa, heading for Interstate 5. Evigan's response would determine whether I went north or south.

"No. I called her, but she didn't pick up. Why?"

"Is that normal?"

"Why? What's going on?" Quick. High-pitched.

"Probably nothing. Just answer the question. Is it normal for Naomi to ignore your calls?"

"Well, yes." Grudging. "Has something happened? Is she okay?"

"Call me if she contacts you or when she arrives at the station." I hung up.

I felt for Evigan, but I didn't like him. Probably not his fault. He was in a tough spot and he'd hired me to help him get out of it. But he was management and I had a dislike for authority, down to the DNA level. Even when I'd managed Muldoon's Steak House, I didn't like management. I liked being the boss, not for the power, but for cutting through the bullshit and getting things done.

There were a few sergeants I liked when I was on the Santa Barbara Police Force. Most only cared about keeping you and the citizens alive and putting the bad guys away. I couldn't think of a single lieutenant who wasn't more politician than police. All ass-covering and looking for the next rung up the ladder.

Management. Evigan fit the mold.

I got onto 5-North and called Naomi again.

"Rick?" Semi-purr. Not the throaty thrum for over the air, but sultry enough to make a man think. Or not think.

"Where are you?"

"I just got out of the shower. Why?"

"Just checking in. We need to talk."

"About what?" A light tease in her voice.

"The gun."

"What about it?" Calm.

"We need to talk in person." She made a living speaking as a disembodied voice coming out of the night. A believable voice. I needed to see her face when we spoke.

"I can't. I'm just about to drive down to the station." A flutter of anxiety. "Should I be worried?"

"No. I'll meet you there."

I made a quick jag onto 52 heading east and then got onto I-15 South. I made it to the station by 8:15 p.m. Except for Naomi's Camaro, the same cars were in the parking lot as last night. Plus one more. A white SUV with green lettering on the side that said San Diego Security. Good. Someone had listened to me. An armed guard stood in front of the entrance to the radio station.

I got out of my car and walked over to the entrance.

"Good evening," The guard said. He was big and broad and had a Glock 9mm holstered on his side. "May I see your employee badge?"

"I don't have one. I'm here to see Chip Evigan."

"Your name?"

I gave it to him. He pushed the intercom next to the door.

"Yes?" Evigan's voice again.

"A Mr. Cahill is here to see you, sir."

"I'll be right out."

Thirty seconds later, Evigan unlocked the door to the station and let me inside.

"Compliments on the guard," I said.

"Did you talk to Naomi?"

"Yes. She's on her way."

"Did you tell her about the letter?" Big eyes. Nervous. His ass in a vice with ownership squeezing on one side and Naomi on the other.

Not my problem. Keeping Naomi safe and finding the truth was my split mission. Learning the latter might make me change tactics for the former.

"Let's talk in your office."

"You look like you haven't slept in a week." Evigan put his hands on his hips and eyeballed me like I was one of his employees who'd come to work still drunk from the night before.

Management.

"Your office?" I stepped past him through the lobby.

Evigan caught up to me by the time I made it to the news nest. Rachel Riley's eyebrows pinched together and she forced a smile. I must have looked as bad as I felt. We passed the studio. From behind the glass, the voice of Jeff Palet, the six-to-nine host, droned through the station's internal speakers as he commented on the San Diego mayor's fecklessness.

Evigan ushered me into his office. I plopped down in the chair facing his desk without an invitation. He sat behind the desk and stared at me.

"Are you going to answer my question?" He leaned forward. "Did you tell Naomi about the letter?"

"Yes."

"What did she say?"

"She didn't seem concerned." Until someone stole her gun or when she made up a story about someone stealing her gun. That would remain our secret until I decided it wouldn't be anymore.

"Oh? Then I guess there's no reason for me to stick around here." He stood up and grabbed his sweater off the back off his chair, then looked at me and sat back down. "What did you want to talk about? Something new I should know about? Have you made any headway on the letter writer?"

"Nothing new." Possibly. "How did you find Naomi?"

"What do you mean?"

"When you hired her, how did you come across her? Where was she working?"

"She sent me a tape. She'd been doing afternoon drive time at some podunk five thousand-watt station up in Chico." He sat back down. "Why?"

"How long did she work in Chico?"

"A year or two, I think."

"Where before that?"

"I don't know. Why?"

"Why doesn't she post on your social media sites? All your other talent does."

"What?" His face squished up. "What does that have to do with anything? What happened that I should know about?"

"Nothing happened. Why don't you make her post on social media like everyone else?"

"What are you not telling me? We hired you to tell us what you learn. That's the only reason we hired you. I'm starting to think it was a bad idea. You come in here looking like you're on the seventh day of an all-week bender and now you're holding out information on me? Tell me what's going on or we'll cancel your contract and sue for restitution."

Management. But he had a point.

"I'm not holding out on you." Lie. "I'm trying to learn as much as I can about Naomi. Maybe I can get some insight into her stalker." Not a complete lie. "She's your biggest star. Why doesn't she post on social media? Has she posted before and someone harassed her online?"

"No. It's in her contract. No social media. No on remote events. No fully exposed headshot."

"Isn't that a little odd?"

The fact that Naomi was an ex-con would be a marketing bonanza. Nobody loves redemption stories more than Americans, and no Americans love redemption stories more than San Diegans. But Evigan and 1350 didn't know they had a redemption story because they didn't know that Naomi was an ex-con.

"People have all sorts of waivers in their contracts." He didn't look me in the eye.

"An unknown from Chico has a waiver not to do social media and not to have an identifiable photo of her on your website?"

"She didn't have the waivers in her first contract. She probably only posted five or six times on social media. I got flack for not pushing her more, but after the second book came in and she had a 4.3 rating, nobody said anything."

"Did you make her take a photo in the first contract?"

"Yes." Evigan opened his hands in front of himself on the desk. "What's this all about?"

"Just gathering information." I shrugged like it was standard operating procedure. "Did she wear the floppy hat in the first photo?"

"We wouldn't let her. Hmm." Evigan scratched the side of his face. "But the day of the photo shoot, she came in with a short haircut and her hair dyed brown."

"I thought that was her natural color."

"I'm not an expert on women's hair. I don't even know what my wife's natural hair color is. It changes twice a year. But when Naomi started, she was blond and it didn't look like it came out of a bottle."

Naomi didn't want her story of redemption known. Maybe because she hadn't been redeemed or because she knew there was someone looking for her from her past life. The stunning blue eyes covered with brown contact lenses. Blond hair dyed brown for picture day. A past she refused to talk about. I'd spent the last twenty-four hours guarding Naomi or staring at videotape. I hadn't had a chance to

investigate her beyond the sultry voice I heard on the radio. Maybe
I should have done more research before I took the job. If I'd known
what Evigan did about Naomi, I certainly would have.

"Did any of this seem strange to you, Chip?"

"Like I said, women change their hair all the time."

"Not just the hair. The social media. No off-site events."

"What are you getting at?"

"She wanted to be a star, but she didn't want anyone to know who
she was, or where she came from. Don't tell me you didn't figure that
out."

"She got a 4.3 her second book. She's been above 6 for the last year.
I don't give a damn about who she is or where she came from."

"Wouldn't syndication be the next logical step? She'd have to make a
helluva lot more money than 1350 could afford to pay her." I shook my
head. "I don't know the radio biz like you do, but I'm guessing the radio
station and you would benefit from her going into syndication, too."

"You're right. We wouldn't have to pay her anything and still get
the numbers from her show." Chip picked up a pen and tapped it
on his desk, not looking at me again. "She doesn't want to go into
syndication."

"She doesn't want to become a millionaire?"

"Oh, she wants to become a millionaire. She just wants us to pay
her like she's been syndicated in the top ten markets without going
into syndication. That's why we're at an impasse in her contract
negotiations."

"Have you ever known someone in radio who didn't want to go
into syndication?" Naomi was definitely hiding from something. Syndication was a license to print money for a radio host. She picked an
odd profession for anonymity. Maybe she never expected to blow up
and become so popular.

"This station has never produced anyone with the opportunity to be syndicated. Until now." He kept doing a one-handed drum solo with the pen and avoiding my eyes. He knew there was something off about Naomi, but his quest for the next rung up the ladder had kept him from investigating. "But, you're right, I've never heard of anyone turning it down."

The office door flew open and Naomi walked in.

"Did I miss an invite to the meeting?" She plopped her purse down on Evigan's desk.

"This isn't formal." Evigan taped on a weak smile. "Mr. Cahill and I were just discussing ways to improve the station's security." He stood up and tucked his sweater under his arm. "We just finished the discussion. I'm heading home. Have a good show."

Evigan slipped out of the office.

"What do you need to talk to me about?" Naomi checked her watch then took the seat that Evigan just fled. "I have show prep to do before I go on."

"You're sure about the last time you saw the gun and how many stops you made to and from work last night?"

"Yes." A frown. "Why?"

"I spent all day looking at video of the radio station's parking lot last night and three different camera angles of the Night Owl and didn't see anyone break into your car. Or even approach it." I spread my hands out in front of me on the desk. "You're one hundred percent sure about the last time you saw the gun?"

"Yes, I'm sure." No purr. Naomi folded her arms across her chest. "I put it in the glove compartment of my car at seven thirty when I left for work last night. I didn't make any stops. The only stop I made on the way home was at the Night Owl. Did these video cameras all have clear views of my car?"

"Clear enough." The ones of the Night Owl parking lot didn't give a full view of her Camaro, but the surrounding footage from all the cameras didn't show anyone entering the parking lot, either on foot or by car.

"Are you saying I'm lying about someone stealing my gun?" An edge her radio listeners never heard.

"I'm just wondering if you're mistaken."

"I'm not. I want to see the tapes from last night."

"I don't have possession of them. I had to call in a favor from someone at the FBI just to see them. Even then, it wasn't easy."

"The FBI?" Naomi's eyes flashed wide.

"There's nothing to worry about. The agent would probably lose his job if he followed up, and he's not going to. He's a friend." Probably not anymore.

"You're sure?"

"Yes. If you want to see the tapes, we'd have to contact the police and tell them about the theft." I fought to keep my hands from making air quotes around the word theft. "They'd have to get a warrant. Are you ready to get the police involved?"

"No." She squeezed her chest harder. "You promised me no police. Are you going to keep your word?"

"Yes." Either Naomi didn't want the police involved because she was afraid of where an investigation might go, or she made up the whole story. Neither reason gave me confidence about her character or the possibility of a happy ending to this case.

"I appreciate you're watching over me last night and whatever you did today." Her voice softened to almost vulnerable. "Is there anything else? I have to get ready for my show."

I had plenty else, but I didn't want to upset her before she put her voice out in front of tens of thousands of people.

"Just one other thing. Was anything else stolen from your car?"

If the different camera angles of the Night Owl parking lot did miss something and someone really broke into her car, had they known about the gun or been looking for something else? Identity thieves, or feeders to them, steal car registrations to set up fake identities. Or it could have just been a junkie looking for something to fence for his next fix.

"No." She tilted her head and looked up to the left. "I don't think so. I had my purse with me here and at the bar. I didn't have anything else valuable in the car."

"We can talk tomorrow."

I went to the door, but her voice stopped me.

"I really do appreciate what you've done for me, Rick." Soft. Exposed.

I tried to believe her.

CHAPTER ELEVEN

MY PHONE WOKE me on the couch. Midnight was staring at me again. This time from a respectable distance. My laptop lay open on my prone belly. I'd started researching Naomi's background when I'd gotten home from the radio station. I hadn't gotten very far. Sleep had interrupted. But I found one interesting fact. Or hadn't found one. The Naomi Hendrix who lived in Chico for four years and in San Diego the last two didn't have a criminal record.

My phone buzzed in my pocket. Naomi. 12:16 a.m. I answered.

"There was something else stolen." A nervous sizzle. "My car registration."

I didn't know if she was telling the truth or if I was a pawn in some game I didn't understand.

"Are you sure?"

"Of course I'm sure. It's not there."

"Can you say for sure it was stolen last night?" Or at all? "Do you check to see if it's there when you put this gun in the house every night?"

Silence. I had the feeling she wasn't going through her memory.

"No. I don't." The nervous sizzle had turned into an angry boil. "What do you mean *this gun*? You don't believe me, do you?"

"I'm not sure what to believe. The video cameras were pretty definitive. No one approached your car while it was parked at 1350 and no one entered the Night Owl parking lot while we were there. So, you must have gotten your dates or stops mixed up or you're not telling me the truth."

More silence. Seething silence? I didn't care. I was tired of the game. Chip Evigan had hired me to investigate who had sent Naomi a menacing letter, but I'd spent the last twenty-four hours chasing Naomi's ghosts. I'd let her alter my focus. My directive from 1350 was clear. My life's overriding mission was, too. Find the truth. The truth was that Naomi had lied to me. The why was a distraction from everything else. I didn't need to know the why.

Finally, Naomi spoke, "I'm sorry you don't believe me." No anger. Calm. Resolved. "Good-bye."

She hung up. She hadn't protested too much. She hadn't protested much at all. I didn't know if that was confirmation she'd lied to me or she didn't feel the need to convince me. It didn't matter. My hero complex had run its course with Naomi. Tomorrow I'd get back to working on the job I'd been hired to do.

I started to put my phone back in my pocket and head up to bed when I noticed there was a missed call and a voicemail message. I vaguely remembered my phone vibrating me awake earlier and ignoring it for more sleep. The time stamp for the message was 11:07 p.m. A phone number I didn't recognize.

My heart thumped in my chest, and I was suddenly wide awake. A late-night call from an unknown number. Rarely good news for anyone. For me, it could be a command to break the law or worse. And I couldn't refuse it.

I tapped the message and listened.

"Mr. Cahill?" Young voice. Not the voice I'd heard late at night a year ago. The one I hoped would never call. The message continued. "Um . . . this is Rudy Wayne. We met today at Sonic. I'm the manager who showed you the surveillance camera tapes. You gave me your

card, so ... anyway, I was looking at one of the tapes and I noticed
something kind of strange. I thought you might want to look at it
before it erases."

He left his callback number. The video from Sonic only had an
angle of the entrance to the Night Owl's parking lot. All it had shown
us was that no one other than Naomi and I entered the Night Owl's
parking lot while we were there. I couldn't imagine what Rudy had
seen that Special Agent Mallon and I missed. Still, my nerves were
already jangled from the possibility of what the phone call could have
been. A return to sleep would take a while whether I called Rudy back
or not. I tapped the number.

"Hello?" Awake. Good.

"Rudy? Rick Cahill."

"Oh, hi. Yeah, like I said on the voicemail I left you, I saw something weird on the video that I thought might interest you."

"Thanks. I can meet you at the restaurant in ten minutes."

"Oh, I'm not there. I'm home."

"Okay, can someone else at the restaurant show me the tape? The
night manager?"

"Um ... I don't ... no ... because ..."

"Rudy, spit it out."

"The tape was erased at midnight. I thought I mentioned that was
the procedure when you were at the restaurant today. That's why I
called you earlier. Sorry."

"It's not saved in some cloud storage?"

"The videos from inside the restaurant are for two weeks, but we
only keep the outside ones until midnight the next night. The inside
tapes are more important in case someone tries to rob us or employees
are stealing from us."

"Did you make a copy before it was erased?"

"Um, no. That's against company policy."

Sleep deprivation. It makes cowards of us all. If only I'd roused myself out of that first sleep. Probably didn't matter. What could Mallon
and I have missed that some kid manager saw? "Okay. Can you tell me
what you saw that Special Agent Mallon and I missed?"

"Yes, but . . . um . . . you didn't really miss it because we didn't really
look at it today."

This kid would be a master at circuitous arguments.

"Why don't you tell me what you saw and start from the beginning."

"Well, like I said, I didn't really see it at first."

Hmph.

"Go on."

"I was leaving to go home around about seven tonight when a carhop who works the night shift complained about a customer who
parked his car in one of the stalls last night and ordered a Coke, but
disappeared from his car after she brought it out. She said he never
came back to the car. When we closed at one last night, the car was
still there, and no one was in it. People aren't supposed to park in the
carhop area and leave their cars there. We have a parking lot on the
other side of the restaurant if they want to eat inside. Alicia complained to the night manager, and of course, Larry didn't do anything about it, so—"

"Rudy, can you skip the inner-restaurant politics and tell me what
you saw on the video?"

"Sure." Hurt. I didn't care. Nice kid, but he needed an editor.
"Anyway, I went home without doing anything about it, because
there weren't any cars in the carhop area when I got in this morning so
there was nothing I could do. But something about it stayed with me,
then I remembered the black car on the video you and Special Agent
Mallon wanted to look at. I figured it had to be the same car as the
one Alicia complained about because the car we saw on tape parked
in the carhop area around twelve thirty last night."

"Is that it?" Now I wished I hadn't checked my voicemail. Ten minutes of nothing that was going to cost me an hour of sleep. "Somebody parked where they weren't supposed to and got out of their car and you didn't even see the tape? This is all thirdhand information and supposition?"

"No, Mr. Cahill." More hurt. "I did see the tape. I went back to the restaurant and watched the tape all the way through because I thought I might see something that would help you and Special Agent Mallon. I would have called him, but I didn't have his card. Only yours."

That made two of us who were disappointed.

"Did you see anything on the tape other than an empty car?"

"Yes. The car that parked in the carhop spot was the same one that we saw on the tape at 12:33 a.m."

The car that had been behind me last night when I turned left onto Balboa Avenue from Mission Bay Drive. The same car that passed by the Night Owl after Naomi and I turned into the parking lot.

"And?"

"The driver sat in his car and ordered a Coke through the intercom in the stall, then got out of the car and walked away."

"Which way did he walk?" It couldn't have been out to the sidewalk on Balboa, because we didn't see anyone on the sidewalk through any of the different camera feeds we watched.

"He walked toward the back of the lot until he went off camera."

"What's behind you?"

"A-1 Self Storage."

That's right. A-1 Self Storage sat behind Sonic and the Night Owl. There was a chain-link fence that separated it from the other businesses. I didn't imagine it was open at 12:30 a.m. It had a security camera on the fence side, but it pointed in the opposite direction of Sonic and the Night Owl.

"Did the video catch him coming back?"

"Yes. That's the strange part. He appeared on the tape at 1:21 a.m. But his head was down like he was staring at the ground the whole time he walked back to his car. I could only see the top of his head. His ski cap, really."

1:21 a.m. The time stamp on the Enterprise tape was 1:17 a.m. when Naomi and I exited the Night Owl parking lot. My breath left me. What if the driver of the black sedan had hopped the fence behind Sonic, walked down behind the Night Owl, hopped the fence again, and entered the parking lot from the back? The Enterprise camera only picked up the first third of the parking lot and only the front half of Naomi's Camaro. He could have broken into the car and stolen the gun and registration and gone back the way he came without being spotted on any of the camera views we looked at.

Why hadn't he gone back to his car right away? Was he just some thief who tried to break into other cars or was there another reason he didn't return to his car for forty-five minutes? My stomach dropped. He could have been watching the bar from a hiding place in the back of the lot. Waiting for Naomi to come out and to see if I followed her home as I had to the bar from the radio station.

"Did you see the driver's face when he first got out of the car and walked out of the camera's range?"

"No. He had his face angled away like he knew there was a camera and he didn't want to be seen. And the feed is real grainy."

Shit.

I remembered the graininess from watching the footage this morning.

"Could you at least tell if he was white or black?"

"I'm pretty sure he was white. Like I said, he was wearing a ski cap, but I saw the back of his neck. It looked pale."

That would rule out Naomi's one-night fling, the former call screener, Alex. He was African American, but I still had to make a run at him.

"Did you notice anything else about him?"

"No."

"How about the carhop? You said her name was Alicia, I think."

"Yes, Alicia Alton."

"Did she say what he looked like?" I needed something, anything I could work with.

"No."

"When does she work next?"

"Tomorrow night. I mean tonight, now that it's already Wednesday morning."

"Please have her call me."

"Okay. I will. Can I ask what this is all about?"

"I can't tell you, but the information you're giving me might help keep someone safe." If I wasn't already too late.

"Oh."

"Anything else, Rudy? Did you get a license plate number?"

"The video is pretty blurry. I couldn't make it out, but I think it was a white license plate like we have in California."

And a bunch of other states.

"How about the make of the car?"

"It looked like a Toyota Corolla or a Hyundai Elantra. Like I said. The images aren't very clear."

"Thanks, Rudy. This is great work."

"Thanks, Mr. Cahill." Not hurt anymore.

I hung up. I didn't have time for more platitudes. I called Naomi.

"What?" A sharp edge.

"Is the address on the registration of the Camaro your home address?"

"No. The registration is in someone else's name. It's a gift, but I don't have to deal with the registration and renewal. It's mine, but it's not in my name."

"The same guy who loaned his house to you?" I wondered what part he played in Naomi's life.

"That's not really any of your business, Rick. Why do you care anyway? You think I'm lying about the whole thing."

"Because if the address on the registration is for the house in Del Mar, whoever stole the gun and the registration knows where you're staying."

"Oh my god." Nervous.

"Where are you right now?"

"On my way home."

"You can't go there. Where are you?"

"I just got onto 5 North, off the 8."

"Plug this address into your phone's GPS." I gave her my address. "You can stay here tonight."

"I don't think so, Rick. I don't want to stay somewhere where I have to explain myself."

"I apologize for doubting you. Let's just get through tonight and we can figure out the rest tomorrow."

"I'll stay in a hotel. Thanks." She hung up.

I couldn't blame Naomi for being upset with me. If the roles were reversed and she'd seen the video I'd seen today, she might not have believed me, either. But that didn't matter.

To be accused of lying when you are telling the truth is unnerving and infuriating. I'd been called a liar too many times over the last fifteen years. Mostly by the police. Sometimes by the media. By my late wife's father. He called me a murderer, too. I'd lied enough to be called a liar, but not when it mattered. Or when I thought it mattered.

I wished I'd believed Naomi from the start, but there was nothing I could do about it now. I had other concerns.

Sleep was still a long way off. I could go up to bed and pretend, but that would just be time wasted. I picked up my laptop and took it over to the kitchen table. Time to do the research I should have done on the letter writer when I'd researched Naomi. I went into the foyer and grabbed my jacket off the coat stand. The copy of the letter I made was in the inside pocket.

I sat back down at the kitchen table and reread the letter. Creepy, but not specifically threatening. I didn't have a background in psychology or psychotherapy, but I'd dealt with twisted enough in my life to recognize it when I saw it.

The last paragraph and signoff of the letter, combined with the last twenty-four hours, restarted my alarm bells.

> *Until that night, that sweet night when our prophesy is fulfilled, I ask that you just acknowledge that you've listened to my words on paper as you have on the air. Just say my name once during the show by the end of next week and I'll know our hearts are twinned forevermore. Don't disappoint me and awaken my rage.*
>
> *Until, sweet Cora,*
> *Yours, Pluto.*

"Until that night, that sweet night when our prophesy is fulfilled." Grandiose language. *Our prophesy fulfilled. Awaken my rage.* This was someone unwinding if not already unwound. He may be able to pass for normal at work or around the few friends he had, but not alone at night. At night, listening to Naomi, he'd let himself spool out. I could feel it even if I had no way to prove it.

Was he the man in the black sedan who parked at Sonic and disappeared? Had he broken into Naomi's car trying to find her address and gotten lucky with the gun and the registration? Was that "sweet night" already on his calendar?

Naomi needed protection, and I couldn't be with her twenty-four seven. She also had to come clean to me or the police about her past.

If there was someone from her other life whom she feared, I needed to know who it was. That would be a giant leap forward from chasing a phantom who mailed a letter without a return address from a US Postal mailbox somewhere in San Diego.

He'd signed the letter, though. *Pluto*. Evigan hadn't gone any deeper than prescribing the name to the onetime planet. But it was also the name of a Roman god. I Googled "Pluto Roman god." The air sucked out of me when I read the description.

Alternate name for Hades, ruler of the underworld.

The person writing to Naomi saw himself as the devil. And he might have her gun and know where she lived.

I Googled the name Cora. The first thing that came up matched what Evigan said yesterday—Cora was the heroine in *The Last of the Mohicans*. I scrolled down the page and found another definition. Derived from Kore, an alternate name for the Greek goddess Persephone. I Googled "Persephone." Greek goddess of the underworld.

Kidnapped by Hades and became his bride.

CHAPTER TWELVE

I PUNCHED NAOMI'S number on my phone. Voicemail. I left a message to call me back immediately. The fallacy of Naomi's safety hit me like a left hook to the ribs. The radio station had hired a security guard, and I'd convinced Naomi to stay at a hotel. Neither mattered if Pluto simply followed Naomi from the radio station. He didn't even have to be parked near the station to follow her. All he had to do was wait on Aero Drive and pick up her iconic Camaro as she headed down to the freeway. Just another late-night driver heading home.

He'd probably done the same thing last night. I'd had my eyes in the rearview mirror as much as the windshield as I followed Naomi away from the radio station. No one followed us out of the business park. With no headlights in my rearview mirror, I'd relaxed once we hit Aero Drive. From there, my focus had been on following Naomi, not on reflected headlights. Even at 12:15 a.m. on a Tuesday morning, there was enough traffic on the freeway to be unconcerned with the smattering of tailing headlights. Maybe the black sedan that parked in Sonic had taken that exact course last night.

I called Naomi again. Voicemail. I hung up and tried three more times until she finally answered.

"What!"

"Come to my house or tell me where you're staying."

"No."

"This creep could be following you right now, waiting for you to stop somewhere so he can kidnap you."

"Nobody's following me. Don't you think I've been paying attention to cars behind me when I leave the station?"

"He doesn't follow you from there. All he has to do is wait on Aero Drive. The only way to the freeway is east on Aero. He knows you take the freeway, whether you're taking the 15 north or south."

"Why the sudden urgency, Rick? Twenty minutes ago, you thought I made the whole thing up. You probably even thought I wrote the letter. Now you're convinced this guy is going to kill me tonight."

"Not kill you. Kidnap you. At least, for now."

"You're a little schizo, Rick." She dropped down into her *Naomi at Night* voice. Mocking me. "Call my show tomorrow night and maybe we can work it out on the air."

"This isn't a joke, Naomi. Come to my house or tell me where you are or where you're going. I hope I'm wrong about this, but we can't take that chance tonight."

Silence. Finally, "Give me your address again."

I gave it to her.

"I can probably get there in fifteen minutes."

"Great. I'll fill you in on what I found out when you get here." And try to squeeze some of her past out of her.

"No thanks." Harder edged. "I just want a place to sleep tonight. I'm not going to be your friend. I'm not even going to be your sidekick in figuring things out. That's between you and the station, now. Just keep your promise to me about the gun. The best you can be to me now is a man of your word."

She hung up.

I put on my jacket and went upstairs. Midnight followed me up, probably wondering why I was putting clothes on instead of taking them off as I prepared for bed. I grabbed my Smith & Wesson .357 Magnum off the nightstand in my bedroom and went back down-stairs. Midnight followed me down, but from a distance. He didn't like guns. He knew they were loud and knocked people down. He'd seen and heard it for himself. Up close.

I kept the gun to my side and went out the front door. I walked to the end of my street, which T-intersected with Moraga Street. Moraga ran up a hill for about a quarter mile above my street. A good view for oncoming headlights. I walked across the T intersection and stood behind a dwarf palm tree.

Headlights appeared at the crest of the hill about fifteen min-utes later. The car passed under a streetlight. Metallic blue Camaro. Naomi, right on time. I texted her a message to park in my driveway and wait in the car until I greeted her.

The Camaro slowed and I caught Naomi's profile as she made the right-hand turn onto my street. I shifted my focus back up Moraga. No headlights. I waited a solid minute. Clear. Naomi texted me.

I'm here. How long am I supposed to wait?

Me: *Be right there.*

I slid the gun down the back of my pants and walked to Naomi's car.

Naomi sat facing my house, waiting for me to come out the front door. She snapped her head toward me when I got within ten feet of her car. Eyes wide. Terrified. This wasn't a joke to her. The tough-gal persona could only cover up so much. She was scared. And not just from my warning. There was something in her past that scared her as much as a letter from some twisted fan. I needed to find out if she thought the past terror and the present one were the work of the same person.

She threw open her car door and jumped out.

"What the hell are you doing? Trying to scare me into believing I'm in danger?" She shoved me in the chest. "Someone broke into my car and stole my gun and knows where I live. I'm already convinced."

"I was just making sure you weren't followed. Sorry."

"Can we just go inside?" She pushed her hair out of her eyes.

"Sure." I put my hand out toward the house, and she walked in front of me.

"Let me go in first," I said when we reached the front door.

She took a step backwards, and I opened the door. Midnight growled when he saw Naomi, teeth bared. I snapped my fingers and pointed at the living room. He slunk away and laid down, his eyes at full alert. He growled again when we entered the living room. I snapped my fingers. He kept growling.

"Hey! Go in the other room." I pointed toward the kitchen. Midnight scooted out of the living room, low to the ground with his tail between his legs.

Maybe it was because he saw me grab a gun earlier or something about my and Naomi's body language was off, but Midnight always settled quickly when I brought a woman into the house. Naomi was in jeans and a leather coat, but neither hid the fact that she was a woman. I let it go. Everyone was entitled to an off night.

"Sorry. He's a little tense tonight." I pushed a hand toward the couch. "Would you like a drink?"

"No. Just a room." She remained standing and glanced at the staircase.

"Fine. Upstairs, second door on your left."

"Thank you." Curt. She started up the stairs.

"We have to talk about the threat and where it might be coming from, Naomi. Soon. You're either going to have to talk to me or Chip and let him decide if he should call the police."

She looked down from the top of the staircase. "I'm not talking to anyone tonight."

She hurried down the hall to the guest bedroom out of my view.

I went into the kitchen and shut down my laptop. Midnight sidled up to me, and I scratched his head. He was as confused as I was. I led him upstairs to the master bedroom. The pungent skunk smell of marijuana seeped under the guest room door as we passed by.

A bit of weed at the end of the night might help Naomi forget about her problems for now. But it wouldn't make them go away.

CHAPTER THIRTEEN

I WOKE UP at 7:40 a.m. Late for me, but only after I got about four and a half hours of sleep. Not enough when running on a dry reservoir. I thought about trying to fall back asleep, but heard the thrum of running water through the bedroom wall. Naomi was taking a shower. I didn't want to let her sneak out of the house before we talked.

I threw on some shorts and a sweatshirt, went downstairs, and let Midnight outside. I followed him out and went over to my fenced-in herb garden and picked some basil, then went back inside. The water had stopped running upstairs by the time I returned to the kitchen. Naomi was probably already planning her escape. I let Midnight back inside. He'd let me know when Naomi came downstairs.

I put my flattop griddle over two gas burners on my Viking stove, whisked some eggs with a splash of milk, and poured them on in two separate puddles. Once they firmed a bit, I chopped the basil and sprinkled it onto the eggs, then grated some Parmigiano-Reggiano over the top. I used a spatula to roll up each portion into eggritos and transferred them onto plates. I grabbed some strawberries, apples, and carrots out of the fridge and juiced them into orange-red liquid. I transferred the eggs to the kitchen table and put napkins and forks down. Breakfast was ready. I just didn't know if I'd be eating it alone.

Midnight's ears peaked and he bolted to his feet from his spot on the kitchen floor.

I told Midnight to stay and walked into the living room. Naomi stood at the bottom of the staircase. "I made breakfast. Your timing is perfect."

"I'm not hungry. Thanks for the room." She walked toward the front door.

"Bullshit. You probably haven't eaten since before your show last night. Let's eat, talk a little bit, and figure out our next move."

"*We* don't have a next move, Rick." She ran a finger between the two of us. "You're on your own and so am I."

"I think you'll want to talk to me before I talk to Chip." I nodded toward the kitchen table. "Let's eat."

She blew out a long breath, tossed her purse onto the couch, and walked into the kitchen. Midnight didn't growl, but he didn't wag his tail either. Naomi kneeled down and showed him the back of her hand.

"What's his name?"

"Midnight."

"Midnight, come here, honey." Her voice, high and sweet. "Let's be friends. I'm not that bad once you get to know me."

Midnight walked slowly over and let her scratch him behind the ear. He settled, but his ears were still on alert. What did he sense that I couldn't see? Or were we both on the same wavelength? Wary.

Naomi had secrets. Everyone did. But I had the feeling hers were darker than most. Maybe I was giving Midnight's instincts too much credit. Then again, he'd already saved my life once.

"Have a seat." I pointed to the table. "Juice, milk, or water?"

"Juice." Naomi sat down in front of an eggrito. "Thank you."

I grabbed a couple chilled glasses out of the freezer, filled them with juice, and sat down at the table.

Naomi tried a forkful of the eggs. Then another.

"This is really good." She took a sip of juice. "I didn't expect you to be so domesticated. You're a little rough around the edges."

"I used to run a restaurant. I know my way around a kitchen." I tasted the eggrito. She was right. Fluffy, herbaceous with a tang from the cheese. "Just because I live alone doesn't mean that life can't have flavor."

"You said you live alone instead of calling yourself a bachelor." Just a hint to the radio purr. "Why?"

"I don't know if I qualify as a bachelor. I was married once. My wife died. I live alone. By choice."

"I'm sorry about your wife." Blue eyes consoling. Mouth drawn down. "When did she die?"

"A long time ago."

I let her work me. She'd try to coax me into talking so I'd forget about questioning her. She was good at it. So good that thousands of people tuned in to listen to her on the radio five nights a week. She knew people loved to talk about themselves, especially about their own pain. If that pain was deep enough, other people would listen in.

There was plenty of pain in my history, but no one was listening. Just Naomi. And she was only listening for the next hook she could turn back on me and open a dark hole I could get lost in. I had to give her something real, something horrible that might bring her guard down and open a crack into her own past.

"What happened?" she asked.

"She was murdered, and the police thought I did it."

"How awful." Sincere. "Did they arrest you?"

"Yes, but I was never tried. Lost my job as a cop." My stomach turned over. Not because of the memories of Colleen's death. I dealt with them almost every day. Because of my betrayal of her, to use her murder as a poker chip. I'd never done it before. It was the invisible, yet indelible, line I never crossed.

Until this morning.

"Did they ever find the person who killed your wife?"

"I'm not going to talk about it." I pushed my plate away and stood up. Sweat gathered at my hairline. I thought I might throw up. I bent over and put my hands on my thighs.

"I'm so sorry." Naomi stood up and put her hand on my back. "The pain you must fight every day."

She rubbed my back in slow circles.

"Stop." I stepped out of her reach and straightened up. "I was working you just like you're working me. I thought if I gave you something I could get you to open up about your own past."

"You lied about your wife being murdered?" Naomi tilted her head and put her hands on her hips.

"No. That happened. And I used it to try to get information out of you." I walked to the sink, turned on the cold water, and splashed some on my face.

"What do you want to know?" Naomi sat down at the breakfast table.

"I don't care anymore, Naomi. The game's up."

"It's not a game to me, Rick." She snapped off my name.

"Your whole life's a game. A con."

A blush bled across Naomi's cheeks. Her eyes stayed blank, but she couldn't hide the engorged blood vessels under her skin.

"What do you mean?"

"Naomi Hendrix doesn't have a criminal record." I walked back to the table, but remained standing. "You probably thought that was a good thing when you choose the name for your new identity when you got out of prison. But you never figured someone would steal a gun from you. You can't report the gun stolen and risk the police delving too deeply into your background. They might question why

Naomi Hendrix's record of employment only started seven years ago. A single woman, never married, in her late thirties didn't start receiving paychecks until she was thirty-two. I'm sure that name change wasn't done through a court. A felon has to have a public hearing to change her name. You couldn't allow that."

"What are you trying to prove, Rick?"

"Just that, sooner or later, it's all going to come tumbling down. I suggest you get out in front of it now."

"And if I don't, do I have to worry about you getting out in front of it on your own?"

"Nope. I gave you my word."

Naomi strode into the living room and grabbed her purse off the couch. I followed her to the front door.

"Where are you going?"

"Wherever I want to."

"Listen to me first." I put my hand against the door. "There's a man out there watching and waiting for just the right moment when he can grab you and put you in a dark room where you'll spend the rest of your life as his wife. In a cage or a basement, never to see the light of day again. His name is Pluto or Hades and he thinks he's the ruler of the underworld and Cora is to be his wife. That's you."

"Where did you come up with all of this?"

"It's easy to find. Chip could have found it if he'd dug a little deeper online. But that's not his job. It's mine. I found it. I know this sicko's plan. If you let the police get involved, you'll be much safer."

Tears welled in her eyes. Real tears. Not phonied up for an unseen radio audience. And not phonied up for me. Naomi was my responsibility. And her wall had finally come down.

"No police." She wiped her eyes and blew out a breath. "God damn this fucking little freak. He's ruined my whole life."

"Not yet."

"No, the damage is already done whether he kidnaps me or kills me or whatever. I'd made a new life. I'd gotten away. And now some fucking psycho listens to me on the radio and gets a sick little crush and destroys everything. Seven years gone."

"You do all your time?"

"Yes."

"Get a lawyer. Maybe hire a publicist. Like I said before, the police are more interested in putting a psychopath behind bars than a popular radio personality. The public will be on your side. You'll be the redemption story of the month. If you're tried for falsifying an identification, you have every swinging dick politician in this town hoping some of your popularity will rub off on them as they stand up in court as your character witnesses."

"No, they won't."

"Why not?"

"I did three years for fraud. No politician is going to get next to that." A tear streamed down her cheek. "And no radio audience, no matter how large, is ever going to believe another word I say when they find out I scammed people out of money as a psychic."

CHAPTER FOURTEEN

"YOU MEAN LIKE a gypsy?"

"No. We're called Travelers."

"Irish Travelers?" My people's name for gypsies. "Where?"

"South Carolina." Naomi stood up and wiped another tear from her eye.

"What was your name then?"

"I had many names and many social security numbers." She sat down and Midnight ambled over to her, tail wagging low. He sat on his rump and leaned against her leg. Her tears had broken down the barrier for him. Mine was still up. "I need your help, Rick. Please, you have to trust me."

"Trust goes both ways."

"I can't go back to Murphy Village and the clan."

"The Klan? Do you really expect me to believe that you were a member of the Ku Klux Klan?"

"No. My clan in Murphy Village."

"Your clan? You mean your family?"

"Sort of." She suddenly stood up, and her tears had dried on her face. "I changed my identity to get away from them." She ran a sharp hand through her hair. "My family. My clan. My husband."

"They don't have divorce attorneys in Murphy Village?"

"I had an arranged marriage. I was chosen to marry someone when I was nine."

"What? You were forced to get married when you were nine years old?"

"The actual marriage didn't happen until I was fourteen, but an arrangement was made when I was nine. I was promised to someone and that's a promise Travelers keep. He was twenty-five when we were married. I can't remember a time as a child when I didn't know that I would have to spend my whole life with someone I hated."

"Do you think he could be Pluto?"

"No. That's not their style. If they knew I was out here, they would have already taken me back to South Carolina."

"You're a grown woman. You tell them you're not going. You get a restraining order."

"You don't understand. They always get what they want."

"Maybe when you first came to California, but now you're a celebrity. You have leverage now. You're not some nine-year-old child."

"If the police or the press get involved in this, my family will hear about it. They'll come after me."

"You picked a strange occupation for someone supposedly trying to stay under the radar."

"It was kind of an accident, but I've taken precautions. I changed my look, my name. I don't allow myself to be photographed. I changed my voice completely. I was born and bred in South Carolina. I had an accent and much higher voice back there. No one could recognize it now. I spent three years in prison working on it every day. My voice. My walk. My posture. I changed it all and I'm not going to give it up now. I need your help."

My help meant me. All of me. Consumed to keep her safe and find her stalker. Possibly risking prison and certainly my PI's license by knowingly helping her to perpetuate her fake identity.

Naomi was a job. A case. And she wasn't even the one paying me. My fiduciary responsibility was to Chip Evigan and the radio station. And I'd already breached that trust for a woman who'd spent most of her life conning people. Was I her latest mark?

She hadn't asked for money. She'd told me her secret. She was all alone with a psycho stalking her and a past waiting to run her down.

"Okay." I knew about secrets and the damage they could do when exposed.

CHAPTER FIFTEEN

ALEX EVANS ANSWERED the door to his tiny condo in Normal Heights. Tall, skinny, close-cropped hair, midtwenties, African American. I'd called ahead. He'd looked as happy to see me as he sounded on the phone. But at least he agreed to see me.

"Rick Cahill." I stuck out my hand. He gave it a weak shake and didn't invite me inside.

"Like I told you on the phone, I only have a few minutes. I have to be at the station soon."

"Ten minutes, max. How about we talk inside?" I needed to see the inside of the condo. Were there books on Greek and Roman mythology on a bookshelf? Pictures of Naomi on the wall?

"Okay, I guess." He let go a breath and let me in.

Sparse, but neat. No photos of Naomi, but there was a bookshelf in the tiny living room next to the TV. I examined the books. *Private Parts* by Howard Stern and a biography about him. Books about other radio personalities. No books on Greek or Roman mythology or anything else. All radio. The kid was a junkie and he was on the way to living his dream.

Did he have another, darker dream he was working his way up to?

"When was the last time you saw Naomi?" I turned from the bookshelf and looked at him.

"Like I said, I haven't seen her since the trial about a year ago." Irritated, not nervous.

"When was the last time Pluto saw her?"

"Pluto? Who the fuck is that?" No tell. Just more irritation.

Time to switch gears.

"You used to screen Naomi's calls, right?"

"What? Yeah."

"Anyone call in who gave you the creeps?"

"Yeah. Every damn one of them. Bunch of messed-up people whining about their problems." He put his hands on his hips. "Is that what this is about? Is someone calling in and creeping out Naomi?"

"Something like that. Any callers you can remember who gave you a bad feeling? Something about them that was more than just socially awkward?"

"Not really. It was a while ago." He folded his arms across his chest. "The dude who gave me the creeps was Chip. He was crushing hard on Naomi and flipped out when he found out we hooked up."

"How many times did you hook up?"

"Just once."

"But it was more than a hookup for you, wasn't it?"

"Maybe, but I got over it." He smiled. "And I got over Chip firing me once I got paid."

* * *

My phone rang on the drive home from Alex Evans' house. I didn't recognize the number.

"Mr. Cahill?" A woman's voice. High. Young. Unsure.

"Yes?"

"This is Alicia Alton from Sonic. Rudy Wayne said you wanted to talk to me?" A question more than a statement.

"Yes. It's about the man who ordered a Coke around twelve thirty Monday night and disappeared, but left his car parked in the drive-in spot."

"Yes. I remember him."

"What did he look like? White? Black? Hispanic?"

"I think he was white."

"I thought you said you remembered him." Neither Rudy nor Alicia could give me a race. I guess millennials didn't see race, which was a good thing. Unless you were trying to get a description of a possible sicko stalker.

"He avoided my eyes when I dropped off his Coke, so I didn't get a great look at him. He was wearing a beanie that covered most of his head. I guess he could have been Hispanic. I'm not sure. Sorry." Apologetic, like she'd disappointed her father. Made me feel a little guilty. And old.

"That's okay. This is helpful." At least now I'd gotten two negatives on African American. That solidified my feeling that Alex Evans wasn't Pluto. Progress. "What about approximate age? Height? Build?"

"Oh." Thinking. Trying to remember. "Older than me. Like I said, I don't really remember what he looked like. Maybe twenty-five or thirty. Or thirty-five. Younger than forty, for sure. I think."

"How about height and weight? I know he was sitting down, but was his head high up near the roof? Down near the steering wheel? Muscular? Fat? Thin?"

"I really don't remember. I'd say normal."

"Okay. Last question. Do you remember what kind of car it was?" Alicia was a carhop. She roller-skated up to cars every night. Either she'd become discerning about them or they all blended together into the background.

"I think it was black."

Option two.

"Thanks, Alicia. I appreciate you taking the time to call."

"I wish I could have been more help." Earnest. A good kid. She hadn't given me much, but I liked her.

"Can you do me a favor and call me if you ever see this guy again?"

"Sure, but, obviously, I don't remember him very well."

"That's okay. Your subconscious probably took in a lot more than you know. If you see him again, everything may click into place."

She promised she'd call and we hung up. I felt like I'd moved the ball an inch. Better than going backwards.

* * *

Naomi stayed at my house all day. I followed her to work that night at 8:15 p.m. and watched her go inside the radio station. The security guard was still on duty. I let him handle the radio station and I patrolled the surrounding area. First stop was the Lansing Business Park. The center was the most likely lookout for a creep peeping at Naomi. The back offices had windows that faced the front of the radio station. Plus, the Lansing Security camera pointed its way. The security office closed at 6:00 p.m. when the center did, but that didn't mean that Quint or someone like him wasn't sitting in the tiny office watching the camera's feed on his computer.

There were only eight cars in the large parking lot. I parked and tried the door leading into the building. Locked, as I expected.

I circled the area in my car for the next hour and a half while I listened to Naomi on the radio. She was as smooth and sultry as ever. No hint of the tumult exploding in her life.

My phone vibrated in my pocket at 9:50 p.m. I didn't recognize the number. But I did the voice.

"Mr. Cahill." Guttural. Heavily accented. Russian. "Do you know who this is?"

"Yes." Sergei Volkov. Head of the Russian Mafia in San Diego. And God knows where else.

I pulled to the curb and turned off the car. The call. Even after a year of silence, I knew it was coming.

"Now is time to live up to our agreement. You must meet with Tatiana tomorrow. She will give you instructions."

"Where and when?"

"She will find you." He hung up.

Tatiana. His daughter. We hadn't met under friendly circumstances the first time. And we left under even unfriendlier ones. I had no way out. I could only hope that the Russian would be true to his word. And that paying my debt wouldn't involve robbing a bank or beating somebody up.

Or murder.

CHAPTER SIXTEEN

I WOKE UP at five a.m. the next morning. Early, even for me. Woke up may be a bit optimistic. I stopped the spin cycle at five. I'd really spent more time not sleeping than sleeping the previous five hours. My new world order—thanks to an old-world mob boss.

Midnight and I padded quietly downstairs. I didn't want to wake Naomi, who'd spent the night in my guest room again. There were no more kisses like the one we shared at her house. Just an unstated understanding that nothing could happen between us until the Pluto threat was over. After that was an unanswered question.

Still, the call from Sergei Volkov might complicate our short-term living arrangement. I didn't want the Russians anywhere in my life. But I didn't have a choice. Hopefully, after I carried out whatever chore they had planned for me, they'd leave me alone. At least for a while. Whatever the deed, I didn't want it bleeding over onto Naomi. She'd have to stay in a hotel until I dispensed with the Russians or Pluto.

I let Midnight outside. He didn't stop at his food bowl looking for his breakfast. Early, even for him. I opened the front door and grabbed the newspaper, then realized the news would have to wait. Something more pressing than the world's miseries just came up. Everything in my life was about to go on hold. Hopefully, I'd be able to start it up again.

A black Hummer sat next to the curb in front of my house. A bald
man in tight leather everything stood holding the back-passenger
door open. We'd met before. It hadn't turned out well for him. I was
in shorts, a tee shirt, and no shoes this time. No weapon. I could dive
back into the house and gain access to a small arsenal in thirty seconds. But it wouldn't do any good. There would just be more black
Hummers.

I tossed the newspaper inside the house, shut the door, and walked
across the front lawn to learn my fate.

"Rick, have you missed me?" A woman's voice. The dead emotion of
a millennial covering a wisp of a Russian accent. Tatiana. The devil's
daughter. "Because I've missed you. Get in."

I stepped into the Hummer and Leather Man swung the door shut
behind me then ran around and jumped into the driver's seat. Tatiana had softened the Goth look that she wore like a weapon last year.
Not that she needed any extra. Still dressed in all black leather, but
less severe bangs to her dark hair. No more racoon-eye makeup, but
there were a couple circles under her eyes like she was ending her day
instead of just starting it. Still, without all the Elvira excess, she was
quite attractive. In a millennial hit woman sort of way. I doubted her
disposition matched her new softened look.

"Tatiana."

"New car?" She nodded in the direction of my driveway where
Naomi's 1969 Camaro was parked. "Sporty."

I should have had Naomi park her car in my garage. If Pluto tracked
me down, he could have already driven by my house and seen it
in the driveway. Too many late nights and not enough sleep. Plus,
Tatiana had just stumbled across a weakness although she didn't
know it. My energies divided between protecting Naomi and tackling
whatever task the Russians had for me made me vulnerable. More
than usual.

"I trust you're here for a reason?"

"You are lucky my father has found a use for you." She pulled a stiletto switchblade out of the top of her stiletto boot. She pressed the button on the handle and a four-inch knife blade sprang into place. "Otherwise, we would have finished our little game."

"I'm overjoyed." I looked at the knife, then back at her dark lifeless eyes. "You want to get down to business or do you want me to take that knife away from you again?"

Leather Man pointed a handgun at me over the top of his seat. Tatiana dangled the knife in front of me. Familiar territory. Sometimes it's better to just show true fear than raise up the façade of a tough guy. Old habits.

"Do you have your cell phone?" she asked.

"No."

"Write down this email address."

"I don't have a pen." I wanted to stuff the words back in my mouth as soon as I spoke them. Tatiana's replacement for a pen and pad might be her knife and my skin.

Luckily, Leather Man produced a pen in his non-gun hand. I grabbed it.

"T. Randolph45 at gmail.com."

I wrote the address on the palm of my left hand. "Who is T. Randolph?"

"That is the person you will send all of your correspondence to."

"What correspondence?"

"The information you learn about the person you're going to follow at night." A Goth grin.

"And who's that?"

"Peter Stone."

Stone. The Damocles Sword hanging over my head for the last six years. The philanthropic face of the partnership between him and the

Russian mob. He had another face that the public never saw. I had and never wanted to see it again. But even Stone was afraid of Tatiana's father.

"Why do you want me to follow Stone? I thought he and your father were partners."

"Rick, you don't seem to understand what you agreed to. You do what I tell you to do and you will pay off your obligation." She pressed the flat side of the knife's blade onto her lower lip and smiled at me. A psychopathic come-hither look. "If you don't do as I say, you'll die. Painfully. If you go to the police, you'll die more painfully and so will people you care about."

"I remember the deal." I'd thought about it every day for a year. "And all I have to do is follow Stone and send status reports to the T. Randolph email address? That's the deal?"

"Yes."

"When do I start and for how long? I'm working another case."

"You start tonight. Do you want this other case to be the last one you work, Rick?" She chopped her teeth on the blade.

"No. But I need to have the deal confirmed by your father."

"My father told you to do as I say, right?"

"Yes, and I intend to. But he's the person I made the deal with last year. I need him to tell me that my obligation is to follow Stone and report to T. Randolph and then our partnership is done."

"You are not a partner. You are an employee."

"However you want to phrase it. I just need to hear from your father that if I do as you just instructed that our business relationship is concluded."

"You don't trust me?" The come- or die-hither look.

"No."

"Such a stubborn, stupid man. You make everything so difficult. I could kill you right now and tell my father that you attacked me. Simple. You're dead and my life is easier."

"I just need to hear confirmation from the person I made the deal with. You'd do the same thing in my position."

"Rick." A snarl for a laugh. "You see Petrov's gun? You see my knife? I'd never be stupid enough to be in your position."

She had a point. But I needed to hear directly from the devil, not his spawn.

"Your father?" I said.

Tatiana stabbed the stiletto into the upholstery of the seat back between us. I flinched. Luckily not enough to attack her and get myself shot. Tatiana sliced down on the leather upholstery exposing the padding underneath. Petrov still held the gun on me, but he pinched his lips and blinked like it wasn't the first time he'd have to take the Hummer to the dealer to get a new seat back.

"Get out!" This, directed at Petrov.

He threw open the car door and jumped out. I took a couple of long breaths through my nose, trying to loosen the tension between my shoulder blades. Tatiana had stabbed me before. She'd caught me by surprise that time. I was ready now, although I wish I were wearing Petrov's leather jacket to lessen the slash wounds I might have to endure to take the knife away from her. Though prepared, I didn't think I'd have to go to battle. My guess was that Tatiana had sent Petrov away so he wouldn't hear her give me what I wanted.

She snapped the blade shut and stuffed the knife back into her boot.

"If you make one mistake following Peter or are late with a report, I'll kill you. No matter what my father says."

She yanked a cell phone out of her jacket pocket and punched a number. "Papa?" Her voice had lost its edge and melted into a little-girl-lost tone. I couldn't understand what she said because she spoke in Russian except for the one time she spoke my name.

After a minute or so of speaking and listening, Tatiana handed me her phone.

"You have insulted my daughter. Again." The guttural tone of last night now a bark. "Follow Stone and report to the email address. When you are done, pay Tati $10,000 and our business is concluded."

"I don't have $10,000." And I'd have to walk away from a paying case.

"This is not my problem. You are a hard man. You must pay the price. Hand the phone back to my daughter."

I handed the phone to Tatiana. She and her father spoke for ten or fifteen seconds and she hung up.

"You should have listened to me, Rick." The snarl smile again. "Your life would be much easier. Wait for emailed instructions. Get out of my car."

I got out of the Hummer and Petrov got back in. The massive SUV peeled out, leaving behind smoke, the stink of burnt rubber, and another debt I didn't know how I was going to pay.

CHAPTER SEVENTEEN

THE RUSSIANS. PETER Stone. The police? Not an option. If I went to them, the Russians would kill me. There was no negotiating, no pleading, no paying them off. My fate was preordained. Do, or die. I did have a Hail Mary sitting in a safe deposit box in a nearby bank. But using it was an invitation to play Russian Roulette. With real Russians. From the Russian Mafia.

If all I had to do was follow Stone and give Tatiana ten grand, I'd gotten off easy. Too easy. Somewhere in this nothing job was a bomb waiting to be detonated. All I had to do was find it, disarm it, and not let the Russians kill me. Or throw the Hail Mary and pray.

The first step was figuring out who T. Randolph45 was. I went quietly upstairs past the guest room to my office. I didn't know how to explain to Naomi that I'd have to abandon her. At least at night. And I wasn't sure for how long. A bridge to cross when she woke up.

Right now, the Russians had all of my attention.

I got onto my computer and searched some people finder websites for T. Randolph in San Diego and various iterations of the name from Anthony, in case the T was short for Tony, all the way to Trent. Nothing particularly nefarious about any of the people attached to the names I researched. I spent hours digging through the names and couldn't find any connection to the Russian mob or Peter Stone.

Naomi emerged from the guest room at 9:15 a.m. I scrambled some eggs and cooked some bacon while my brain searched for the perfect way to tell Naomi I couldn't protect her 24/7 and that she had to move out of my house. Empty.

"We need to talk." I put the plate of food down on the kitchen table in front of her, then sat down with my own.

"Are you breaking up with me, Rick?" Her eyes didn't match the whimsy of her words.

"You can't stay here anymore. It's not safe."

"Did something happen while I was asleep?" Her eyes went a fraction wider, but she kept her voice steady.

"Yes, but it has nothing to do with Pluto." I had to give her some truth so she wouldn't think I'd tossed her aside for something trivial. I doubt she'd asked for help much, if ever, in her life. She'd asked me and now I was abandoning her. But I couldn't help her if I was dead. "Some dangerous people have come back into my life, and I have to deal with them before I can help you 'round the clock."

"What dangerous people?" Eyes full wide now. "Can't you go to the police?"

"No, I can't go to the police." She should be able to understand that. "I'm going to get you a bodyguard, twenty-four seven. The best there is. I'll cover the cost, continue to investigate during the day."

"Thanks for breakfast." She left the kitchen and hurried upstairs.

She was mad, but at least she'd be safe.

I pulled out my phone and called the toughest person I knew who saved my life two years ago.

Naomi came downstairs a half hour later with her buckskin leather purse over her shoulder.

"Thank you for the hospitality." No smile. "I appreciate all you've done. Good-bye, Rick."

"Hold on. First, I'm still on the case. Just not twenty-four seven. At least for a while. Second. Where are you going?"

"The house in Del Mar, then a hotel. I need to get some clothes."

"Okay, but please wait until your bodyguard gets here. Should be just another couple minutes."

"I'll be fine. I've traveled these roads before."

She walked toward the front door, but I cut her off.

"Naomi, please." I put my hand on her arm. "I know you're strong and smart and have been through a lot and come out stronger. But we don't know who we're dealing with, yet. Please wait for the bodyguard."

Midnight growled and someone knocked on the front door. I checked the peephole, then opened the door.

"Rick. I've missed you." Miranda Jennings gave me a long hug. I hugged back. I didn't get too many hugs and never knew when the next one might come.

We released and she smiled. Her blond hair in a ponytail, exposing her grown-up tomboy good looks. She wore a gray and pink sweatshirt and black yoga pants, which gave outline to her muscular, but shapely legs. Flip-flops on her red-toenailed feet. I'd never seen Miranda in shoes. But I'd never seen her wear gloves on her hands either. All four were potent weapons. I'd seen her foot up close before we were friends.

"I've missed you, too." I let her inside.

"Hi." Miranda smiled at Naomi.

I shut the door and turned to see Naomi laser-eyeing Miranda up and down.

"This is the bodyguard?" She focused the lasers on me. "A yoga instructor in flip-flops. No offense." The last remark aimed at Miranda.

"None taken." Miranda's sweet high-pitched voice, no doubt, putting an exclamation point on Naomi's assessment. Miranda held out her hand. "Miranda Jennings. Nice to meet you."

"Naomi Hendrix." She shook Miranda's hand, then quickly pulled it away and rubbed it. "I get it. You're strong. I'd still rather have a football player–type with a gun guarding me."

"Miranda was an undefeated MMA fighter and she saved my life." I led the women into the living room. "She's the best bodyguard I know."

Miranda reached around her back under her sweatshirt and smoothly produced a Smith & Wesson M&P 40 handgun. She racked the slide, chambering a round. Presumably to impress Naomi. It seemed to work. Naomi pursed her lips and nodded her head.

"You'll be safe at my house." She re-holstered the gun behind her back. "I promise."

Miranda hadn't carried a gun when I first met her. Maybe the mess I'd gotten her into a couple years back had made her more cautious. And deadly. That was okay with me. I didn't know what or who we were dealing with, but I was pretty sure he was armed. With Naomi's gun.

* * *

My cell phone pinged the arrival of an email at noon. The sender, T. Randolph45. The instructions were to stake out Peter Stone's house tonight from sundown until midnight. If he left his house, I was to follow and report his movements to T. Randolph at the end of the night.

An hour later, a driver for Enterprise picked me up and delivered me to the location in Pacific Beach next to the Sonic. I wasn't there to look at video today. I needed a car. A nice one. I rented an Audi A8 L.

I didn't normally go bucks up when I had to use a rental, especially when I couldn't expense it and had to find ten grand somewhere to pay off a spoiled psychopath. But my target was Peter Stone. His base camp was a fifteen-million-dollar lair hanging off a cliff with a view of the Pacific Ocean from here to Hawaii. My three-year-old Honda Accord would stick out like a wooden nickel in the collection plate at La Jolla Presbyterian Church. Besides, Stone knew my car. He'd ridden in it once.

One car wouldn't be enough. Not for someone like Stone who lived life straddling both sides of the law. He would sniff out a one car tail by rote. I needed help. I needed a friend. I had one. But what I had to ask would push our friendship to its limits.

I made a phone call in the Audi.

"What do you need now?" Moira MacFarlane's jackhammer voice had become the background percussion of my conscience rattling around in my head over the past year. "A plate run? Copy of an arrest report? An extra set of eyes?"

"Bingo."

"Extra eyes?"

"Yes."

"Can't help you. I'm working a case of my own right now."

"Twenty-four seven?" My voice rose in a plea.

"No."

"This is a nighttime gig."

"You're really pushing this friendship thing, Cahill."

"It gets better." I tried to make it sound like a good thing.

"I'm afraid to ask."

"I can't pay you. At least not for a while."

"You make it sound so enticing. Where's the target and what time tonight?"

"Seven o'clock. Hillside Drive in La Jolla."

"Hillside?" Her voice rose almost to a women's tenor. "You don't mean . . ."

"Yes. Peter Stone."

"You're tailing Peter Stone?" Her high-throttle voice redlined. "Are you out of your mind?"

"I don't have a choice."

I debated how much to tell her. She deserved to know what she'd be getting into if she agreed to help me. But keeping her ignorant might be the safest thing. No, the safest thing would be to tell her never mind. I'd supposedly ordered my life around finding the truth, no matter the repercussions. Was it fair to withhold the truth from someone I'd asked to help me so I could stay alive? How did the quest for the truth and dishonesty coexist? How many segregated compartments did I have left in my head?

"What have you gotten yourself into now, Rick?" Scold with a hint of concern.

"You working surveillance right now?"

"Yes. Worker's comp fraud."

"Where are you?"

"The parking lot of Torrey Pines Golf Course."

"I'll be there in thirty minutes."

"You can't explain over the phone? You're in that much trouble?"

"Yeah."

CHAPTER EIGHTEEN

THE PARKING LOT at Torrey Pines Golf Course was packed. No surprise. It's packed every day it doesn't rain, and, sometimes even when it does. The course holds a PGA event every year and will get its second US Open in 2021. Torrey has two eighteen-hole courses that have the same view Peter Stone did, except that they sit atop a cliff hovering right above the beach. Close enough to hear waves breaking on the shore if the wind is blowing in the right direction. Maybe the most beautiful municipal golf course in the US, if not the world. Not cheap, and getting a tee time is damn near impossible.

My rental Audi A8 L may have looked more at home at La Jolla Country Club, but there were plenty of luxury cars jamming the parking lot at Torrey Pines. Everyone wants to play Torrey. Even those who could easily afford to play somewhere else. Anywhere else.

I circled the lot and found Moira's white Honda Accord parked along the fence with a gallery view of the ninth green and the first tee beyond it on Torrey North. She must have gotten lucky, arrived with the dawn patrol, or circled the lot until just the right spot became available.

Two full circumnavigations later, a car pulled out of a spot fifty or so yards away from Moira. I grabbed it and walked to her car. White clouds lazed above in the October sky, occasionally giving shade from the autumn sun. I wore a coat, but didn't need it, except to conceal the gun holstered underneath it. Fall in San Diego.

With the Russian mob playing Simon Says.

Moira held binoculars up to her eyes pointed down the course. A green floor to the blue-sky ceiling and ocean beyond. She dropped the binos and turned her head toward me as I approached the passenger side of her car.

Her head barely visible above the window. Saucer brown eyes staring at me. Her puffy lips poised for a wisecrack. Everything was big about Moira, except her physique. Including her personality. TNT wrapped in a hundred-pound frame. But all of it fit together perfectly. Moira was beautiful, but not pretty. Tough, but not hard. Honest, but not cruel. Somehow over the last year, she'd become my best friend. Someone I didn't see that often, but who I couldn't imagine my life without. I opened the car door and got in.

"You trying to impress me with the Audi?"

Eyes in her binoculars or not, Moira didn't miss anything.

"That's for tonight. Tailing Stone."

"Yes. Stone." She pulled a brown lock of hair from her bob cut away from her eyes. "Who do you owe a favor, or has someone kidnapped Midnight?"

Now or never. I had to come straight with her or not ask for her help. I could still try the tail alone. The Russian told me to follow Stone. They didn't say don't get spotted. Of course, that was implied. Just like the implication that if I didn't pay Tatiana the ten grand, I'd die. Important to read between the lines when dealing with the Russian Mafia. And the fine print that wasn't written down.

The Russians expected me to do the job right. I couldn't do that without help. I needed Moira. To stay alive. But it wasn't fair to endanger her life to save mine.

"The Russian Mafia."

"What?" Her eyes bulged wider.

"I made a deal with them last year. I didn't tell you about it. I didn't tell anyone." A cloud passed over the car, throwing a shadow across the ninth green. The night that everyone was pointing guns but me flashed through my mind. "As you can guess, the deal was one-sided. I didn't have a choice. Agree or die."

"And following Stone is your end of the deal?" She blinked and her eyes were unsteady. Lacking their constant certainty. I'd never seen them like that. "There's nothing else?"

"There's something else, but it's not what you think." I knew what she meant. "They didn't ask me to kill him. Just follow him and report back. The other thing is an add-on. A punishment for questioning a sawed-off psycho. It's monetary and has nothing to do with the assignment."

"Go to the police and tell them the Russians are extorting you."

"I can't do that. This is the Russian Mob. I take down one boss, another one takes his place and sends soldiers after me. Forever. They don't forget."

"There has to be another way."

I thought of the flash drive I'd hidden in a safe deposit box. It wasn't leverage. It was a suicide vest. All it would do was take down Stone and Sergei and a few others, but I'd still be dead.

"There is no other way." I patted her hand. "But all I have to do is follow Stone for a few nights and then I'm free." And pay off the psychopath. "I wanted you to know the players before you decided to enter the game."

"Why does the Russian Mafia want to tail Peter Stone?"

I'd given that question a lot of thought since I got the five a.m. visit from Tatiana. Even as I seesawed with the notion that ignorance isn't bliss with the Russians involved, but could equal continued breathing. My unnatural curiosity and albatross for the truth won out.

Stone and the Russians were in some kind of twisted partnership. Or, at least they had been a year ago. A partnership in which Stone had been very much the junior partner. Maybe Sergei Volkov thought that Stone wanted to move to a more senior position and, thus, needed to be watched. Then what? I'd figure that out after I got to "then."

"I don't ask the why. I just ask the what and the when. And then the when the hell are we even?" I looked out at the ninth green and hoped there'd be a time soon when the only thing hanging over my head was the doubt that I could get home with a three wood in my hands. "But I will tell you that Stone and the Russians have done a deal or two over the years."

"And how do you know this?"

"By accident. I wish I didn't, but wishes are as useless as hope."

"You never make it easy, Cahill." She put the binoculars back up to her eyes. "Here comes my boy. Hand me the Canon from that backpack."

Two golf carts pulled up to the first tee box.

"What's the story?" I pulled out the video camera and gave it to her.

"Drives a forklift at Callaway Golf's warehouse in Carlsbad." Moira pointed the camera at the tee box. "Supposedly got whiplash when he ran into another forklift. Went outside the company health plan to find just the right doctor. Even got a prescription for Percocet."

A man in khaki pants and a blue golf shirt got out of the cart and teed up a golf ball. He was tall, average build. Too far away to know for sure, but probably late twenties. He waggled the club a few times and then took a vicious hack at the ball, snap-hooking his drive at a ninety-degree angle down onto the eighteenth fairway.

"Fuuuck!" The injured forklift driver and healthy hacker launched his driver after the ball with the form of an Olympic hammer thrower. Much smoother and more on plane than his golf swing.

"Jackpot," Moira said. Still filming with her left hand, she blindly held out her right toward me above her head. I wasn't big on public displays of affection or celebration, but I high-fived her anyway. I had asked her a pretty big favor.

The forklift driver tromped over to his ball before his cart-mate could even hit his drive. Now I hoped this guy did life in worker's comp prison. Defrauding your employer and the state of California was bad enough, but bad golf etiquette was unforgiveable.

"You get enough or are you going to wait five hours until he comes hacking up eighteen?"

"I already got him lugging his golf bag a quarter mile from his car to the starter's window." Moira took the camera away from her eye. "Then down the stairs to the golf cart. Plus, I got him lifting weights at a gym yesterday. He's done and so am I."

"So?" I raised my eyebrows and felt like an ass as soon as the word left my mouth.

"So." Moira handed me the camera, which I put into the backpack at my feet. "Why can't you ever take a worker's comp case like this or follow an overweight middle-aged man who's cheating on his wife?"

"I do. I just don't need help with those cases."

CHAPTER NINETEEN

I COULDN'T SEE Stone's house from my vantage point parked along the curb on Hillside Drive above where Via Siena T-boned into it. The Stone mansion hung off a cliff less than a couple hundred yards away, but was blocked from my view by two twists in the road. Moira was parked about a mile away, down the hill in the other direction. Her Honda Accord was less likely to stick out on the section of Hillside where homes didn't have an ocean view and were worth a mere two or three million. Hillside was ancient Rome narrow, and any cars not parked in driveways or garages would flash like neon lights to Stone. Luckily, Hillside only had a couple exit points. Moira and I had them both covered.

I let my mind drift, but kept my eyes on Hillside Drive. No action. I'd been parked on the curb for an hour and a half. A total of five cars had turned onto the street since I'd been there. None had exited. The rich packing it in for the night. When you had a view of La Jolla and the Pacific Ocean beyond, where were you going to spend an evening with anything better to look at? I jogged down Hillside after each car went down the street to get a glimpse of Stone's house. None of the cars parked in Stone's driveway or anywhere near his house.

I listened to *Naomi at Night* through my iPhone app. The beep of an incoming text interrupted Naomi's liquid smoke voice.

Moira: *Lights just went on in another wing of the house.*

Me: *No cars though?*

Moira: *I'm going to ignore that.*

Me: *Thanks for the update.*

Moira: *um hum.*

She loved when I asked stupid questions while she was helping me pro bono.

*   *   *

Ten and eleven o'clock came and went. Naomi's seductive radio voice in my earbuds and the comfortable Audi seat lulled me into serene relaxation. My eyelids hung at half-mast. My body whispered in my ear to give in. *Ping!* Moira saved me again. This time with a text at 11:35 p.m.

Moira: *Stone's caddy just passed by my intersection.*

I snapped to attention. The quickest exit from the narrow windy confines of Hillside would have been to come in my direction and take Via Siena to Via Capri where his Caddy could better maneuver and have quicker access to the freeway or Torrey Pines Road, the main artery in and out of La Jolla. Choosing the winding route must have meant that he was headed into The Village. La Jolla's original township.

I started the Audi and turned right on Via Siena and left down the rolling S of Via Capri. I gunned it down the hill and braked hard for the left-hand turn onto Hidden Valley Road. I called Moira through the Audi's Bluetooth.

"Unless he's stopping by a neighbor's, he's got to be headed to the Village, exiting on Prospect to cross Torrey Pines. Give him some rope. I'll catch up."

"Roger. I think you're right. He's not in a hurry."

I was. I raced around the turns of Hidden Valley and swooped down to the light fronting Torrey Pines. Red light. Finally, green. I gunned it, sliding left and pushed hard to make the light at La Jolla Shores Drive.

Moira's voice came through the Audi's speakers. "Behind him on Prospect at Torrey Pines."

I zoomed up Torrey Pines Road at sixty miles an hour, twenty over the speed limit. I could see the green light on Prospect at the top of the hill. I moved to the far-right lane. The light turned red. I saw Stone's Caddy cross Torrey Pines. Perfect.

"Turn left and circle back to Prospect via Park. I've got him," I said to Moira.

I turned right at the light and rolled down the soft hill into the Village. Stone's taillights were fifty yards ahead. No hurry. I cruised behind, giving him room. He pulled into a valet parking spot.

Right in front of Muldoon's Steak House. The restaurant I managed for seven years and once had a sliver of ownership. Until Stone got involved. He now owned fifty percent. The other fifty belonged to Turk Muldoon. My onetime best friend. We weren't close anymore, but Turk did let me use a booth in the dining room to meet clients during the restaurant's slow hours. And we were closer than Stone and Turk would ever be. Their partnership was a forced marriage. With Stone doing the forcing.

But Stone was a hands-off partner. I'd never seen him in the restaurant during my frequent rendezvous with clients.

Yet, here he was, entering the restaurant at eleven forty-five on a Thursday night.

Why?

It would be up to Moira to find out. Stone would easily spot me in the small confines of the bar. He didn't know Moira.

"He went into Muldoon's." I passed the valet's stand and drove down the block. "The dining room's closed at this hour. Hopefully, he went into the bar. See if he meets anyone and try to get some shots with your iPhone."

"Roger. I just turned onto Prospect. I'll be inside the bar in less than a minute."

Parking was tight, even late on a Thursday night. I turned left onto Ivanhoe and a few spots were available. But I kept moving, letting the cool night air coming through the window flow across my face like seawater over a shark's gills. Too restless to stand still.

I was working a case I hadn't chosen. My life was in someone else's hands. Maybe whatever Moira saw tonight would be what the Russians needed, and I'd be off the hook.

I circled Prospect, Cave Street, and Ivanhoe. Naomi's voice thrumming through the car's speakers. The ping of a text.

Moira: *He's not in the bar.*

Me: *Go into the dining room like you're going to the bathroom and look around.*

Silence.

Maybe Stone was back in the tiny restaurant office talking to Turk. Perfectly innocent.

Except the office was once a small pantry and could barely hold Turk and his desk. I couldn't imagine Peter Stone being in a space where he couldn't spread his peacock feathers for long. He needed room

Moira: *There's someone up in one of the booths. Sounds like two men talking. One could be Stone. I can't make out the conversation.*

Me: *Hang there.*

I finished my second pass by Muldoon's and pulled into the first parking spot I found on Ivanhoe, half a block down from Prospect. I popped the trunk of the Audi and pulled out my Nikon and hustled down to the T intersection. When Stone or his boothmate exited Muldoon's, I'd have photos for Sergei. Proof that I wasn't just sitting on my ass.

Moira: *Man left. Headed outside. Blue pinstriped suit, six two, mid-forties, Thin. Blond hair.*

My instructions from the Russians through T. Randolph were to follow Stone and email back a report about where he'd gone and what he'd done at the end of each night. Simple. No room for interpretation. My "get out of Russian mob jail free" card. But what if it was too simple? There was a play underneath the surface that I couldn't see, but knew was there. There had to be.

Me: *Stay on Stone.*

Moira: *What are u doing?*

Me: *Following Pinstripes.*

Pinstripes emerged from Muldoon's staircase looking exactly as Moira had described. I took a string of zoomed-in pictures of him as he handed his slip to a valet. Then I busted it back to the Audi and sped the half a block to the corner of Prospect. Pinstripes was still waiting for his car. I sat at the stop sign and waited. A silver Tesla pulled up in front of Pinstripes and the valet jumped out. Pinstripes gave him a tip, hopped in the car, and drove toward me on Prospect.

The silver Tesla kept heading south, and I pulled out a block behind it. I got close enough to read the license plate number, then drifted back, giving it plenty of room as it took Prospect down to La Jolla Boulevard.

Moira: *Stone's leaving.*

Me: *Follow him unless he crosses Torrey Pines on Prospect. Just go home if he does.*

Moira: *Roger.*

She called me a minute later.

"He just crossed Torrey Pines up Prospect. I'm heading home."

"Thanks for the work. Same time tomorrow night?"

"Roger." She hung up.

The Tesla turned onto Marine Street and then made a left onto Olivetas and pulled into the half driveway behind a classic old Spanish cottage–style home. I drove past just as the electric garage door lifted up. The Tesla disappeared into the garage in my rearview mirror.

I had Pinstripes' license plate number and home address. I'd be able to attach a name to the house on Olivetas when I got home and got onto a paid real estate website. Maybe he was just one of Stone's legit business associates or a fellow philanthropist. If that was the case, why not a simple phone call instead of a five-minute drive for a five-minute meeting?

No. My gut and my years as a cop and a PI told me the meeting wasn't about the next real estate project or donated wing. It had something to do with why the Russians wanted Stone followed. I needed to find out if there was anything I could use in their meeting for leverage before I reported back to T. Randolph.

I raced home.

Midnight greeted me at the front door. I let him out into the backyard for his last shot at bladder freedom, then we both headed upstairs. I went into my office and turned on my laptop. Midnight plopped down under the desk. I'd run over the report I needed to send to T. Randolph in my head on the way home. Before I typed it up and emailed it to him or her, I had to find out who the man who'd met with Peter Stone was. I logged onto Property Shark, a subscription website that had information about real estate, including home ownership. I typed in the address on Olivetas. A name popped onto the screen.

Obadiah Thomas Randolph. That was a mouthful.

Any kid festooned with Obadiah as a name would grab anything normal to take its place.

Like his middle name. Thomas.

T. Randolph.

Trandolph45@gmail.com.

CHAPTER TWENTY

WAS THIS A trick? A game? A trap? Why give me instructions to follow Stone when T. Randolph knew he'd be meeting him that night? Was I supposed to report to T. Randolph that I followed Stone to Muldoon's to meet him? Was this the angle I couldn't see, but knew was there when I took the case? Had he met Stone without the Russians knowing? Was he playing his own game against the Russians?

I thought about calling Moira to ask her opinion. She was smarter than me and wasn't physically invested in the case like I was. There was a reason she wasn't as invested as me. The more I told her, the more invested she became. And the more dangerous her life.

Ping.

She'd read my mind.

Moira: *U make it home ok?*

Me: *Yes.*

Moira: *What did u find out on Pinstripes?*

There it was. The opening I needed. A second brain, bigger than mine, to run scenarios by.

Me: *Best to leave you out of that part of it.*

I wasn't desperate enough to pull her in deeper. Yet.

Moira: *Cahill I'm already in. What happened? Did he spot the tail?*

Me: *No. I got it covered. Thanks. I'm about to send off my report. Maybe that will be enough and the case will be over. I'll call you tomorrow.*

Moira: *Don't be stupid. Talk to u tomorrow.*

I wasn't sure I knew how not to be stupid. Asking Moira's opinion would have been stupid and, possibly, reckless. Not asking her may have just been stupid.

I brought up my email account on the computer and replied to the email I'd gotten from T. Randolph earlier with the instructions to follow Stone.

Subject left his home at 11:35 pm and went to Muldoon's Steak House. He met briefly in a booth in the dining room with a man. Midforties, 6'2", slender build, blond hair, well dressed. He stayed for approximately five minutes and left the restaurant. The subject left five minutes later and returned home at 11:55. I was unable to get close enough to the booth to hear either conversation or take any photographs without bringing attention to myself. I await further instructions. If I don't receive any by noon today, I'll consider our business concluded.

I hit send and stared at my computer, hoping for, and dreading, a reply at the same time. I'd gone all in on a bluff. But maybe I wasn't the only one gambling. Randolph might be playing his own game. If he was, he could alter the email I'd sent him to say anything he wanted it to and show it to the Russians. If he was playing straight with the Russians, and knew I'd followed him home but hadn't reported it, I wanted the bad news right away. Best to know where I stood even if it was in quicksand.

I downloaded the photos I'd taken of Obadiah Thomas Randolph outside Muldoon's from my camera onto my computer. I pulled up the best shot I'd gotten of his face and split-screened it, then I Googled Obadiah Thomas Randolph in the other browser. Exactly one listing came up. Obadiah "T" Randolph was the CEO and founder of

LiveStem Technologies, Inc. A global leader in regenerative stem cell research.

His photograph was a match for the ones I took on Prospect Street. Bingo. The man supposedly sending me emails to tail Peter Stone had met with Stone last night. What was the game and who was in charge? And what the hell did a CEO of a stem cell biotech company have to do with the Russian mob or Peter Stone? The mob and Stone were more on the degenerative side of things, not regenerative.

I read further. LiveStem claimed to be the leader in clinical-grade, ischemic-tolerant, allogenic stem cell products. Whatever the hell that meant. Stem cell *products*. The whole idea creeped me out. *The Island of Doctor Moreau* with hybrid humans all around. Whatever it was, there was obviously money in it. That would be the only connection between LiveStem, Stone, and the Russians. Green. Their favorite color. Still, strange bedfellows.

LiveStem was located in Mira Mesa, a twenty-minute drive from Randolph's home. I looked up LiveStem's Board of Directors. There was the connection. Peter Stone's smiling countenance. The side he showed to the public, not the smirk I saw when he held leverage over my head. His accomplishments as a real estate developer and philanthropist were listed. Nothing about his casino days. The last sentence stated he was in charge of charitable outreach. I wondered whose pocket his hand went into at the end of that outreach.

If Stone was involved in LiveStem, the Russians were, too. Just not in a public way.

This put a sideways spin on things. That angle I'd been concerned about under the surface since I said yes to Sergei was sharp-edged. Even if I still couldn't figure out what it was. I wondered if Stone had been invited onto the board or had wedged himself in. With a Russian crowbar.

Obadiah T. Randolph was the key to figuring things out. Tomorrow, I'd start trying to figure out how to use that key.

Tonight, I'd try to stay safe.

I checked all the doors and windows before I went into my bedroom. Midnight found his spot at the foot of the bed. I always kept a handgun on the nightstand to my left. A Smith & Wesson .357 Magnum. Tonight, before I spent two hours staring at the ceiling, I practiced rolling over and grabbing the gun in the dark.

CHAPTER TWENTY-ONE

THE CLICK OF an incoming email on my phone woke me out of a fitful sleep at 5:45 a.m. I grabbed the phone off the nightstand, right next to the Smith & Wesson. T. Randolph. The Russians and their surrogates started their days early. I held my breath and opened the email. *Stake out Peter Stones house on 7453 Hillside Drive from sundown until midnight and note any visitors he has, complete with the license plate numbers of their cars. Follow Mr. Stone if he leaves the house and note where he goes and who he meets documented with photographs. Report all details by replying to this email after midnight, tonight.*

It looked like he just forwarded yesterday's email. No request for elaboration or follow up on the report of a man visiting Stone at Muldoon's. I had to find out more about the man who played middleman between me and the Russians.

I got to Obadiah Thomas Randolph's neighborhood by 6:40 a.m. This time, I took my car. A Honda Accord wouldn't stick out so much in this part of La Jolla. Plus, Randolph may have seen the Audi last night.

Olivetas was part of old La Jolla. A quarter mile back from the beach, the original Spanish cottage homes were still worth a couple million dollars even without views of the ocean.

I parked a half a block south of Randolph's home on Dunemere with a view of his front door and the detached garage at a right angle behind the house. No action on the street except for a couple of middle-aged women out for a morning walk. They both gave me long looks as they passed by my car. Probably the unofficial keepers of the neighborhood. I'd have to move soon if Randolph didn't venture out of the house. It was possible that he'd already left, but I doubted it. There was a newspaper sitting on his front porch.

I spotted the women returning up the block twenty minutes later. Still nothing from Randolph's house. I started my car and made a right-hand turn before the women made it back to my car. I took a wide circle, using La Jolla Boulevard to go down a couple blocks before I entered Olivetas from the other end. I parked five houses down from Randolph's home. Close enough to see him leave, but far enough away not to be spotted by him.

Unless he was looking.

The newspaper was still on the porch. No sign of the walking neighborhood watch patrol. I sat and watched for twenty-five minutes. Finally, Randolph stepped out onto the porch in a robe and slippers and grabbed the newspaper. He retreated back into the house. I figured I had at least another half hour before he left for work. Or somewhere else. I hoped the neighborhood watch ladies weren't spying on me out their windows.

Five minutes later, I got my answer. An LJPD cruiser flashed his lights and rolled up behind me. At least he didn't hit the siren.

I slowly put my hands on the steering wheel. I had a reputation with LJPD. Not a good one. I didn't recognize the cop who got out of the cruiser. Good. No history, except of the institutional one everybody had of me down at the Brick House.

The cop walked confidently up to my driver's window. No gun out. That was a plus.

"License and registration, please." His brass nameplate read, *Keefer*. Young. Strong command presence. Good. It was the nervous ones who shot you.

I slowly reached across to my glove compartment, took out the registration, and handed it to him. Then took out my wallet and handed him my license. I gave him the registration first, because I didn't want him to be reading my license and catch me reaching for the glove compartment out of the corner of his eye. Never knew when that command presence could disappear and the nerves took over.

"Mr. Cahill, can you tell me why you've been sitting alone in your car here for the last hour?"

"Actually." I gave him an oh-shucks smile. "I've only been in this spot for about twenty-five minutes."

"What about other spots in this neighborhood?"

"Point taken, Officer. I'm a private investigator surveilling a target." Every once in a while, I start with the truth. Even with a La Jolla cop. "I can show you my license, if you like. I just have to reach into my wallet again."

"That won't be necessary. I know who you are."

Damn. Just when I thought we were getting along.

"Oh?"

"I read the article about your father in the newspaper last year. He was the TO for my dad on La Jolla PD."

TO. Training Officer. A retired *San Diego Union-Tribune* reporter wrote an article for the paper last year addressing twenty-seven-year-old allegations about my dad.

"Oh?"

"My dad never believed the stories about your father."

"Good."

"But you can't sit here and loiter in your car." He handed me back my registration and driver's license. "Move along."

I could have argued with him that I did have a right to sit in my car on the street, but why make an enemy when I'd almost made a friend?

Besides, I could sit across La Jolla Boulevard with a view of the Dunemere intersection and wait for the Tesla to emerge and turn right or left.

I drove down to Windansea Beach and watched a couple surfers ride the morning break for a few minutes. The sun hadn't even hinted at pushing through the marine layer yet, but the salty tang in the air and gray-blue sky against the whitewater of the ocean was enough for me. I was Irish and didn't sunbathe on the beach. I never surfed, but could still admire the beauty of human and nature coming together in unison.

A surfer wiped out going over the falls, his board shooting skyward, then snapping back on its leash. Unison broken.

I drove off to find a new lair from which I could tail the man who grew tiny pieces of one human to try and prolong the life of another.

* * *

Obadiah T. Randolph appeared at the intersection of Dunemere and La Jolla Boulevard at 8:15 a.m., turning left against the traffic. I followed him through La Jolla and onto Highway 52 East. He took the 805 and got off on Mira Mesa Boulevard. I stayed way back. I knew where he was headed. To LiveStem. Three minutes later, I made a couple turns and saw him pull into a parking space with his name on it in front of a large industrial building. LiveStem, Inc. was on the door to one suite that looked to take up about a third of the building. A couple other biotech businesses also had their names on suites in the same building.

I parked in a spot in the back of the lot. My phone vibrated before I could pull it out and fill up what looked to be a long day by reading more about LiveStem.

Moira. I'd forgotten to call her.

"Well?" A jab more than a word.

"We're on for tonight. Same time. Let's work the same spots."

"That's not what I'm asking about."

I figured that, but wasn't ready to volunteer what I'd found out yet.

"I can't tell you anything else. The less you know, the better."

"The less I know, the worse for you."

She was right, but that didn't mean I had to make my life safer by making hers more dangerous.

"Text me tonight when you're in position. I really do appreciate all your help."

"Save it, Cahill." She hung up.

I hadn't had too many friends since my wife died thirteen years ago. I'd been the main suspect in her murder. Still was to a lot of people. People whom I thought were true friends turned out to be the easy kind. There when things were easy, gone when they got tough.

So, I had Moira. She'd started out by not liking me and sometimes it felt like she still didn't. I'm not even sure she liked being my friend. Or even why she chose to be my friend. I think she'd seen a need in me. A void that needed to be filled. And the woman and the mother in her forced her to take the job.

And I was a lucky man for it.

I spent the next hour searching the Internet on my phone for stories on LiveStem, glancing up to check the building and Randolph's car every couple of minutes. Both still there. Stories about LiveStem were scarce, but I did learn that they had clinics in Bermuda, Tijuana, and Amsterdam where they sold hematopoietic stem cells, which, I learned, come from red bone marrow, which is used in the treatment of cancer and other immune system disorders.

So, LiveStem appeared to be doing work to help mankind. And making a tidy profit. As it should. But was there room in there for Peter Stone and the Russian Mafia? I kept digging. While LiveStem sold hematopoietic stem cells, which were not from embryos, they also did research using embryonic stem cells. They received federal funding for their embryonic research. Federal funding. Free money that would attract Stone and the Russians.

At 1:10 p.m., a black Nissan Pathfinder parked near the front of the parking lot. A man, late twenties in a skinny suit, got out and carried a mini hard-sided cooler into LiveStem. The cooler was about the size that could fit a six-pack or a lunch in it. The man came out fifteen minutes later with the cooler and drove away. Lunch? Frozen stem cells from another lab? Who knows. The drop-by had been the highlight of the stakeout.

Randolph left at 5:30 p.m. I followed him home. He didn't stop and meet anyone in an ushanka or have a Putin bumper sticker on his car. He just went to his home in La Jolla like twenty other biotech CEOs did.

I went home, too.

CHAPTER TWENTY-TWO

I arrived at my spot on Hillside above Via Siena at 6:45 p.m. Randolph's instructions had been to stake out Stone at sundown. I had no way of knowing whether or not he was home, short of knocking on his door. I'd driven up Hillside past his home before I took my position. No car in the driveway, but he had a garage. The front of his house had no windows, so I couldn't see if he had any lights on when I passed by. Even if there had been, they could be on automatic timers.

Ping. Text.

Moira: *In place. I walked up the road around the bend to get a look at the house. Light just went on. Someone inside. Too far away to know for sure, but looks like Stone. Standing in front of the window. Just staring.*

Stone's house was almost all glass from the back, facing the ocean. You could catch glimpses of it driving up the back side of Hillside. If I had his view, I'd stand and stare, too. Even in the darkness of that mind, he could appreciate beauty. Maybe sketching out a plan how to harness it for his own benefit.

Me: *Roger.*

Moira: *You come to your senses yet?*

Me: *Not yet.*

Moira: *Roger and out.*

No further texts from Moira for the next hour and no movement from Stone. At least, not outside his house. Four cars exited Hillside, three entered from my end. I jogged down to check Stone's house after each. No cars in the driveway or on the street near his house.

I slipped a single earbud into my left ear at five after nine and turned on 1350 AM through the iHeart Radio app on my phone. Naomi's intro music stopped playing and her seductive purr vibrated in my ear. Guilt slipped into the other side of my head. I told myself that I hadn't abandoned her. That she was in good hands with Miranda. At least the second part was true.

"The sun is down, the moon is up, and it's just you and me alone here in the dark. Fear not. Take my hand. We'll find our way together."

I kept my eyes on the street ahead of me, but let Naomi's voice take me where she wanted to go. Like thousands of other listeners.

One of those listeners had broken into Naomi's car and stolen her gun. And wanted to steal her. Forever. So he could have her by his side as he ruled the underworld. Or maybe I'd read too much into the creepy letter someone had sent her. And maybe the person who snuck away from Sonic and around the back of the Night Owl hadn't followed us from the radio station that night. Maybe he was just a career thief who knew to stay out of the line of surveillance cameras and had tried to break in to all the cars in the Night Owl parking lot and Naomi's had been the easiest.

Whatever the case, he'd have to find Naomi before he could lock her in a dungeon and put a ring on her finger and a shackle around her ankle. He wouldn't find her at the radio station. I'd convinced Chip Evigan to let Naomi broadcast remotely from Miranda's house in North Park. She was safe for now.

Probably safer than me.

No action on Hillside. Eleven o'clock came and went. Moira texted at eleven thirty to say all the lights went out in the house. Stone in for the night? Maybe. Or, maybe he'd figured out that he was being watched and was planning an excursion after midnight. I doubted it, but I did wish I'd heard the conversation he'd had with T. Randolph last night at Muldoon's. A conversation he could have easily had over the phone.

I had the feeling something in that talk would be leverage that I could use against the Russians and their hidden agenda.

Moira had been silent since the lights-out text. I texted her at 11:50 p.m.

Me: *Head home. Thanks. Are you up for another night if I need you?*

Moira: *Yes. U do need me. Call me in the morning and I'll explain why.*

Me: *Yes ma'am.*

Moira: *Roger and out.*

I stayed in position.

Naomi at Night had served as white noise as I contemplated my future with the Russians. But a change in Naomi's voice caught my attention. Uncertainty? Fear? Subtle, but not to someone who'd heard her speak on the radio and in person.

"What did you say your name was? You told the screener it was Joe."

"You heard me, dear Cora. I have many names, but tonight it's Pluto."

I shot up in my seat. The stalker claiming his name on the airways. More escalation. My instinct screamed to drive over to Miranda's house, heavy. Strapped with my Smith & Wesson and two-handing the Mossberg tactical shotgun. But there was no way Pluto knew Naomi was working remotely. The station, usually big about announcing remotes, kept this one a secret. And even if the stalker knew where Naomi was hidden, he'd have to go through Miranda. And her gun.

Plus, I was still on the clock with T. Randolph. I did the next best thing and texted Miranda and told her to peek through her windows and look for anything out of place.

"That's okay, Pluto. We all wear the masks we have to wear to make it through another long hard day out in the world." Certainty returned to

her voice. He was on her turf. The world she created. *"But you're here with me now. You can be yourself."*

"I've never been more myself than right now, sweet Cora."

Baritone voice. But artificial in some way. Like the caller was speaking through an electronic voice changer. Why? To give his voice more authority or to disguise it because he knew Naomi would recognize it? Had he called before and given his real name, or was it someone she knew in her former life? Alex, the fired call screener who'd had a fling with Naomi? Or maybe the caller had a voice he wasn't proud of. Maybe effeminate or childlike?

"My name is Naomi, Pluto. You know that. I'm not a character in your fantasy world. I'm real." A slight scold in the purr. An ineffectual lover being taken to task. *"What makes you feel so yourself tonight? Talking to me? Do you find some of yourself in me, Pluto?"*

"You will know me." An edge to the artificial voice. *"And you will find some of me in you."*

"Let's keep it G-rated, Pluto. The clock is ticking toward midnight. The show ends in two minutes. Tell everyone, our thousands and thousands of listeners, why you called tonight."

"This is for Hercules, your watcher. Have you looked for Persephone's twin?"

"You've gone a bit Greek, Pluto. We only deal in truth and honesty here. Take off your mask and quit speaking through a machine and talking in riddles." Scolding, baiting. A side her listeners had never heard before. I understood. She wanted it over. She was calling him out for battle. Risky when you didn't know who he was or what he was capable of.

"Roman. Not Greek. Until we meet, sweet Cora." Dial tone.

Naomi fell back into character and said something about tortured souls and ended the show. I tapped her cell phone number on my phone.

"You heard?" A residue of anger.

"Yes. Tell your producer to make a loop of the phone call and send it to me in a link."

"Carl's at the station. He ran the show from there. I'm the only one remote."

"Give me his cell phone number."

She gave me the number and I called it.

"Hello?"

"This is the guy Evigan hired to find out who's harassing Naomi." I carved an edge on my voice meant for management and not this poor guy. "You realize that was the guy, right?"

"Yes. I read the letter."

"Good. Send me a loop of that call as soon as you can."

"I have to check with Chip. I can't do it on my own."

"Fine." I let my anger stretch out the word. "I don't care whether you have to go over to his house and wake him up, but get me a loop of that fucking phone call tonight."

"Okay."

"Did the caller's phone number come up on your screen?"

"Yes, but I can't give that to you either."

"Carl, do you want to see Naomi hurt?"

"No." He let go a long exhale. "But I need this job, man. Chip will fire my ass if I go behind his back. I'll talk to him and tell him how important it is that you get the phone number, but he has to give the okay."

"Got it. Do me a favor, though. Call me tonight right after you talk to Chip."

"Okay."

I gave him my number and hung up.

My phone rang before I could email T. Randolph the nightly report. I checked the screen hoping for Carl's number and good news. Naomi.

"Is Carl sending you the recording?" she asked.

"He has to ask Chip. He's also going to try to get me the phone number of the caller so I can try to get a reverse listing physical address online. If I can't, the police should be able to track down who the phone number belongs to."

"Police?" The uncertainty returned to her voice. The voices in the background faded away like she'd gone into another room. "We don't have to get them involved."

"I think we should. This guy is escalating. Talking about when you two will meet. Plus, this talk about Hercules and Persephone's twin. He knows about me and he's got something planned. And soon. Everything about this guy screams momentum. The letter, the voicemail, stealing your gun, and now this. He's cramming a year's worth of kink into one week. He's about to go off. I can feel it."

"We don't know if he stole my gun." She whispered "gun." "You said yourself it could have been anyone who broke into my car. A junkie. An identity thief. Anyone. I always knew he was going to call the show and boast. He probably has his little weenie in his hand right now. That's his rush. He'll call again and I'll embarrass him and that will be the end of it."

"You know that's not true. This guy is dangerous. You wouldn't have agreed to bunk with Miranda and do the show remotely if you thought he was harmless."

"Just taking intelligent precautions, Rick." Almost pleading. Another new side. "You promised you wouldn't get the police involved."

"Until things got out of my control. I can't keep watch at night and this guy is nocturnal."

"I've worked too hard to get where I am now. The police can ruin everything. There has to be another way."

"I'll see what's possible after I get a loop of the call and Pluto's phone number." I let go a long exhale of my own. Going against my gut was almost physically painful. "Goodnight, Naomi."

I called Miranda.

"Hi, Rick." The sweet, earnest voice from someone so badass always took me aback.

"Anything unusual?"

"No. I checked the street and the backyard. No cars I don't recognize. Nothing out of place."

"Good. Be on high alert. I think this guy is getting ready to make his move. I don't think he knows about you or where you live, but he's smart and resourceful."

"I'm ready."

"I know. Do you need to leave the house for anything tomorrow?"

"No. I'm stocked for two weeks. Just like you said. I have plenty of bullets, too."

"Good. Talk to you tomorrow."

CHAPTER TWENTY-THREE

I EMAILED T. Randolph my nightly report from my phone, then headed home. The report was two sentences. The second sentence was another ultimatum stating that if he didn't contact me by noon, our arrangement was over. I'd spent the last few days chasing the ghost of one psychopath and avoiding another, who I now "owed" ten thousand dollars. I wasn't a psychologist, but even I knew that my ultimatum was more for my benefit than for T. Randolph's or the Russian mob's. An obvious bluff to try to convince myself that I had some control of my fucked-up life.

Midnight met me at the door. We went into the backyard. I sat in my patio lounger and looked out at where the ocean was hidden by the night miles away. Midnight circled the yard looking for a place to splash down some yellow rain.

My phone rang at 12:35 a.m. Evigan.

"Tell me Carl is emailing me a phone number and a loop of the call," I said.

"He's sending you the call, but I have to check with legal about the phone number."

"Chip, you hired me because people told you I'm good at what I do. You trusted whoever recommended me, so now you need to trust me. Get me that phone number. Tonight. By the time your lawyers run through every possible contingency, Naomi could be dead or in some guy's basement dungeon as good as dead."

"I listened to the call. Both live and on replay. And, although I do find the call a bit creepy, there's nothing threatening about it. What am I missing?"

What he was missing was that Pluto had broken into Naomi's car, while expertly avoiding four or five security cameras, and stolen her gun and car registration, which had the address of where she was house-sitting. But I couldn't tell him that. I'd promised Naomi. A promise she was willing to risk her life on. A promise I knew I'd have to break at some point. Each day that I didn't, I went all in with Naomi on her gamble. How much was my word worth?

"Chip, you put your trust in me. You have to ride it out. Naomi is in danger. She doesn't want the police involved for her own reasons. Either send me what I need or call the police and watch Naomi pass on the new contract you're offering and go work for some other radio station." Reasoning hadn't worked so far. Maybe a baser need would. "You had the foresight to hire a virtual unknown and turn her into a star. I'm sure you're now known beyond San Diego. What will you be known for if you lose Naomi, one way or another?"

Quiet, but I could hear him breathing and almost hear him thinking. Finally, "What would you do with his phone number? You wouldn't call and threaten him, would you?"

"Of course not." Progress. "I can find out who he is with the phone number, or at least where he made the call. If I find out where he lives, I can surveil him. From there, we can figure out whether or not to get the police involved."

"Naomi doesn't want the police involved. You are right about that. She told me she'd quit if I called them." The precariousness of his situation cracked his voice high. "Please don't call the police."

"I won't unless I absolutely have to. You and I want the same thing, Chip, to keep Naomi safe. When the time comes, maybe between the two of us, we can convince her to bring in law enforcement. In the meantime, help me keep her safe."

The silence built again. He was thinking. Weighing the blowback he would get from the station owners if he gave me what I wanted without consulting legal against what could happen to Naomi and his career if he delayed giving it to me.

"I'll call Carl back and have him send you the number. But you have to agree to consult me if you find out who this Pluto is and what you plan to do."

"Will do."

I hung up and went inside. I grabbed a Ballast Point from the fridge and led Midnight upstairs to my office. My laptop had the time at 12:57 a.m. I stared at my inbox, willing the email from Carl to appear. I began to worry if Chip hadn't followed through or if Carl had gone to bed. The idea of sleep seemed foreign and inviting all at once. I doubted I'd get much of it until I finished with the Russians and dealt with Pluto.

A new email appeared in my inbox. CarlD@1350sandiego.com. I opened it and my phone rang simultaneously. A number I didn't recognize. My luck hadn't been very good with unknown phone numbers. Sergei, T. Randolph, a new threat? I answered anyway.

"This is Carl. I just sent you the information you wanted. Just click on the link to listen to the call."

"Got it. Thanks. Before you go, I need to know one other thing."

"Tell me what it is and I'll tell you if I can help."

I was starting to like Carl.

"Does the station keep a database of call-in numbers to the show?"

"I'm not sure. I'd have to ask IT on Monday. Why?"

"To see if there's a match for the number Pluto called in on tonight. If there is, we could—"

"Listen to any other calls associated with that number and see if Pluto, or whatever name the caller used, gives away any personal information to help you track him down."

"Exactly." Yeah, I liked Carl just fine.

"I'll talk to IT, but won't tell them why I really need the information."

"Perfect. And, maybe don't—"

"I won't tell anyone. Not even Chip. I feel ya, Cahill. I want to find this son of a bitch, too."

"Okay. Just don't go rogue."

"I won't, but if you decide to drop in on Pluto unannounced and need some backup, I'm available."

"Good to know. Call or email me Monday with what you find out."

"You got it." He hung up.

One more on Team Naomi.

I opened Carl's email. The phone number had a 619 area code—619 covers the largest swath of land in San Diego. Pluto could have called from anywhere. If he used a cell phone, the police could ping cell towers with a warrant. But even if I convinced Naomi to let the police in, they didn't have anything near a justification for getting a warrant.

I fought the urge to call the number to hear Pluto's voice unaltered. But that would just spook him and send him deeper into hiding. Instead, I fed the phone number into a subscription reverse address website and it came up a blank. Shit.

Tomorrow, or later this morning, I'd have to try to enlist another pro for Team Naomi. Moira. She had police contacts that my reputation and cops' elephant memories would never allow. Plus, she had me beat in the looks and charm department, which helped when it came to nudging cops to give out information they shouldn't.

I clicked on the link in the email that contained the phone call. The link took me to the 1350 website and a box with *Naomi At Night* and the time of the call. I pushed the play button and listened to the call again.

I'd missed the beginning of the call while sitting in my car because I'd been in my head worrying about the Russians.

"Welcome, Joe. You're safe here. What burden would you like to lift from your soul tonight?"

"My name is Pluto and my soul is already unburdened tonight and in the afterlife." The afterlife? Was he thinking murder-suicide or referencing the Roman underworld where Pluto or Hades was ruler? I didn't like either choice.

"What did you say your name was? You told the screener it was Joe."

"You heard me, dear Cora. I have many names, but tonight it's Pluto." Many names? Had he used other names and called in before? Hopefully, Carl and 1350's IT department could help with that. Or maybe he just meant Hades or Satan or any other name for the ruler of hell.

"That's okay, Pluto. We all wear the masks we have to wear to make it through another long hard day out in the world. But you're here with me now. You can be yourself."

"I've never been more myself than right now, sweet Cora." Confident. The night creeper and anonymous letter writer wanted to be acknowledged and get the notoriety his sad little life had been missing. Was he associating more and more with his fantasy self and losing touch with reality? If so, people, coworkers, might begin to notice.

"My name is Naomi, Pluto. You know that. I'm not a character in your fantasy world. I'm real. What makes you feel so yourself tonight? Talking to me? Do you find some of yourself in me, Pluto?"

"You will know me. And you will find some of me in you." Sex? Or a metaphor for putting his knife or his bullet into her.

"Let's keep it G-rated, Pluto. The clock is ticking toward midnight. The show ends in two minutes. Tell everyone, our thousands and thousands of listeners, why you called tonight."

"This is for Hercules, your watcher. Have you looked for Persephone's twin?"

In the Greek mythologies I'd read up on since the Pluto letter, Hercules was commanded to go into hell and bring back Cerberus, the three-headed hellhound of the underworld. I was Hercules. Pluto had seen me go into the Night Owl with Naomi. But he must have seen more than that to call me Naomi's watcher. Had he followed her home that night and been hidden outside when I came to her house in Del Mar? If so, why not call me her lover or boyfriend? How would he know that I was watching over Naomi?

I'd only been to her house the one time. She'd stayed at my house two nights. I'd checked to make sure no one was following her each night. I'd gone to the radio station three times. The first time I'd staked out the parking lot for the majority of her show. Had he been watching the parking lot? Is that why he called me the watcher?

Another possibility popped into my head. This one more twisted than the others. What if Pluto worked at 1350? Chip, Carl, and the board op knew I'd been hired to, more or less, watch over Naomi. Did someone else at the station, aside from the owners, know? Carl and the board op couldn't have made the Pluto call because they were working. I guess the board op could have made the call with his cell phone to the switchboard from the station and patched himself in. Very risky and he'd have to have been completely alone at the station. But he wasn't. Carl was there along with the news reader, Rachel Riley. It wasn't her and it wasn't Carl. And it wasn't the board op.

That left Chip Evigan or an unknown station worker. I couldn't fathom what kind of game Chip was playing if he was Pluto. He'd hired me. Even if it came from the owners, once I was hired he'd have to figure his game was up. And there wasn't a game that made sense. Maybe, once being behind the mike himself, he was jealous of Naomi's notoriety. Why would he care now? Naomi's success had made him a genius program director. His star was on the rise and it was tied to Naomi. Couldn't be Chip. That left someone else at the station I didn't know about or someone from the outside who was watching the station. I had to find out from Chip who else knew about the real reason I'd been hired and who they might leak it to.

Have you looked for Persephone's twin?

Persephone was the alternate name for Cora. Either name meant Naomi. I knew he was coming for her. But who was the twin? My brief reading of Persephone didn't reveal a twin. Why would I be looking for a twin? By his words, I was Naomi's watcher. Did Naomi have a sister I didn't know about? She was stingy with information about her past. If she had a sister in the area, surely, she'd have told me when I asked her if there was someone she could stay with that first night.

If not a sister, then who was the twin Persephone? Another female radio personality in town?

"You've gone a bit Greek, Pluto. We only deal in truth and honesty here. Take off your mask and quit speaking through a machine and talking in riddles."

"Roman. Not Greek. Until we meet, sweet Cora." The gnawing in my gut since I heard the phone call for the first time told me that attempted meeting would be coming sooner rather than later. Much sooner.

CHAPTER TWENTY-FOUR

ANOTHER EARLY MORNING click from my cell phone signifying the arrival of an email pulled me from the half sleep I'd grasped onto. I grabbed the phone off the nightstand and read the email. T. Randolph. Same instructions as yesterday. The Russians and their surrogates loved the crack of dawn. I used to. Back when I could sleep for more than two hours at a time. Before I met them.

I waited until 7:00 a.m. to call Moira.

"You finally come to your senses, Rick?"

Some may think this was less than a cheery greeting, but there was a time when Moira would only address me by my last name. Without a mister in front.

"Not yet. Just wanted to ask if you can play it again tonight."

"I suppose."

I sensed clenched teeth on the other end. Not the best time to ask for yet another favor. I didn't have a choice. Moira would.

"You still have friends on LJPD?"

"You know I do. Nice try." A release of breath that could have been a laugh or exasperation. "You wanted me to say 'Yes. Why?' so I'd be the one to ask a question. For someone who leads with his chin most of the time, you can be a real passive-aggressive jerk. Ask me your favor."

She knew my faults and weasel moves like a wife or a mother would. Maybe I should just ask her to marry or adopt me.

"I need a reverse address with this phone number. It came up empty on Spokeo. Hopefully, the police have it." I gave her the number Pluto used to call into Naomi's show last night.

"Does this have something to do with the Stone surveillance?"

"No. It's another case I was working when I got the call to surveil Stone."

"Give me some background. I don't want to use up a favor for something I wouldn't do."

"The number belongs to a stalker who's harassing a public figure. This person doesn't want to go to the police, so they hired me."

"The public figure is a woman. I got that much. I guess you're not going to tell me who she is."

"Why do you think it's a woman?"

"You used 'they' instead of instead of 'he' or 'she.' If it had been a man, you wouldn't have been so protective about the pronoun. You would have just said 'he.'"

I wondered, not for the first time, why anyone in San Diego who needed a private detective would call me before they called Moira. Maybe none of them did. Maybe I got all the cases she didn't want.

"No, I can't tell you who she is. But the guy after her is escalating, and I think his next move is to try to kidnap her."

"And she still doesn't want the police involved?"

"It's complicated."

"I don't think I've ever helped you on a case that wasn't." A brief chuckle. Good. She was going to help me. "If you think the pervert is about to make a move, aren't you worried about her at night while you're staking out Stone?"

"I hired a bodyguard. Someone I trust. But I still need to find this guy and shine a little sunlight on him."

"My guy is out this weekend. It will have to wait until Monday."

"Roger. Thanks."

CHAPTER TWENTY-FIVE

MOIRA CALLED AT 10:35 a.m. Monday morning. We'd had an un-eventful weekend on Stone watch. No visitors. No late-night rendez-vouses. Fine by me.

"The phone number is connected to a pay phone." No preamble, as usual.

"A pay phone? There can't be that many left in San Diego. Do you have an address?"

"Surprised me, too. Yes. The address is 9871 Aero Drive."

A frozen finger went up my spine. Aero Drive. The main thorough-fare on the way to the 1350 radio station. Someone had watched me in the parking lot of the station the first night I went there. From out-side of 1350. Or inside. From whatever vantage point, Pluto had been two steps ahead of me the whole time. His taunt on the call to Naomi was born out of confidence. But now I knew he knew. That made the game even. Or at least, less one-sided.

"You're not saying anything, Rick," Moira said. "Does the address mean something to you?"

"It's near where the woman works."

"You think it's an inside job?"

"I'd already considered that possibility and eliminated it. But now I have to recalculate."

"I'm turning in my report on the worker's comp fraud case today at noon and picking up a check. I can meet you down on Aero Drive around one thirty if you want another set of eyes."

"Deal. Call me when you're done with the cheating golfer. Thanks."

Aero Drive leads up to residential housing east of Interstate 15 and commercial businesses just west of it. The address associated with the phone number had me turning right onto Aero. West.

The 9871 Aero Drive address was a block up from Interstate 15. A McDonald's restaurant next to a strip mall. I pulled into the parking lot and spotted the pay phone. Just off the entrance with a view of Aero Drive. Pluto had made his phone call Friday night two minutes away from the 1350 radio station. Had he hung up the phone and waited for Naomi's car to drive by on Aero? What did he do after he waited and the classic Camaro never drove by? Did he go up to the radio station and look for the Camaro in the parking lot? Had he already driven by and seen that Naomi's car wasn't there?

I got back into my car and drove to the radio station, clocking the time. It only took a minute, forty-five seconds and that included being stuck at the light turning left onto Aero. With little traffic late at night, Pluto might be able to make the trek in a minute.

I drove past the station and turned left into Lansing Business Park. Maybe my old friend Quint was working in the Lansing Security office. Maybe he'd let me look at tapes from last night without my FBI sidekick. I parked, but didn't get out of the car. No way. Quint had liked lording his power over me too much. He'd never let me see the tape and I'd used up my FBI goodwill.

Maybe there was another in. How about a woman with a badge? Paper like mine, but still sexy and with an attitude. Quint had closed the computer he'd been looking at in a hurry when Special Agent Mallon and I walked into his office the other day. I'd guessed porn. Without judgment. Now I hoped it was.

I pulled out my phone and checked the time. Eleven forty a.m. I still had almost two hours before Moira thought she could make it over to Aero Drive. I texted her and asked her to call me as soon as she could.

I drove across the street to the radio station. No security guard during the day. Chip Evigan's Beemer was in the parking lot. I didn't recognize any of the other cars in the lot. None were black sedans that looked like Toyota Corollas or Hyundai Elantras like the one Rudy, the night manager at Sonic, saw the mystery man get out of on the tape.

I parked and went up to the front door of the station. A woman sat behind the desk in the lobby. I buzzed the intercom and told her who I was and that I was there to see Evigan.

A minute later, Evigan came out and opened the door for me.

"My office." No hello. No smile. No bro hug.

He didn't bother introducing me to the news person at her computer or tell me who the talent was in the broadcasting booth. All business. So was I. He closed the office door behind me and sat down at his desk without offering me a seat. I sat down opposite him anyway.

"Did you learn anything with the information Carl and I broke company rules to give you Friday night?" He leaned back in his chair, folded his arms, and squinted at me like he already knew the answer was no.

"Yes. The sonofabitch who made the call did it from a pay phone next to the McDonald's on Aero Drive."

"How do you know?" He cupped his chin and scratched the side of his face. "Are you sure?"

"Yes. A hundred percent." Sort of. "The important thing is that Pluto is escalating and he's going to make his move soon."

"What move? What's he going to do?" Evigan scratched harder.

"Try to kidnap Naomi."

Evigan's eyes widened.

"How do you know that?"

I told him about the mythologies. Both the Greek and the Roman. And the part about Hades kidnapping Persephone.

"Jesus. You really think this guy is going to take it that far?"

"Yes. Soon."

"Why do you think it's going to be soon?"

"He's escalating at a rapid pace. A letter two weeks ago. The angry voicemail. The call Friday night from a pay phone within walking distance of the station. Linking himself to the letter by calling himself Pluto over the air. He's growing bolder by the day." Even without knowing about the car break-in and theft of Naomi's gun, Evigan should be alarmed. Naomi's secret was on life-support.

"Anybody here drive a black Toyota Corolla or Hyundai Elantra–type car?"

"I don't think so."

"Who here at the station knows the real reason you hired me?"

"You don't think someone here is Pluto?"

"Due diligence. Answer the question."

"Just the owners and me." He scratched his face again. "And now Naomi and Carl."

"Bullshit. What about Naomi's board op and Rachel Riley? They saw me in here two days in a row."

"They don't know the real reason you were here. I didn't tell them."

"Come on, Chip. You manage people. People gossip. People tell other people things they're not supposed to and swear those people to secrecy who tell other people. Who's friends with who in here?"

"Well, Carl probably told Dave, Naomi's board op. Especially since she's doing the show remotely and Dave's being left at the station. He might tell Greg, the morning show board op. Everyone would tell Rachel. She wouldn't tell anyone else."

"What about the other on-air talent? The morning guys. Steve and Ben, and your other shows."

"The word might have gotten around that we hired a security consultant, but I doubt everyone knows the real reason why we hired you or that we hired you at all."

"Any of the other show hosts jealous of Naomi's success and income?"

"Probably all of them. That doesn't mean that they want to kidnap or kill her. Professional jealousy is like oxygen in the radio business. Nobody's ever gotten killed over it."

"Anyone who works here pay any special attention to Naomi? Ask personal questions about her?"

Evigan was probably the first person there to show inappropriate attention to Naomi. So he should know all about anyone else with the stench of lust musk on them.

"She's a beautiful woman. All the men who work here look at her when she walks by, but none of them are writing letters to her."

"You sure about that?"

"Well, pretty sure."

"You got someone in mind?"

"No. It's just that sometimes people are different in their free time than they are at work."

My whole job depended on people acting differently in their secret lives than they did in public.

CHAPTER TWENTY-SIX

MOIRA MET ME in the parking lot of Lansing Business Park at 1:15 p.m. She would have gotten there a half hour earlier if I hadn't asked her to stop by her house and dress in something sexy on her way over. I'd only seen her in something other than jeans and a sweater or sweatshirt once in the three years I'd known her. That had come from a request from me, too. Another case she helped me with.

Moira looked great in jeans, but I'd needed something a little more revealing if my plan to get Quint to show us last night's security tape had a chance to work. She didn't disappoint in a low-cut, high-hemmed red dress. I hadn't imagined she owned such a dress, and found myself reevaluating our friendship.

"What the hell's wrong with you?" Moira said as she walked from her car. "Quit staring."

"I'm not sure I can."

"Get in line, Cahill." She put one hand up to her hair and the other on her waist then thrust out her hip.

"Perfect. Bring that attitude inside."

I led her through the lobby of the main building to Lansing Security. She took the lead and went up to the drive-thru window and my pal Quint. Except he looked different. He'd shaved his muttonchops.

"May I help you?" His voice even sounded different. Still flat, but devoid of condescension. Maybe that was just because he'd directed the question to Moira and not me. Then I noticed that the sewed-on name tag on his shirt read Caleb, not Quint. They had to be brothers. Twins.

"We are private investigators working on a case." She put her hand on the wall next to the window and leaned down a bit to the seated Caleb revealing another inch of cleavage. "We need to see your security tapes from last night. Someone's life might depend on it."

Caleb moved his eyes from Moira's breasts off to the side. "I'm sorry. I'm not allowed to do that."

"Quint showed me security tapes last week." I stood next to Moira.

"You know Quint?" An ember of life seeped into his voice. There was something slightly off about him. He wouldn't look me in the eyes.

"Yeah. We met last week when he showed me the tapes from the night before. And that's what we need to see today. Tapes from last night. Just like your brother Quint showed us."

I smiled at Caleb even as guilt gnawed at me for taking advantage of him. Manipulating people didn't bother me much. Not when I was working a case. Most of the people I maneuvered had already lost their shine. But Caleb seemed innocent. An innocent. Another speed bump to roll over on my quest for the truth.

"I'm not allowed to show the tapes to anyone. Except Quint and the police if they show me a warrant."

"I didn't show Quint a warrant. He showed me that tape because he wanted to help me keep someone safe."

I could feel Moira's look more than see it out of the corner of my eye. My conscience in human form. She'd known what the gig was when she agreed to help me. She'd manipulated people on her own cases to get what she needed. Her lines were similar to mine. She just didn't cross them as often as I did. If ever. Trying to take advantage of a damaged innocent was on the other side of a line she'd never cross. I didn't see any other way to keep Naomi safe.

"I don't know." Caleb pulled down his lower lip with his index finger. "I better call Quint."

"Okay. I just hope he doesn't get mad at you."

Moira clasped my hand below the window and squeezed. Hard. She could have cracked a walnut. I took the pain. I wished she'd squeezed harder.

"I have to . . ." Caleb shook his head. "I have to call Quint."

Moira let go of my hand and walked over to the corner of the small room. I stayed by the window and watched Caleb dial a phone next to the computer on his desk. I preferred Moira's vice grip instead of the look she no doubt was giving me.

Caleb explained the situation into the phone, then quietly listened to the bad news for me that Quint had to be giving him. After ten or fifteen seconds, Caleb handed the phone receiver through the window to me.

"Quint wants to talk to you."

I held the phone to my ear. "This is Cahill."

"That's cold, bro." The disinterested voice. "Taking advantage of my brother. He's got Asperger's Syndrome. You know, autism. You knocked him out of his routine. He's going to be messed up for the rest of the day. I should troll the shit out of you on social media. Caleb's going to show you whatever the fuck you want to see, but the next time you want to look at security video, talk to me."

"Roger." I wondered why the sudden cooperation, but wouldn't look a gift Quint in the mouth. Or anywhere else.

"Give the phone back to Caleb."

I gave Caleb the receiver. He listened for a bit, then hung up. He picked up a business card from a card holder on the desk and handed it to me through the window. It read Lansing Security, Quint Lansing, Owner.

"Quint said I can show you whatever you want to see." Blank expression. "Come through the door and turn left."

"Thanks, Caleb." I gave him a big smile that made me feel worse.

I put my hand on the doorknob and glanced back at Moira.

"You got what you needed." She looked down at her dress then back at me. "I'm going home to take a shower. I'll be on my post below the target's house tonight. I'll text you when I'm in position and if I see anything. Otherwise, let's go radio silent. For a while."

I nodded and she left the room. I could have tried a different tack with Caleb, but I'd seen his vulnerability and knew it was the best way in. It hadn't really worked. I'd just gotten lucky. But I'd try the same tack again. I'd just try not to do it in front of Moira. Or any other decent person. The guilt would still be there. And I'd still be trying to keep someone safe.

I went through the door and took the path I'd followed yesterday to the small office. Caleb already had the split-screen security video feed cued up on the computer.

"Which area would you like to see?" A hint of animation in his voice. He sat more erect in his chair. "We have the lobby and the front and back parking lots."

"Back lot from 8:30 Friday night."

Caleb's fingers whizzed across the keyboard and a single shot of the parking lot, the street, and the 1350 parking lot came on the computer screen. The time stamp was exactly 8:30 p.m.

Maybe I had to rethink Caleb. Autistic or not, he seemed very proficient at his job.

Nothing happened on the upper part of the screen until about 9:10 p.m. when the evening show host, Jeff Palet, exited the station with his producer. They got into their cars and left.

Neither car resembled a black Toyota Corolla or Hyundai Elantra.

I watched the video on fast-forward for the next twenty minutes. No black economy cars passed by the parking lot. Very few cars passed by at all and none loitered or looked suspicious.

At 11:55 p.m. on the video, I had Caleb slow to live action. Pluto had talked to Naomi from the phone at McDonald's less than a mile from the radio station then. I let the video roll. After midnight passed, I kept an eye on the lower right portion of the computer screen where any car coming from Aero Drive would appear. None did. Cars started exiting the 1350 parking a lot at 12:10 a.m. No cars came the other way. The lot was empty by 12:20 a.m. I watched for another five minutes then gave up.

My ruse with Caleb had blown up in my face, but I'd still managed to see the video. And nothing came of it. I'd worked an innocent, been called out by his brother, and dropped a few degrees in Moira's eyes. All for naught.

I took out one of my business cards and held it to Caleb. "If you ever need a private detective for anything, give me a call. I won't charge you."

"Thank you." He took the card without meeting my eyes.

I went out to my car and was about to get in just as the car opposite me pulled out of its spot and gave me a view to the back of the parking lot. And the car parked in the outer ring of parking spots.

A black Toyota Corolla.

CHAPTER TWENTY-SEVEN

I DROVE TO the outer ring and parked in the space opposite the Corolla. It was a late model in mint condition. White California license plate. There were probably five hundred to a thousand Black Toyota Corollas on the streets of San Diego. Hell, there was probably more than one that parked in this lot every day. There would be no way Rudy Wayne from Sonic would be able to ID the car against what he saw on the grainy security camera feed. He wasn't even sure the car was a Corolla.

But this Corolla was parked across the street from the radio station where Naomi worked. Plenty of office windows in Lansing Business Park that faced the parking lot of 1350. When grasping at straws, don't miss the ones right in front of you. I took a photo of the license plate with my phone.

I was about to text Moira and ask her to run the plate with one of her cop buddies when I remembered her last words to me today. "Let's go radio silent. For a while." I didn't know how long she meant by a while, but I knew it was longer than an hour.

I got out of my car and scanned the parking lot. Someone had just exited their car in the front part of the parking lot and walked toward the main building. No one else around. I looked through the driver-side window of the Corolla. The inside of the car was like the outside. Immaculate, except for a crossword puzzle book on the front passenger seat. Nothing on the back seats. Nothing to indicate whether the car was driven by a man or a woman.

The car registration was probably in the glove compartment. I thought about checking the door to see if it was locked. Even if it was, I had a lock pick set in a duffel bag hidden in the spare wheel well of my car. I'd broken into cars before. I'm sure I'd break into them again. But I'd always needed what I considered solid probable cause before I'd cross that line. Good reason or not, I broke the law every time I picked a lock. The law didn't give me discretion. My personal code did. Today the code said I didn't have enough to breach someone else's privacy.

That and the faint alarm light blinking under the dashboard. Decisions were easier when physical barriers prevented you from broaching moral ones.

I could try the door handle or rock the car until the alarm went off, then wait for the owner to come out and check on his car. But people tend to just wait for car alarms to run their course during the day. Sometimes even at night. And I knew there was a security camera pointed at the front parking lot as well as the one pointed at the back. I couldn't afford that kind of exposure on this case. Yet. And I couldn't afford to get arrested.

My only options were to text the plate number to Moira or stake out the parking lot until the Corolla's owner came out and got into his car, then follow him home. Tough to do without getting spotted during the daylight hours. Plus, I had to leave the parking lot by 6:00 p.m. and head over to Peter Stone's for my life-or-death assignment.

I texted Moira.

Me: *I know I disappointed you today. And not for the first time. I'm sure I'll do it again.*

Moira: *I'm sure u will too.*

Me: *I need your help.*

Moira: *Didn't take u very long.*

Me: *I wouldn't ask if it wasn't important.*

Moira: *It's always important. To U.*

Me: *I need a plate run. Might be the stalker's car.*

Moira: *I can't push my guy anymore. I just got u the phone number info u needed.*

Me: *Do you have someone else?*

Moira: *Not that I want to use up for u.*

Me: *I understand. I'm just trying to keep this woman safe.*

I texted her a photo of the license plate.

No response.

I did have one other option. Barely. I called Special Agent Mallon's cell phone. Voicemail. I left a message asking him to call me. I wouldn't hold my breath. I hadn't burned that bridge yet, but there was smoke coming from it.

I moved my car to the far end of the second-to-last row of cars, still with a good view of the Corolla. The car remained empty as the rest of the parking lot thinned out. John Mallon hadn't returned my call. It had been over two hours. The smoke from the bridge grew a bit thicker.

Naomi's producer, Carl, called me at 4:20 p.m.

"We don't have a database that saves call-in phone numbers to the show. But, I got Chip to give me a copy of the most recent phone bill and I checked the numbers against the one from last night. Unfortunately, no matches."

I wasn't surprised after finding out Pluto had made last night's call from a phone booth. I was convinced he'd called the show before last night. He'd even hinted at it in his letter. But I figured his early calls came during his incubation period. Before his feelings for Naomi had grown to full kink or his fantasy self had reached maturity.

I thanked Carl and hung up.

I called my next-door neighbor and asked if her daughter could let Midnight out and feed him. Tasks she performed with love and care. I didn't know what I'd do when she graduated from high school and left for college. I might have to find a girlfriend or just a friend. Hadn't had much luck in either category lately.

The parking lot mostly emptied out over the next few hours, but no one claimed the black Corolla. The descending sun chased me out of the parking lot. The night, Peter Stone, and the Russians couldn't wait any longer.

* * *

I should have waited for however long it took to see who drove the Toyota. Peter Stone stayed in all night. Another pro bono night of boredom for the Russians.

I listened to Naomi's show. No return of Pluto. Maybe I was wrong about the escalation. Maybe the only thing that was escalating was the speed of his hand on his private part when he thought of Naomi.

The show ended and rolled over to the news, and I ran over the scenarios of what I'd learned and hadn't learned about the Pluto case today. The only certainty was that I had to find out who owned the black Corolla and eliminate them as a suspect or focus on them as one.

Something on the radio pushed itself out of the background noise and I concentrated on Rachel Riley's voice.

"... as a carhop. Ms. Alton was reported missing by her roommate Friday, but she was last seen leaving the restaurant after her shift early Thursday morning at 1:45 a.m. If anyone has information on her whereabouts, please call 911 or Crime Stoppers at ..." She gave the number, but I'd already moved ahead of her.

There was only one chain of restaurants in San Diego that had carhops. Sonic. There were at least three Sonics in the city. The odds were at best one in three that the missing carhop worked at the one in Pacific Beach. Or maybe, at worst. The odds of her being Alicia, the carhop who'd complained about the black Corolla-like car the night Naomi and I went to the Night Owl were much lower. Still, I needed to know tonight.

I called Rudy Wayne.

"Hello?" Alert.

"Rudy. Rick Cahill. Is the missing carhop from your restaurant?"

"Yes." His voice brittle with emotion.

Shit.

"Is it Alicia, the employee who complained about the black car the other night?"

"Oh my god." His voice cracked high. "I hadn't even thought of that. Yes. It's Alicia."

CHAPTER TWENTY-EIGHT

I CALLED THE phone number of the SDPD detective Rudy had given me when I got home. The phone picked up after four rings.

"Detective Skupin." Groggy.

"Detective, my name is Rick Cahill. I'm a private investigator and I think I may have some information regarding Alicia Alton's disappearance."

A pause. A long one. I couldn't tell if he was searching for a pen and pad or had fallen back asleep.

"You call me on my personal number at 12:23 in the morning and you *think* you *may* have some information on the disappearance?" He made a grunt like he'd moved his body from horizontal to vertical. "You trying to insert yourself into the case for a little free publicity, Mr. Cahill? I've already gotten calls from two other private dicks and three psychics. I'm all full up on unsolicited theories. You'll have to make your calls to the media without my input. I'm not buying."

I'd finally made the phone call I should have made last week. The delay may have cost Alicia Alton her life. The call would probably cost me a lawsuit with 1350 and unknown drama from Naomi, and now this cop took me for a scheming publicity hound.

"Are you stupid or just lazy, Detective?" Another cop I'd never be able to ask a favor. Fine. I doubted this guy would ever get off his ass long enough to have anything of value anyway. "I don't give a shit about the press. Do I have to talk to your lieutenant to find someone who will work this case?"

"All right." A groan with a lot of air. "Let's have it, gumshoe. What's your theory?"

"I don't have a theory. I have facts. You put them together any way you want, but you know as well as I do that the clock is ticking on Alicia Alton. If we're not already too late."

I told him about taking the case for 1350, the letter from Pluto, the myth of Hades and Persephone, having drinks with Naomi at the Night Owl, the missing gun, the black car parked in the Sonic drive-in, Rudy Wayne and the security tape, Pluto's call into Naomi's show, and the license plate of the black Toyota Corolla parked in the Lansing Business Park's parking lot.

"So, you think the disappearance of Miss Alton has something to do with this Pluto character?" He'd dropped the distain from his voice. A cop working a case the right way. Fine by me. I didn't hold grudges.

"It's too coincidental that the woman who delivered a Coke to the guy who disappeared from his car and may have stolen the gun from Naomi's car would go missing two nights later. I don't like coincidences. Especially when it comes to kidnapping.

"Neither do I." Skupin was wide awake now. Engaged. "So, you think he grabbed the girl as some sort of dry run for Naomi?"

"Maybe. Pluto did direct a question at me on his call to Naomi's show about me looking for Persephone's twin. That was Friday night. Alicia was already missing by then. Hopefully, he's got her locked away somewhere and hasn't killed her."

"That's if your Pluto is the guy. I'm not convinced yet, but I'll have someone at the station run the plate you gave me."

"Don't wait until morning. He might have had another reason for kidnapping Alicia." The hole in my gut that opened when I heard about the missing carhop grew bigger.

"What's that?"

"From what Rudy Wayne told me about how the guy in the Corolla kept his head angled away from the security camera, he knew he was being taped. He had to figure someone would put together his disappearance from his car and the theft of Naomi's gun and check the tapes."

"But you just said he knew where the cameras were and angled his face away from them. No one would be able to identify him."

"There was one person who could. Alicia Alton. She delivered his Coke to him before he left his car. Maybe he doesn't want her for a dry run. Maybe he's getting rid of potential witnesses."

"I sure hope you're wrong."

"Me, too."

"Thanks for the call, Rick. This is helpful information. You might be onto something with this Pluto character. Sorry I rode you earlier. A case like this attracts all kinds trying to get their names in the paper." An exhale of breath like he stood up or was about to broach a touchy subject. "I need to ask you a favor."

"Sure."

"Don't talk to the press or anyone else about what you told me tonight."

"I don't search out the press, Detective. And I'd never tell them anything about an ongoing case. But the radio station hired me, and I report to them. I'll tell them and Naomi everything I have to if I think it'll help keep her safe."

"I get that. Why didn't the radio station or Naomi alert SDPD about this Pluto?"

"They did when they got the letter. Whoever they talked to didn't think the letter was enough to start an investigation."

"Okay, but what about after the gun was stolen?"

The gun. Naomi. I couldn't cover for her anymore. I shouldn't have this long. Her paranoia about involving the police and my acquiescence had put her life in danger and may have gotten an innocent killed.

"The radio station doesn't know about the stolen gun and Naomi didn't report it to the police."

"Why not?"

"Ask her." I gave him Naomi's cell phone number and Miranda's number and address. "I've already breached my agreement with both the radio station and Naomi by talking to you. Finding that poor carhop comes first."

"Do you have some connection to Alicia Alton, Rick? I'm sure you're an altruistic guy like every PI I've come across, but you seem particularly invested in a woman's safety who you've never met."

"You're right. I only talked to her once on the phone, but she's my responsibility now."

"Just don't go working this case on your own. I appreciate the information, but we'll take it from here."

"I'll stay out of your way." But I wouldn't stop working the case. Find Alicia Alton and I find Pluto. Find Pluto and I find Alicia Alton. Hopefully, I wouldn't be too late.

CHAPTER TWENTY-NINE

My phone woke me at 7:45 a.m. The equivalent of 10:00 a.m. for most people. I'd planned to get up at 6:00 a.m. as I normally did and stake out the Lansing Business Park parking lot, hoping to catch the arrival of the black Corolla and its owner. I didn't set an alarm because I always woke at six or earlier. Except when I didn't get more than three hours of sleep for a week.

I picked up the phone, surprised that the first correspondence that morning was a call and not the daily email from T. Randolph.

Naomi. I answered.

"So, you're not a man of your word, after all." More sarcasm than anger. I preferred anger. "A Detective Brian Skupin just called me and he's going to be here to talk to me in a half hour."

"Where's here? Miranda's?"

I hoped Naomi hadn't snuck out to some unguarded address.

"Yes, Miranda's. But what does that have to do with anything? You made a promise to me. Promises are supposed to mean something, like vows, and you broke yours."

"I should have done it a week ago. There's a woman missing because I waited to go to the police. That's on me."

"What are you talking about?"

I told her about Alicia Alton and how I put the pieces together to get to Pluto.

"You can't be sure there's a connection." Disdain in her voice. "Detective Skupin didn't even say anything about a missing woman. He wants to question me about Pluto."

"It's all tied together. Tell him everything. A woman's life depends on it."

"Why didn't you tell me you talked to the police? That's the least you could have done after you broke your word. I didn't take you for a coward. I guess I was wrong."

"Because a woman's life is at stake and I thought you might run instead of telling the detective everything you know that might help him save her."

"Good to know how you really feel about me." A statement. No emotion. "For your information, I'm sticking around here to wait to talk to the detective."

She hung up. I didn't blame her. I didn't blame me, either.

I flipped on the TV as I got dressed and found local news on channel 6. A reporter stood in front of a faded beige house. The reporter had brown hair and intelligent blue eyes behind horn-rimmed glasses. Beautiful. I'd seen her before. Cathy Cade. She held her microphone up to a man in his fifties. Tears streamed down his face.

"She's a sweet girl. She's never hurt anyone. She goes to college during the day and works at night. She's a good girl." He wiped tears from sleepless eyes, but they kept coming. "Please, if anyone has seen Alicia or knows anything, please call the police. I just want my baby girl to be safe."

Alicia. Alton. The carhop from Sonic. My stomach dropped and my mouth went dry. A photo of a young woman with brown hair and a big smile popped up on the corner of the screen. Eighteen or nineteen. Now I had a face to go with the voice I'd heard on the phone. A lovely innocent face.

Cathy Cade turned to the camera, tears in her own eyes. "Please, as Dennis Alton, the father of Alicia, just said, if anyone in the viewing public knows anything about Alicia Alton's disappearance, please, please call the police hotline at 619-555-1212." A tear ran down her cheek. "Let's do all we can to help reunite the Alton family. A very sad scene here in Pacific Beach. James, back to you."

Alicia Alton was a real person, not just a sad news story you forget about a day later. I had to find her.

*　*　*

I got to the Lansing Business Park by 8:40 a.m. The black Toyota Corolla was already there. Parked in the back of the lot like yesterday. In fact, it could have been in the same spot. I wished I'd paid more attention to that detail. I pulled up alongside it and looked into the front seat. Still immaculate, with just the crossword puzzle book on the passenger seat.

Maybe the owner never came back to the car yesterday. Maybe someone had abandoned it in the parking lot.

I parked near where I had yesterday, a row forward and twenty spots or so away from the Corolla. I called Detective Skupin. No answer. He was probably at Miranda's questioning Naomi. And running into a brick wall. I left a message. I knew he wouldn't tell me if he found out who owned the car when he had someone run the plate. He'd never tell me anything. He was working a case and had gotten something useful from me. I was a source, not a compatriot. He had a badge and a gun. I had a piece of paper and a reputation. Not a good one.

And a lot of guns.

I watched the car all morning. No one came near it. Maybe not the best use of my time. I called Detective Skupin again and left another message. I even called Moira in hopes that she had another friend on the force who could run a license plate for her on the sly. She didn't pick up either.

Quint Lansing pulled up in a black Ram 2500 truck at ten until noon and went inside the main building. It couldn't be a coincidence that he and his brother had the same last name as the Business Park. If they or their family owned the park, why were the brothers relegated to security duty in a tiny cubbyhole office in the back? Maybe that's why Quint was such a pleasure. Dad was making him work his way up from the ground floor right alongside his socially challenged brother.

Or maybe he didn't like me bigfooting my way into his office to watch his security tapes. Wouldn't be the first time I hadn't made a friend on a first impression. Or third.

I scanned the parking lot with my binoculars for the twentieth or thirtieth time, then settled in on the main office building. A few minutes after Quint went in, his brother Caleb came out. He walked into the parking lot. I dropped the binos and watched him from afar. He walked through rows of cars without stopping to get into one. Until he finally pulled a key fob out of his pocket and a disarmed car alarm chirped. He opened the door and got into the car.

The black Toyota Corolla.

CHAPTER THIRTY

CALEB? THE AUTISTIC Lansing brother with the lightning-quick fingers on the computer keyboard? Twisted came in all different kinds of packages, and autistic people were obsessive. But did he have the creative flourish to write the letter? Doubted it. Maybe the car Rudy Wayne saw on the security tape wasn't a Corolla. Maybe it was, but not this one. Maybe the car in the Sonic parking lot had nothing to do with the disappearance of Alicia Alton.

Maybe it was time to stop thinking and act.

I followed Caleb out of the parking lot from a good distance. He turned onto Granite Ridge and then right onto Aero Drive like he was heading to Interstate 15. But he pulled into a parking lot before he made it to the I-15 exit.

McDonald's. Where he and unnamed others from the business park probably had many meals. And walked right by the pay phone on their way to and from the restaurant. I parked in the back of the lot as Caleb pulled in behind three other cars in the drive-thru lane. He exited five minutes later and continued east on Aero until he got onto 15 South.

I'd expected him to head back to the office once I saw him go through the drive-thru. He couldn't be going far with hot food.

You can reheat McDonald's fries, but I wouldn't try it with their hamburgers.

Caleb went west on the 8 and then south on 805 and into South Park. He parked in the driveway of a remodeled mid-century modern home in a cul-de-sac on Nutmeg Street. I pulled to the curb on a slight hill a hundred yards back from the house. Caleb went inside, seemingly oblivious to the fact that he'd been tailed. But I'd already started to question Caleb's obliviousness and lack of cunning. Maybe he wasn't such an innocent, after all.

I called Detective Skupin for the third time that day and left another message. This call was to give him information instead of asking for some. He probably already knew the Corolla belonged to Caleb Lansing, but he hadn't talked to Caleb like I had. At least not face-to-face.

I sat in my Accord and waited Caleb out. I couldn't exactly kick down his door and demand he tell me where he was hiding Alicia Alton. Not without a lot more evidence. Even then, I didn't have a badge. I did have a gun, though. And if it came down to saving the woman's life, I'd use it. She was an innocent. And if Pluto had kidnapped her, she was my responsibility. Whether Pluto was Caleb Lansing or not.

I studied the house through my binoculars. Two stories, in a nice neighborhood of South Park, a quaint little community east of Balboa Park loaded with hip, independent businesses. The house sat above a forestry canyon and looked to have views of Balboa Park and Downtown San Diego.

Nice house for the autistic half of a brother team running a commercial security company. Maybe it was a family home. I pulled out my cell phone and logged onto a real estate pay website and looked up who owned the home.

The home had been owned by Caleb Stephen Lansing since 2017. Caleb owned this million-dollar home. Stephen Kenneth Lansing owned it the previous thirty-one years. Caleb's father? Must be—and Caleb inherited the house upon his father's death in 2017. I Googled Stephen Kenneth Lansing. He'd been a commercial developer who specialized in private/public projects. Lansing Business Park was the only development I could find online that he'd named after himself. He left behind an ex-wife and his twin sons, Caleb and Quint.

I wondered what Quint got out of his father's will. Maybe a three-million-dollar home in La Jolla, or an $850,000 one in Pacific Beach, or a couple mil in investments. If so, why did the brothers still run what looked to be a two-man security shop on just the one property? Did someone else get the ownership of the business park? Maybe the bank owned it. Maybe the house in North Park was the only thing left of value when Stephen Lansing died, and Quint had been left out. Didn't matter. Caleb was my concern right now.

I got out of my car and walked down the sidewalk. The house was two stories, the top story level with the street. The rest of the house hid below the street, cut out of a sloping hill. It looked like it had a third floor or an aboveground basement at the bottom of the hill. The front of the house had only one window, perched over a wooden deck. The rest of the windows must have been in the back where the view was, much like Peter Stone's house in La Jolla. A blind was pulled down over the front window. A nice sunny day in San Diego and Caleb Lansing was keeping the sun out.

Now I wished I'd been smart enough to follow Caleb through the drive-thru at McDonald's and had asked the attendant what the guy in front of me ordered. Did he get enough for just himself, or did he order lunch for two? The extra lunch for a woman tied up down in the basement.

I had to get inside that house. Alicia Alton had been missing almost a week. How much time did she have left, if any at all? I took out my cell phone and called Detective Skupin again. Voicemail. How many messages did I have to leave Skupin that it was urgent he contact me right away before he finally did? Zero for four so far. A fifth wouldn't make any difference. I needed to try a fresh vein. The police hotline wasn't an option for a quick response. They'd catalog my call, and I'd be lucky to get a call back in twenty-four hours. I needed something more urgent.

I hustled back to my car and called 911.

"911, what's your emergency?"

"My neighbor has been acting strange the past couple days. Ever since that Sonic carhop girl went missing."

"Here's the number to the crime hotline, they'll—"

"There's no time for that! I heard a woman screaming inside his house. You need to get someone over here right away! I think he's hurting her."

"What is the address?"

I gave her Caleb Lansing's address.

"And what is your name and address?"

"Joe Tate. I rent a room in the house next door." I gave her the next-door neighbor's address.

I didn't feel guilty about lying to the 911 operator. This one went into the ends justifying the means category. I sat in my car and waited.

Ten minutes later, an SDPD black-and-white cruiser rolled past me and parked in front of Lansing's house. I sank down in my seat and watched through the binoculars, just over the dashboard. A male and female team got out of the car. They didn't rush the house, but walked up showing confident command authority. The woman had a sergeant's chevron patch on her sleeve. She knocked on the door and stepped back, wide stance, hands on hips, right one near her service weapon on her Sam Browne duty belt. The other officer, large and square, took the same stance.

The sergeant waited ten or fifteen seconds, then knocked again. What was Caleb doing in there? Hiding evidence? Putting tape over Alicia Alton's mouth? The sergeant raised her fist and the door opened before she could knock again.

Caleb Lansing stood in the doorway, a blank look on his face. The sergeant said something, and Caleb opened the door wide to let the police officers in. Everyone disappeared inside the house, leaving the door halfway open and blocking my view to all but the first few feet of the foyer.

I kept the binoculars pinned to the front door and strained to listen for any noise or command even though I was too far away to hear anything. A minute, then two, passed. No one appeared in the doorway. Had the cops found Alicia Alton? Were they arresting Caleb Lansing? Had he made a run for it down some back staircase I couldn't see?

I got my answer ten seconds later. The two cops and Caleb appeared in the doorway. They smiled at Caleb and left without him.

Had I been completely wrong about Caleb or had he already killed Alicia and disposed of her body? In his call to Naomi's show, Pluto asked if Hercules, meaning me, had looked for Persephone's twin. I'd thought that meant he must be holding Alicia somewhere. Was I wrong and he'd already killed her? Maybe he never took her to his house.

Or maybe, I was wrong about everything. The black Toyota Corolla could have been completely unrelated. I'd let my imagination off its leash and it had stacked one fact wrapped in boundless speculation on top of another until I had a tower a hundred feet high with no connecting foundation. The cops leaving without Caleb was the sound of the tower crashing to the ground.

Maybe I wasn't responsible for Alicia Alton's disappearance, after all. Maybe there wasn't any connection to Pluto. But that didn't soothe the ache in my gut for the missing woman.

It almost made it worse. Whether responsible or not, I now felt connected to Alicia Alton. If her disappearance had nothing to do with Pluto, I had no way to help find her.

CHAPTER THIRTY-ONE

STAKEOUT DUTY ON Hillside Drive. Stone was home. Alone. As usual. He had fewer friends than I did. Moira was at her spot below the house, but the ice wall was still up. Maybe Stone and I had the same number of friends.

A few cars had turned down Stone's block, but none stopped at his house. The same with below the house.

My phone rang at 8:45 p.m. Detective Skupin. A little late. Just as well. Better not to lead him down the rabbit hole I sent the two cops on at Caleb Lansing's house.

"What's your angle, Cahill?" Gruffer than his wake-up voice this morning.

A fair question most of the time, but I didn't have an angle right now. Despite staking out a crooked philanthropist's house as ordered by the Russian Mafia, who would kill me if I refused, the question seemed out of place just then. All I did was leave a few voice messages that Skupin ignored until now. Eight hours later.

"What do you mean?"

"I asked you politely to leave the missing girl case alone. Should I have threatened you instead? I thought we'd come to an understanding. I thought you were a stand-up guy."

"I had some pertinent information, so I left you a couple of messages." Screw this guy, I was trying to help. "Sorry to intrude."

"Oh, that's not all you did." Louder. He was getting revved up. "You called in a 240 on Caleb Lansing over in North Park and sent a couple uniforms on a wild goose chase."

Oh, that. I hadn't thought to block my phone number or worry about the repercussions. Alicia Alton's life came first. Now, with the woman missing for a week, apparently the police had the time to check up on a false report of a crime. A lot of energy used to chase down a misdemeanor. I'd committed more than one felony in my life. A misdemeanor seemed like a waste of time.

"I had a good-faith belief that a crime was being committed." Or had been committed. Or I just needed a way for someone to get inside Lansing's house and make sure Alicia Alton wasn't being held there.

"Bullshit. You found out Caleb Lansing drove a black Corolla like your mystery car at Sonic and you had to play cop without a badge."

Nailed it.

"I maintain I had a good-faith belief that a crime was being committed, but let's say you were in my shoes. What would you have done if you thought you'd found the guy who kidnapped Alicia Alton?"

"I'd never be in your shoes, Cahill. I didn't get busted off the force after three years and now have to peep through motel windows to make a buck." Another cop who'd done his homework on me and the second person in a week who couldn't imagine themselves being stupid enough to be me. One a cop, one a con. I guess that left me somewhere in between.

"I was in a tough spot, Detective. You wouldn't return any of my calls and the car belongs to someone who had a view of 1350's parking lot where Naomi comes and goes every night. Seems like a pretty big coincidence."

"Not your call to make." He snapped off each word. "And you don't know what a tough spot is, yet. I'm not asking this time. Stay away from the case or I'm going to start thinking you're a bit too interested in it and bring you down to the station for some questioning. Am I clear?"

"Perfectly. Just tell me if you questioned Caleb Lansing and if he checks out."

"Keep it up, Cahill, and the next time we talk will be eye-to-eye in the box. I know you've been in one of those before." He hung up.

The box. A police interrogation room. He was right, I'd been in plenty. And one of my goals in life was to never go back into one. The odds weren't in my favor. Pluto was out there somewhere and Skupin's phone call hadn't done anything to confirm or deny that he was a suspect in Alicia Alton's disappearance. Even if there was no connection, I had to find him because I was certain, no matter who Pluto was, that his plan to kidnap Naomi was real and he was close to putting it into action.

I was also certain I'd get no cooperation from the police.

*   *   *

Moira texted me at 9:20 p.m. with a car alert. The routine was she'd text me that a car had passed by her going up the hill in Stone's direction. I'd get out of my car and walk down the street and around a couple turns until I had a view of Stone's house to see if the car stopped there. Six nights and none had yet.

Moira: *A silver Tesla just passed me going up the street.*

Silver Tesla. The car and color that Obadiah "T" Randolph owned and drove the other night when he met Stone at Muldoon's Steak House.

Me: *Roger.*

I grabbed the dog leash I kept with me on surveillance and jogged down the street toward Stone's house. If anyone spotted me, they'd think I was chasing after my dog who I'd let off the leash. I got within range of the house just as a Silver Tesla turned into the driveway. The night had pulled down into full dark, but there was a lone security light over Stone's driveway. I watched in the darkness as Obadiah "T" Randolph got out of his car and walked up to Stone's porch. He carried a leather portfolio with him. I couldn't see the front door from my position, but Randolph soon disappeared from my view.

I called Moira and ran toward my car.

"The Tesla driver went inside Stone's house. Drive up to the spot where you can see the house and get eyes on him."

"Roger. Why are you breathing hard?"

"I'm running."

"Oh." I heard her ignition start up. She spoke again just as I got to my car. "I can see them through the window. The visitor is thin, almost as tall as Stone, blond hair. Could be the same guy who met Stone at Muldoon's Steak House. Hard to tell. Stone has the house dimly lit tonight. They're standing in the living room talking. He just opened a binder or something and handed Stone some papers."

"Thanks. Wait until I get there and we'll change positions."

"Roger." She hung up.

I drove down Hillside doing the speed limit, which was fifteen miles per hour along the winding street. No action in the front of Stone's house. The Tesla was still in the driveway. I made the slow right banking turn below the house and then a few more turns down the narrow street and spotted Moira standing under a tree limb over-hanging the side of the road. I drove past, did a three-point turn into a driveway, then parked behind her car around the bend. I grabbed my binoculars and hustled up to her.

"Looks like an argument. Neither one of them has sat down, yet."

"Thanks. Good job. I'll take it from here."

"Don't 'good job' me. Who is this guy?"

"His name is Obadiah Thomas Randolph." I pulled down the binoculars and looked at Moira. "And my emailed instructions to follow Stone come from a T. Randolph. And he is the same guy who met Stone at Muldoon's the other night."

"Yes, he is." She put her hand on my shoulder. "What do you think the Russians are up to?"

"I don't know. I'll email a report on what I observed tonight to T. Randolph just like all the other nights. Whoever is receiving these emails, whether it's really T. Randolph or the Russians, doesn't know that I know who the visitor is."

"I don't like this, Rick."

"I know. It wasn't fair to get you involved. You can head home and be done with the whole thing right now."

"I'm not talking about me. I'm worried about you. And the Russians." She walked back to her car and drove up Hillside.

I watched Stone and Randolph through the binoculars. Stone was now seated, probably on his throne, a massive black leather recliner that he'd sat in when I'd had the misfortune of speaking to him at his castle. Randolph sat opposite Stone with his head in his hands.

What the hell could they be talking about that would have Randolph so upset? Did Stone know Randolph was a plant for the Russians? Did Randolph even know he was a plant?

My phone dinged the arrival of a text message.

Moira: *In place. Tesla still in driveway.*

Me: *Still talking. Randolph is upset.*

Moira: *I'm here for the night. Text any movements.*

Me: *I owe you.*

Moira: *We're good. Out.*

All it took to get Moira back on my side was to have my life become more dangerous and more complicated. I was glad to have her back, but not happy about the circumstances that put her there.

Two meetings with Stone by the man who supposedly gave me the commands to follow him. Something was off on a case that was already off. On top of that, I somehow had to come up with ten grand to give to the millennial psychopath to stay upright and breathing. Easy to understand why Moira wanted to be my friend.

Stone and Randolph remained seated. Randolph's posture was slightly better. No more face in hands. Stone was talking. I could just make out the knifepoint of his gray widow's peak in profile pointed at Randolph. I'd been lined up in those sights before. Staring down malevolent self-interest. Stone used leverage, the threat of violence or some kind of personal destruction, to bend you to his will. I wondered what he had on Randolph and what he wanted from him.

Stone as a vice was a scenario I understood. Squeezing for as long as it took. But there was something else in the game that Stone didn't know about. The Russians commanding me to follow him, supposedly through the man he was now turning the screws to.

Stone always saw the angles. Even when they were turned against him, he saw their slope and vertex. What was the angle here? Did he know I was following him? Was Randolph a stooge he was turning back against the Russians? Or against me?

You could keep a cobra confined in a basket, but it still had venom. And was always waiting for the lid to come off.

Stone suddenly stood up and Randolph did the same. They shook hands and Stone put his free hand on Randolph's bicep. A warm gesture that didn't reflect the man I knew, but was the perfect image of the glad-handing philanthropist that the public saw.

Stone led Randolph out of the living room with his hand on the back of his neck, like they were pals. Not around the front of his neck, which would have made more sense to me. They disappeared out of my view.

I called Moira, put her on speaker, and watched Stone's house through the binoculars.

"Randolph's leaving. I'm going to stay with Stone."

"What do you want me to do?"

"It's a big ask. Follow Randolph. He's probably heading this way on his way home to Olivetas."

"Easy, not a problem."

"It could be. If he doesn't go home and meets the Russians instead."

Stone came back into his living room and stood in front of the massive sheet of glass that made up the back wall of his house. I'd seen him take that stance before. Staring out over the view of La Jolla, the Pacific Ocean, and beyond. Master of his domain, and all others. I couldn't make out his face perfectly, but was sure he wasn't wearing the usual self-satisfied grin.

"If he does, the Russians will be looking for you, not a woman. I got it."

"Be careful. I don't—"

"Don't get sappy, Cahill. I'm coming your way."

"Roger. Call or text when he lands for the night."

"Roger." She hung up.

Stone remained staring out at the world he used to control. I couldn't tell by his expression whether he knew he was no longer king of the realm, but the fact remained. The Russians had control now. Maybe they always had and neither he nor I had known it. I ran to my car and drove up Hillside, but had to veer into a driveway as the silver Tesla appeared around a narrow turn. It wasn't speeding, but was going too fast and too wide for Hillside Drive. Reckless. I remained in the driveway until Moira passed behind me five seconds later.

Despite the late glad-handling by Stone, Randolph appeared to still be upset. What had he and Stone talked about? What was on the document he'd shown Stone? Did it have something to do with LiveStem or the Russians? Both?

I drove by the front of Stone's house. The security light was still on. He could have made a quick exit while I drove up Hillside, but I doubted it. Stone didn't do anything quickly, except think. Even if I could get inside that head, I didn't want to. I had enough darkness in my own life.

I found my perch across Via Siena and parked. I had to gamble that, if Stone took off, he'd come this way. I waited fifteen minutes, then hedged my bets, grabbed the leash, and walked down past his house. Quiet. I walked far enough around the turn to get an angle on the back of the house. The lighting hadn't changed since I'd looked at the house through binoculars from down the hill twenty minutes earlier.

Moira sent a text stating that Randolph had gone straight home to Olivetas. Good. One less worry. I made her text me when she got home. I changed stakeout positions in my car from below and above Stone's house a couple times in the next hour and a half. All the while, I listened to Naomi's show through my phone and earbuds. No calls from Pluto. Why not? If Caleb Lansing was Pluto, maybe the cops' drop-in at his house had shaken him. Or was Pluto someone else and he was just listening tonight, plotting his next move?

Midnight came and went. I sent off my report, which included Stone's guest. I stayed at my post in case Stone made a late-night sojourn. For myself. Randolph had been Stone's only visitor in the week I'd been watching his house. Something had changed. I needed to know what it all meant and how it could help me escape the Russians.

But Stone stayed inside. I gave up at 12:30 a.m.

I put my finger on the ignition button when I saw an SUV turn right off Via Siena onto Hillside. A Hummer. Black with tinted windows. And a familiar license plate.

CHAPTER THIRTY-TWO

I COULDN'T SEE through the tinted windows of the SUV, but I knew who was inside. Tatiana and, at least, her armed driver. Maybe more. The Hummer could hold a squad of armed leather-clad bad guys. And it was headed toward the home of a partner or foe.

I grabbed the leash and jumped out of the Audi. The taillights had already disappeared around the bend. I sprinted down the road, staying on the left side where there was some overgrown tree cover and out of the line of the Hummer's rearview mirrors. I slowed around the turn and hugged up into the tree line.

Red circles glowed around the corner. The taillights of the Hummer. It passed slowly by Stone's house. I watched it go out of sight down the hill and kept my eyes pinned on the corner it disappeared around. After a solid three minutes, I figured the Hummer and its dangerous cargo weren't coming back for another look.

Thirty minutes after I sent T. Randolph a report about the visitor to Stone's house, Russian Psychopath Junior cruises through Stone's neighborhood. Why? Because the emails I sent to T. Randolph were being read by the Russians and they wanted to see who the visitor was? Or, maybe they drove by Stone's house every night and I'd hadn't seen them before because I'd headed home earlier the other nights.

The first solution made the most sense. The Russians wanted to get a look at the person Stone met with twice in the last week. They had to know it was Obadiah T. Randolph. One thing seemed certain now—T. Randolph was some kind of a front and the Russians were really getting my reports. Did Randolph even know about them?

What was the Russian connection with the founder of a stem cell research company? There had to be billions of dollars connected to stem cell research. The black market? A tiny percentage of that kind of money could buy a lot of black Hummers.

* * *

I went home and to bed without any answers and woke up the same way. I didn't have answers to what the Russians were up to or who Pluto really was. But the clock was ticking on both. The Russians were now circling behind my stakeouts of Stone. What would they do next? How many more nights of surveillance? Should I be happy or worried when they finally called me off?

Alicia Alton had now been missing for a week. How much time did she have left if she wasn't already dead? The odds got worse with each hour that passed. According to Naomi, the police were more interested in her than they were in Pluto. Had they already eliminated him as a suspect? Discounted him as a threat to Naomi? Had they written him off as just some harmless socially awkward guy with too big an imagination and too much time on his hands?

If so, they were wrong.

But, Pluto hadn't threatened my life, and Naomi had twenty-four-hour protection. Detective Skupin had warned me off the Alicia Alton disappearance. I could follow Caleb Lansing's Corolla around all day, but the police had already given him a free pass. If I really heard a woman screaming at his house and called it in, the police wouldn't come. Unless they came to arrest me for falsely reporting a crime. Alicia was still my responsibility, but I couldn't think of a way to help her.

I had to help myself.

CHAPTER THIRTY-THREE

THE WOMAN OPENED the door to the vault area and led me through the opening. She stopped in front of a bank of safe deposit boxes. I'd rented the smallest they offered. What was inside didn't take up much space. But the thought of what damage it could do left a sucking hole in my gut.

"Number 1210, right?" She smiled. She had no idea that when we put the keys in the lock and twisted them we'd be opening my Pandora's box.

"Yes." My mouth went dry.

"Here we are." She tapped box 1210 at eye level. "If you'll just put your key in."

We each did the key thing, and she opened the mini-vault that contained the box that held my salvation. Or doom. She pulled out the long, thin box and handed it to me. I went into the privacy room and set the box down on the table. Did I really want to do this? Once I set the plan into action, there would be no way of stopping its momentum or possible repercussions.

I knew the moment I'd signed my soul away to the Russians that this day would come. They'd never stop at my soul; they'd want my body, too. They could use me, but I was also a liability. They didn't know how much I knew. Hell, I wasn't even sure what I knew, but the Russians risked the possibility that I knew enough to take them down.

That's why I'd taken precautions and hidden my insurance in the safe deposit box. Seeing Tatiana's Hummer circling Stone's house told me it was time to cash in.

I didn't have a choice. Even if it got me killed.

I opened the box and took out the letter envelope. There was a thin two-inch bulge in the bottom of it. The flash drive. Sealed inside and hidden away for almost a year. Still, I had to look at it, touch it, to make sure it was really there.

I tore open the envelope and poured the flash drive into my hand. Two inches of freedom. Or doom. I wouldn't know which until I let loose the information inside. I put the drive in my pocket and left the viewing room. The woman returned the box to its vault and we did the key thing again and I left the bank and got into my car.

The police might be interested in what was on the flash drive. The press most certainly would be. Giving it to either would probably get me killed. I needed an entity quieter but with more power than either. The power of the largest, most rapacious bureaucracy in the entire world. The Federal Government of the United States of America. Specifically, its policing authority. The FBI.

I didn't have fans or contacts in any of the police departments in San Diego County. Or in any other county. But I did have a "friend" in the San Diego field office of the FBI.

That is, if Special Agent John Mallon would still talk to me.

I pulled out of the bank parking lot and drove down Clairemont Mesa Boulevard toward the exit onto the 805. The FBI field office was located in Sorrento Valley, a tiny community wedged between La Jolla and Mira Mesa. I'd been to the field office before. It hadn't gone well. In fact, the only meetings I'd ever had with Special Agent Mallon had all been off-site. That's because they'd all been clandestine.

Off the books. Today I had something that Mallon could actually open the books to investigate.

Still, probably better to check with him before I showed up. It had been two years since the last, and only, time I'd been inside the office. I'm guessing that Special Agent in Charge Richmond still held a grudge. I'd yet to meet anyone in a law enforcement command position who didn't. Going all the way back to my days on the Santa Barbara Police Department. But maybe it was just me.

I pulled into a gas station before I reached the exit onto the 805 and called Special Agent Mallon from my cell phone. This time he answered.

"What is it now, Rick?" His voice, only slightly less irritated than his words. "I can't help you with any more security camera footage viewing. You've used my shield enough. Aren't we even, yet?"

Thank God, we were still friends.

"We're more than even." The truth. Now came the lie. "I'm not looking for a favor today. I have something that could make your career. Get you an office with the view on the fifth floor."

"You're selling awfully hard, Rick."

He was right. I felt a little slimy. But just a little.

"I've got a paper trail with laundered money from shell company to shell company all the way back to the Russian Mafia in San Diego."

"Unless any of this laundered money buys and resells weapons to terrorists on the international arms black market, I'm not interested."

"This is the biggest player in organized crime in San Diego. Isn't that the reason the FBI was created? To bring down the mob?" A Christmas present wrapped in a bow and it turns out Mallon's an atheist.

"That may be, but it's not the reason I joined the FBI and you already know that. And I'm not alone. The command directive for my division is tracking the money trail of terrorists, not the local mob."

"Who knows where the trail will take you? We live in a port city that is the eighth largest city in the country. Money, especially the laundered kind, is fungible. This might take you exactly where you want to go."

"No thanks, Rick."

"Okay, then tell me who I need to talk to. Surely, someone at the FBI still cares about organized crime. Or, maybe, I'll just show up at the field office and ask for Special Agent in Charge Richmond, your boss."

"He'd never see you. You didn't make a good first impression."

"Alright. Then maybe I'll take it to the *Union-Tribune*." A lie. "After I show them what I have, they might wonder why the FBI wasn't interested."

Mallon didn't say anything for a while. Neither did I. First one to talk loses.

"Meet me at the Starbucks in UTC in a half hour." He hung up.

* * *

University Towne Center was in the Golden Triangle, north of La Jolla. The Golden Triangle was made up of retail and commercial office buildings and a smattering of residential housing units. Technically in University City, UTC was considered part of La Jolla by everyone but native La Jollans. With over a million square feet of retail space, UTC was large for San Diego, but only a little over a third of the area of the Mall of America in Minneapolis and with none of the glamour of the Grove in Los Angeles. But it had a Starbucks.

Special Agent Mallon was already sitting at a two top against the wall sipping some fair-trade coffee concoction topped with whipped cream and ribbons of caramel made from unfair-trade refined sugar and milk from machine-milked cows.

I bought a two-dollar bottle of water and sat down opposite Mallon.

"Let's get this over with. What do you have?" Mallon was finding it easier and easier to adopt the attitude shown to me by all law enforcement in San Diego.

Maybe it *was* me.

I scanned the coffee shop for Russian assassins clad in tight leather. None. Just some scruffy student types and hipsters peering into laptops, tablets, or smartphones while sipping $4.00 coffee. Maybe the Russians didn't care about fair trade.

I pulled the flash drive out of my pocket and slid it across the table to Special Agent Mallon. He looked at it, then at me.

"What's on it?" Mallon took a sip of his coffee froth.

"Like I told you over the phone, money trails, shell corporations. I'm sure you can find a lot more criminal activity than I did."

"Why the sudden interest in the Russian Mafia, Rick? What's in it for you?"

How much could I tell him? He worked for the FBI. The most feared law enforcement agency in America. Even the Russians feared the FBI. Should I tell him everything and hide behind the power of the Feds? Would that keep me alive? If I did tell all and somehow managed to stay alive, would I have to change my identity and move to a tiny town on the outskirts of small town USA in the middle of nowhere?

What would I be losing? I talked to my sister once a year on Christmas and to my mother once a decade. I could do that from anywhere, under any identity. I had one true friend who could get along fine without me. I'd learn how to get along without her. Life would be less enjoyable, but I'd manage. I had a dog and I could take him with me. There was nothing holding me to this town.

Except, somehow, I'd made it my home.

"It doesn't matter what's in it for me. And it's nothing nefarious. These guys are vicious and have no fear of the local police agencies.

The Feds are the only people who can bring them down. Bring him down."

"Who?"

I scanned the room again. I'd never said his name out loud before, not even while alone, much less in public. I leaned forward and whispered, "Sergei Volkov."

"I've never heard of him." Mallon frowned. "Is this some sort of personal vendetta, Rick?"

Not on my end.

"No. Look at the files on the flash drive. Follow the money. It will take you to Volkov." And his psychopathic daughter. "He's the kingpin. You get him, you can take down the whole Russian mob in San Diego and God knows where else."

"There's something you're not telling me, Rick." FBI Special Agent Mallon put the flash drive in his inside coat pocket. "When I find out what it is, I won't cover for you."

He was more right than he even knew. There were a lot of things I hadn't told him. That my life might depend on how strong a case he could make and how quickly he acted. But the more I told him now about my involvement, the greater my potential exposure. His wanting to keep me safe would involve more people up the chain. People I didn't trust, with their own agendas. The other important thing I didn't tell him was that I wouldn't testify in court or have my name associated with the investigation in any way. No need to give him that information, yet. Not when I had him half on the hook.

I wasn't going to live the rest of my life under an assumed name in an assumed city. San Diego was my home. I'd never live anywhere else. I planned to die there. Just not on the Russians' timetable.

I'd read all the files. In many ways, they were Greek to me, but I'd understood enough to see that the Russians were using a number of shell companies to launder money. That was right in Mallon's wheelhouse—the flow of money throughout economies, light and dark. Clean to dirty to clean, again.

"That's fine. I don't want any cover. I don't want any exposure, either."

Mallon frowned and I knew I'd said too much.

"What's that supposed to mean?"

"Just that I don't want to be a hero. I'm not looking for any credit on this." True, but a lie as to the main reason I didn't want exposure.

"I wish you'd give me the whole story, Rick. Just one time." He stood up. "I'll give this a look in my spare time. In the meantime, you might consider coming clean with me about why you brought me this gift. If I even get a hint that you're playing some crooked angle with this, I'll turn my investigative attention and the full force of the FBI onto you."

"Roger, Special Agent." I stood up. "Just don't take too long to connect the dots."

I strode to the exit and left without another word.

* * *

Two and a half hours later, Special Agent Mallon called me.

"Was this some kind of a joke, Rick?"

Not a good start.

"Was what a joke?"

"This big career-making case you foisted on me."

"No. What did you find?"

"It's what I didn't find." Exasperated. "Your shell companies all ceased doing business last year."

"When?"

"One in October. The other four in November."

"Those businesses were worth millions of dollars. How could they just cease doing business at the drop of a hat?"

"I didn't say it was at the drop of a hat. The construction company stopped bidding on jobs in October and sold to a new buyer in November. The title company transferred its last title on October 27th and went out of business."

I returned the flash drive to the Russians in October. They must have started closing up shop as soon as they realized it was stolen. They just needed to make sure the flash drive stayed out of the hands of law enforcement until they could liquidate their assets. I was their stooge then just as I was now.

"Where did the money go? Who benefited from the sales of the companies?"

"There wasn't that much money, Rick, and most of it went to creditors."

"Who are the creditors? What about Sergei Volkov?"

"What about Sergei Volkov? He owned twenty percent of the deed company. Hardly the Mister Big you made him out to be."

"Did you dig any deeper, Agent Mallon? It's only been a couple hours since I gave you the flash drive." Fear and anger rose together in my voice. My get out of jail free card was counterfeit. "Did you follow the damn money trail from the sales of these companies? Doesn't it seem strange to you that all these companies dissolved at the same time?"

"Of course, it seems strange, but there's nothing I can or want to do about it. There's no national security threat here, Rick. I can't give it any more time. If I dig deeper on my own, my SAC is going to want to know what I'm doing, and I don't have a good explanation for that. I did what I could, Rick."

"What about handing it off to your RICO people?"

"National Security and Terrorism, Rick. That's all our SAC wants to hear about. I did what you asked. I hope we're finally even now. I suggest you take this to the police." Special Agent Mallon, my lifeline to escape the Russians, hung up.

The FBI took a pass on the Russian Mafia. Maybe Sergei wasn't as connected as I thought. Or maybe he just knew how to make himself look that way on first glance. Anyone who scared Peter Stone was high up the food chain. My only other alternative was to take the flash drive to the police or ride out the Stone surveillance. The Russians had eyes in LJPD and probably SDPD.

There was one other alternative. Find out why the Russians really wanted me to spy on Stone.

CHAPTER THIRTY-FOUR

OBADIAH T. RANDOLPH'S silver Tesla was in the LiveStem parking lot when I got there at 1:15 p.m. Fifteen minutes later, the same black Pathfinder from the other day parked near the front of the lot and the same hipster-suited guy got out of it. He carried a small cooler the same size as the one he'd had a couple days ago. Ten minutes later, he came out still carrying the cooler. He got into the SUV and exited the parking lot. Randolph's car was in the same spot it had been in two days ago where it didn't move until he went home from work at 5:30 p.m. Decision time.

I started my car and exited the parking lot. The Pathfinder was twenty seconds ahead of me and out of sight. I'd given it too long of a leash. I turned onto the street that fed to LiveStem and gunned it up to the next street until it T-boned into Mira Mesa Boulevard. Another decision. Turn right and head deeper into Mira Mesa or left and head toward the freeway. Freeway. I sped through a yellow/red light, sliding into the next lane, then righted the car and cleared the next light.

Two entrances onto the 805 Freeway. North to the right or two lanes over and left to the South. I punched it and swerved across two lanes and made the light onto the freeway. One hundred yards ahead, the black Pathfinder.

I slowed to the speed of traffic and let the Pathfinder roll out in front of me. The driver wasn't in a hurry. I stayed three or four cars back, a lane over to his right. He got off on Clairemont Mesa Boulevard going east. A couple minutes later, he pulled into a strip mall parking lot. Emphasis on strip. I drove past the mall and watched the Pathfinder's driver go into the Alley Kat Gentlemen's Club. Odd habits, this one. Totes a cooler around to a stem cell research lab, then stops for an afternoon lap dance.

I'd never seen many gentlemen in a gentlemen's club. There was a time in my life, after I'd lost everything, that I was one of them. One forty-five in the afternoon was not an ideal time to see high earners on the poll. Or in your lap.

I circled the block and pulled into the parking lot and parked in front of an auto supply shop one door down from Alley Kat's. A one-stop shop mall. I walked behind the Pathfinder on my way to the club and took a picture of its license plate with my iPhone. Maybe Moira had one more favor left with the cop who ran plates for her. For me.

The blacked-out-windowed club was nighttime dark, where any time of day was the midnight hour. The cloying scent of post-dance perfume hung heavy in the air. A couple of senior citizens sat in front of the stage, nursing five-dollar Budweisers and, no doubt, lecherous fantasies as a bored topless dancer twisted slowly around the pole to timeless strip club music. She could have been thirty. She could have been fifty. However many years, they'd all been hard.

A hint of the empty I could never fill years ago in a place like this settled into my gut. My life had improved since then, but my prospects for a long life hadn't. Life had come full circle and dropped me into this dump in an effort to figure out what the Russians were up to and maybe stay alive a while longer.

I scanned the tables back from the stage. No sign of the Cooler Kid. Must be in a back room getting a private dance. I ordered a five-dollar Budweiser that I wouldn't be able to expense and took a seat at a table in the back. Darkest part of the club. An employee in a lacy bra, G-string, and sheer wraparound approached to tell me she liked champagne. I spotted Cooler Kid come out through a curtain in the back with a woman in jeans and a leather jacket and the heavy eye makeup of a stripper.

They exited through the front door. I handed my Bud to the champagne aficionado and went outside ten seconds after the Kid and his date. The Pathfinder was just backing out of its parking spot as the sun reminded me it was midafternoon and not midnight. I hustled to my car and followed the SUV onto 163 South toward Downtown San Diego. Anyone looking for a tail could have easily spotted me. The Pathfinder cruised along at seventy miles per hour. No lane or speed changes to confirm a tail. I think Cooler Kid had other things on his mind.

He stayed on 163 for a few miles then got off on University Avenue. He pulled to the curb next to the Fifth and Palm Street building. The woman from the strip club got out of the car and entered the building. Carrying the cooler. The Pathfinder pulled away from the curb. Another tough decision to make. Follow the car or the woman?

I found a parking spot across the street as the SUV disappeared down Fifth Avenue. I hopped out of my car and ran through traffic into the three-story building. The elevator doors clinked shut twenty feet away across the lobby. I hustled over and pushed the button, but the doors didn't open. I watched the floor lights above the elevator. The light on number three finally blinked on. I ran over to the enclosed staircase and sprinted up the two flights of stairs.

The third floor had three offices. All doctors. All OB-GYNs. I popped my head into the nearest office. Two women in the waiting room in various stages of pregnancy. Second office, three women, the same. The third office had three women in the waiting room. None showed any signs of being pregnant. All in their twenties. All thin with hard veneers. One of them was the woman from Alley Kat. She was more attractive than the other two and didn't have their razor-sharp edges. The cooler was on the floor at her feet. She looked at me, but showed no surprise or recognition.

I walked over to the half wall that separated the patients from the staff. A woman in her thirties with cop eyes looked at me without smiling.

"Hi. My girlfriend told me to meet her here at two fifteen. Is she already in with the doctor?"

"What's her name?"

"Jill Anderson."

"No one by that name has an appointment today." The cop eyes got harder.

"This is Doctor Rich's office, right?" I remembered the sign on the door.

"Yes."

The door to the back opened and a woman in a white coat stepped out. "Audrey Hastings? The doctor will see you now."

The woman from the Alley Kat picked up the cooler and followed the white-coated woman through the door. The other two women in the waiting room looked at each other, then at the woman I was talking to with puzzled looks. Like how come she gets to see the doctor before us when we've been here longer?

"Do you mind if I wait for Jill to get here?" I said to the woman manning the desk. "I'll text her to make sure I'm at the right place."

"That's fine." She dismissed me with a roll of her eyes.

I sat down and tapped my phone like I was texting my faux girl-friend. I actually pulled up a paid people search site and typed in Audrey Hastings, San Diego, age 20–35. No matches came up. The closest was a sixty-two-year-old woman who lived in Chula Vista.

Audrey Hastings didn't sound like a stage name. Not like Bambi Bountiful or Annie Ample. Her real name was less important than what was in the cooler. Or what had been in the cooler when the Pathfinder driver took it into LiveStem. Was he making a delivery or a pickup at LiveStem? If a pickup, why did he have to use a stripper to make the delivery at the doctor's office? Or had the delivery been from Dr. Rich and Audrey Hastings was just returning the cooler?

Had to be one or the other. What would a stem cell research company have that an OB-GYN wanted? Then it clicked. I wasn't a doctor or a scientist, but I'd watched enough news to know where stem cells came from. The most valuable ones came from embryos.

Was the Cooler Kid delivering stem cells from aborted fetuses to LiveStem? Nothing about Dr. Rich's office read abortion doctor. I looked him up online and he was listed as an OB-GYN. He had privileges at the top hospitals in San Diego. No mention of family planning on his website. Often a euphemism for abortion clinics.

The only thing that might hint that Dr. Rich performed abortions was his clientele. At least the patients in the waiting room right now. If pregnant, they were probably in the first trimester and not showing. No wedding rings, not that they were the ultimate determiner. Both were thin, twitchy, and had the thousand-yard stare of someone who'd spent the majority of their adult life on the street.

Possibly junkies and prostitutes, not high-end call girls. They didn't look like they could afford lunch, much less an appointment with Dr. Rich. If Rich was performing abortions, his office wasn't a Kermit Gosnell horror chamber. How were they paying for his services? Maybe hookers had better health insurance plans than I did.

Or I was wrong about everything.

I walked over to the front desk. The assistant was less happy to see me than when we'd talked five minutes ago.

"My girlfriend hasn't texted me back yet." I tried to look befuddled. Not a stretch for me. "Maybe I am at the wrong doctor."

"As I told you before, no Jill Anderson has an appointment scheduled for today or any day this week."

"I feel so stupid." I glanced to the side, then leaned in a bit and spoke in a low voice. "But you do perform, ah, family planning services here, right?"

"As I just told you again, there is no appointment for Jill Anderson, so it would be best if you didn't use up a chair in our waiting room. They are for confirmed patients only." She gave me a mouth-only smile. "Good luck finding your girlfriend."

Neither a yes nor a no, but I took the dismissal as a confirmation. Maybe there was no mention of family services on Dr. Rich's website because abortions were only a small part of his practice. Judging by the women waiting to see him, I guessed they weren't that small a part.

I went to the door to leave the office when it opened in front of me. Cooler Kid walked in and I had to step back to avoid running into him. He held a Starbuck's coffee cup in his hand. A Grande or a Venti, or a Veni, Vidi, Vici. I wasn't up on my Latin.

"Oops." He smiled and slid by me. No recognition from him, either.

I held up my hands in front of me and smiled, then grabbed the door handle.

"That's why we don't allow food or drink in the offices." The cop-eyed assistant's voice floated over my shoulder.

I went through the door, but caught the Kid's voice before it closed behind me.

"Relax, Kira, I'm just here to pick up Jana."

I walked toward the elevator. Jana. Not Audrey. Was it the same person or was he running a car service for Dr. Rich's patients? He knew the cop-eyed assistant's name and the tone of their voices suggested they knew each other. How often did he drop off and pick up patients at Dr. Rich's office? And did he leave with a cooler each time?

I exited the building and scanned the street for the black Pathfinder. Didn't see it. I walked around the corner of the building and saw that it had an underground garage. I jogged into it and spotted the Pathfinder.

Would Cooler Kid emerge from the doctor's office with another cooler along with his next fare? What was next? Another trip to Live-Stem? I had to put on another tail, but he'd seen my face now and had probably seen my black Honda Accord a couple times in his rearview mirror today without registering that someone might be tailing him. If he saw the Accord again, he might put it all together.

I pulled out my phone and tapped the Uber app. The closest driver was three minutes away. I scheduled a pickup. Now I just had to pray the Uber driver beat Cooler Kid to his car. I stood in the shadows of the garage near the entrance, ping-ponging my eyes from the Uber app on my phone and the elevator in the garage.

The Uber driver won. I met him in front of the building and hopped in the back of his silver Chevy Malibu.

"Change of location," I said to the driver. I'd put in the Muldoon's Steak House address as my destination. "I want to stay here and wait for a black Pathfinder to come out of the garage and then follow it."

"Where is it going?" The driver had a Middle Eastern or North African accent. A guess. I'd never been to either area.

"I don't know. That's why I need you to follow it."

"Hmm." Not a fan of spontaneity.

I took a ten out of my wallet and held it above the front seat. The driver looked at me in the rearview mirror for a short game of Blink, then reached back and grabbed the ten.

The mighty dollar is a universal language unto itself.

A couple minutes later, the Pathfinder emerged from the garage. A woman who was not Audrey Hastings sat in the passenger seat. Dark hair. Pale. Presumably, Jana. The SUV took Palm Street and turned right on 4th Avenue going south into the Gaslamp Quarter.

The Gaslamp is a historic district with vintage buildings once known for bordellos, now for trendy nightclubs. I had my driver stay a couple cars back. On-the-job surveillance training.

The Pathfinder went into a six-story parking structure on Market Street.

"Follow them into the garage," I told the Uber driver. We entered the garage just in time to see the SUV go up a ramp to the right. "Follow them until they park."

The Pathfinder had to go up four stories before it found a parking spot.

"Go past and drop me off around the corner."

The driver did as told, and I hopped out of the car, quietly closing the door. The Malibu drove off and I peeked around the cement pillar on the corner down at the Pathfinder. Cooler Kid helped Jana out of the passenger-side door. She was thin and hard like the women in Dr. Rich's office, but with slightly softer edges. She moved slowly like she was impaired. He steadied her with his hand around her waist as they walked to the elevator. I waited until they got to the elevator, then sprinted down the ramp to the stairwell. I busted down the stairs. The ding of the elevator's arrival greeted me as I exited the stairwell. I spun around the elevator shaft and waited on the other side.

"It's a couple blocks to the club," Cooler Kid's voice. "Are you sure you can make it? You can wait until tomorrow."

"No. I want money now." Slavic accent.

Or Russian.

"Okay."

I heard them shuffle out of the garage, then followed on the opposite side of the street. It took about five minutes, but they finally made it to a three-story brick building. A sign attached to the building read *Club Quartz*. The club was closed, but Cooler Kid hard-knocked the front door. Ten seconds later, someone from inside opened the door, and he and Jana entered the club. I crossed the street and sat at an outside table at a pub right next to Quartz. I ordered a BLT and a water and paid in advance in case I'd soon be on the move again.

I ran through scenarios as I waited for the food. Jana came wobbly out of an OB-GYN's office. Not likely she went there to get buzzed. She'd been sedated for a reason. She'd had a procedure done. An abortion. What other in-office procedure would an OB-GYN perform? Was Cooler Kid delivering aborted fetuses or parts to LiveStem? To what effect?

I pulled out my phone to expand my knowledge on embryonic stem cells. Turns out that they had to be harvested in the first week after fertilization, long before a woman would know she was pregnant. Thus, most embryonic stem cells are harvested from eggs that have been fertilized in vitro. Then why would the Cooler Kid deliver something in a cooler to LiveStem?

Maybe I was all wrong and the only eggs he had in the cooler were deviled, which he ate for lunch every day with someone on the staff at LiveStem. And maybe Audrey Hastings delivered the leftovers to Dr. Rich for an afternoon snack. I checked the sky for soaring pigs.

I was halfway through my sandwich when the door to Club Quartz opened. Jana and the Cooler Kid walked out, then he held the door open.

Tatiana Volkov stepped out onto the sidewalk.

CHAPTER THIRTY-FIVE

I DROPPED MY head and stared at the table. If Tatiana saw me, the ten grand I "owed" her would go toward a pine box and my final resting place. Or hers. I closed my eyes to try to focus my ears past the street noise and listen for any hint that Tatiana recognized me. If she did and wanted to go to battle, I was ready.

My Ruger .357 was in a pancake holster on my hip. Snub nose, not as accurate as my longer-barreled Smith & Wesson, but accurate enough to hit Tatiana's limited center mass from my position. And Cooler Kid and Jana, if I had to. But Tatiana wouldn't do battle on equal terms during daylight. She'd come at night with men shouldering Kalashnikov semiautos. If she spotted me, I'd die. Just not today.

"Take a day off, then back to Alley Kat," Tatiana's voice cut through the street noise. Maybe because I'd heard it before. Too many times.

"I can work tomorrow. I just can't give any private sessions after hours for a while."

"Yes. Give your snatch a break for a few days." Tatiana smiled and patted Jana's cheek.

The pyscho princess hadn't spotted me. I scratched my forehead and lifted my head, peeking through the fingers covering my face.

The black Hummer of my nightmares pulled up alongside Club Quartz facing me. Shit. I dropped my head back down like I was looking at my phone. I heard two doors slam shut. Either Tatiana and Cooler Kid and Jana had gotten into the Hummer, or more than one person had gotten out. Maybe those men with Kalashnikovs were working the day shift. I slid my hand under my jacket and grasped the handle of my Ruger on my hip. I took a peek up as I pulled the gun free, but kept it under my jacket.

The Hummer pulled away from the curb and drove north on Fifth Avenue. I let go a long breath I didn't know I'd been holding.

The Cooler Kid. LiveStem. Tatiana. The Russians were the thread that ran through them all. They were involved. Beyond Peter Stone being on the board of LiveStem. Whatever was in the cooler that the courier either delivered to LiveStem from Doctor Rich's office or vice versa was controlled by the Russians. And whatever it was made them money. The lifeblood of their organization. Sergei Volkov had tighter control over its flow throughout his businesses than did a CEO of a Fortune 500 corporation.

The cooler and LiveStem were my out from the Russians. They'd outsmarted me with the information on the flash drive. How much time did I have before they outsmarted me with LiveStem? Or killed me? Time I desperately needed to find out what was in the courier's cooler and how I could use that information to take down the Russians and save my own life.

* * *

Moira called me at four thirty.

"The Toyota Corolla belonging to the license plate you sent me is owned by Lansing Construction."

"Lansing Construction? Not Lansing Security?"

"Like I said, Lansing Construction. Located at 6546 Marindustry Drive. Now, I take it we're still on at Hillside tonight."

"I can go solo. I appreciate all you've done for me on—"

"Don't be such an ass, Rick. Same time tonight?"

"Yes. Thanks for the info on the license plate." I cleared my throat and pulled up the photo I'd taken of the Pathfinder's license plate on my cell phone. "I have one more."

"Sorry. My guy told me the shop's closed on favors for a while. His sergeant has been snooping around. Let's give it a few weeks."

She hung up. Friends again.

Lansing Construction, Caleb and Quint Lansing's father's business. The Toyota wasn't owned by Caleb, or Quint for that matter, but by the corporation. The wrong corporation. Still, Caleb was the person I saw drive it out of the Lansing Business Park's parking lot.

Was it on loan from the construction business? Who was in it last Monday night when the driver parked at the Sonic drive-in and left it there unoccupied for forty-five minutes? I still didn't know if it was the same damn car or if the driver was really Pluto. My imagination forced me to fill in the gaps. Had it run wild and pulled in the disappearance of Alicia Alton to give Pluto the sense of menace I felt but couldn't prove?

Detective Skupin had to have run the plate number of the Corolla I gave him. I'd taken him for lazy at first, but I'd been wrong. He would have done his due diligence. Yet, no arrest. Caleb Lansing had been all but exonerated by the cops I put on his house.

My lead on the black Corolla had gone nowhere. A woman's life was still in the balance and any way to help save her was beyond my grasp.

* * *

I sat in the rented Audi, which I was now into for four hundred and fifty bucks, above Peter Stone's house. The endless surveillance. Maybe the Russians were trying to kill me through attrition. I listened to

Naomi's show through earbuds connected to my phone, but she was background ambience tonight. My concentration was on the Russians.

The Russians. Peter Stone. Obadiah T. Randolph. Doctor Rich. The pieces of the puzzle that just wouldn't fit together. Black-market fetal tissue made sense in a sick Russian Mafia kind of way. Working girls the Russians control have abortions, and they harvest the stem cells of the dead fetuses and sell them. The Russians wouldn't be the first to make that coldest of calculations. But did the science work? Fetal stem cells and embryonic stem cells were two different things. Only the embryonic stem cells were used in the kind of research Live-Stem did. None of it made sense.

The white noise of Naomi's show cut through my musings.

"Hello, Pluto." Naomi's sultry voice. No fear. "I was hoping you'd call again. It seems we have some unfinished business."

"That is true, for no imposter can take your place beside me on my throne." The puffed-up voice sounding like it was coming out of a well.

"Emerge from your fantasy cocoon, Pluto. Drop the mask. You're a real man, aren't you?" More taunt than sultry. "Not a daydreaming boy. Tell me your real name. Come out of the shadows."

"For imposters there is only the darkness below. But I grow weary and feel the pull from my eternal home. You'll not hear from me again until your rebirth where the River Styx flows through the wall of the two worlds."

"Let's meet in a bar like grown-ups and you can tell me your real name and why you mash Greek and Roman mythology together." Sultry whittled down to contempt.

"Until, sweet Persephone."

"It appears Pluto has retreated to his cocoon of fantasy. The rest of us will speak as adults after the news."

I called Naomi's cell phone as soon as Rachel Riley started in with the news.

"You heard?" Calm.

"You pushed him too hard."

"I didn't push him hard enough. This thing has got to end. Miranda is a sweet girl, but I need to get back to Del Mar and my old life."

"Give me a little more time. I'm making progress." A hope.

"Maybe you should get back to your life, too."

"Give me time."

"I have to get back to the show." She hung up.

Naomi did the last hour and a half of the show flawlessly. Like the pro that she was. I texted Miranda to be extra vigilant tonight. She was way ahead of me.

I played Pluto's words over and over in my head the remainder of my shift above Stone's house. He'd said that no imposter could take Naomi's place and that for imposters there was only the darkness below. He'd mentioned Persephone's twin in his last call and Alicia Alton went missing.

Had he killed Alicia, the imposter? Or was she in the darkness below him in his basement?

I went home and exchanged the Audi for my Accord. Where I was going, I might need something hidden in the trunk.

* * *

Clouds high in the sky diffused moonlight like sheer lace hung over a light bulb. I parked at the crest of the hill overlooking Caleb Lansing's house. I didn't come with a plan, just a responsibility. It had tugged at me since I found out about the carhop's disappearance. Something that might have never happened if I'd just gone with my gut instead of Naomi's wishes. My guilt, my gut, my responsibility brought me back here. Pluto might be inside that house down the hill. So might Alicia Alton. If she was still alive, I had to find her. I pinched my left arm against my chest and felt the reassuring density of the Smith & Wesson .357 in the shoulder holster under my coat. Insurance for whatever plan I came up with.

No sign of the Corolla in Lansing's driveway. All the lights in the house were off. A dark shadow at the dead end of the cul-de-sac. Was the Corolla in the garage? Was Caleb inside asleep? It was 12:40 a.m. on a weeknight—most people would be. But was he alone?

I got out of my car and quietly closed the door, then opened the trunk. The trunk light didn't go on. I'd disabled it long ago. What I needed was best kept unseen. I pulled up the cover over the spare tire and opened the nylon duffel bag snugged against the spare tire. All without seeing. My hands were my eyes and they'd performed this routine in the dark many times. I unzipped the duffel and searched until I felt a small leather case, thinner than a pack of cigarettes. I put the case in my back pocket, then searched the bag until I found a plastic bag containing unused nitrile gloves. I slipped a pair on my hands, then quietly closed the hood of the trunk.

Lansing's home sat outside of the reach of the streetlight one house over. No hint of light inside his house. I shone my penlight flashlight into the crack between the garage door and the doorjamb. The angle was too tight to get a view, but I thought I saw the shadow of a tire. No way to tell if it was connected to a black Corolla. Didn't matter. The tire gave me the information I needed most. Someone was home.

I stepped away from the garage and eased myself onto the front deck. Dark. Quiet. I pointed the penlight at the lone front window. Kitchen island. Floor. Nobody. I backed off the deck onto the sidewalk.

Had the cops checked the basement when I called 911 the other day? The third floor below the hill? It wasn't even visible from the angle they'd approached the house in their car. I'd only noticed it because I'd walked down the sidewalk where I was right now. I ran back the scene with the police entering the house in my head. They weren't inside long enough to check every room. My gut told me they hadn't checked the basement. Maybe that's what I wanted to believe so I could justify creeping around someone's house after midnight.

Justification or not, I was here now. Dennis Alton's halting voice and rolling tears as he pleaded for his daughter's return on TV cycled inside my head. I owed him a look. The cops owed him. Life owed him.

I stepped off the sidewalk onto the dirt and sloping hill the house was built upon. I pointed the flashlight at the ground and found a path through a patch of ice plant down to the bottom of the twenty-foot decline. There were no windows on this side of the house. The view and money shots were out the back, around the corner to the right and above. A door loomed in front of me, built out of the pale wood siding. I tried the handle. It really didn't matter whether it was locked or unlocked. If the handle turned and the door opened, and I entered, I'd be breaking and entering just as if I'd picked the lock. The handle didn't turn.

The first barrier to keep me from making a bad decision. But for whom? Me, yes. Alicia Alton and her father, no. There was only one decision.

I removed the leather case in my pocket that contained my lock pick set. One of the tools in my burglar kit duffel bag. I'd never used its contents for personal gain. But every time I did use it, I broke the law.

I worked the Allen wrench–shaped tension wrench and the curved rake until I'd manipulated all the pins and unlocked the door. I pushed the door open and stepped to the side to avoid leaving my body as a shadow target. No sound or movement from inside the basement. I stepped inside and eased the door shut. No window to allow cloud-refracted moonlight. I waited for my eyes to adjust.

I'd use the penlight only after I had a sense of the room. I didn't want to turn it on and have the light shine through a doorway or under a door I couldn't see. A dank, moldy odor crawled up into my nostrils. With something else. Fecal matter? A broken sewer pipe? I was in the bowels of the house. Maybe the stench was rodent waste.

I concentrated on my eyes and tried to ignore the stench. My vision slowly adjusted, but I still couldn't see much. There was a large structure to my left, which I figured must be the staircase heading down from the second floor. Empty space in front of me. I think. Some sort of wall to my right that didn't correspond with the outside of the building. Too close.

My vision didn't get any clearer. I took the penlight out of my pocket, pointed it at a forty-five-degree angle at the ground, looked straight ahead, and flicked the on switch. A thin strip of light ran along the cement floor of the basement. No doors visible. I lifted up the light and saw all the way across to the back wall. I scanned the large room. I was right about the staircase to the left. It was enclosed and the stairs ran away from me. A water heater sat in an opening underneath the staircase and a pipe traced along the ceiling and dropped down into the cement floor.

I swung the penlight to the right. The large room was segmented on that side with three walled spaces, one by one by one next to each other. Openings were cut into the walls without doors, like large cubbyholes or office cubicles. I went into the one nearest me. There was a little desk and chair against the back wall. I flashed the light above the desk. Photographs were taped to the wall. Rows and rows of them covering the entire wall.

All of Naomi.

CHAPTER THIRTY-SIX

MY BODY FLASHED cold. I grabbed my gun from inside my jacket and spun around. The gun followed the light around the room, only blocked by the walls dividing the rooms. Nothing had moved. No one was there. I was still alone. Reflex. I was in the lair of an evil force and instinct had taken over. My nerves settled. I returned the gun to its holster and turned back to the Naomi wall. Most of the photos were of Naomi in the parking lot of 1350, taken from a distance. Still shots pulled from the feed of the Lansing Business Park security camera. Caleb Lansing sitting in that tiny office and watching her every night. A sick presence hidden behind a computer screen.

Other photos were more concerning. Naomi sitting in a bar, obviously taken without her knowing. Her home in Del Mar. At night. Coming out of the Night Owl. With me.

Pluto was there that night. He'd followed us from the radio station, perched somewhere along Aero Drive and parked at Sonic. He kidnapped Alicia Alton two nights later. After I'd gone snooping around looking at security camera footage. Maybe Quint told his brother in passing that the FBI and a private investigator had come to the office and looked at the camera feed that faced the radio station.

Caleb Lansing was socially awkward, but intelligent. And evil. He'd deduced that Special Agent Mallon and I would check the security cameras around the Night Owl and ask questions of the businesses. Alicia Alton was the one person who could ID him. So he kidnapped her.

But where was she now? My stomach sank as the finality of her situation struck me. She was dead. Lansing had probably killed her that first night. She'd seen him. A witness to what was to come. He couldn't take the chance. She wasn't a trial run for the real Persephone. She was cleanup. Collateral damage.

And I was going to make him pay.

I pulled out my cell phone and took flash pictures of the photographs, to show to the police. The police. How was I going to explain being inside the basement? They couldn't use the photographs I'd taken after I broke into Lansing's house as a basis for a search warrant. The evidence obtained from such a warrant would be disallowed in court. Fruit from the poisonous tree. It could blow the whole case.

I'd think of something after I finished my sweep of the basement. I checked the drawers of the desk. Empty. Nothing else in the small room. I went into the room next door. It held the kind of things you'd expect to see in a basement. Paint cans, strips of faux wood paneling, old window blinds, and other dreck a house sloughs off after a remodel or years of wear and tear.

I went into the last room. Empty except for a plastic shower curtain rolled up on the floor. Too thick for a single shower curtain. Maybe two or three all rolled together. Each end closed off with swirls of duct tape. The curtains had an odd color, beige but see-through.

The hair on the back of my neck spiked. The shower curtain wasn't beige. It was clear. The color came from skin wrapped in plastic.

A body.

I whipped the flashlight up to the head. Naomi stared back at me. Through layers of plastic, eyes open. I sank to my knees and vomit rushed up my throat. I fought it back down and stood up.

It couldn't be Naomi. I'd just heard her on the radio less than an hour ago. I steadied the light on her face. Through the plastic, I saw a small mark on her forehead. A staple. Used to attach the picture of Naomi's face onto someone else's.

Alicia Alton.

Had to be. I'd found the missing carhop. The young woman who probably would still be alive if I'd followed my gut and not Naomi's wishes. I wouldn't disturb the evidence to make a positive ID, but I didn't have to. An innocent caught up in the twisted game of a depraved little man who put his malignant fantasy above all else. Including the life of a woman just doing her job. Living her life.

I exited the room and noticed a nook to the left of it. I flashed the light inside. A six-foot-tall wooden stand sat in the five-by-five space. It formed a large X. Large enough to hold a human being. At the top and bottom of the four corners of the X were leather restraints, big enough to fit around wrists and ankles.

My jaw clenched. Air pistoned in and out of my nose. Sweat boiled out of my forehead. I backed out of the nook and pulled the gun from the holster and walked toward the staircase on the other side of the basement. I flashed the light at the bottom steps, but sensed something dark, looming at the top of the staircase. I whipped both hands up, gun on top, flashlight underneath.

The light beam caught Caleb Lansing in the left eye. It didn't blink. It stared. At nothing. Lansing's head hung to the side, a rope dug into his neck. The neck that no longer had a pulse. I followed the rope with the light, up to the metal pipe it was tied around.

Lansing had tied a rope around the pipe, then his neck, and stepped off the stairs into eternity. Where he could meet the real god of the underworld. And rot.

There was probably a suicide note in heavy block lettering inside the house. Maybe murder in real life didn't live up to his bent fantasies.

What was the point of going on when murder was a disappointment? Just once, I wish a murder-suicide would start with suicide first. Too late for this one.

I backtracked out of the basement and closed the door behind me.

Alicia Alton was dead. Pluto was dead. The threat to Naomi was over. If I walked from the scene, I wasn't endangering the public by leaving a madman on the loose. If I called the police, the only person in danger would be me. A vindictive cop could arrest me for breaking and entering. Detective Skupin didn't read vindictive, but he had told me to stay away from the case. It wouldn't be a stretch for him to stick me in a cell for a few days to teach me a lesson. I'd had enough of life's and cops' lessons.

Eventually Quint Lansing would come looking for his brother when he missed work or the stench of decaying bodies would waft out under the basement door and alert neighbors who hadn't seen the quiet guy who kept to himself and lived in the dead end of the cul-de-sac for a while.

I walked back to my car and put my burglary tools back in the duffel bag in the trunk. Alicia Alton's father flashed back on the screen in my head. There was someone who would be hurt by my not calling the police. Dennis Alton would never get over his daughter's death, but he deserved to have the agony of not knowing come to an end.

I pulled the duffel bag out of the trunk and walked up the street until I found a house that kept its trash containers under a carport. I silently lifted up the lid of one container and placed the duffel bag inside. I'd tell the cops that I entered the house. They just didn't need to know that I kept a duffel bag full of tools that helped me to do so. That would guarantee me a night or two or more in a jail cell.

I took off the nitrile gloves, balled them together, and threw them onto the roof of the house next to the one with the carport. I went back to my car, got in, and pulled out my cell phone and tapped a number. The phone on the other end rang a full five rings before someone picked up.

"What the hell do you want now, Cahill?" Skupin's voice rumbled in my ear.

"I found Alicia Alton and Pluto. She's dead. So is he."

"Jesus Christ, Cahill. You didn't kill him, did you?"

"No. I didn't get the chance."

CHAPTER THIRTY-SEVEN

Two SDPD cruisers beat Skupin to the scene. One parked in front of Lansing's house. The other parked behind me and flashed its light bar. I was near a crime scene. Fair.

I checked the rearview mirror and saw both doors of the cruiser open and two uniforms get out. They cautiously approached my car, one on my side, the other on the passenger's. They pulled their service weapons and two-handed them low in front of themselves. Not fair.

I rolled down my window and slowly placed my hands on the steering wheel and hoped the cops would start a conversation with their mouths and not their guns.

The cop on my side pulled up behind my left ear. The other appeared just outside the passenger door, pointing a gun and flashlight at me through the closed window. Sweat bubbled along my skin all over my body. My stomach folded in on itself and my breath caught in my throat.

"Slowly step out of the car with your hands over your head, sir." The cop on my left.

"Before I do, I want you to know that I have a conceal carry license and there is a Smith & Wesson .357 Magnum in a holster under my left arm."

"Step out of the car. Now!" He took a step back, spread his feet, and went into a shooter's stance.

Shit.

I slowly opened the door and got out of the car.

"Lie facedown on the ground! Now!"

I did as told as smoothly, but as quickly, as I could. A knee in the middle of my back. The other cop must have circled around. He grabbed my right hand, bent my arm behind my back, and snapped a handcuff around my wrist. Same with the left hand. My head was pointed down the street, and I saw a police officer rise up from the hill next to Caleb Lansing's house. He shook his head at his partner who was over by the deck. He must have accessed the basement from the same door I did and seen the same things.

A Ford Taurus plain-wrap detective car rolled up in front of Lansing's house. A woman in slacks and a blazer got out and walked over to the cop who'd just come up the hill from the basement. Probably Skupin's partner. Maybe she lived closer to the scene. She and the uniform disappeared down the embankment.

The cop kneeling on me patted me down then rolled me over onto my back. Above my head, the barrel of a gun pointed down at me. The other cop. The one who flipped me over reached inside my coat and removed the Smith & Wesson from my shoulder holster. Good. Less chance of getting shot now.

He opened the cylinder of my gun and took out the bullets, then put them and the gun on the roof of my car. He bent down over me, and I got a good look at him. Midtwenties, Hispanic, close-cropped hair. I thought he was going to say hello, but he slipped his hand under my ass and came out with my wallet. The other cop, white, taller and broader than his partner, holstered his gun and walked over.

"Rick Cahill," the shorter cop said.

"I've heard that name before." The white cop smiled and nodded his head.

Nothing good ever followed that statement. Especially coming from the police.

"What are you doing at a 187-crime scene?" He used the penal code for murder. He must have known I'd been a cop once. Everybody seemed to know pieces of my history.

"I'm the one who called it in, Officer." I rose to a sitting position. "So maybe you could take off the bracelets and treat me like a civilian."

"But you're not really a civilian, Cahill. I watch the news." He was old enough to know the whole story, not just pieces. Everyone his age in San Diego who paid attention knew the whole story. Or what the news and crime shows told them it was. "You're the guy who got away with murdering his wife."

"And you're the guy who's going to have another citizen's beef on his record unless you take these cuffs off."

He took a step closer to me, widened his stance, and put his hands on his hips. Showing me who was boss. A blue Ford Taurus plain-wrap detective car pulled up alongside us before the white cop could pull out his prick and lift his leg.

The window rolled down and a man in his late fifties, short curly gray hair, looked down at me, then up at the uniforms.

"What's going on here, Officer Barnes?"

Now I had a face to go with the voice. An unhappy voice. Detective Skupin.

"Found the suspect parked up here, armed, and spying on the crime scene, Detective," the white cop said. Less command presence in his voice than when he talked to me.

"Suspect?" I said.

"Uncuff him, Officer." Skupin got out of his car and looked at the top of mine. "And give him his gun back."

Barnes twisted his neck. The other cop knelt down and took off the handcuffs, helped me to my feet, and handed me my wallet. Barnes let out a loud breath and grabbed my gun and bullets off my car and thrust them at me.

"Thank you, Officer." I took back my property. "I'll skip the citizen's complaint this time."

"Officers Barnes and Salazar, go down and help secure the crime scene. Make sure the first officer on the scene has started a personnel log." The two cops nodded and went back to their car. "And, boys, make sure no one tramples all over my crime scene. Especially you."

The cops got into their cruiser and drove down the hill to the death house. "Thanks, Detective." I stuck out my hand. "Rick Cahill."

"I'm not shaking your hand, Cahill. I should have let those two idiots take you downtown." He put his hands on his hips, inadvertently or advertently opening his blazer to expose the gold shield on his belt and the gun on his hip. "I know all about you. I should have trusted my instincts the first time you called me. When is the press due to arrive? Did you call them or me first?"

"I didn't call the press, Detective. I understand you're angry that I didn't heed your command." I put my hands on my own hips, exposing nothing. "I had to follow my gut this time, but I was too late. I just wanted to find that twisted fuck hanging from a sewer pipe down there before he could do what he did to that poor girl. She's dead because I waited too long to alert you to Pluto. And because the uniforms that searched the house the other day on the anonymous call didn't check the basement. We both fucked up. I'm not about to dance on her grave by calling the press and bragging that I found her body."

"Is that a threat, Cahill? You going to hold the welfare check here over SDPD's head?"

"Skupin, things will run a lot smoother once you believe I don't want anything to do with the press. Just like I don't want anything to do with SDPD or any other police department. I'll answer all of your questions. Help any way I can, and then you and the press will never hear from me again."

"Time will tell, Cahill. Now tell me exactly how you came to find the bodies."

I told him. Just not exactly. I left out the part about picking the lock on the basement door and added a part about the door being unlocked. I'd still broken the law, but he didn't need to know how adept I was at it.

"How do you know the body was Alicia Alton if there was a photograph of Naomi stapled to its face?"

"I just assumed. Am I wrong? I saw a detective go down toward the basement while San Diego's finest were handcuffing me. Didn't she identify the body? Is it someone else?"

"Maybe, maybe not." The body was Alicia Alton. Skupin just didn't want to give me anything. "So, do you have a legitimate reason for unlawfully entering Caleb Lansing's house?"

"I had probable cause. Pluto—"

"Probable cause?" Skupin raised his voice. "You got a badge somewhere I don't see, Cahill? Because, I'm pretty sure you haven't been a cop for over a decade. And even then, you only lasted a couple years. What gives you the right to unlawfully enter a citizen's house armed?"

"Okay, Detective, I didn't have a right, and probable cause doesn't apply to me. But I had a responsibility to find Alicia Alton."

"I don't see how this explains why you broke into the house tonight."

"Pluto called Naomi's show tonight. He said that the imposter was in the darkness beneath. Alicia Alton was his imposter." I could see by Skupin's expression that he wasn't getting it. "I took this to mean he had her in his basement. I thought if I called you or 911 with Lansing's address you'd think I was crying wolf again. I didn't have a choice. He also said he was weary and that his eternal home was calling him. I guess that's why he offed himself."

"You had a choice, Cahill. But none of that matters now." Skupin rubbed his forehead. "Here's what's going to happen. We're going to go down to the station and you're going to tell me all of this in an interrogation room on video. I'm going to try to talk my lieutenant out of arresting you for breaking and entering and tampering with evidence."

"Tampering with evidence?"

"You walked all over the crime scene. He likes to get creative. You're lucky I don't lock you up on suspicion of murder."

"What?"

"You called in the murder. You were at the scene of the crime. You probably left some DNA in there. I could justifiably sweat you in jail for a couple days, but I'm not going to."

"Why not?" Why did I suddenly deserve a break? Especially from a cop I'd openly defied.

"Because, even though you're a bullheaded asshole, you tried to save that girl's life." He closed his eyes and let out a long breath. "But you didn't and neither did I. And now I have to go tell her father something he already knows but hasn't let himself believe. Your cowboy escapade will at least let Mr. Alton begin his grieving process."

I could see the pain in Detective Skupin's eyes. With just the faint luminance of the flashing lightbars from the cop cars down in the cul-de-sac, I could see it. But I felt it more than saw it. In his voice. In his posture. The job wasn't just the job to Skupin. Lives mattered. The lives of the dead and the lives of those left living.

"I should have listened to my gut."

"You're not a cop, Cahill. You're not allowed to have regrets over something out of your control. So save it." His body found it's full six-foot height again and his eyes went back to hard. "And if I find out you called the press or I see you on TV saying you knew Lansing had Alicia Alton in his house all along, I'll throw your ass in jail quicker than you can cry false arrest."

"Got it."

"Show up at 1501 Broadway downtown at 6:00 a.m. sharp or I'll send a BOLO out for your ass."

San Diego PD headquarters.

"I'll be there, Detective, but I'm ready to go now."

"I'm not. I have to go tell a father his daughter's been murdered."

CHAPTER THIRTY-EIGHT

SAN DIEGO POLICE Headquarters looked like a six-story parking structure with windows. Two-tone windows, the bottom having a beachy blue racing stripe. We were in San Diego, after all.

I met Detective Skupin on the fourth floor in the Homicide unit. Skupin was working with Homicide to close the Alicia Alton missing persons case. He took me into a square white room a lot like the others I'd been in over the years. A more modern camera over the door than LJPD, but the chairs were just as uncomfortable. The female detective I'd seen at the crime scene walked in just as I was sitting down.

"Detective Ava Ganz." She held out her hand. I stood up and shook it. She had dark hair pulled back in a ponytail. Brown eyes. Late-thirties. Fit. Gym rat. Chiseled facial features that read more handsome than pretty. She smiled, which may have been more theater than sincere in an effort to put me at ease. The jury was out. My history in square white rooms hadn't been pleasant.

She stood while Skupin sat kitty-corner across from me.

I repeated the story I'd told Skupin four hours earlier. Neither detective interrupted me. Detective Ganz's expression turned stoic when I got to the part about opening the door and entering the basement. Skupin had obviously clued her in. I wondered if she was clued in on the part about not arresting me, too.

Ganz spoke first after I finished.

"Where were you when you were listening to the radio show?"

"I was working surveillance in La Jolla."

"Where in La Jolla?"

"It's confidential." I lifted my hands and splayed my fingers. I didn't want the cops anywhere near Stone and the Russians. A certain end to a short life. "Sorry, Detective. The nature of the business."

She remained stone faced. Chiseled jaw pointed at me.

"Can anyone verify you were in La Jolla when you claimed to be?"

I didn't like the direction Ganz was angling toward. I looked at Skupin. He gave me nothing.

"Yes. Moira MacFarlane." I gave Ganz Moira's phone number. She wrote it down on a small pad she pulled from the inside pocket of her tan blazer.

"Did you stop by your home to get your weapon before you went to Caleb Lansing's house?"

"No. I already had it on me. I have a conceal carry permit." I stopped at home, but for something else. "Do you want to see it?"

"Not necessary." Ganz put a hand up. "What did you intend to do with the gun once you were inside Caleb Lansing's house?"

A good question. And a bad one. I didn't intend to kill Pluto when I took off from Hillside Drive. I just wanted to free Alicia. I'd use the gun on Pluto if I had to to keep Alicia alive. After I saw that she was dead, I was going to back out of the basement and call the police. Then I saw the wooden rack with the restraints. Kidnapping her and killing her hadn't been enough for Lansing. He had to torture her to get his rocks off.

At that point, I intended to kill Pluto. But he took the coward's way out.

"Nothing. It's just a part of the wardrobe, like a belt."

"Well, Mr. Cahill, as far as I know, you haven't killed anyone with your belt. Can't say the same about your gun."

Everyone knew pieces of my history.

"I've used my weapon lawfully to defend myself, Detective." Once, as far as most of law enforcement in San Diego knew. A couple more some of them knew about and claimed as their own. And once, not so lawfully, that no one but me and an accomplice after the fact knew about.

"Was that your intention last night, Mr. Cahill? To use your weapon somehow in self-defense after you unlawfully entered Mr. Lansing's home?"

"No." The familiar flop sweat I'd experienced in other square white rooms over the years returned. Coming down to headquarters to give a statement had seemed like a good idea four hours ago. Especially after Skupin's reassurance. "I'm beginning to think I should have brought a lawyer with me." I looked at Skupin. "Do I need a lawyer?"

"I don't think so, Mr. Cahill." Skupin looked at Ganz, then back at me. "I just have one question for you. Were you wearing gloves when you opened the basement door at Mr. Lansing's house?" He air-quoted "opened" with his fingers.

Fingerprints. SDPD had probably already checked my prints with AFIS against any that were on the basement doorknob. And didn't find any because I'd been wearing gloves. Malice aforethought. The gloves showed intent to commit a crime and that I was aware that I was committing a crime by breaking in. Once I'd decided to call the police, I should have taken off my gloves and put my hand on the door knob to leave some prints. That would have squared with my story. The police could say I'd entered Lansing's house with evil intent. But what did it matter now? Lansing was dead when I got there.

Now I worried how long Lansing had been dead before I got to his house. If he'd killed himself right after he called Naomi's show, he'd have been dead for around two hours by the time I got to his house. Real-life TOD—Time of Death—determinations aren't as precise as they are on TV. A two-hour window left a lot of room for suspicion to fall on me if there was something hinky about Lansing's hanging. The police didn't think I'd killed Pluto. Or did they? Even if I had, would they charge me? I'd be a hero in the press. This PD seemed to be pretty press conscious.

If I admitted I'd been wearing gloves, I'd have to tell them why. I didn't have a good answer for why.

"No." I thought about the nitrile gloves sitting atop the roof of the house I threw them on. Were they visible from the street? My DNA would be inside.

"That's all, Cahill." Skupin stood up. A crooked smile on his face. "For now."

CHAPTER THIRTY-NINE

I pulled into my driveway at 7:25 a.m. A TV truck was parked next to the curb in front of my house. Chanel 6 News. Shit. Someone had called the press. The garage door remote was in the Audi so I couldn't slip inside without facing them. A cameraman and a female reporter were at the door of my Honda by the time I opened it.

"Mr. Cahill, what can you tell us about the scene at the death house?" The reporter stuck a microphone in my face. Cathy Cade. I'd always liked her. Until now.

I kept my mouth shut and angled around her and the cameraman onto the walkway leading to my front door.

"Why were you there?" Microphone over my shoulder.

Fifteen feet from the front door.

"What did you know that the police didn't?"

Shit. Five feet.

"Do you think the police dropped the ball and Alicia Alton should still be alive?"

Shit. Shit. Shit.

I got inside and closed the door before she could ask if I thought the police were responsible for Alicia's death. Midnight growled at the closed door. Good dog.

I went upstairs and laid down on my bed, even though I knew sleep wouldn't come. I'd somehow managed an hour before I went down to

SDPD. That was before they put the subtle screws to me. Midnight settled down at the foot of the bed. My protector. I could have used him in the square white room down at SDPD.

I prayed that neither Skupin nor Ganz nor their lieutenant watched Channel 6 News. The leak to the press had to be on their end, but they could play it any way they wanted. In their minds, they'd have an excuse to charge me for breaking and entering. Put me in jail for a couple days. Delay the release of the determination of Lansing's death and leak that I was a person of interest. Payback for making them look bad. In their minds, at least.

I tried to sleep, but it didn't take. I called Naomi at 8:30 a.m. There was some good news to deliver in between all the bad. The phone rang four times before she picked up.

"Christ, Rick." Husky. Not in her sensual radio way, but in an interrupted sleep way. "Why are you calling so damn early? After that call from Pluto last night, I didn't get to sleep until after three."

"That's why I'm calling." No joy or satisfaction in my voice. All I could think about was Alicia Alton and her father. "You don't have to worry about Pluto anymore. He's dead."

"What?" Wide awake. "What happened? Who is he?"

"Caleb Lansing. The sonofabitch who kidnapped and killed Alicia Alton, the carhop from Sonic." It came out hard and accusatory. But it wasn't Naomi's fault. She'd just been trying to protect the life she'd made for herself when she begged me not to go to the police. At the time, she didn't know that Alicia had been kidnapped. Neither did I, but I knew the right thing to do and hadn't done it. If I had, Alicia might still be alive.

"Oh, that poor girl." Sincere. "It's not your fault, Rick. Pluto is to blame, not you."

She was good. She could read people over the phone. That's why tens of thousands of people listened to her every night. But I didn't feel any better.

I recapped my actions for the night after I'd talked to her on the phone. Entering the basement, finding the photographs of her, finding Alicia Alton's body, then Lansing's, calling the police, the cops pulling guns and cuffing me, my interrogation at SDPD, and finally, the press staking out my home. I left out some of the specifics just as I had with the police. Nobody needed to know everything. Except me.

"Are you okay?" A hint of her husky radio voice, but without the sultriness.

"Yeah." If the cops didn't throw me in jail and the Russians didn't kill me.

"What did you say to the reporters?" The huskiness replaced by an anxious soprano.

"Nothing, like I just told you."

"Are they still outside your house?"

"I don't know. I haven't looked."

"Are you going to talk to them?" Higher.

"Naomi, I'm not going to talk to the press. I have no desire, and if I do, I'll probably end up in jail."

"Why?" Concern. Real or well-acted.

"Nothing to worry about. Anyway, the press has no idea that you're tangentially involved. They don't know about the letter, the calls to the show, or that Lansing called himself Pluto. Unless the police leak them, your secrets are safe with me. The ones I know and the ones I don't."

"Thank you for everything, Rick." The confidence returned to her voice. "You really are a good man. Let me reciprocate for the drinks you bought at the Night Owl. How about Sunday night? The house in Del Mar."

I'd had worse offers. The memory of the one kiss Naomi and I shared brought back warm feelings. I could use some warm feelings. Anything other than the awful ones I'd just experienced. Naomi wasn't a client anymore. I could get involved if I wanted to. I didn't know what I wanted. Just something to make the awful go away for a while.

"Is twelve thirty too late? I'm working a case."

"See you then."

* * *

I somehow fell asleep and my body played catch-up for the last couple weeks and I woke up at noon. I felt rested and relaxed for the first time in over a week. Then I remembered what had happened in the last twelve hours. I flipped on the TV and Channel 6, hoping not to see video of Cathy Cade questioning me in front of my house.

Her image appeared on the screen and I held my breath. The shot was live, but not in front of my house. Highlight of the day.

"Yes, Ted, I'm here at the death house in North Park where Caleb Lansing is believed to have tortured and murdered poor Alicia Alton before he hanged himself in his basement. The bodies were discovered by a local private investigator, Rick Cahill." Not such a highlight. The cameraman panned back from Cade to show the police taped-off front of Lansing's house. "But the story gets even more frightening as I've just learned that Lansing had a wall full of hundreds of photographs of San Diego radio personality Naomi Hendrix."

Shit. Naomi and I both outed on local TV. Skupin would think I talked to the press and told all.

A headshot of Naomi popped onto the screen next to Cade. The photo wasn't the one with Naomi's face shrouded by the floppy hat that the station had on its website. This one was a full face shot of Naomi. Must have been her original headshot they took before she became famous. The photo took up half the television screen. No place to hide.

Naomi's biggest fear about the Pluto investigation had come true. Second biggest.

At least she was still alive.

But the looming invasion into her privacy was her problem now. I had my own to deal with. Someone had leaked to the press. It had to have been someone on SDPD or the coroner's or medical examiner's office. I was sure of two things. I hadn't been the leak and SDPD would think I was. I couldn't hold my breath and hope Detective Skupin and his command structure decided to let it go.

I called Skupin on my cell phone.

"Cahill, this might be news to you, but the young lady I've been trying to find for the last week was murdered and I'm assisting on the homicide investigation."

I understood his irritation. I wanted to talk to him even less than he wanted to talk to me. And he obviously hadn't even seen the news yet. But I figured he'd have free time soon enough. The homicide "investigation" was open and shut. The twisted social misfit, Caleb Lansing, started living his fantasies, stalked Naomi, kidnapped, tortured, and murdered Alicia Alton as a practice run, then offed himself when the reality of murder didn't live up to the fantasy, or he simply short-circuited. His wiring was faulty from the beginning.

"Somebody leaked to the press and it wasn't me."

"What the hell are you talking about?"

I told him about Cathy Cade's live shot on Channel 6 News.

"Son of a bitch!" His voiced reverberated in my ear. "If I find out you're behind this, I'm going to throw your ass in jail and charge you for breaking and entering and as an accessory to murder."

I knew the accessory charge was a bluff. Didn't matter. The breaking and entering was enough to pebble sweat on my forehead. I'd been in jail. A week was plenty of time to decide I never wanted to go back.

"The leak is on your end, Skupin. Why the hell would I alert you to it if it came from me?"

"To try and convince me it wasn't you. Just like you're trying to do now."

"Tighten up your own ship, asshole." My patience had limits. My stupidity, none.

"Listen, you Peeping Tom gumshoe mother—" He stopped suddenly. "Son of a bitch. My LT is calling me. Probably just saw the news. This isn't over, Cahill." He hung up.

LT. His lieutenant. He was right. This wasn't over.

That went even worse than expected. Now I had enemies on all agencies on the bright side of the law and one on the dark side. At least with the cops, I could see where they were coming from. With the Russians, all I saw were shadows.

* * *

I listened to Naomi's show during my Stone stakeout that night. Her connection to Pluto and Alicia Alton's murder wasn't missed by her audience. Even the emotionally wounded watch the news. Naomi deftly steered the conversation away from her anytime a caller brought it up. Still, at the end of the night she told her audience that she'd be off the next night. She didn't answer my post-show call, but answered with a text telling me that she needed some time alone and that she'd let me know on Sunday if our late-night drink was still on.

That warm feeling might have to wait.

The Stone watch was uneventful. No visitors. No trolling Russian Hummer after midnight. All good, but it felt like the lull before the storm.

CHAPTER FORTY

THE COOLER KID made another delivery or pickup at LiveStem at 1:00 p.m. the next day. He stayed inside the building the usual fifteen minutes and came back out with the cooler. I could follow him back to Dr. Rich's office, but until I found out what was being picked up and delivered in the cooler, it wasn't worth the trip.

I could mug him on one of his deliveries or pickups. But that wouldn't do me any good. If I picked the wrong end of the delivery, there'd be nothing inside. If I picked the right end and found a test tube, I wouldn't know what I was looking at anyway. I'd have to extract the information from the courier and, unless I killed him, word would get back to the Russians and I'd take the mystery out of whether or not I was in a life or death situation.

I still had to figure out what was in the cooler, but there was another way.

Maybe.

* * *

I got to the Alley Kat by 2:00 p.m. I had to make a quick stop at home for a prop and then go by my bank. The reserves were running low, but I still took out three hundred dollars. In five-, ten-, and twenty-dollar bills. My plan required cash. A credit card would also work and give me an extra thirty days to pay, but that would leave a paper trail. I didn't want the real owner of the strip bar, which I'd bet was Tatiana or her father, to come across a credit card charge with my name attached. So, cash I couldn't afford to give up, it was.

I pulled a Philadelphia Eagles hat out of the trunk of my car and went into the strip club. I needed a change of appearance from when Audrey Hastings saw me in Dr. Rich's office the other day. I pulled the cap down low, hiding my eyes.

I felt blind and naked framed in the doorway with the sun behind me and darkness in front of me when I entered the Alley Kat. If there was a Russian connection to the strip club, being seen there by the wrong person could get me killed. I felt eyes on me that I couldn't yet see until my own eyes adjusted to the darkness of the room.

I went over to the table in the back of the room where I'd sat briefly the other day. My eyes found the texture of the room and no one seemed to care about my presence except the waitress heading my way. A dozen or so men, from day laborers to slumming CEO types, were scattered around the room enjoying the daytime fare. A topless dancer, nearing the senior circuit, twisted around a pole onstage without much enthusiasm. No sign of Audrey Hastings.

"What can I get you to drink, sugar?" The waitress had black hair cut short in a bob and big brown eyes made bigger by enormous fake eyelashes. She wore a mesh top over a bulging brassiere and short shorts. A hint of modesty to be discarded when it was her turn on the pole.

"A Bud." Another five bucks gone. "Hey, I was here on Wednesday and I enjoyed watching a dancer, but I didn't get her name. She's maybe five-five, dark blond hair parted in the middle with little waves, real boobs." I was sure about the hair. Her breasts were a guess. I'd only seen her in clothes, not on the pole. I didn't ask for Audrey because a customer would only know her stage name.

"I'll be on stage in about fifteen minutes, hon." She thrust out her pert backside. "I'll give you what you're looking for. And more."

"I have no doubt you will." I pulled the wad of cash I'd withdrawn from the bank and slipped a ten under her garter belt. "I look forward to it. I'd like to see the other dancer again, too. I'm sure you know her. Is she here? What's her name?" I chased the ten in her garter belt with a five.

"That sounds like Honey. She's in the dressing room. I'll tell Honey she has a fan." She put her hand on my thigh. "I'm Fantasia. Where fantasies begin." She ran a finger down my thigh and walked away looking at me come hither over her shoulder.

I didn't doubt her claim about fantasies. As long as the dreamer had the cash to make the fantasy come true.

Fantasia came back with my beer and a seductive wink, then went behind the stage in an alcove, presumably to the dressing room. I kept my eyes under the bill of the Eagles cap pinned on the alcove. A minute or two after Fantasia went through it, Audrey Hastings' head peeked around the corner. The lights pointed at the stage washed over into the edge of the alcove. I had the sight advantage up in the dark corner of the room. She put a hand up to shade her eyes and looked in my direction. She eyed me for a second then disappeared back into the alcove.

A couple minutes later, the music changed, and the bored dancer on the pole left the stage. A cracking came over the PA speaker and a disembodied carny barker's voice came out of the darkness.

"Ladies and gentlemen, here comes a slathering of honey." The only ladies in the room were the ones working it.

The woman I knew to be Audrey Hastings strutted out in six-inch platform heels wearing a black sheer lace top over a tiny bikini top and a pair of shorts with about four Band-Aids' worth of fabric. Her hair jounced with each hip-twisting stride. She grabbed the stripper pole with one hand, anchored her stiletto against it, and did a three-sixty spin around it with her free hand held out and high in a dancer's pose. She let go of the pole and strode to the far end of the stage with one hand in her hair and the other on her hip.

The somnambulant crowd woke up with hoots and whistles and outstretched hands full of one- and five-dollar bills. Honey stopped in front of each depositor and thrust out a thigh for him to slip the cash under her garter belt. With the last stop she put an index finger in her mouth and looked up at me. I pulled my bankroll out of my pocket and snapped a twenty in front of me with two hands and then placed it on the table.

Honey slinked down to the other end of the stage and slithered out of her lace top and flung it over her head to the bartender twenty feet away. A seemingly spontaneous move, but must have had many repetitions as the bartender didn't have to move an inch to catch the discarded clothing.

More hoots and whistles and cash deposits. Next a sensuous unsnap of the shorts, a hips shimmy and four inches of fabric fell to the stage, revealing a tiny red thong. Honey hooked a platformed-toe under the shorts and flicked them to the bartender. Again, not an inch of move-ment. She strode back to the pole and did another three-sixty and spun out to the far end of the stage again. She did a little peekaboo with her bikini top, then finally crossed her arms in front of her and pulled the top slowly over her head as her hips swayed back and forth. She slingshot the top to the unmoving bartender. The men erupted, and Honey proceeded on another deposit run.

I'd been correct about her beautifully proportioned natural endowments.

She glided over to the pole and easily lifted herself onto the apparatus with two hands and climbed to the very top without the aid of her shapely legs. Once at the top, she straddled the pole with her legs and let go with one hand at a time and slowly lowered her torso into a horizontal plank position with her arms, hands, and fingers in dancer's repose. The move was more elegant than sensual and required Olympic-level core strength. That move told me something I already knew, but had let myself forget in my quest to beat the Russians.

Every stripper has a story and is a real person.

Whatever Honey's, or Audrey Hastings', story was, if her appointment at Doctor Rich's office meant she was pregnant, she wasn't showing an ounce. She could rake spoons along her abs and play in a Zydeco band.

She twisted and writhed around the pole in more crowd-pleasing positions for the next few minutes until finally dismounting and collecting her biggest round of deposits. With the last one she gave me the look again and I snapped another twenty.

Honey did a showgirl one hand on the hip and another aloft pose, then descended down the three steps from the stage and pranced back to the dressing room.

Fantasia took the stage and started a routine without the elegance or athleticism of Honey, but oozing with hip-thrusting sexuality. She got her share of hoots, whistles, and deposits, but they didn't match Honey's.

Halfway through Fantasia's routine, Honey emerged from the hallway in a different set of shorts, bikini top, lace, and platform heels. Only now, the heels were a mere four inches. A few of the connoisseurs in the crowd ogled her and applauded as she made her way up to my table.

Up close, underneath the big-eyed makeup, she was pretty. Not glamorous, but lose-your-heart naturally pretty. Midtwenties. I stood up, but made sure to keep my head titled slightly down so she couldn't get a good look at my face.

"A gentleman." She smiled a natural smile with no strip-club sensuality hanging off it.

"Sometimes." I smiled back.

She looked at the two twenties sitting on the table and then up at me. Commerce. "I put on a new garter just for you." This time the smile came with strip-club artifice. She straightened a leg out in front of me. Sure enough, her black garter had been replaced with a red one.

I am a man. Unattached. And she had lovely legs. The idea of putting my hands on her legs was hardly unappealing. But it was a prerequisite of her employment, not really a consensual choice. Under the circumstances, I would have preferred to just hand her the forty dollars or slide it across the table. But that would have been out of the ordinary and thrown up a red flag. And wouldn't coincide with my upcoming request.

"How thoughtful." I picked up one of the twenties. She laid a ruby-red toenailed foot in my lap. I slid the twenty under the garter on the outside of her thigh, then picked up the other bill and slid in under on the inside of her thigh.

She lifted her leg slowly up above her head at ninety degrees, then brought it back down to the floor. Sensual and elegant at once. If Honey, or Audrey, hadn't danced professionally, as in, on a stage in a theater, not a bar, she'd at least taken classes. Years' worth, I'd bet. After she gave up gymnastics.

Before I could make my request, a cocktail waitress appeared in the Alley Kat scant uniform. She was a bottle redhead. Too tan to be natural.

"Honey must be thirsty after that sexy dance." Strip-club smile. "Are you going to help her quench her thirst?"

"Of course." I looked at Honey. "I'm guessing champagne."

"Yes." She nodded. "Just a glass, Vixen."

"You sure, darlin'? That was quite a strenuous dance."

"I'm sure." Honey blushed.

"How about you, pardner? Maybe you'd like to share a split?"

"Another Bud would be fine. Thanks, Vixen." I hadn't even sipped my first one yet, but I knew the rules. Two drink minimum—those bought for the dancers didn't count.

She looked at Honey for a couple uncomfortable seconds, then sashayed off to the bar.

Honey had broken the code, and probably club rules, by not trying to upsell me. Had she correctly sized me up and my limited resources and determined if she ordered a split of champagne that I wouldn't have enough left over for a private dance and generous tip? The dancers had to pay the house for dancing at the club, but they kept their tips. Their time on the stage was tied into how much they could get the patrons to spend on alcohol and private dances.

The thought that she'd taken a liking to me and didn't want to see me gouged also floated through my mind. The strip club fantasy.

"You should be headlining here at night, not working the afternoon shift." I nodded down to the stage.

"I like having my nights free."

"How many years were you a gymnast?"

She studied me for a few seconds. No smile, real or fake. Just trying to figure out what I was about. Finally, "Until I was fifteen."

"How far did you go?"

"You ask a lot of questions." Stripper smile. "I have one for you. What's your name?"

"Ross." I lied. I lied a lot in my quest to find the truth. The irony of lying to learn the truth wasn't lost on me.

"Well, Ross, Fantasia said you told her you'd seen me dance in here before, but I don't remember seeing you."

This was good and bad. She didn't recognize me from Dr. Rich's office, but questioned whether I'd told Fantasia the truth about seeing her dance. Alley Kat Catch 22.

"I like to keep a low profile and, unfortunately, I wasn't able to stick around and tip you the last time I was here. I'm trying to make up for that today."

Vixen returned with our drinks.

"That will be twenty dollars, pardner." Vixen gave me a smirk. I liked the stripper smile better.

I handed her a twenty and a five and she slipped off.

"How do you plan to make it up to me, pardner?" She winked and smiled.

"I was hoping you'd give me a private dance."

"I'd love to." She stood up and took my hand. "Let's go."

I remained seated and nodded at the $15.00 flute of champagne sitting unsipped on the table. Probably Cooks or some other cheap brand similarly marked up 1,000 percent. "Aren't you going to finish your champagne?"

"Oh, I don't drink during the day." She pulled on my arm with surprising strength, unless I thought back to her climbing the stripper pole. "Come on."

I stood up and left both bottles of beer on the table and let Honey lead me down past the stage and the short hallway behind it. There was a door straight ahead and ones on either side of the hall. A bouncer-sized man stood outside the door on the right. Bald, black, and buff.

"Thumper, my friend Ross, here, would like a VIP room."

"That will be a hundred dollars for half an hour." His voice came out of a deep hole in the ground and almost had its own echo. I didn't think his name came from an old Disney movie.

I pulled five twenties of my dwindling wad and handed them to him.

"Room one," he said to Honey. He turned to me. "I'm coming through that door in exactly thirty minutes and ten seconds if you haven't come out yet."

VIP service.

CHAPTER FORTY-ONE

THE VIP ROOM was actually all glass, given privacy by the red curtains throughout. I sat on a faux leather love seat. The small room wouldn't have had space for another one. Honey stood in front of me. She pulled off her lace and bikini tops and shorts with less elegance and more fervor than onstage. She poked the tip of her tongue between her teeth. Her eyes dropped to feline slits. She put her hands on my thighs and leaned into me, hovering her breasts an inch from my face.

I hadn't been with a woman in a while. My body reminded me that everything still worked.

"You gonna make it up to me, Ross?" she whispered in my ear.

She turned around and started grinding her rear end into my crotch. A groan slipped out of me.

"For another fifty dollars, I'll keep going until you tell me to stop."

"Let me think about it."

She turned around to face me again and leaned forward.

"Why are you hiding your handsome face?" She pulled off my hat before I could stop her.

I smiled like I was handsome and it was no big deal. But the seduction left her eyes, and she stared at me, then took a step backward.

"I've seen you before and it wasn't in the club." She put her hands on her hips and now her half-moon expression was a squint. "You were at Dr. Rich's office the other day. What do you want, Ross? If that's even your real name."

After watching Honey perform and talking to her, I didn't feel so good about what I was about to do.

"My name's not important." I stood up and pulled my late father's La Jolla Police Department badge out of my pocket and flashed it in front of Honey's face. Just long enough for her to see it was real, but hopefully not long enough to see it wasn't SDPD. "I could write you up for solicitation right now."

She made a move for the door, but I stepped in front of her. If she screamed for Thumper and it got back to the Russians, I'd be a walking corpse. Time of death to be determined, but outcome certain.

"I don't care if you're a cop." Her eyes had gone from feline to feral. "If you don't let me out of here, I'll cry rape and let's see who believes who."

"I said I could write you up. I didn't say I would." I pointed at the love seat. "Sit down. Let's talk."

Honey stood still for a five count, then sat down. I waited until she was completely settled before I left the door and grabbed her discarded clothes off the floor. I sat down next to her and handed her the clothes.

"Put these on."

"What's the matter?" She shifted gears again and the stripper smile was back in place. "Don't you like what you see?"

"Let's play it straight. Okay, Audrey?" Her eyes went round when she heard her real name. "Just a man and a woman talking. None of the fake come-on bullshit."

"How do you know my name?" She put her scant stripper wear back on.

"That's not important." I turned toward her. "And I don't care how you make a living. I'm sure you could get a job with a dance troupe anywhere and I'm also sure you wouldn't make nearly as much money as you do on the pole."

"Then what do you want from me, Ross?"

"Why were you at Doctor Rich's the other day? Are you pregnant? Did you get an abortion?"

"That's none of your business. What kind of a question is that for a cop to ask a woman he claims just propositioned him?"

"I'm not asking you as a cop." The truth for a change.

"Then why are you asking me?"

"Because my life depends on finding out what happens in that office?"

Audrey studied me. A competitive gymnast as a kid, a stripper as an adult. She'd been trained not to give into physical pain as a child and hide emotional scars as an adult. Her life depended on her ability to read men's true intentions and the darkness of their souls. I might be able to fool her with a badge, but she'd see the truth in my motives.

"You're not a cop, are you?" Not an accusation.

Today, my life depended on being able to read a stripper who was a real person and had a life.

"No."

"Then why did you threaten me?"

"Because I'm desperate." The truth.

"Then why didn't you just talk to me like a decent human being?"

"You're right. I should have. I'm sorry." Also true.

She studied me for a few seconds. With soft eyes, not the hard ones of an afternoon stripper.

"I had an abortion." She looked down at the floor. Her breaths, audible and quick. Her shoulders shuddered and a sob erupted from deep within her. She put her head in her hands and cried. Soft huffs of grief. I gently rubbed her back.

She cried for a minute or two, her head still in her hands. I stayed silent and continued to rub her back. Finally, she lifted her head up. Her blue eyes were surrounded by red tendrils and puffy skin.

"It must be hard." I didn't know what to say.

"I didn't want to do it. They made me."

"Who's *they*?" I was pretty sure I already knew.

"Kevin. And Tatiana." She said the second name like a swear word. I shared her revulsion.

"Who's Kevin?"

The tears came again. No sobs or shudders, just two thick lines of tears.

I waited. I pulled out my phone and checked the time. We'd only been in the room for ten minutes. Plenty of time before Thumper came charging through the door.

"He's my boyfriend."

"Does he work here at the club or for Tatiana?"

"He works for Tatiana." She straightened up and wiped her eyes. "He cares more about her than he does for me. Or anyone else."

"Is Kevin the guy who drove you to Dr. Rich's office?"

"Yes. He didn't even stay with me during... the procedure."

I put my hand on her shoulder and gently squeezed.

"What does Kevin do for Tatiana?"

"How do you know Tatiana?"

I'd tried to use a badge I couldn't wear to coerce Audrey to tell me about what had to be one of the most painful experiences of her life. My pursuit of the truth. My quest to stay alive. But Audrey had a life, too. And right now, it made mine seem tolerable.

"I don't really know Tatiana." I was all in now. "I've had the misfortune of talking to her a couple times. If she knows I'm talking to you, she'll have me killed or try to do it herself."

A huge gamble. I'd just given Audrey the chance to extort me by buying her silence or have her report our talk to Tatiana. I wasn't gambling on Honey and the stripper fantasy. I'd put my faith in Audrey. The woman I'd met in a strip club's back room.

"She's evil."

"What does Kevin do for her?"

"He's just a gofer. He thinks he's more, but he's stupid. I see it now. I wish I'd never met him."

"What was in the cooler that you took to Dr. Rich's office?"

"Nothing."

The stops by LiveStem, made by Kevin, must have been deposits from Doctor Rich and not vice versa.

"How about when you left? Did the doctor put anything in the cooler? Did you give it back to Kevin?"

"Kevin told me to leave it with the doctor. That's what I did."

"Who paid for the abortion?"

"A bill was never discussed, but it had to be Tatiana."

"How much contact do you have with her?"

"She comes into the club sometimes and inspects the girls. Harry Abrams supposedly owns the club, but everyone here knows Tatiana is the real owner." Audrey put her knees together. "She looks at our arms and between our toes to see if we're shooting up. She doesn't care about cocaine or weed, but she doesn't want anyone on heroin or crack. I don't do any of it. I dance here to keep a roof over my son's head and put money away for his college fund."

"When did she last come in?"

"A couple days ago. I found out I was pregnant and I told Kevin. I thought he'd be happy, but he told me I had to get an abortion. I told him I wouldn't. The next day, Tatiana came by the club. She told me she'd give me a thousand dollars after I got the abortion."

"Did you tell her you didn't want to?"

"You don't tell Tatiana no." Her eyes welled up.

I put my arms around Audrey and pulled her close. She tucked her head into my shoulder. I stroked her hair. She hugged me. Softly at first, then harder and harder. I could feel resolve building through her in her tensing arms.

"I'm going to bring Tatiana down, Audrey. Her and her whole fucking organization."

"How are you going to do that? You're not a cop. And even if you were, she has cops on her payroll. They're in here all the time. They get free lap dances and more with some of the girls in rooms like this. You can't touch her. And if you could, she'll find out and kill you."

"Do you know of someone's she's killed?" I knew someone the Russians killed. I just didn't have enough evidence to go to the police. Even if I did, I wanted to stay alive. If the Russians were ever questioned about the death, they'd know I'd been the one to put the cops on them. Maybe there were other bodies that I could pin on them without them knowing I was involved.

"Not directly. But there was a dancer here last year, Sheila Ames. She was dating Petrov, Tatiana's driver. After Tatiana made him break up with her, Sheila started telling the girls that Petrov was in the Russian Mafia."

Petrov, my old gun-pointing friend.

"What happened to her?"

"She died of a heroin overdose two days after a Tatiana inspection. She didn't have any needle marks then. She didn't suddenly start doing heroin two days later."

Another hearsay case against Tatiana that would never stick.

"Do you know what Dr. Rich gives to Kevin in that blue cooler?"

"No. Not really." Audrey shook her head.

"What does *not really* mean?"

"I was with Kevin once when he picked up a girl at Dr. Rich's office after she had an abortion. I think her name was Kendra. She was one of Tatiana's high-end girls—"

"You mean call girls?"

"Yes. The girls who work the hotels around the convention center. They charge $1,000 a trick, but they only keep about two hundred— the rest goes to Tatiana." And some of that money is used to buy off cops to look the other way. Audrey continued, "Anyway, Kendra gave Kevin the cooler when we picked her up and I freaked. I thought the fetus was inside. I have an eight-year-old son. A fetus is a baby to me. I wouldn't stay in the car if I thought there was a dead baby in the cooler like a piece of garbage. Kevin got mad, but he finally opened the cooler to show me there wasn't a fetus in it."

"What was?"

"Four or five sealed test tubes in a glass or plastic case surrounded by dry ice."

"Did you ask Kevin what was in the test tubes?"

"Yes, but he wouldn't tell me. He just said, 'See, I told you it wasn't a fetus.'"

"Were the other two women in the waiting room at Dr. Rich's office the other day getting abortions?"

"I don't know. I didn't talk to them, but they had the look of Tatiana's motel girls. Cheap hookers, not from the convention center crowd."

Someone knocked on the red-curtained glass door.

"Honey, finish up in there." Thumper's voice. "Tatiana is here and she wants to talk to you."

CHAPTER FORTY-TWO

AUDREY'S EYES AND mouth went oval. My heart double-tapped, but I kept it inside. I didn't have my gun to shoot or intimidate my way out of the club, so I had to use my wits. I'd feel more comfortable with a gun.

"Give us a minute, Thumper." Audrey's voice was surprisingly composed. "We're at the point of no return."

"You don't want to make Tatiana wait." Thumper through the door.

"I know, hon. I'm keeping the customer satisfied and then I have to get properly attired."

No response from Thumper. No way to tell if he was still outside the door without peeking through the curtain.

"Will Tatiana be in the bar or in the office?" I whispered into Audrey's ear.

"In the office," Audrey whispered back. "She's probably here to pay me for killing my baby."

"Who else will be with her?"

"Just Petrov."

"In the office, the bar, or in the car?"

"In the bar. He sits up where you were and watches everything from there."

Shit. Petrov could recognize me. Even in the hat.

"Is there a back exit out of here?"

"Yes, but you have to go around the bar to get there."

"Is there anyone here right now you can trust?"

"Fantasia. She's like a big sister to me."

"Will you ask her to talk to Petrov and block his view of the exit before you talk to Tatiana?" I pulled my head back from her ear and looked her in the eyes. My life was in her hands. We'd known each other for a half hour, and she'd be deceiving a woman who could have her killed or do it herself. But we'd shared a moment of humanity that was probably rare in her life. It was in mine.

"Yes. She's probably in the dressing room changing after her dance." Audrey took my hands in hers. "Wait about two minutes and then leave this room and turn right around the bar when you come out of the hall. The exit is around the back to the right."

"Call me later tonight." I handed her a business card from my wallet.

"Why?"

"I want to make sure you're all right."

Audrey kissed me on the forehead and slipped the card into the crotch of her micro shorts. "Wait here two minutes before you leave."

"I lied about my name. It's really Rick."

"Nice to meet you, Rick."

Audrey stuck out a hand and we shook. She stood up, put one hand over her crotch, and went through the door. Thumper must have been outside the room because I heard Audrey's voice.

"Give me one sec, Thump. He made a little mess on both of us. I have to run into the dressing room for a minute and then I'll go right into the office. Promise."

"One minute. Tatiana's not going to be happy." The double baritone voice. "Where's the customer."

"Give him a couple minutes. He's cleaning himself up."

I hit the stopwatch icon on my phone and timed the two-minute warning down to the second. Now or never. My safety in the hands of a woman who danced naked for a living and possibly turned tricks on the side.

Every stripper has a story. And is a human being.

I opened the door with my hand over my own crotch. Thus, the mess I'd made. Thumper wasn't in the larger room. I opened the door into the hallway, and the big man was standing right outside, hands on his hips.

"'Bout time, buddy."

I didn't say anything and walked quickly around him with my hand over my crotch hiding my phantom mess and head down. Just another satisfied and embarrassed customer. I maintained my posture down the hall and around the bar. No Tatiana. I didn't risk a look over my shoulder to see if Fantasia was keeping Petrov occupied. I went through the rear exit, and the sunlight hit my eyes, blinding me.

CHAPTER FORTY-THREE

AUDREY CALLED ME that night to tell me that Tatiana had been at Alley Kat to pay her the $1,000 for the abortion. Audrey said she was going to put the money toward her son's college fund and hung up.

The Russians were lying low if they'd caught onto me. The T. Randolph emails continued to arrive and the stakeouts remained dull over the weekend. But the war of attrition had taken its toll. I couldn't afford the Audi anymore and planned to return it to Enterprise Monday morning.

* * *

The lights were on in Naomi's house when I got there at 12:25 a.m. She hadn't called me to follow up on our drink or returned the phone calls and texts I sent her. I would have left it at that if Miranda hadn't called me during my Sunday night stakeout to tell me that she hadn't heard from Naomi since Friday and was worried. Apparently, they'd become friends during Naomi's sequestration.

I parked in front of Naomi's neighbor's, one house up. I took a penlight flashlight from the new duffel bag of tools I'd purchased after I hid the last one from the police. Plus my new lock pick set. And I grabbed my gun from its nylon case.

The classic Camaro with the racing stripes wasn't in her driveway.
I flashed the penlight between the garage door and its frame. All I
could see was what looked like the shadow of a car. I didn't know if
the homeowner had another car or if the Camaro he gave Naomi
was it.

I texted Naomi before I went to the front door to tell her I was outside. No response. I knocked on the front door. And waited. Nothing.
No sound of footsteps or movement from within. No shadows across
the light coming from the front window. I rang the bell and knocked
once more. Loudly. Nothing. I tried the doorknob. Locked.

The porchlight wasn't on, affording me the cover of darkness. Still,
I felt exposed on the porch. I walked around the side of the house
and entered the backyard through the gate to the wooden fence. No
lock on the gate. Zero protection. I went up the steps to the deck and
over to the sliding glass door. I put on the nitrile gloves and tried the
handle. Unlocked.

I stopped cold. Had Naomi relaxed her guard after Pluto committed suicide and left the door unlocked? Or had someone tripped the
lock as I'd intended to?

I went inside, gun out. The open floorplan living area looked much
the same as it did the only other time I'd been there. A lone floor lamp
next to the sofa was on, as were the recessed lights in the kitchen.
No sign of disturbance anywhere. A living room intact, as if someone
went out to run a quick errand.

I walked down the hall to the bedrooms.

"Naomi."

No response.

I checked the two guest bedrooms and two bathrooms on my way
to the master. Beds made, probably unused since the homeowner was
last home. Naomi wasn't one for guests. Again, nothing out of place.
Same with the bathrooms.

The master bedroom showed no signs of disturbance either. The bed was unmade and the closet door was open. In my house that would be considered immaculate. But my recollection of Naomi's bedroom when I'd checked the house before was that the bed was made and both closet doors were shut. She was organized, if not quite a neat freak.

I holstered my gun and walked back down the hall and noticed Naomi's purse in a chair next to the dinner table. Naomi's cell phone and wallet were in it, but no key chain. I looked at the last texts sent and received. Incoming ones from Evigan, Miranda, and me, but no outbound since Friday. I went back further and found texts to Evigan and Carl, her producer, but none to anyone else over the past month. She didn't send many texts or make many calls.

I listened to all her voicemails. They were all from me and Miranda since Friday. None before that. She must have been in the practice of listening to voicemails and then deleting them immediately. Spoken words were transitory and easily erased. Just like her past. No outbound since Friday. The calls before were to numbers I recognized. Mine, Miranda's, Evigan's, and the radio station's.

Naomi led a very insular, private life. That someone may have disrupted.

I put the purse back, went into the garage, and flicked on the light. The Camaro sat on the left side of the two-car garage. I opened the driver's door. Again, no sign of disturbance. The interior neat and clean. I leaned across the passenger seat and opened the glove compartment and checked to see if Naomi had replaced her stolen gun. Even if she had, she would have taken it into the house. No gun.

I was just looking for something out of place to agitate the itch I had that something was off about the house and Naomi's absence. Or looking for something that would quell that itch and clear my mind. The car gave me neither. I walked behind it to open the trunk. I found a body in a trunk once. I didn't want to do it again, but I had to check.

The trunk was locked. I used the lock pick set I'd taken from the duffel bag in my trunk and picked the lock. I held my breath, opened the lid, and looked inside. A spare tire, full size like the Ford Fairmont my dad drove when I was a kid, sat in the trunk. Along with a car jack and jumper cables.

No body.

I shut the trunk and walked to the door that led back into the house. I put one hand on the light switch and the other on the doorknob and stopped before I could turn either of them. There was a button next to the doorjamb wired through the rafters to the motor of the automatic garage door. I hadn't noticed it when I came into the garage or it hadn't even registered because automatic garage doors were so prevalent nowadays. And all were paired with remote controls.

I hustled across the cement floor back to the Camaro and whipped open the door. No remote clipped to either sun visor. There wasn't one in the console compartment, either. I opened the glovebox and looked inside again to validate what I already knew. No remote control inside.

I walked toward the door leading into the house and noticed something in the middle of the garage floor. A few tiny brown stains dotted the cement. Again, I'd probably seen them earlier and hadn't taken notice. Oil stains that were wiped up, but not completely eradicated. In the middle of the garage floor. Where someone with one car would park in a two-car garage.

I used the fingertips of my gloved hand to turn the doorknob so as not to smudge possible fingerprints and reentered the house. I searched the purse. Again, reaffirming what I already knew to be true. No remote control to open the garage door.

Someone had taken Naomi.

The unmade bed and opened closet door, the missing car keys, the Camaro parked on the left-hand side of the garage instead of the middle. The missing remote. Someone broke into the house, subdued Naomi, then moved her car to the left side of the garage so they could pull in their own car and put her in it without being seen and drive off with Naomi hidden in the trunk or on the floor.

I ran back into the garage and hit the door opener without turning on the overhead light. The garage door rumbled open, but the light bulb connected to the casing around the motor didn't go on. I stretched up on my tiptoes and gently twisted the light bulb into the socket. The light went on. I loosened it until it went out. Whoever kidnapped Naomi had made sure the light wouldn't go on when they opened the garage door.

The last ten minutes caught up to me and my stomach flipped over. Pluto was dead, but Naomi had been kidnapped. Her past had reached out and pulled her back into it. And it happened under my watch. I'd stumbled upon Pluto in time to save Naomi, but not Alicia Alton. And I hadn't taken the threat of Naomi's Traveler past seriously enough. I'd let my guard down and Naomi paid for it.

I took out my cell phone to call 911. I tapped the send button, then quickly hung up. I needed to go over the facts one more time before I got the police involved.

Had Naomi orchestrated her own disappearance?

She was smart and had been living by her wits under a false identity for years. The clues were subtle. No sign of a struggle. If she wanted to make it seem as if she'd been abducted, she'd left scant clues. Why? And why make it look like an abduction at all? Why not just disappear?

If she just disappeared, Evigan and the radio station may try to track her down. They'd hire a PI, like me, who had limited skills and resources. They might try to get the police involved, but with no evidence of foul play, the police would quickly conclude that Naomi just didn't want to be found and drop the investigation if they ever picked it up the first place.

If Naomi had made it look like an abduction, she'd be inviting a police investigation. All the resources and dogged determination of San Diego's finest. If Naomi disappeared on her own, why enlist the one agency with the know-how to find her? Was she hoping that her disappearance would be ruled a homicide so her Traveler clan would stop looking for her forever? If that were the case, she would have left more evidence of a struggle.

No, the Naomi self-disappearance didn't play. She'd been abducted.

CHAPTER FORTY-FOUR

I CALLED 911 and reported Naomi missing. I got the San Diego Sheriff's Department, as Del Mar was in its jurisdiction. The dispatcher wanted to know how long. I told her forty-eight hours. A guess. I didn't care. I needed law enforcement involved.

I went outside and left the front door unlocked.

Five minutes later, a Sheriff's cruiser pulled up in front of the house. A female deputy got out. Shortish and lean, hat brim pulled low. She flashed me in the face with her flashlight. I told her who I was and that Naomi had been missing since Friday.

"Wait here, please." She walked to the front door and knocked on it. "Ms. Hendrix? San Diego Sheriff's Deputy, open the door."

She repeated the exercise and added the doorbell. I willed her to check the door to see if it was unlocked. She didn't. She walked back to me instead.

"I'm afraid there's not much else I can do." A car turned up the street and the headlights flashed across the deputy. Her nameplate read Dep. Shane. Red hair dangled out the back of her hat. She was young. Midtwenties.

"Her car's in the garage. The lights are on in the house. She could be injured inside."

"How do you know her car is in the garage?"

"Because I shined my flashlight into the crack between the door and the frame and saw it."

"Stay here, please." Deputy Shane walked over to the garage and shined a light through the crack on the side of the door.

She walked back toward me, and I braced for another excuse why she wouldn't check the door. But she walked past me down to her cruiser. She got in the car and grabbed the receiver to her car radio. I couldn't quite make out her words with the door to the car closed, but my guess was she was calling her sergeant for instructions or calling for backup before she attempted to enter the house. I welcomed either.

After a couple excruciating minutes, she got out of the car and walked to the front door. I started to follow her.

"Mr. Cahill, please stay by your car."

I retreated to my car. I needed to get inside that house and see what she saw. Deputy Shane couldn't have been more than a year on the job. She worked patrol. Would she connect the dots the way I did? How could she? She didn't have the knot in her gut that I did.

She reached the front door, knocked, and called out Naomi's name again. Shit. Round and round. She waited a couple seconds, then twisted the doorknob. When it turned, she looked back at me. I couldn't clearly see the expression on her face, but I sensed an accusation. Like she'd figured out that I'd already been inside. Prove it.

She turned back to the house and went inside, leaving the door open behind her. I edged up to the house and peeked inside. Deputy Shane stood in the living room with her hand on the handle of her gun in her holster and her head turned away from me. I watched her from outside the door. She walked out of my sight and called out Naomi's name. She must have taken the same trek I did and checked the bedrooms. The muscles twitched in my legs. I put my hand on the doorframe to restrain myself from entering the house.

Deputy Shane returned and called out Naomi's name, and I backed away from the door into the night. She passed by the front door. I took a couple steps forward and to my right to get a view of her. She was at the dinner table examining Naomi's purse. Hopefully, she spotted that Naomi's keys were missing. I willed her to check the garage and Naomi's Camaro, but she turned and spotted me.

"I asked you to stay by your car."

"Naomi's my friend, and I'm worried about her. I can't just sit idly by."

"Well, you can't enter the house. It could be a potential crime scene."

"Why do you say that?"

"Please go back to your car, Mr. Cahill."

I obeyed and went back to my car. A few seconds later, light leaked under and around the garage door. Deputy Shane may have been young, but she was thorough. Hopefully, observant, too. The light went out. Ten seconds later, Deputy Shane exited the house. But she left the front door open. Good. She had the same reservations I did. She approached me, all business.

"Would you mind waiting here for a while, so you can talk to a detective?"

"Sure." Yes! Deputy Shane was on my team.

She went into her cruiser and got on the radio again. Thirty minutes later, a detective sedan pulled up. A man in slacks and a blazer got out of the car. Slowly, like he thought he was important and you should, too. Six feet, slight paunch, early fifties, gray hair combed back and a porn mustache. A relic from the 1990s. He reminded me of paper pushers when I was a cop in Santa Barbara. Putting in just enough effort to stay on the job until the retirement bonanza.

Or maybe I just had too many bad memories of Santa Barbara.

Deputy Shane walked over and told him about my story and her search of Naomi's house. The detective looked bored until he heard my name. He slowly turned his head and eyeballed me. I don't think he liked what he saw.

Shane finished her report and the detective went into the house and returned a few minutes later. He ambled over to me and stuck out a hand.

"Mr. Cahill." A smile with a lot of gums, but no mirth. "I'm Detective Deacon. What makes you think Ms. Hendrix is missing?"

"I was supposed to meet her here tonight and she hasn't answered her phone or texts for two days."

"Hmm." A sour note. "That's hardly conclusive. The house isn't in disarray. No sign of a struggle. She's an adult and is allowed freedom of movement. Maybe she went somewhere to be alone."

"Without her car or purse?" I clenched my teeth.

"Maybe she took a cab or called a friend." He tilted his head and raised his eyebrows like anything was possible. "Whatever the case, I'll send her information to the National Crime Information Center. If she pops up somewhere, the San Diego Sheriff's Department will be alerted. That's all we can do at this point."

I was right about this guy. A clock watcher.

"That's it?" I threw up my hands. "She's in danger right now. We don't have time to hope for a sighting somewhere. How about questioning her neighbors here and at her primary residence to see if anyone has been asking about her? Or question the radio station employees?"

"I'll contact you just as soon as something comes up, Mr. PI." He knew me and my reputation. "You can go on home now."

I stared at him for a few seconds and he stared back at me. I'd played blink with a lot of cops over the years. I always lost. The badge never blinks. I turned away and got into my car.

CHAPTER FORTY-FIVE

MY PHONE RANG five minutes into my drive down Interstate 5. A blocked number on the caller ID. I answered anyway. Curiosity. Cat.

"Rick?" A hushed woman's voice.

"Yes?"

"This is Audrey." A slight slur. She was drunk. "You know, Honey the stripper."

"Why are you whispering?"

"I'm in the bathroom and I don't want Kevin to hear me."

"Okay. Tell me why you called."

"They put stem cells from the aborted fetuses in the cooler and sell them through LiveStem."

"How do you know this?"

"Kevin told me. I got him drunk and he told me LiveStem sells them as in vitro stem cells, which is a lie. Kevin says they don't work like the in vitro ones. Tatiana pays the girls a thousand dollars for every abortion and her father sells the stem cells for fifty thousand dollars a strand."

The cooler made sense now. So did the Russians' involvement. Sell inferior stem cells as in vitro on the open market through a reputable research firm like LiveStem. A steady source of assembly line abortions with fake in vitro stem cells and wash the profits through Live-Stem. Create fetuses so they can be destroyed for their parts, which aren't even what they're purported to be. A modern-day Soylent Green racket. The perfect profitable money laundering business for the Russians. And they had Peter Stone as their inside man on the LiveStem board of directors.

This might be the out I needed to free myself from the Russians. Fraud. I'm sure the aborted stem cells were sold all over the country, if not the world. That had to make it a RICO crime and under the purview of the FBI. This was bigger than mere money laundering and shell companies on the flash drive I gave Special Agent Mallon. This was people with serious illnesses paying exorbitant sums for treatment that could never work. Fraud. Racket. RICO.

But that was a secondary concern right now. Audrey's safety was first.

"Audrey, you have to get away from Kevin." When he sobered up, he'd realize that he'd made a big mistake telling Tatiana's secrets to Audrey. Or Honey. Or anyone. "Where are you? I'll pick you up."

"I don't want to do this anymore, Rick."

"Do what?"

"Dance in Alley Kat. Dance for Tatiana."

"You don't have to. I'll pick you up right now. Where are you?"

I heard a man's muffled voice, maybe through the bathroom door.

"I have to go."

"Tell me where you are."

But she'd already hung up.

Shit.

Audrey might be in danger, and I had no idea where she was. I hadn't met her until a couple days ago, but I felt responsible for her safety. And my own. If Tatiana found out that Audrey knew about the scam the Russians were pulling with the aborted stem cells, she'd kill her. And if she found out that Audrey told me, she'd try to kill me, too. I wouldn't have to worry about what happened when the Stone surveillance was over. I'd be over before it was.

I wanted to help Audrey but I had to find Naomi first.

I called Chip Evigan's cell phone. Voicemail. I called again. He answered.

"Jesus, Mr. Cahill, it's after two o'clock."

"Naomi's missing."

"What?" Panic. "How do you know?"

I told him what I'd just discovered at the house in Del Mar. I spoke calmly, but firmly. Command presence. An echo back to my days as a cop.

"I need you to question everyone at the station from the receptionist to the on-air talent and find out if they spoke to anyone either on the phone or in person about Naomi and her schedule. This would be in the last two days. Since the Pluto story hit the news."

"They know they're not supposed to do that." Defensive.

"I know, but people make mistakes. You have to convince your staff that they won't be in trouble if they come clean. Does the station have a record of the phone numbers from calls into the station? Not just calls into shows, but any that come into the station."

"Yes. Why?"

"If someone cops to giving out information about Naomi via a phone call, make copies of the phone numbers from calls made to the station around the time the information was given out and give them to me."

CHAPTER FORTY-SIX

I TURNED ON the early morning news when I woke up the next morning. Cathy Cade stared at me through the TV screen from in front of the SDPD headquarters on Broadway downtown. Except it was nighttime. Film from last night. She relayed the news that SDPD had finally ruled the death of Alicia Alton as a homicide and that of Caleb Lansing as a suicide. A suicide note had been recovered inside the house in which Caleb claimed responsibility for Alica Alton's murder and said he couldn't live with what he'd done. Cade also reported that the police had reason to believe that Lansing was responsible for Alicia's death, but that the case was still open.

What the hell more did they need? They even had a confession in Lansing's suicide note. How many T's and I's were left to cross and dot? I couldn't help but think that the slow roll had something to do with me finding the bodies. That SDPD wanted to have other dots to connect to show that they'd figured everything out on their own.

I didn't want the credit. I already had the guilt.

I turned off the TV and led Midnight downstairs and outside for his morning relief. The morning haze wafted through crisp, heavy air. Fifty degrees and fall fog, San Diego's version of the changing seasons.

I called Chip Evigan. No answer. I left a message telling him that I needed answers on the inquest of his staff about giving out information on Naomi. A day of waiting for Evigan's call and the sun to go down to revisit my Stone surveillance post rolled out in front of me. My actions dependent upon other people's. Not the way I operated.

I returned the Audi A8 L rental to Enterprise. If Stone spotted my car up the street from his house, maybe he'd stop and tell me what the hell was going on. Or try to have me killed. Either one would free me from the nightly pro bono work for the Russians. Lemons to lemonade.

Moira picked me up from the Enterprise at 8:15 a.m. She greeted me with her version of good morning as soon as I opened the passenger door of her white Honda Accord.

"Does this mean we're finally done with that damn Stone surveillance?" Gray sweater, blue jeans. Big brown eyes above soda-pop lips. Her short brown hair banded back in a chef's bun. Ready to take the day face-on. Just like every day.

"Unfortunately, the surveillance continues. Just with my own, already paid for, wheels."

"How much longer do you think this is going to continue?"

"I have no idea." I thought about the information Audrey Hastings gave me on the Russians last night. Information that might interest the FBI. If it came from anyone other than me. "But I may have found a way to put some heat on the Russians."

"Spit it out, Rick. Don't get shy now."

I told her about LiveStem, Kevin—the cooler courier, Dr. Rich, Alley Kat, Honey—Audrey, and the aborted fetal stem cells. She drove without saying anything for a block.

"You up for a little door to door?" I asked.

"Sure. Where to?" Always up for the next puzzle.

"This is for the other case I'm working on." I gave her Naomi's address in Pacific Beach and then told her the whole Naomi story, from Pluto to what I found at the Del Mar house last night. Moira listened to the evidence I stacked up into a neat pile.

"Someone grabbed her, Rick."

"Yep. And Detective Deacon at the Sheriff's Department is going to sit on his ass and wait for a hit from NCIC. There's no time to wait."

Moira pulled out on to Balboa Avenue and turned right up Soledad Mountain Road. We turned onto Beryl and finally settled in front of a pale-yellow mid-century home that hadn't been remodeled like most of its neighbors. Naomi's house. But not for the last few months.

Moira and I hustled up the two sets of steps to the split-level house. I knocked. Hard and loud. Nothing but the echo of empty. I rang the bell and knocked again. More nothing.

"Go stand on the sidewalk with your back to me."

"What are you up to now, Rick?" Moira put her hands on her hips and looked up at me.

"You don't need to know 'cause you're not going to watch." I flicked my hand toward the sidewalk. "Go."

She eyeballed me, then walked down to the sidewalk. I pulled out my pick set I'd grabbed from home for just this reason.

I picked the lock and entered Naomi's house. It had Navajo stylings that the blanket she kept in the Del Mar house hinted at. But no Naomi in the two-bedroom house. And on quick glance, nothing that said she'd been here in months or where she was now.

I exited the house and locked up.

Eight thirty on a Monday morning. Probably not the best time to question people about the comings and goings of neighbors. I didn't care. Sitting and hoping or picking the perfect time weren't options. Action was the only answer.

I knocked on the door of Naomi's next-door neighbor to the west. Moira went in the other direction. No answer. Next house over. An elderly woman in a bathrobe stared at me through a window in the front door. I held up my PI's license like it meant something and asked loudly if I could talk to her for just a minute. She shook her head.

"I'm calling the police!" The woman turned and hurried out of the foyer.

Next house, on the corner. A younger woman, early forties, said she hadn't seen Naomi in months. Didn't even know her name and no one had been around asking questions about her in the last few days. Or ever.

I crossed the street and got similar responses from the three homes where people answered their doors. I knocked on door four and no one answered. I went back out to the sidewalk and Moira approached from the other direction.

"Anything?" I asked.

"Nope. Only one person even knew that Naomi was a radio personality. She saw the report about Pluto on the news and recognized Naomi's picture. Said that in the year that Naomi has lived here, she'd only spoken to her once. She brought Naomi a housewarming cake and that was it. Said Naomi wasn't very friendly."

"That's her." I put my hands on my hips. "Nothing here either. How 'bout you give me a ride home so I can get my car?"

"Roger."

We crossed the street to Moira's car. A green Nissan Murano came down the street and turned into the driveway of the last empty house I'd checked. I looked at Moira.

"One more."

She nodded and got into the Accord and I crossed the street. A thin older man, maybe late eighties, got out of the driver's seat and opened the back door to the SUV and pulled out three Target shopping bags. The new thick ones that will never biodegrade. He must have gotten to the Target on Balboa just as it opened at eight o'clock.

"Excuse me, sir." I approached him on his driveway. "Do you have a minute to answer a couple questions?"

He looked down at the bags in his hands then back at me with a "what do you think" expression that made me realize the stupidity of my question without uttering a word.

"How about I help you carry those bags to your house?"

"How about you don't?" He started shuffling toward the walkway that lead to his front door. The house had a green, trim lawn and perfectly leveled hedges in front. Immaculate, just like his SUV. This gentleman liked attention to detail.

"Sir." I held up my paper badge. "I'm a private investigator investigating the disappearance of your neighbor across the street. Naomi Hendrix."

"Oh, the looker." He stopped shuffling and glanced at me over his shoulder. "I listen to her radio show every once in a while. They don't make many women like her anymore. She's missing? I thought the guy who was stalking her killed himself after he murdered that poor girl."

"He did, but now Naomi's missing."

He handed me the heaviest Target bag, and I followed him onto his porch. He gave me the rest of the bags, then unlocked his front door.

"I'm not going to invite you in." He stuck out his hands. "Give me the bags and I'll be right back."

I handed him the bags and he went inside and closed the door, eyeing me until it shut. A moment later, he opened the door again.

"Ask me what you want to know."

"Has anyone come around asking questions about Naomi in the last few days?"

"No. Next question."

I didn't have another question. He'd already told me that last time he'd seen Naomi was on the news. Another strikeout and Naomi was still in the wind. Or worse.

"That's it. Thank you for your time." I turned and walked back to the sidewalk.

"There was a guy who used to park on the street and watch her house sometimes. Sometimes he'd park right in front of my house. But that was about a year ago, so I guess that doesn't answer your question."

Probably Caleb Lansing. Back when the crush grew into an obsession. Something dark. Evil. Best hidden behind the name of a Roman god. He probably followed Naomi home from work one night. Just like he followed her to the Night Owl and came across Alicia Alton. I hoped the underworld was giving him the treatment he deserved.

But with Pluto gone, there were other evil forces at work.

"The car was a black Toyota Corolla, right?"

"Sometimes."

"He drove another car?" I stepped back onto the driveway.

"A truck. A black pickup. One of those big ones."

My mind racked the vehicle. I'd seen a black pickup truck recently, but couldn't immediately place it. "Did you ever get a good look at the man? Was he the man who stalked Naomi and killed Alicia Alton?"

"Can't say. It was always dark, and I only saw his profile. Could have been the sicko. Except he had those hipster sideburns."

My stomach dropped into a void.

"What do you mean?"

"You know." He raised his hand to the side of his face. "The long ones. Muttonchops."

Muttonchops. Black Ram 2500 pickup.

Quint Lansing.

CHAPTER FORTY-SEVEN

I SAT IN Moira's car and stared straight ahead.

"Well, what did you find out?"

I pulled out of my haze and looked at her.

"The wrong Lansing may have hung himself. Or gotten help from his brother doing it."

I told Moira what the old man told me.

"Let's not jump to any conclusions. Quint and Caleb were twins." Moira raised her eyebrows and tilted her head. "In the only encounter I had with Caleb, it seemed obvious that he looked up to Quint. Maybe he wore his hair like him sometimes. Some twins are like that, even as adults. And with Caleb's autism, maybe more so for him."

"What about the Ram truck? That's Quint's car."

"Maybe they borrowed each other's cars. Also, not unheard of." Moira unbuckled her seat belt and turned toward me. "In fact, we know that Caleb was smart, staying under the radar, avoiding the security cameras around the Night Owl and Sonic. Maybe, he borrowed his brother's truck without Quint knowing to give neighbors peering out the window a different look."

"One of them was smart and one of them wears muttonchops."

"I'm not convinced, but what's your plan?"

"Drive."

* * *

I pulled up in front of Quint Lansing's condominium in Tierrasanta. I'd found the address on a people finder website. Moira had followed me east after she dropped me at my house to get my car. She parked in a visitors lot above the entrance of the cul-de-sac where Lansing lived.

I got out of the car. No black Ram truck in Lansing's driveway. No vehicle at all. I walked past the garage to the front door inset behind it, hidden from the street. The condo was split-level and with an enclosed brick patio below the front entrance. The blinds were closed on the sliding glass doors that opened to the patio. They were the only front-facing windows. I knocked on the steel security door then turned my head down to the sliding glass doors. No movement. No mutton-chopped Lansing peeking out. Doorbell. Another hard knock. No answer at the door, no movement behind the blinds.

I didn't see any security cameras. Strange for the owner of a security company, unless the condos' HOA didn't allow them.

I went back out to the front and peeked through the gap between the garage door and frame. The high sun in Tierrasanta, too far inland to get any of the haze from the coastal morning marine layer, backlit the crack into the garage. No SUV on the left. I walked to the other side and peeked in. No car on the right, either.

I walked back to my car holding my right thumb down so Moira could see it from the parking lot. The plan was for her to stay and watch Quint's condo for his return while I checked the death house and his work.

* * *

No more crime scene tape at the North Park house. No Ram truck either. I knocked on the door. No answer. I peeked into the garage and saw the side of the black Corolla, but no truck.

* * *

I arrived at Lansing Business Park at 10:45 a.m. I didn't call and check to see if Quint was at work because I wanted to surprise him. Maybe he figured it out on his own or was somewhere grieving the death of his twin brother. I doubted the latter.

No black Ram truck in the parking lot. I parked and went inside the main building and down to Lansing Security in the far corner.

Quint wasn't behind the drive-thru window in the office. An African-American man in his midtwenties sat there instead. He wore a black Lansing Security shirt with the name "Curtis" in white embroidery across the breast pocket.

"Has Quint Lansing been in today?" I asked.

"No." He tilted his head when he looked at me. His eyes went big. "Wait a second, aren't you the guy who found . . . ah, the woman and Caleb? I saw you on the news."

Which answer had a better chance of me gaining some information on my visit here, yes or no?

"I don't watch the news. When do you expect him in?"

"What's this concerning?"

Wrong choice. I didn't have a good answer to his question. I needed to find out if the man sitting in a car outside Naomi's house about a year ago had been Quint or Caleb. What if it was Quint? Did that make him Alicia Alton's killer and Caleb a patsy? Could he have kidnapped Naomi and fulfilled his fantasy?

"It's personal." I smiled to try to take the edge off.

"Then you probably have Quint's personal cell phone number, so you don't need me." He folded his arms and gave me his own smile.

I pulled out my wallet and took out my PI license and a twenty. I stuck the wallet back in my pocket and held the license in my left hand and the twenty in my right.

"Let's trade." I waved my left hand. "Information for information." I waved my right hand. "Or information for money."

"What information could you possibly have that I'd want?"

I remembered how his eyes lit up when he recognized me. Not because I'd been on TV, but because I'd found the bodies. Nobody takes a business park security job as a first choice. Unless your father leaves the company to you.

You take this level security guard job because you couldn't cut it in the police academy or hadn't even been accepted. Or you liked spying on people with security cameras. Like Caleb. Or Quint. Either way, getting the gory details from a murder scene might be too good to pass up.

"That was me on the news. Rick Cahill. What do you want to know about the crime scene?"

"I'll take the twenty." He stuck his hand through the open window. "And the information."

"I'll give you both, but not all at once. I'll tell you what you want to know about the crime scene and then you give me Quint's cell number." I waved my PI license again.

"How do I get the twenty?"

"You answer a couple questions about Caleb for me. What do you want to know about the crime scene?"

He peeked around me to make sure no one was outside the office door. Clear.

"Did the smell of decomp lead you to the bodies?"

A *CSI* fan. Everyone was a crime scene tech now.

"No. Alicia Alton was wrapped up tight in plastic." The image flashed through my mind again. For at least the hundredth time in the last couple days. I didn't need the reminder, but a deal was a deal. "Looked like clear shower curtains, but may have been a tarp. Both ends where heavily duct-taped. Caleb had probably only been dead for an hour or two. No smell."

Except for the smell of feces from Caleb's muscles relaxing after death, but why fuel the fire?

"Could you tell if the woman had been tortured?" He leaned forward into the window. A little too eager. How many sickos manned that little office at Lansing Security?

"No." I thought of the wooden stand with the ankle and wrist restraints. Alicia Alton's death was known. Her horror and pain in the last hours of her life didn't need to be. "Time to give me Quint's cell number."

He gave me the number and I punched it into my phone.

"Question number two, did Caleb ever have muttonchops like Quint has?"

"Why do you want to know that?"

"I didn't ask you why you wanted to know about the bodies."

Curtis scrunched up his mouth for a second then said, "He did. He kind of idolized his brother in a weird way."

Caleb had worn muttonchops in the past. Case closed. All the worry for nothing. But that still didn't tell me where Naomi was. It just narrowed the target down to someone from her Traveler family.

"Thanks, Curtis." I handed him the twenty and spotted a picture of Quint standing in front of his truck on the opposite wall in the little office. Quint leaned against the Ram truck with his arms folded like a proud owner. "Hey, did Caleb and Quint ever use each other's cars?"

"I'm not sure. Quint may have used Caleb's car, but no way he let Caleb use his truck. He loves that thing much more than he did his brother. Hell, I don't think he even liked Caleb."

That didn't mean Caleb hadn't taken Quint's truck without him knowing. Maybe he stole the second set of keys from his brother. He was a lot cleverer than his disorder may have let on. Still . . .

"How long ago did Caleb wear muttonchops?"

"Hmm." Curtis' eyes went up to his left. "Right after I started working here."

"When was that?"

"About two years ago."

Naomi's neighbor across the street in Pacific Beach had spotted someone watching her house about a year ago. Maybe Caleb had just recently shaved his sideburns.

"How long ago did he shave them off?"

"Oh." He laughed. "Quint didn't like Caleb having the same look he did at all. He made him shave them within a month."

"So, Caleb hasn't worn mutton-chop sideburns in a couple years?"

"Right."

"Did you think Caleb was capable of doing all the things he was accused of?"

"He was a hard guy to get to know with the autism and everything. But I always thought he was a decent guy underneath his awkwardness. I guess I was wrong."

Maybe we'd all been wrong.

CHAPTER FORTY-EIGHT

I SAT IN my car in the Lansing Business Park parking lot and stared at my phone. I'd given Quint my card the first day I met him. It had my work number on it. If I called him, I'd use my personal number so he wouldn't recognize it, but he could still recognize my voice. I needed a ruse to get him out in the open.

I called Moira.

"Anything?"

"I think I can remember the plan, Rick. I call you when Quint Lansing shows up." The usual playful sarcasm. "If I don't call you, like right now, that means he hasn't shown up."

"Not today, Moira."

"What's wrong?"

"Quint is Pluto. I'm certain of it." I told her what Curtis told me about the muttonchops and Quint and his truck.

"Maybe he got the dates wrong or maybe the old man in Naomi's neighborhood did. Rick, you found the girl in Caleb Lansing's house where he committed suicide. He drove the black Corolla that followed you the night you and Naomi went to the Night Owl. The same car that the manager from Sonic saw on the video. I'll help you find Naomi, but the Quint angle is a dead end."

"Quint could have borrowed Caleb's car. It was a company car. He might have his own set of keys. Curtis said he wouldn't let anyone drive his truck and I believe him. He looks like the kind of prick who doesn't share. His brother takes the fall for killing Alicia Alton, then conveniently commits suicide."

"I think you're letting your dislike for Quint taint your view, Rick. Maybe you should let the police handle this."

"They don't seem to want to. I have Quint's cell phone number. I need your help."

"I'm staking out his condo in Tierrasanta in the middle of a perfectly good day. That's not helping you?"

"I was thinking of something more proactive."

"I'm not breaking into his house."

I'd do that on my own if it came down to it.

"No. The gas leak ruse."

A loud exhale. "Give me the number."

I gave her Quint's cell number and told her to call me with the results.

The gas leak ruse involved calling the target as a San Diego Gas & Electric employee and telling him that neighbors have complained about the smell of gas coming from his home and there's a technician waiting on his front porch to check for leaks. Moira and I had each used the ruse to get people home so we could serve them as process servers. Had worked every time so far.

Moira called me back in less than a minute.

"The call went straight to voicemail. I didn't leave a message."

You never leave a message if the target doesn't answer as he could call back from a different number and you'll have to answer as SDGE until he called back. If he ever did.

"Okay, call me if . . . you know."

"What are you going to do?"

"Try to get the police to believe me." I didn't have much of a chance considering I couldn't even get my one friend to believe me. "After that fails, I'm going to talk to one of the last living Lansings not named Quint."

* * *

Detective Skupin answered on the fourth ring.

"What is it now, Cahill?"

"Why haven't you buttoned up the Alton murder yet?" My ego and my own gut had begun to tell me that the delay had more to do with questions about Caleb's guilt than taking the glory from me.

"Don't believe everything you see on the news."

"So, then it's a done deal and there'll be a press conference led by the brass with you standing in the background real soon?"

"What do you want, Cahill?"

"Quint Lansing is Pluto and he kidnapped Naomi."

"What?"

"Why isn't the Alton case closed, Skupin? Who has the doubts? What evidence is missing?"

"Stay out of it, Cahill."

"Is it the rope? The crime techs couldn't find Caleb's DNA on the rope, could they?"

"We sent the DNA we found on the rope to the lab. No results yet."

"You didn't find any DNA on the inside of the knot, did you, Skupin?" I kept my voice steady. "If Caleb hung himself, he tied the knot, and DNA should be there. You know I'm right. Ping Quint Lansing's cell phone. He's got Naomi caged somewhere."

"That takes a warrant. Like I said, Cahill, there's not enough here." He hung up.

Skupin wasn't sold on Caleb either, but his hands were tied. I had to get him more.

CHAPTER FORTY-NINE

LANSING CONSTRUCTION WAS located in Miramar, east of the Golden Triangle and home to the Marine Corps Air Station Miramar. Birthplace to the Navy's Top Gun program long before Tom Cruise had a need for speed. Miramar is also the industrial park capital of San Diego. Flat, desert-like, and spacious. With occasional flyovers by Tom Cruise types. Except they're the real deal.

Lansing Construction had a massive warehouse a couple streets back from Miramar Road on Marindustry Drive. I entered the office attached to the warehouse. Edward Lansing owned the business alone since the twins' father died.

"May I speak to Edward Lansing?" I asked the woman behind an industrial desk in the small lobby area. Industrial park, industrial desk.

"Do you have an appointment?" The woman was in her late fifties, sturdy, natural gray hair mixed in with the brown. She read me the second I entered the office. Trouble.

"No. My name's Rick Cahill. I found the body of his nephew in the North Park house."

"And why do you want to talk to Ed?" If she'd had hackles, they would have just risen.

"I'll tell him when you take me to his office."

She stared at me. I didn't flinch. Detective Skupin couldn't make me flinch holding a badge. Neither could Tatiana Volkov holding a knife. Ed Lansing's gatekeeper armed with nothing but a nasty scowl didn't have a chance. One of Ed's nephews killed Alicia Alton. He was going to help me figure out which one. And if I was right, he was going to help me find Quint. And Naomi.

I won the game of blink, and the woman picked up the phone on her desk. "That Rick Cahill is here to see you." She listened and then spoke again. "He won't say."

I was a "that." A something. I had standing.

The woman hung up the phone and stood up. "Follow me."

She led me down a narrow hall with small offices on each side. The hall dead-ended into one large office. The woman opened the door and stuck her head in. "Rick Cahill."

At least she dropped the "that." She gave me one last nasty look and walked back down the hall. I went inside the office. Nothing fancy. More industrial furniture. A bald man with a horseshoe of gray hair stared at me through black horn-rimmed glasses. The look was nasty enough to make me wonder if he and the woman up front were related. Bulky, with the extra heft that comes with age for some people. White shirt with a pocket protector full of pens and pencils. A steel nameplate on the desk read Ed Lansing.

Lansing didn't get up or offer me a seat. I sat in a chair in front of his desk, anyway. Industrial. Uncomfortable.

"Please get to why you're here, Mr. Cahill, so I can address it and get back to my work."

"Where's Quint?"

"Why would I know that?"

"I take it you don't have a close relationship with your late brother's only remaining heir."

"I don't see how my family's dynamics are any concern of yours." Lansing clasped his hands together on the desk and leaned onto them.

"Just because you found my nephew's body doesn't give you special access to my family. I don't know where Quint is. You can leave now."

"Did you ever suspect Caleb of a twisted hidden life?" I stayed seated. "Did he torture animals as a kid? Ogle girls inappropriately in high school?"

"Am I going to have to call security?"

I doubted he had official security guards, but didn't doubt that he had plenty of large men in the warehouse who could remove me from my seat.

"Go ahead. Then I'll make a call, too. To Cathy Cade at Channel 6 News. She can't get enough of your nephew's twisted story. I'm sure she's already contacted you. She might be interested in some of the things I found out about your nephews that haven't surfaced in the news yet."

"What are you talking about?" His shoulders tensed and his brow furrowed. I'd found his weak spot. I'd done my research and knew he was in negotiations with the city to construct a new freeway off-ramp on the 805. I'm sure Lansing would do all he could to squelch any further bad publicity for his family and business name.

Dirty, but the clock on Naomi was ticking.

"I was hired by *Naomi At Night's* radio station to find who was stalking her. I did, but too late to save that poor girl that your nephew murdered. Cathy Cade from Channel 6 News calls me every day for an interview." A lie, but she'd listen if I called her. "You want me to talk to her, or do you want to answer a few questions and get on with your bid to construct that new off-ramp on the 805?"

Lansing's posture went weak. He had a lot to lose.

"What do you want to know?" Tired. Resigned.

"Where would Quint go if he wanted to get away from everything?"

"I don't know."

"Is there a family retreat he has access to somewhere?"

"No. Why are you looking for him?"

If I told him the real reason, he might clam up or tell me the truth. The only read I'd gotten on him was that his construction company was probably the most important thing in his life. No wedding ring, no pictures of children on his desk or walls. Did he care about the innocent life of a radio personality beyond what damage her death's connection to his last name might do to his company? Or did he care at all about the last remaining child of his brother?

"Tying up loose ends for the radio station." I wasn't ready to gamble yet. "Back to my earlier question, are you surprised at the things your nephew did?"

Lansing sat in his chair and stared at me. Not a nasty look this time. In fact, I don't even think he saw me. He stared at his family's past through me.

"I'm not convinced that he did the things he's been accused of."

Bingo.

"Then who did them?"

This time he registered me in his stare, but he didn't say anything. His silence said more than anything he'd said out loud so far.

"Do you think Caleb would take his own life?"

"That I don't know. I don't think so, but people surprise you."

They sure did.

"Why did your brother leave his house to Caleb and not Quint? What happened to the rest of his fortune?"

"There was a trust. Left to Caleb."

"Why was Quint left the scraps and everything else went to Caleb? Does the trust go to Quint now that Caleb is dead?"

"I think I've said enough, Mr. Cahill. Make your phone calls. I really don't care anymore." He'd slumped down in his chair a half a foot since I'd been in his office. My quest for the truth seldom brought joy to the people I used to find it. Mostly sorrow. Some days it got to me. But Naomi was still out there somewhere, probably under the command of the real Pluto. If she was still alive.

Ed Lansing's feelings didn't matter.

"He left everything to Caleb because Quint was the black sheep, wasn't he? Caleb had a disorder, but Quint was the one who tortured animals and creeped out his female classmates, wasn't he?"

Lansing stared at his desk, no doubt the tragedy of his extended family running through his head. The reality that the last child who could continue his family's name was defective. Evil. And yet, still family. He stayed silent.

"If Caleb didn't commit suicide, then somebody killed him. And framed him for the murder of Alicia Alton. And kidnapped Naomi Hendrix three days ago." I stood up, planted my hand on the desk, and leaned. "Where's Quint, Ed? I have to find him before he kills Naomi!"

"I honestly don't know." Tears pooled in the bottoms of his eyes.

"Your family has made a lot of money, Ed. There has to be some family property that Quint could escape to."

"There's a ranch in Idaho, but he doesn't like it out there."

"Is it a working ranch? Does anyone live there full-time?"

"Yes, a foreman and a few ranch hands."

"Have them contact you if Quint shows up."

"Okay." He bit his lip and looked down.

"What is it, Ed?"

"The company owns a condo in La Jolla that we use to entertain some of our clients. It's set up as an entertainment center and doesn't even have a bed in it. I guess he could be there if he found an old set of keys in the house in North Park."

"Who else has keys?"

"Just me."

"Give me your key and the address."

Lansing stood up, whipped open a desk drawer, pulled out a key-chain and handed it to me. A single house key was attached to the Lansing Construction key chain.

"1020 Prospect Street, unit 1. Are you going to call the police?"

"I already did. They're not interested."

"Call me if you find him." He grabbed a card from a holder on his desk and wrote a phone number on the back and handed it to me. "That's my cell. I don't care what time it is, call me."

CHAPTER FIFTY

THE LANSING CONSTRUCTION condo on Prospect Street was just a couple blocks down from Muldoon's Steak House. It was in a large modern four-story building with twelve total units sitting above the ocean a quarter mile away. The Lansing condo was on the first floor, but still had an ocean view. The floor plan was completely open. The décor and fixtures minimal and ultra-modern. Everything funneled to the magnificent view through the floor-to-ceiling moveable glass wall facing the ocean. The wall opened to a concrete deck. Another sunny day in paradise highlighted the soft blue of the sky against the dark, deep blue of the ocean.

Blissful. Serene. Empty. Like my gut, knowing Naomi was out in the real world somewhere with a psychopath and I couldn't find her.

The condo was less than one thousand square feet and probably worth no less than three million dollars. Immaculate. No sign of human interaction. I checked the lone bedroom, which had been converted into an office. No sign of Naomi, Quint, or anyone. I checked the drawers in the desk. A couple notepads and pens. Nothing else.

The refrigerator contained a case of beer without a bottle missing. A case of bottled water, the same. Six unopened bottles of white wine. No food. None in the pantry either. An inset in the wall contained a glassed-in wine rack. The condo was staged for entertaining, not living.

Nothing but expensive patio furniture on the deck. I walked to the front door noticing the stark white walls for the first time. Nothing hung from them lest they distract the eyes from the ocean view. Just one wall hanging right next to the front door. A four-by-six foot black-and-white photo of the Cave Shoppe, an old wood-shingled curio store a few blocks north on Coast Boulevard. The store got its name because the original owner of the property dug a tunnel that led down to one of the limestone caves along the shore that opened up to the sea.

A La Jolla landmark and kitchy, but the picture didn't fit in with the ultra-modern décor of the condo. I guess Ed Lansing liked it and won the battle with the interior decorator. Good for him, but his condo was a zero for leads to finding his nephew and Naomi.

I locked up and walked back to my car wondering what dead end I would find next.

CHAPTER FIFTY-ONE

MOIRA CALLED AT 6:15 p.m. from the parking lot above Quint Lansing's condo. "The sun's setting, Rick. You want me to continue to watch Lansing's condo or take my post below Stone's house?"

"Stay there until ten then head to my location on Hillside."

"Why not my normal spot?" Wary.

"You're taking my place for a bit."

"Where are you going to be?"

"Best that you don't know."

"Rick." A scold. "We help each other because we're friends not business associates. I can't help you if you're always leaving the important stuff out. Don't be stupid. Where are you going?"

Moira was right. She always was. But she was wrong, too. If I told her I planned to break into Lansing's condo, she'd be an accessory. Another casualty in my quest for the truth. No.

"I'm going to stay stupid on this one. I'll wait until you get here before I leave." I hung up.

Four hours later, Moira pulled in behind me on Hillside Drive. I drove away without acknowledging her. My cell phone pinged with an incoming text. I ignored it.

No lights were visible in Quint Lansing's condo when I drove by and circled out of the cul-de-sac at 10:30 p.m. I parked in the visitors parking lot above the street and pulled a flashlight, pick set, and nitrile gloves from the duffel bag in the trunk. I slipped on the gloves and put the pick set in the pocket of my jacket. Opposite the pocket that held my gun.

In blue jeans and a black Callaway hat, I was camouflaged on the streetlightless end of Lansing's street. I flashed a light into the crack between the garage door and the frame. No car or shadow of one that I could see. I slipped past his garage up the walkway to the front entrance and knocked on the front door. Nothing. Again. Nothing.

I swung over the railing protecting the sunken patio and dropped down onto the red brick flooring. No sound from inside the house. I ran the flashlight along the side of the sliding glass door and found an opening between the blinds inside. I couldn't see much except a wooden dowel on the inside track of the sliding glass door.

My face flashed hot when I remembered that Lansing had probably entered Naomi's house through the unprotected sliding glass door.

I climbed up over the railing and went to the front door hidden from the street by the garage. A steel security door was the first line of defense. I rang the bell. Nothing. I had to gamble that Quint Lansing hadn't forked out for an alarm system with his limited resources. I got both the security and front doors opened in less than two minutes.

The house opened into a landing above the kitchen and living room and below a staircase that must have led up to the bedrooms. All the lights were off. No beeping alarm, waiting to be unarmed. I slowly went down the staircase that led to the lower living area, clearing each room with the flashlight and my gun. No sign of anyone in the house. Next, I cleared the bedrooms upstairs. I took more time knowing the whole house was empty.

The master was modest in size and decoration. I poked the flashlight around the room, looking for any sign that Naomi had been there. Nothing. I left the lights off in case Quint had notified his neighbors that he was out of town. The closets and bureau had nothing but men's clothes in them. Same with the master bathroom. Just men's toiletries, no sign of a woman. I checked the sink and shower drains for long dark hairs. Nothing.

The house was immaculate, like it had just been deep-cleaned or the occupant was a neat freak. The home had the feel of the latter. Someone who never made messes and cleaned regularly.

If Quint was Pluto, he'd made a mess of Alicia Alton and cleaned up after her. But there was no evidence of it in his condo.

Nothing under the bed or in the other two bedrooms. No photographs of Naomi, either. The smallest bedroom had a desk with a computer on it in the place of a bed. The computer wasn't password protected, and I spent a few minutes going through the online search history and photograph files. The photos Quint saved were mostly of cars. A few had car show models in them, but those were the only photos with scantily clad women in them. No girlfriend shots, either.

Apparently, Quint hadn't had a girlfriend since he'd owned the computer. Or, he'd deleted all photos of ex-girlfriends. And what else? I clicked the computer's trash icon. No new deletions. I didn't know enough about computers to be able to resurrect files or images deleted from the trash.

There was nothing in the computer even hinting at the kind of perversion that led to Alicia Alton's death or Pluto's psychopathy. No snuff videos, no twisted pornography, no porn of any kind. Here in Quint Lansing's house, the belly of the beast, there should be some evidence of Pluto's psychosis. Nothing. The only oddity was the lack of oddity. All the upright citizens I knew, good people, had a little kink hidden somewhere. A pressure release. A guilty pleasure. A hidden shame. Quint Lansing had nothing I could find. His life, seemingly as clean and ordered as his home.

I walked downstairs to the foyer. A door led into the garage. I opened it, scanned with the flashlight, and went inside. No car. Wherever Quint Lansing went, he took his truck with him. I left the light off for fear of light leaking under and around the garage door. The garage was immaculate like the rest of the house. A small recessed area to the left of the door held a workbench and stacked washer/dryer. There was a large upright metal tool chest next to the recessed area. Shelves covered the entire wall on the left-hand side of the garage. They held mostly car products: motor oil, rim cleaner, upholstery cleaners, car wax, a wheel rim, and a few model car boxes. Quint loved his cars. There was also a set of luggage, a couple storage boxes, and a portable table saw.

A table saw. Used to cut wood, like the stand that Alicia Alton had been tortured on. I searched the garage for two-by-fours like the ones that made up the torture rack. None. No wood at all. A coincidence? Maybe. There were plenty of people in San Diego who had table saws in their garages. They just didn't happen to be the sicko who murdered Alicia Alton. But, I wasn't completely convinced that Quint Lansing was either. The lack of any sign of pathology had weakened my certainty.

I opened one of the storage boxes and found a stack of photo albums inside. I took the box over to the workbench and set it down. The bench had a small desk lamp on it. I sat down on a wooden stool next to the bench, turned on the light, and risked giving myself away. The light's beam was narrow and centered over the desk. It's lowest setting only illuminated half of the garage.

I pulled the first photo album out and opened it. It contained pages and pages of wedding photos. One of the twin's wedding. I couldn't tell which. Seeing that the photo album was in Quint's garage and considering Caleb's disorder, I guessed it had to be Quint's. Whichever one was the groom; the other was the best man. Judging by the age of the twins, the photos looked to be at least ten years old. The bride was beautiful and out of either of the twins' league. Maybe that's just how I looked at things. Always keeping score.

There were the requisite photos of the bride and groom exchanging vows, exchanging rings, exchanging cake. The families, the wedding party together, the bride and bridesmaids, the groom and grooms-men, reception revelry. The usual. No hint of the darkness that lay within the groom or the best man. Or, maybe, both.

Uncle Ed Lansing was in a couple photos. His smile looked plastered on. Maybe he'd already seen hints of the darkness and knew that the marriage wouldn't last or that only misery would come from it.

I examined the extended family photo more closely, looking for someone else who shared Ed's lack of faith. There looked to be plenty of fake smiles. Maybe all weddings were that way. Filled with some true believers and some fakers. Mine wasn't. It was filled with all true believers and one up-front skeptic. My bride's father. He only smiled in one photo. The one of just him and Colleen. He scowled in all the others. It got so bad that the photographer quit asking him to smile.

I studied the faces in the photo. One I'd missed earlier jumped out at me. My stomach dropped. I pushed my face closer, almost touching the picture. A woman in a sun hat and a dress that didn't match the elegance of everyone else's.

It was Naomi. But it couldn't have been. Maybe an older sister. But that was impossible, too. Naomi was from an Irish Gypsy family, Travelers, from South Carolina. She had to be someone else, some-how connected to the Lansing family. The photo looked to be a fam-ily shot. There was one of the twins' family and one of the bride's. The woman was on the end next to Ed Lansing, but they weren't touch-ing each other. They didn't look like they were together. The woman didn't look like she belonged, but there she was in the family photo.

I pulled out my cell phone and took a picture of the woman with Ed Lansing in the frame and texted it to the handwritten cell number on Lansing's card. I asked who the woman was in the photo. The time on my phone read 11:10 p.m. Lansing told me to call him if I found Quint. I hadn't but still expected a response. I got one thirty seconds later.

Ed: *Where did you find that?*

Me: *That's not important. Who is the woman in the photo?*

Ed: *That's the twins' mother, Louise. She wasn't invited to the wedding, but Caleb asked her to come.*

Me: *Why wasn't she invited? Quint was the groom, right?*

Ed: *She walked out on the family when the boys were twelve. Yes, Quint's wedding. The marriage lasted two years. Did you find him?*

Me: *Not yet. Where's the mother now?*

Ed: *Dead. Committed suicide two years ago.*

Me: *How? Before or after your brother died?*

Ed: *Sleeping pills. Before. A few months after Stephen was diagnosed with pancreatic cancer.*

Me: *Did she still have a relationship with him at the time?*

Ed: *No. He divorced her immediately after she abandoned the family and refused to let her see the twins when she tried to reconnect three years later. Caleb was the only family member who still talked to her. What does all this have to do with finding Quint?*

Me: *I don't know. I'll call you if I find him.*

I didn't know. I was just collecting blank puzzle pieces and trying to fit them together. None of them fit yet and Quint Lansing was in the wind. Naomi was either with him against her will, dead, or starting a new life somewhere else. Again.

I pulled out another photo album and started turning pages.

The albums were a slow-motion movie of the twins' lives told in reverse order starting with the wedding and backing up all the way to their birth. There wasn't one photo where I could be certain which twin was which. But in almost every early picture of the twins with their mother, one was always smiling and the other always scowling. Quint might be smiling and Caleb scowling in one photo and their expressions reversed in the next. I couldn't tell. Caleb's condition would point to him as the unhappy child in each photo. Yet, my gut, still roiling, told me it was the reverse.

Maybe I felt that way because of my immediate dislike for Quint. I didn't like a lot of people. That didn't make them all psychotic killers. It didn't help, either.

I checked my watch. 11:31 p.m. I had to get back to Hillside Drive before midnight. Moira had the Stone surveillance covered, but I wouldn't feel right unless I closed the night down myself.

The second to last photo album had pictures of the twins from about the ages of four to six years old. Even at this early age, the boys had polar opposite expressions when photographed with their mother. I still couldn't tell who was who, but I had the feeling that the scowling twin and the smiling one were the same in every photo. One boy loved his mother, the other hated her. The woman who bore a remarkable resemblance to the woman who started working across the street from the twins' place of work two years ago.

Naomi.

If only I could be certain that Caleb was the twin who hated his mother, I could move to the Traveler angle or convince myself that Naomi had disappeared by her own design. Alicia Alton's dead body and Caleb's own in the basement of his house told me and the police that Caleb was Pluto. Case closed. But my gut told me something else.

A photo on the last page of the album sent a shiver through my body. One of the twins stood on a dark staircase looking back at the camera. The other one was eight or ten steps below looking at the camera, too. Neither boy smiled or scowled, just blank expressions, but the dim lighting made them look demented. A chill froze along my spine. One of the six-year-old boys in the photo was showing his dark soul, the other was just caught in wrong light. Which was which?

The next three pictures showed the boys standing on a deck in a cave above the sea. A huge crack in the limestone wall that opened onto the Pacific Ocean. I knew the cave. It was the hole in the sandstone coast at the end of the stairs down from the Cave Shoppe.

In the last call Pluto made to Naomi, he talked about the underworld where the River Styx had bored a hole out of hell. The ocean was the river and the hole was the opening of the cave.

CHAPTER FIFTY-TWO

ED LANSING ANSWERED on the second ring.

"Did you find him?"

"No. What does your family have to do with the Cave Shoppe in La Jolla?"

"The company owns it. Stephen took ownership when a developer in La Jolla who owed us money went chapter seven. Why?"

"What about Quint? Did he like going there as a kid?"

"No. He hated it. It scared him. Caleb loved it, though. Why?"

Caleb. Again. If he was still alive and I'd found Quint hanging in the basement in North Park, I'd be convinced that Caleb was Pluto and had murdered and set up his brother and was now holding Naomi in the cave under the Cave Shoppe. Caleb made all the sense. Quint didn't. But he had the photo albums in his garage. The family historian after the death of his father? Or did the photos in the albums have special meaning to him?

The cave. The Naomi look-alike. Naomi and Quint both missing. It didn't matter what should have been. Only what was.

"Does Quint have a key to the Shoppe?"

"What is this all about, Cahill?"

"Does Quint have a key?"

"No. I don't think so. The store has been closed since a woman slipped on wet stairs and broke her arm. She's suing us and the city. The city shut us down on a code violation even though we'd had a grandfathered waiver on it. Anyway, the store's been closed for almost a year. What's going on?"

I hung up before I could give him an answer. I shoved the albums back into the storage boxes and put them back on the shelves, then retraced my steps out of the condo and ran up to my car. I got in and bolted out of Tierrasanta and onto the 52 Freeway headed west.

I called the La Jolla Police Department and told the dispatcher that a woman was being held in the Cave Shoppe. A guess, but so what? I could risk being wrong, but not being right. The dispatcher told me that there'd been a fatal car accident on Soledad Mountain Road and that she'd get a unit to the Cave Shoppe as soon as she could.

Moira called as I turned down Prospect Street.

"Where are you?"

"I think Quint's holding Naomi at the Cave Shoppe in La Jolla."

"What? Why?"

"I don't have time. Call you late—"

"No! I can be there in ten minutes. Wait for backup."

"No time." I hung up.

*　*　*

The Cave Shoppe sat at the top of Coast Boulevard below Prospect Street. The small parking lot was empty. The entry to the parking garage for Coast Mall sat across the street. The mall was closed at this hour and the main entrance was above on Prospect Street. I scanned the street. Empty. No sign of Quint's truck. I still had to check inside the store. I hopped out of my car and peered through the front window with my flashlight. No movement inside.

The wooden double front doors were locked. I went to work on the door with my lock pick set. Forty-five seconds later, I had the door unlocked. One more scan of the street. Still empty. I cracked the door open, pulled out my gun and held it snug against the flashlight pointed forward in my other hand and slipped inside the store.

Brandishing a weapon while breaking and entering. The number of laws I'd broken tonight kept stacking up. No movement in front of my flashlight. The faint hum of the ocean below the tunnel strobed up through the floorboards.

Time had stopped inside the store when the city shut it down. Displays of La Jolla–themed shirts were still in place. Shelves were still full of knickknacks and curios. Posters of the cave hung on the wall.

I cleared the first floor then crept up the stairs to the second level. Offices, storage, a bathroom, but no Naomi or Quint Lansing. I went back downstairs and walked over to the entrance that led down into the tunnel. There was another locked door at the bottom of the five steps that led to the tunnel. I picked the lock and opened the door. A waft of cold briny air pushed up from the black tunnel below.

I pointed the flashlight and gun down the steps I'd last descended in high school while trying to impress a date. Condensation from the shushing ocean below dampened the narrow wooden steps and handrail. Slippery. I put the gun in my jacket pocket and held onto the rail with my right hand as I pointed the flashlight down the tunnel with my left. There were well over one hundred steps down to the wooden platform and railing that sat above the ocean. I stopped every ten steps or so to listen for human sounds. Nothing above the whoosh of the ocean.

I finally reached the bottom and walked out to the wooden deck. A sliver of light from the moon knifed in through the opening of the cave off to the right. I three-sixtied the flashlight around the cave. Nothing but damp limestone walls. Water rushed against the rocks below the deck and receded. High tide. I scanned the water line below

the pier, looking for anything that gave clue to Naomi or Quint having been in the cave. Nothing.

All the clues I'd tacked onto Quint added up to nothing. Maybe I'd
already found the real killer in Caleb Lansing and Quint and Naomi
had disappeared separately on their own. Maybe Quint just wanted
to get out of town until the fervor over his murderous twin brother
died down. Who wouldn't want to disappear?

Another wave rolled through the cave opening and splashed against
the rocks. I started to swing the flashlight back toward the stairs and
make my retreat when something below caught my eye as the tide receded. A rock lighter than the others. No, wood. But not driftwood,
milled wood. Like the end of a two-by-four. The kind used in the torture rack I'd found in Caleb Lansing's dungeon basement.

I vaulted over the railing into the water. My foot caught a rock
under the water and my ankle rolled, splashing me down onto my
side. My hand hit another hidden rock, and I dropped the flashlight.
I steadied myself and sloshed in the thigh-deep water over to where I
thought I'd seen the wood. I stumbled over boulders hidden beneath
the tide.

A passing cloud shrouded the moonlight. Another wave roiled in
and pushed me forward into the rocks below the platform. I regained
my balance and ran my hands through the receding tide, searching
for the wood. My hand grazed something hard. Grainy. I moved
it back slowly through the water. Hit it again. I circled my hand
around it.

A two-by-four.

I pulled hard. It moved from side to side but wouldn't rise out
of the water. I grabbed with my other hand, and a big roller came
through the cave opening and rammed me against the rocks, knocking me over. But I held onto the wood, and it broke free with the
receding water.

I slid one hand down to get a better grip and grabbed something soft. My feet found the bottom, and I stood up and pulled with all I had.

The cloud passed, and the moon splashed a narrow spotlight into the cave.

Naomi's eyes stared blankly through mine.

CHAPTER FIFTY-THREE

"NAOMI!"

Silence.

I bent down and threw my arms around her waist and the cross she was strapped to and hoisted her up. Her naked torso cleared the water. Another wave hit and pushed me into her. I managed to stay upright, but her expression didn't change.

I had to get her onto the deck to try CPR. The tide moved back to the ocean. I pushed her against the rocks and slid down underwater, holding my breath, and found the strap around her ankle. My hands slipped off, but I stayed down and grabbed it again. I pried the strap's buckle, but it wouldn't budge. Another wave crashed in, sending me sideways against the rocks. I lost my grip on the strap and came up for air.

I dove back under and found Naomi's secured ankle again as we drifted out with the tide. I ripped my gun from my jacket and felt along the strap with the barrel. It banged into my hand holding onto the strap. I pressed the barrel against what I thought was the strap against the wood and fired under water.

Naomi's leg came free. I grabbed it and stood up out of the water. Another wave. I slid across and found Naomi's other leg as we crashed against the rocks again. I tried the gun again, but it wouldn't fire. I jammed it into my coat pocket and tried both hands on the strap as we drifted again with the receding tide.

Free.

I let go of Naomi's leg, and she and the cross floated on top of the water. Another wave pushed through the opening. I grabbed the strap around her wrist with both hands just as the wave hit. I maneuvered the buckle and Naomi's wrist came free as the wave slammed my head against the rocks. Stars in the black cave. I lost my grip on Naomi's wrist. She floated on her back, free from the rack except for her right wrist. I dove for her as she started to drift with the retreating tide. Caught her, found her wrist, and freed it from the strap.

I grabbed her around the waist from behind and strode against the current to the right side of the cave where a rocky outcropping rose from the water. A wave knocked me down, but I held onto Naomi. I backed my way to the higher ground, Naomi's heels banging off underwater rocks. No cries of pain. Nothing.

I finally cleared the water and laid her on the rocks and moved her head to the side. Water trickled out of her mouth. I centered her head, tilted her jaw forward, pinched her nose with my fingers, sealed my mouth over hers, and blew as hard as I could. Her lips were ice. Her chest rose. I pulled my head up, grabbed air, and blew into her again. Again. Again.

I checked the pulse on Naomi's frozen wrist. Nothing. I pressed my hands on her chest and pushed.

"One, two, three. One, two, three." Over and over. Nothing.

Back to her mouth. Blow. Again and again.

I pulled my head up and the moonlight splashed across Naomi's face over my shoulder. Her eyes still stared through mine, but couldn't see. They never would again. I put my thumb and finger on her eyelids and gently pulled down.

I fell back onto the rocks. The adrenaline spilled out of me and took whatever strength had been there before with it. A wave splashed up at me, saltwater washing the tears from my eyes.

Naomi had needed my help, and I'd failed her. My gut told me the whole time I investigated Pluto that something was off, and I hadn't listened hard enough. Naomi had grabbed her second chance and built a new life. She'd looked over her shoulder at a hellish past and missed the bogeyman right in front of her.

So did I.

I took my cell phone out of my soaked pants to call 911. Too late to save Naomi, but Quint Lansing was free out on the streets somewhere, and the police had to get involved now. I tapped the phone icon on the screen. Frozen. Waterlogged. I had to leave Naomi's body and climb the stairs up to the street and find a phone.

I didn't want to leave her. Naked and alone, splayed out on cold jagged rocks. She deserved better. In life and death. But I didn't have a choice. I stood up, then grabbed Naomi underneath her arms and pulled her up, as gently as I could, further onto the rocks above the water. I didn't want a rogue wave to wash in and pull her out to sea.

I slogged over to the railing and clambered over. Spent from everything that had happened tonight. The seawater heavy on my clothes, multiplying the pull of gravity. Naomi's death, even heavier. The chill in the cave and the cold seawater turned my sodden clothes into an ice blanket. My body shook.

I wanted to lie down and not feel. But Naomi's body needed care. And her death needed to be avenged. I took a step toward the stairwell and a light shone in my face. Moira or the police. Too late. Just like me.

"She's gone. I couldn't save her."

The light stayed on my face.

"And she couldn't save herself." A voice from behind the light.

Adrenaline shot back through my body. The chill of my falling internal temperature replaced by the primal chill of fear. Quint Lansing was behind the flashlight, not Moira. The light was at least twenty feet away. If he had a gun pointed at me behind the light, he was close enough to hit his target but too far away for me to reach before he pulled the trigger. The gun in my pocket, useless from the saltwater. Moira, the police, or the sea were my only hopes.

"Why did you come back?" I asked then bent over and coughed hard to camouflage my backwards step toward the railing.

"I saw your car pull up when I was leaving." A nasal laugh. "I had just gone into the Coast Walk garage to get my truck and Hercules shows up looking for Persephone."

"I was looking for Naomi. A real human being. Not some pawn in your infantile game of revenge with Caleb because Mommy liked him better." Quint was a psychopath; I gambled that he'd take my taunt as a chance to show me how superior he was. Time. I needed more time for the police or Moira to arrive. "Killing Alicia Alton and your brother wasn't enough? How many people do you have to kill to make up for being forever Mommy's second choice? Two wasn't enough? You had to kill Naomi, too?"

"You're not as smart as you think you are, Mr. Fake Detective." The laugh again. I was already sick of it. I didn't want it to be the last thing I heard before I went to heaven. Or the other place. A hand appeared in front of the flashlight. It was holding a gun. It disappeared back behind the light. "Just wanted to make sure you don't try anything stupid. Or stupider than trying to catch me in my own game. Back to the count. Naomi was actually four and you'll make five."

Alicia Alton. Caleb. Naomi. Had Quint made a practice run before he started stalking Naomi? His father died of cancer. His mother . . . his mother. Overdosed on sleeping pills just a couple weeks after his father had been diagnosed with pancreatic cancer. One less person to contest the will after his father died.

"Killing your mother once wasn't enough for you?" More coughs and shivers and inches backward. "You had to kill her look-alike, too? Why? You have all your father's wealth now. You killed your brother and framed him. Case closed. You were on your way. Why couldn't you just quit when you were ahead? Why did you have to kill Naomi? To make up for the love your mother never gave you?"

"I heard her on the radio before I even saw her. That sexy voice, teasing me every night. I knew I had to have her. I even called into the show. But then one night I watched the radio station parking lot through our camera and I couldn't believe it when she stepped out of that cherry Camaro. The woman who gave me an erection every night while I listened looked like my mother. What would you do, Mr. Fake Detective, if the woman's voice you beat off to in your office every night was coming out of your dead mother's mouth?"

"I'd see a shrink." Another cough. Another couple inches backward.

"Oh, I did as a child. Didn't take." The laugh. "Your girlfriend begged when I raped her and at the very end. The sexy, confident lady on the radio begged for her life at the end as the tide creeped up higher and higher. She promised to do anything for me if I just let her go. Kind of disappointing. They all beg at the end. I expected more from her. I watched her last breath bubble up to the surface. She looked surprised. I don't know why. She knew what was going to happen. I tied her to the cross and weighted it down with rocks and she laid there for two hours while the tide rose. Begging for her life. Are you going to beg, Rick?"

I almost abandoned my plan and charged the twisted fuck. Quint Lansing had to be put down. He had no place in this world. A malignant disorder that had to be eradicated. He had to die, but could I reach him before he shot me first? A deadly gamble.

Then I saw it. I wasn't sure what it was at first. A wisp of fog appeared above the flashlight Quint pointed at my face. No. A light coming around the corner of the platform. Whoever was holding the flashlight hadn't appeared yet. No warning shout from the police.

Moira.

I had to warn her. She probably couldn't hear our voices over the back and forth of the waves in the cave. If I yelled that Quint had a gun, he'd know someone was coming. I could think of only one way to warn Moira without giving her away.

"Time is running out, Fake Detective. Time to beg." The flashlight shifted to my chest, like he'd taken aim with the gun.

"Please don't kill—" I spun, grabbed the rail, and leaped into the darkness. The cave lit up and a boom echoed at the same time. I hit the water and plunged down as the cave lit up again. I didn't hear the boom under water. My nose banged against a rock and stunned the air out of my lungs. I swallowed water. Liquid salt choking me. I pushed off the bottom and rose out of the water.

Boom! Light! I dove back down and banged off the bottom again as a wave receded and pulled water back off me. If Quint shot me now, there wouldn't be enough water to keep the bullets from penetrating my skin. I pulled the water past me along the bottom. Deeper. Toward where I sensed the cave opening was. I came up for air. No boom, but I heard something as I dove back under.

"Rick!"

When I came up again, the flashlight was turned back toward the cave. Shining up at Moira's face. She held the flashlight in her hand.

"It's me. Everything's okay. He's dead."

Moira moved the light to the floor of the pier, and I could just make out the outline of a body.

CHAPTER FIFTY-FOUR

MOIRA THREW UP over the railing into the ocean before the police arrived. She'd never fired a gun at a living creature before. Now she'd only done it once, but that one shot hit home. It went through Lansing's back and came out his front. Judging by the pool of blood around his body, I guessed the bullet ripped through his heart on the way out. No sympathy on my part. His heart was just an organ without a soul attached.

Moira was having a hard time though. Killing someone, no matter how evil, doesn't wash off in the next shower. Saving someone's life doesn't cancel out taking another. Not if you have a soul. Moira had one. I prayed I still did.

"You saved my life." I rubbed her back as she gripped the railing and dry-heaved over it. I wiped away at the blood leaking out of the bump on the bridge of my nose. Courtesy of the underwater rock I dove into. The cold seeped back into my bones and I shivered.

Moira took a deep breath, stepped back, and turned toward me, still holding the railing with her left hand. Moonlight caught her face. Tears trickled down her checks. I'd only seen Moira cry once. When someone threw a cannister of tear gas into her house. Her tears scared me. She was the toughest woman I knew. Hell, the toughest person I knew. And I'd put her in a position that would scar her for the rest of her life.

"He killed Naomi and he would have killed me if you hadn't gotten here when you did." I pulled a strand of hair away from her eyes.

"Shut up, Rick." She pushed me in the chest with both hands. "I know it was him or you. I had to shoot him. Just let me be a girl for a second."

"The toughest girl I know."

"Shut up."

"Let's get our story straight before the police arrive. I'm the one who shot him. I found the body, he shot at me and missed and I shot him."

"You want to be the hero now?"

"I don't want you to have to deal with this."

"So how is it you shot him in the back, idiot?"

"He shot at me. I dove away and he spun around and I shot him."

"You're an idiot. I don't need a savior, Rick. I know in your emotionally stunted way, you're trying to help me." A smile or a frown. I couldn't tell in the bad light. "That's sweet, but the truth is the only way this makes any sense. I have a conceal carry permit. Everything was legal."

"It's still going to be a headache you don't deserve."

*   *   *

We spent three hours at the police station in separate interrogation rooms. Well, I was only in the square white room for two hours. Moira got the full treatment. Luckily, I didn't know the two detectives who interviewed me. When it came to the La Jolla Police Department, familiarity bred contempt. The cops gave me a pair of sweats and socks to wear, but nobody offered medical care for the bump on my nose that had scabbed up. It still throbbed whenever I stopped thinking about Naomi's dead body.

The only lie I told was that the door to the Cave Shoppe was unlocked when I got there. Oh, and a lie of omission by not telling
the detectives that I'd broken into Quint Lansing's house and put
everything together by looking through the family photo albums.
Just in case they pinged my cell phone, I gave them a story that I'd
staked out his condo for an hour before I went to the Cave Shoppe.

I told them I figured out the Cave Shoppe connection after I saw
the photo in the Lansing Construction condominium and asked Ed
Lansing about its significance. They played hard with me because I
was Rick Cahill and they were LJPD. But that only lasted an hour or
so. I could tell by the time they were done with me that they bought
my macro story. Even though I lied about a couple micro details.

Two lies during a police interrogation was about my average. The
big parts, the parts that mattered, were true.

SDPD Detective Skupin walked into the Brick House a little after
2:30 a.m. while I waited for Moira. Rumpled clothes, bloodshot eyes,
tired. Like he'd been awakened after a lone hour of sleep following an
all-night bender.

"Jesus, Cahill." He stopped in front of the wooden bench I sat on
and put his hands on his hips. "You just can't let things rest, can you?"

"We were wrong, Detective. We got the wrong guy and the right
guy completed his sick fucking game."

"They could have been in it together."

"You know that's bullshit, Skupin. That son of a bitch lying in his
own blood in the cave kidnapped and killed Alicia Alton, framed his
brother and killed him, and watched Naomi drown an inch at a time.
All by himself. A sick, twisted game by a psychopath who was born
wrong and never got right. If you've got nothing else to do, you might
want to look into his mother's supposed suicide."

"I would have gotten there, goddammit." Whatever energy Skupin
had summoned to stay upright ebbed from his body. His knees

wobbled, and I jumped off the bench and grabbed him before he keeled over. I directed him to the bench, and he plopped down like a sack of dirt.

"Take it easy, Skupin. Maybe you should head back home. As soon as they're done with Moira, I'll give you a ride."

"I didn't come from home." He rubbed his face. "I've been downtown working the case on my own time. My Lieu told me to close it by tomorrow. He's convinced that Caleb Lansing was Pluto and we need a black checkmark on the board. But, obviously, you were right and he's wrong. I should have put the pieces together quicker."

"You had pressure from your lieutenant, Skupin. The case was giftwrapped. No one else would have taken the case as far as you did. And you were still working it."

Skupin stood up. Old beyond his years. "Naomi Hendrix should still be alive, Rick. We both know that."

He trudged to the staircase and up the stairs to Robbery/Homicide to consult with LJPD and add another extinguished life to a case that his lieutenant thought was already closed.

Skupin was right. Naomi should still be alive. If I'd pushed a little harder, she might still be. And I'd have to live with that and all the other critical mistakes I'd made over my lifetime. Everyday. One day at a time.

CHAPTER FIFTY-FIVE

I WOKE UP at 7:12 the next morning exhausted, but knew I couldn't sleep any more. I had to get busy to keep my mind off of Naomi. I spent the next hour disassembling and cleaning the Ruger .357. The trigger action worked after I reassembled and oiled the gun. One chore done and one more weapon available.

I got to the AT&T store in Clairemont Town Square as it opened at 9:00 a.m. As much as I didn't want to talk to anyone, my phone was my lifeline and I needed a new one to replace the one I'd waterlogged last night.

The screen of my new iPhone lit up with a call as soon as I left the store. That didn't take long. I didn't recognize the number and let the call go to voicemail. I didn't plan on answering any more unknown numbers again for a while. Probably a reporter. I got into my car and the phone rang again. Same number. Now they were pissing me off.

"I don't have anything to say. Talk to LJPD and leave me the fuck alone!"

A laugh on the other end. Female. Caustic. Evil.

Tatiana Volkov.

"Do you have my money?"

"The deal was you get the ten grand after the surveillance is over. Does this mean it's over?"

"You broke the deal when you talked to the police." A sick cat and mouse tick in Tatiana's voice.

"That had nothing to do with you or your father. You'll see it on the news."

"I already have. I want the money now."

"Give me a week." Not that I could come up with ten grand by then. I just needed time. To figure it all out.

"Time is running out." The devil's snicker.

Glee. Malevolent glee. A sick combination from a warped woman. If I broke the extortion contract I'd made with her father, Tatiana would be free to carry out whatever sick and twisted plan she had for me. I'd had enough of sick and twisted. She and her leather-clad skinheads better come heavy.

"You weren't at your post last night. You broke the contract twice in one night."

She had a spy or she made another late-night run by Stone's house last night. Neither scenario made sense. If she had someone spying on me, why not cut out the middleman and have the spy watch Stone's house? And why a drive-by on Hillside if she thought I'd be there staking out Stone? If there was a spy, did he see Moira?

"I stayed there as long as I could, then I had to try to save someone's life."

"Yes." The laugh from hell. "You tried. Did someone take your place while you played hero?"

"No." Shit. Was that a jab at Moira?

"Hmm." The sound rolled out as an accusation. "You have two strikes against you, Rick. One more strike and you and your little helper are out." She hung up.

The call was a warning, but why not just kill me now? The money? Why was I so important? Why to the whole thing? Two weeks of bullshit surveillance when they could have had anyone do it. They wanted me on the job for a reason, and it wasn't because I was good at what I did. Or because I was bad at it. They needed me for some other reason that would benefit them. Whatever it was, I knew it was a zero-sum game.

I called Moira.

"Go up to San Luis Obispo and visit your son. Today."

"What's wrong?" Fear knocked the weary out of Moira's voice. Good. She needed to be alert.

"I want you out of town until this Russian thing is resolved."

"What do you mean by *resolved*?"

"I don't know. Just promise me you'll leave. Today."

"What if the police want to question me more about the shooting?"

"Do it over the phone or tell them you'll come into the station when you get back in town." My voice steady, but adamant.

"And when will that be?"

"When it's over."

"What about you?" Her voice an octave above the usual tenor. "Are you getting out of town?"

"I'll be fine."

"Don't do anything stupid, Rick."

"I won't. Just please promise you'll leave today."

Silence. Finally, "Okay, but you be careful."

"I will." But careful might not be enough to keep me alive.

I went home and took a long hot shower, followed by a short cold one. I needed to be alert.

*   *   *

Special Agent Mallon wasn't happy to see me when he finally exited the elevator into the lobby at the FBI San Diego Field Office in Sorrento Valley. He escorted me out of the modern glass and cement building into the parking lot.

"I thought we were even, Rick." He bit off his words.

The guards at the front gate looked over at us. Mallon grabbed my arm and led me further into the parking lot.

"Are you trying to get me suspended?" He let go of my arm.

"No. I'm trying to stay alive and help you bring down the Russian Mafia in San Diego."

"The Russians again?" He put his hands on his waist. "Go to the police, Rick. I can't help you."

"I can't go to the police. That will get me killed. The Russians have moles everywhere. Hopefully, not in the FBI."

I stuck out the manila file in my hand that had everything I had on the Russians going back to when Tatiana first stabbed me in the leg in her Hummer. If Special Agent Mallon acted on the info, the Russians would probably kill me. If he didn't act at all, they'd do the same. My options were: run and look over my shoulder for the rest of my life or stay and fight.

I'd rather see the gun pointed at my chest than not see the one pointed at my back.

"What's that?" Mallon stared at the file in my hand without moving.

"Everything I have on the Russians. Look at it yourself or give it to your RICO people. Murder, extortion, fraud, racketeering. Take your pick. Just have someone look at it while you still have a potential witness alive."

"It's always life and death with you, Rick."

"Not by choice." I pushed the file out in front of his chest and held it there until he grabbed it.

CHAPTER FIFTY-SIX

I SAT AT my post on Hillside Drive. Night two since the Tatiana warning and since I gave Special Agent Mallon my file on the Russians. He hadn't contacted me, and I'd left him alone. My routine stayed the same as it had since the first email from T. Randolph two and a half weeks ago. Except in addition to the Smith & Wesson .357 in the holster under my arm, I had my Ruger snub nose in my coat pocket, a Glock 9mm in the glove compartment of my car, and the Mossberg 590A1 Pump-Action Tactical shotgun in the trunk.

I'd learned the arsenal approach when I was with the Santa Barbara Police Department. I'd had a partner who'd been a Sheriff's Deputy in San Bernardino County before he opted for a quieter life in Santa Barbara. He always carried three guns on the job. Not to use one as a throw-down at a bad shooting, but so he wouldn't have to take the time to reload in a firefight. Fire until empty, drop the gun and grab another.

I'd never had to use the technique on the job. I figured, after the call from Tatiana, the arsenal method would come in handy. If I could see her and her crew coming. Right now, I couldn't see anything except that I was their pawn and I'd been on the chess board for a long time. Sooner or later the pawn had to be sacrificed.

Moira called me when she arrived in San Luis Obispo. She was still shaken from my call and from shooting Pluto. She would be for a long time. I had nightmares for a year after I killed someone in self-defense. It was easier the next time. I hoped there wouldn't be a next time for Moira. I couldn't do anything about the first time now, but I could pay her for the two weeks of gratis surveillance she'd done for me.

I clicked the bank app on my phone to see just how bad my finances really were. Most of my bills were paid through automatic withdrawal and I hadn't been on top of squaring things with my checkbook lately. Life and death had gotten in the way.

I typed in my password and my account came up. $6,300 in my savings account. That and the $27,000 or so I had in an IRA that I contributed to maybe twice a year was my retirement nest egg. I wondered how many people would hire a seventy-five-year-old private detective. Nothing to worry about. The chances of me living past sixty weren't very good. Especially if Tatiana Volkov wanted her ten grand all at once.

I scrolled down to my checking account. And nearly dropped the phone.

$28,230.17.

This was some kind of joke. A Monopoly card. Bank error in my favor. Except this was more than $200 and I hadn't passed go. More like a $25,000 error. But this wasn't an error. And it wasn't a miracle. My prayers hadn't been answered because I didn't pray for money.

I clicked on my checking account and my recent transactions popped up. There it was. A twenty-five-thousand-dollar deposit into my account made today. But it wasn't *my* transaction. Someone else had made the online deposit.

LiveStem Inc.

Sweat pebbled my forehead. T. Randolph. A Russian puppet. Founder of LiveStem and the person instructing me to surveil Peter Stone. If Randolph was paying me, the Russians were paying me, and if the Russians were paying me it wasn't for surveilling Stone.

Why did they pay me? If the Russians really wanted to pay me for a service, the payment would come in a paper sack full of cash. Untraceable. An online transaction was as traceable as it got. They wanted me attached to LiveStem, the company they were using to defraud sick people. The company they had a connection to, not just through Kevin, the aborted fetus stem cell courier, but through Stone who sat on the LiveStem board. But they weren't connections on paper. The Russians knew how to cover their tracks or not leave any.

The emails from T. Randolph and the deposit from LiveStem were tracks. That led to T. Randolph, LiveStem, and Stone. Who do you leave tracks, clues, for? Law enforcement. Somehow the Russians found my bank account number and planted $25,000 worth of clues.

But there were more clues. Like someone parked in his car on the same street every night for two weeks. The Russians must have had a spy. They knew when I was parked on Hillside watching Stone's house. And when I wasn't. And they must have known when I switched from the rental to my own car. A rental wasn't as easy to trace as a car registered to me. Plus, in Stone's multimillion-dollar neighborhood, the 2018 Audi would just be background noise blending in with all the other high-end cars. My Accord, ubiquitous everywhere else in San Diego, would blink like neon in Stone's toney neighborhood. The whole reason I'd rented the Audi in the first place.

The Russians had to wait me out until I couldn't afford the Audi anymore. Then have me park on the street in the Accord for a few nights in a row. Make sure I'd get noticed. Then what? Set in motion whatever scheme they set up for me to play patsy. The twenty-five grand into my checking account today. That had to be the catalyst that set the plan in motion. They couldn't afford to wait more than a day or two at the most. Sooner or later, I'd check my account and investigate the deposit.

Now was sooner and later. We'd both run out of time.

CHAPTER FIFTY-SEVEN

I DIALED A number I hadn't used since last year and had hoped never to call again. No answer. Voicemail. The message I had for Peter Stone would have to be face-to-face.

I opened the glove compartment, grabbed the Glock, and shoved it in the coat pocket that didn't hold the Ruger. I scanned the street. No movement. No black Hummer. Just a trap somewhere out there in the dark that I had to disarm before it snapped shut on me.

First, I had to figure out what it was.

I got out of my car and walked down to Stone's house. Staying under night shadows of the trees on the opposite side of the street, my right hand on the handle of the Ruger .357 in my pocket.

I made the turn and caught sight of Stone's house. No cars in the driveway. No Hummer on the block. I crossed the street to the castle where evil lived.

All the windows of the house were on the back where the fifteen-million-dollar view was. I couldn't tell if any lights were on inside. I knocked on the massive copper door. Ten, fifteen seconds. Nothing. I rang the bell and knocked harder. My phone vibrated an incoming text in my pocket. I let it go. A few seconds later, the door opened.

Stone, his combed-back gray hair knife-pointed in a widow's peak. Confident dark eyes calculating opportunities for advantage. He wore slacks and a dress shirt, like he was hosting an informal billion-dollar cocktail party. I didn't hear noise from any guests inside. This was Stone relaxing at home alone.

"Rick, do tell, which of my neighbors is in danger of breaking their prenup by sneaking around in the dark? Whose windows are you peeping through tonight?" The smooth arrogant baritone. Smirking at his own inside joke. Stone hadn't changed. But he had. Time had sunken his cheeks and pulled dark circles down below his eyes. And his hand had a slight tremor, which he put in his pants pocket when he caught me eyeing it.

Scared of what was in my hand in the pocket of my coat? I doubted it. He'd stared me down when I'd held a gun on him before. The Russians? Maybe. They were scarier than I'd ever be. But it felt like something else. Time? The clock that not even Peter Stone could control? Maybe. Whatever it was didn't loosen the hand on the gun in my pocket. Stone was a dangerous man, tremor or no tremor.

"We need to talk about LiveStem, Thomas Randolph, and the Russians."

Stone looked over my head at the street behind me.

"No, we don't. If I ever get married again and need someone to spy on my wife, I'll give you a call." He stepped back and started to close the door.

"Sergei Volkov hired me to spy on you."

The door stopped six inches from closing. One dark eye stared at me through the crack. The confidence gone. He pulled the door open.

"In."

I went inside and followed him into his severely furnished living room. Black sharp-angled furniture on white carpet. The room looked more staged than lived in. Stone sat down in an enormous leather chair. A throne. The crown weighed heavy on the head of the king tonight. I sat down on a scale version of Stone's chair opposite him.

"Talk."

Gone was the arrogance that oozed from Stone's pores. His eyes still calculated, but seemed to be turned inward. Rating his own weaknesses. Survival mode. Even his normal pompous loquacious-ness stripped down to the bare minimum. Just the facts.

I told him about Tatiana and Sergei Volkov's intrusion into my life and the T. Randolph emails instructing me to surveil him every night. He took in the information without changing his expression.

"I know you're on the board of LiveStem, Stone. What I don't understand is why the man who supposedly was sending me email instructions to surveil you met with you twice on nights I followed you."

"Did you note those meetings in your reports?" The tremor I'd seen in his hand earlier twitched his head. He took a deep breath and seemed to will his head steady.

"That's an odd question. Why wouldn't I?"

"There's no time for games, Rick."

"Yes, but I didn't identify the man as Randolph. It didn't make sense that the man who instructed me to follow you would meet with you. I figured the Russians were up to something, but didn't know what."

"Do you now?"

"I'm not sure. Why don't you fill in the blanks?"

"Have you told me everything?"

"I know the Russians are funneling sales of stem cells from aborted fetuses and pawning them off as embryonic stem cells." I took the Ruger out of my pocket and rested it on my thigh. "That's fraud, for starters. They're probably being sold overseas. That's federal. That may even be out of the reach of your tentacles, Stone."

Stone looked at the gun, then back at me. He frowned and lifted his right hand from his lap. It twitched in a slight tremor.

"I have Parkinson's Disease, Rick. Embryonic stem cells look to be a cure. That's why I'm on the board at LiveStem. I have nothing to do with Sergei's scheme."

I thought of Randolph's agitated visit to Stone's house last week and showing Stone some papers, probably a report.

"But Randolph thinks you do, doesn't he? I saw him argue with you in this living room last week."

"Did you go to the police?"

How much should I tell him? The Russians had "hired" me to follow him. Whether he was telling the truth or not about not being involved in the Russians' stem cell scheme, Stone and the Russians seemed to be more adversaries than friends right now.

"Not yet." I didn't tell him about the FBI. Whether Stone was friend or foe to the Russians, that admission could get me killed. "But there's something else you should know. A $25,000 deposit from LiveStem showed up in my bank account today."

Stone's eyes went big and he stood up.

"Are you here to kill me, Rick?"

"What?" Then it hit me. The twenty-five grand told him everything it should have told me. The Russians were going to kill Stone and set me up for it. And probably kill me in the process.

Stone bolted down the hall just as I caught a shadow at the left side of the sliding glass door to the patio.

I dove behind an oak coffee table as the glass door exploded inward. Gunshots echoed inside the house and bullets thudded into the coffee table. I thrust my hand up over the coffee table and fired blindly. The intruder had me pinned down, and I didn't know where he was. He'd find an angle and would shoot me dead in a manner of seconds. I pulled down the Ruger, got to all fours, then fired blindly over the table again.

I emptied the gun, dropped it, grabbed the edge of the heavy table, and flipped it up onto its side. Gunshots exploded and bullets imbedded into the table and the wall behind me. I yanked the Smith & Wesson .357 from my holster and fired over the edge of the table until the gun was empty, grabbed the Glock from my other pocket, and dove out from behind the coffee table to the right.

A boom rocked the house and a shadow flew backwards five feet, hit the ground, and lay still. I rocketed to my feet and pointed my gun at the intruder. Dead.

Stone appeared at the edge of the hall, a shotgun braced against his shoulder. He lowered the barrel and turned toward me. A quick up with the barrel and the shotgun would be ready to fire again. At me.

I still held the Glock, two handed—a V shooting platform out from my body. I lowered the weapon, but kept the two-handed grip and turned to Stone.

Gun smoke wafted in the air, its smell in my nostrils. Ears ringing. Stone and I looked at each other. Enemies for five years. One more blast from the shotgun and Stone could be done with me and all I knew about him. He'd be free to paint the picture inside his house anyway he wanted to for the police. The twenty-five grand in my checking account from LiveStem, payment for a hit on him. He could finish the frame that the Russians tried to put around me. But he'd still have to deal with the Russians.

I had fewer options. Stone had tried to kill me once and he'd been a threat hovering over my life ever since. A quick up with the Glock and I'd have one less worry in my life. But I'd have a hard time climbing out of the Russians' frame job.

And Stone had saved my life.

I turned my back to Stone and walked over to the intruder lying on the floor. He was dressed all in black, including a black ski mask. A gaping hole in his chest bled out onto Stone's pristine rug. His gun, a Sig Sauer with a high-capacity magazine, lay a couple feet from his body. I kicked it away even though the man's soul was already on its way up or down. Old habits from my cop days.

I turned back to Stone. He reared up the shotgun. "Down!"

I dove to the floor and the shotgun exploded again. I spun around and saw another black-clad figure bounce off the patio outside the shattered sliding glass door. I shot to my feet and dashed out to the patio, gun up. The man was dead. I kicked his gun away, jumped off the patio, and ran to the steel-barred fence both men had scaled to make their attack. They'd used a multi-pronged hook attached to a rope to get over the fence. They'd studied and come back with a plan.

I peeked through the bars of the fence up and down the street and didn't see Tatiana's black Hummer. Stone stood on the patio and looked down at me, shotgun held down in front of him.

"Any more?"

"I don't know. I can't see the Hummer." I climbed back up onto the patio. "I'm guessing they sent one in at first because they thought you'd be alone and they wanted to frame me, so it had to be a one-man job. When the first shooter didn't check back in, the driver must have come as a backup."

I suddenly remembered that I'd gotten a text. I pulled out my phone to check it.

"You're not calling the police, are you, Rick?" The circles under Stone's eyes had somehow disappeared and his cheeks looked full again. Like the battle had reversed the clock and the disease eating away at his body.

"No. But somebody has to."

"Leave that to me."

I checked the text. It was from T. Randolph.

Come to my house immediately. The text gave the address to a house I already knew.

"Call Randolph and tell him to get out of his house. Now!"

"Why?" Stone, alert.

"Because the Russians are going to kill him and try to pin it on me."

CHAPTER FIFTY-EIGHT

I HOPPED IN my car and called LJPD to report a possible break-in at Randolph's house. I didn't mention the crime scene at Stone's. He'd said he'd handle it, and I didn't want LJPD's limited resources rushing to Stone's house instead of Randolph's.

I got to Randolph's house in less than ten minutes. No cops yet. Shit. No black Hummer that I could see, either. I parked three houses away and walked to the house. The gate to the front yard was open. An invitation. Prudence told me to drive away and leave it to the police. I'd called them and done my civic duty.

Except Obadiah T. Randolph might not be able to wait that long.

Odds were there was a gunman inside the house about to kill Randolph or waiting to kill me when I entered then use my gun on him. I'd made the hit on Stone that Randolph had paid for and now I'd gone to his house to demand more money or kill the only witness. We'd get into a shootout and both die. All cleaned up. The Russians would put some stooge in place of Randolph at LiveStem and continue their dead baby gravy train, and the Stone problem, whatever that was, would be eliminated.

Except it didn't work out. Whether the gunman inside knew that or not didn't matter. He either had Randolph tied up alive waiting to use my gun or he was already dead, shot by some unlicensed gun that the killer would wrap my hand around after he killed me with the gun he'd put Randolph's fingerprints on. The only unknown was whether or not he'd already killed Randolph.

The front door to the house was ajar. Just a few inches, but enough for me to holler in when no one answered. Then, the killer would claim to be Randolph and call out for me to come in.

I turned up Dunemere instead of going inside the gate. A six-foot cement wall ran along the side of the property and attached to the garage. I climbed over the wall and touched down quietly on the backyard grass. Gun out, I went over to the garage and cleared it. Two bedrooms with glass-paned doors opened into the backyard. Both were empty.

The killer would be waiting inside by the front door. He'd laid enough cheese for me to enter that way. I tried the door of the larger bedroom. Locked. I tried the other door. The knob turned.

I eased the door open. The floors were hardwood. Looked original to the one-hundred-year-old cottage home. Probably squeaky. I eased a foot onto the floor. Quiet. Another, no sound. I went silently through the bedroom into the hall. Small dining room ahead to the left, kitchen to the right. The sunken living room was straight ahead, but I could only see the left half of it. Clear. The other half must have been where the front door was. Where the killer waited.

I crept down the hall toward the opening down into the living room. The floor creaked just as I cleared the hall. A leather-clad skinhead spun toward me, gun rising. I fired twice at center mass as his gun went off, shooting the floor. He staggered back and dropped in front of a stone fireplace. I kicked the gun away. Didn't matter. He was dead.

Something caught the corner of my eye just as I heard the loudspeaker outside.

"This is the police. Put your hands over your head and walk slowly out the front door."

I spun and saw Obadiah Thomas Randolph slumped in a chair. Eyes open. Just like the hole in his chest seeping blood. Dead.

The cops and I had both been too late.

The cop outside repeated his commands three times through the loudspeaker. I put all of my guns onto the floor and was at the front door by the time the cop finished his third command. I took two steps down the stairs and was immediately grabbed from behind and thrown to the cement walkway. The scab on my nose opened up and dripped blood onto the sidewalk.

At least I hadn't been shot.

CHAPTER FIFTY-NINE

I'D BEEN IN an interrogation room at LJPD plenty of times. Enough to be a criminal. And I'd lied inside them enough to be a criminal, too. But this was the first time I'd ever been handcuffed inside one. I wasn't as lucky with my inquisitors this time. I had a history with both.

Detective Hailey Denton and Jim Sheets had been going at me for an hour after letting me sweat alone for two. Denton hated me and Sheets was neutral at best. The gold specks in Hailey Denton's eyes got darker and darker with each round of questions. She stuck her face into mine.

"We found the small arsenal you left inside Obadiah Thomas Randolph's house and the burglar kit in the trunk of your car. Care to explain?"

I didn't have a good answer for that, and the truth sounded worse than a lie. I was just about to ask for an attorney and shut the interrogation down when Chief Hardesty walked in and shut it down for me. Dress blues, old-fashioned curled brown hair.

"Detectives, that will be enough." I'd never met the chief, but she didn't look happy. Maybe that had something to do with Special Agent John Mallon standing next to her. "Mr. Cahill is free to go."

The specks in Detective Denton's irises turned to coal. "What? This man is involved in a shooting where two people are dead."

She didn't even know about Stone's house.

"Uncuff Mr. Cahill, Detective." Each word came out individually on an edge.

Denton put her hands on her hips. Defiant.

Sheets leaned over the table where my hands were cuffed on a chain looped through a ring in the table and unlocked the handcuffs.

"Mr. Cahill, you're free to go." The chief wasn't smiling when she said it.

I stood up and Special Agent Mallon spoke for the first time. "Chief Hardesty, do you mind if Mr. Cahill and I have the room?"

"Of course." The chief looked at Denton and Sheets and nodded at the door. "Detectives."

The three of them single-filed out with the chief on the caboose.

"And, Chief, please turn the camera off." Mallon pointed at the camera with the red light on above the door.

The chief grunted and closed the door behind her.

Mallon held up his hand at me and looked at the camera. He turned to me when the light went out.

"This is the deal, Rick." Mallon had aged since I first met him two years ago. Still only in his early thirties, but circles had etched their way under his eyes. "You don't talk to anyone about the file you gave me and whatever you learned from Peter Stone."

"What the hell's going on?"

"I read the report you gave me and gave it to our RICO people. It corroborates information they already had. The only thing they didn't know about was you and the emails the Russians sent you on the fake T. Randolph address. They even sent them via Randolph's router. They hacked into his Wi-Fi when they sent the emails. Anyway, you can testify in the upcoming trial and we can put you in witness protection or you can keep your mouth shut and no one will ever know about the file you gave me. The police won't bother you further on what happened tonight and hopefully you can go on and live your life."

"Hopefully live my life. You know the Russians said they'd kill me if I went to the police. They have a mole in here, and he'll get that information to them. They'll know the FBI came in here and got me out."

"Detective Patterson was arrested two hours ago."

I'd never heard the name before. "Who?"

"The mole."

"How did you get that information?" Then I realized I already knew the answer. Stone. He'd had a connection at LJPD, but maybe he got it from the Russians. Stone was the source whose information I'd corroborated. The Russians wanted him dead because they'd found out or suspected that he'd gone to the Feds and turned state's evidence. They just needed me to be the patsy. He told me at his house not to call the police because he'd take care of it. Or his pals the Feds would.

"You don't have to worry about a mole. There are no guarantees, but I think you have a good shot of getting free of the Russian Mafia. We've just arrested fourteen members here in San Diego, and there will be more to come in other cities."

"Sergei Volkov?"

"Yes."

"Tatiana Volkov?"

"No. We haven't connected the dots to her yet."

Tatiana. Without her in custody, I had a death sentence over my head. And so did she.

I could either wait on her or go find her.

One of us was going to die.

* * *

I caught the news when I got up the next morning, expecting to see a story on the Russian Mafia arrests and praying Special Agent Mallon had been right and I'd been left out of it. Nothing on the Russians and nothing on the shootings at Peter Stone's house. There was a mention of a shooting in La Jolla on Olivetas with two fatalities but no mention of T. Randolph or LiveStem.

Or me.

I reached for the remote to turn off the TV, but stopped dead when the next story came on.

"The police have identified the woman found in her apartment in Little Italy yesterday believed to have died of a fentanyl overdose as Audrey Suzanne Hastings. Ms. Hastings was an exotic dancer at the strip club, Alley Kat. She is survived by her eight-year-old son. Another sad statistic added to the opioid crisis."

I ran into the bathroom and vomited into the sink. Then dry-heaved for another minute.

I slid down onto my hands and knees. Sweat rolled down my face. Audrey. Just another stripper addict statistic. According to the news, her story was a cliché. Nothing special, just the way things are. But she had a real story. Her own. And I'd become a part of it. And because of that, Tatiana Volkov had ended it.

Another story would end soon.

* * *

I screwed the suppressor into the barrel of the 9mm Glock. Both of which I'd bought from a man in a motel room in Las Vegas last winter. No ten-day waiting period. No license from the state. Cash, no credit cards. No connections to me. No serial number. Untraceable. I bought the gun and silencer after Sergei Volkov told me he'd call one day asking a favor. I'd hoped I'd never have to use them, but knew, in the darkest part of my being, that someday I would.

If Petrov and Tatiana followed the same route in the Hummer they had for the last two mornings, they'd arrive at the underground parking garage of Tatiana's Broadway condo at around 4:20 a.m. The one with the broken security camera.

The Hummer rolled into the garage at 4:21 a.m.

* * *

I checked my cell phone when I got home at 5:50 a.m. No incoming calls or texts since I left it in my kitchen at 1:30 a.m. After driving around town depositing pieces of metal and polymer in dumpsters on the morning of their trash pickup.

The temperature was only in the low sixties, but I started a fire in the living room fireplace anyway. And threw in clothing I'd never wear again.

Midnight and I sat by the first fire of fall. The only one. We watched the flames until they finally died out into the ashes of once was. I thought about Moira and the pain she was going through after taking a life. I worried about how little pain I felt right then.

* * *

I called Moira at 7:00 a.m.

"It's safe. Come home."

EPILOGUE

THE POLICE HAD no leads on the murders of Tatiana Volkov and Petrov Korbut, but they were thought to be the first casualties in the struggle for power in what remained of the Russian Mafia in San Diego. The arrests of the surviving Russian Mafia leaders finally made the news two days later. The Feds had kept a lid on it until they made another thirty-three arrests in Orange County and Los Angeles. One of the arrests was Randolph's partner, Victor Greenblatt. He'd been the Russian's inside man at LiveStem. Even Dr. Rich was taken away in handcuffs.

Peter Stone's name wasn't mentioned as the key witness. Only that a prominent La Jolla businessman had been instrumental in putting the case together. Stone's mansion on the hill was up for sale and rumors were that he was living in seclusion somewhere waiting to testify.

In some ways I felt sorry for the man who had caused me so much grief. And saved my life. Twice.

* * *

Moira called me after she saw the news about Tatiana Volkov.

"You called me the morning Tatiana was murdered." She sounded short of breath. "Before her body had even been found."

I didn't say anything.

"What did you do, Rick?"

"I made things safe."

"You made things *safe*?" A shout. "That's not your job. We have the police for that. You should have gone to the police from the start. I should have. Maybe fewer people would be dead."

She may have been right. But that was a chance I couldn't take. I was responsible for my life. And, sadly, too many others.

"I did what I thought was right."

"And now I have to live with what I know. An accessory after the fact. Don't call me anymore, Rick." The best friend I had hung up.

I called her ten times over the next three weeks. She didn't return any of them.

* * *

I went to Naomi's funeral. A small private service that 1350 AM put on. No one had come forward to claim her body. She died in the anonymity that she craved despite her fame. Chip Evigan cried at the service. Genuine tears. I think down-deep, past what Naomi could do for his career, he really cared for her.

So did I. As I did for Alicia Alton, whom I talked to once, and Audrey Hastings, who I knew hardly at all, but too well. I'd pursued the truth no matter the cost, and they'd paid with their lives.

The truth didn't matter much anymore.